THE LYTTELTON
HART-DAVIS
LETTERS
A SELECTION

'In a hundred years' time, I suspect, the letters will be read with as much pleasure as they are today.'
Daily Telegraph

'This book belongs to that wide category, embracing Boswell's *Life of Johnson* and Tuckwell's *Reminiscences of Oxford*, that in a hundred different ways informs, challenges and stimulates . . . This indeed is the secret of their charm. They bring their reading to their observation of life and their experience of life to their reading.'
Richard Ollard

'Their turn of a pungent and pleasing phrase, their ready responses to the quirks and quiddities of life, arise out of complex intellectual processes which it is a sheer delight to observe working with a subtle blend of enthusiasm and elegant ease.'
Yorkshire Post

'One of the most urbane, civilised and entertaining correspondences of our time . . . as rich a feast as ever of gossip and reflection, of bookish jokes and nostalgic asides.'
Kenneth Rose

'A picture emerges of late Roman patricians discussing Virgil, deploring bad manners, observing shadows on sun-dials, light on walls, while elderly traitors grossly flatter the young and barbarians camp outside gates that no longer close.'
Peter Vansittart

'I am left with the feeling that we shall never see the like of such epistolary ebullience again.'
Scotsman

George Lyttelton

Rupert Hart-Davis

Ruth Simon, by Consuelo Haydon, 1950

THE LYTTELTON HART-DAVIS LETTERS

A SELECTION

Correspondence of George Lyttelton
and Rupert Hart-Davis
1955–1962

Edited by
RUPERT HART-DAVIS

This selection edited and introduced by
ROGER HUDSON

A COMMON READER EDITION
THE AKADINE PRESS
2001

A Common Reader Edition published 2001 by The Akadine Press, Inc.,
by arrangement with John Murray (Publishers) Ltd.

First published in 2001
by John Murray (Publishers) Ltd,
50 Albemarle Street, London W1S 4BD

ISBN 1-58579-040-0

Typeset in Adobe Garamond 11/13 pt
by Servis Filmsetting Ltd, Manchester

Printed and bound in Great Britain by
Butler & Tanner Ltd, Frome and London

10 9 8 7 6 5 4 3 3 1

CONTENTS

There is no transaction which offers stronger temptation to sophistication and fallacy than epistolary intercourse.

DR JOHNSON

All letters, methinks, should be free and easy as one's discourse, not studied as an oration, nor made up of hard words like a charm.

DOROTHY OSBORNE

Indulging myself in the freedom of epistolary intercourse, I beg leave to throw out my thoughts, and express my feelings, just as they arise in my mind, with very little attention to formal methods.

EDMUND BURKE

Correspondences are like small-clothes before the invention of suspenders; it is impossible to keep them up.

SYDNEY SMITH

Th' entente is all, and naught the letter's space.

CHAUCER

I rattle on exactly as I'd talk
With anybody in a ride or walk.

LORD BYRON

INTRODUCTION

Letter-writing is a largely dead art, supplanted not merely by the telephone but also by the spreading inability to turn phrases, write sentences, employ a wide vocabulary or construct a paragraph with ease. Claims have been made that e-mail is bringing about a revival, but the proof is yet to appear in book form. Even in 1955, when this correspondence began, there can have been precious few people sitting down each week to write to a friend for the sheer pleasure of it. But this is what Rupert Hart-Davis agreed with George Lyttelton that they should do, thirty years after he had been a member of the latter's English class at Eton. Immediately both parties realised that something out of the ordinary was afoot, and we share their mounting pleasure as they strike sparks off each other, anecdotes are capped and whole new tracts of common ground are discovered.

The same sort of excitement was abroad at John Murray's in 1978 as the ecstatic reviews mounted up for the first volume and the publishers realised they had something of a cult hit on their hands. In the next six years five more volumes were published, taking the correspondence to its conclusion with George Lyttelton's death in 1962. They were then all reissued in three paperback double volumes as well as being published in the USA. Two series of them were read on Radio 3 in evening concert intervals, and they received a backhanded compliment when Craig Brown parodied them in *The Marsh Marlowe Letters* (1984), which also had a brief run when adapted for the stage.

George Lyttelton's background is more swiftly related than Rupert's. From his ancestral home, Hagley Hall in Worcestershire, he went to Eton where he excelled at sport, returning there after his three years at Trinity College, Cambridge, to teach for the rest of his career. In 1945 he retired to a village close to Woodbridge in Suffolk. He was a governor of two girls' schools and two boys' schools and he supplemented his pension by setting and correcting O Level English literature exam papers each year. In his time he had corresponded regularly with the cricket writer and music critic Neville Cardus, and the theatre critic and diarist James Agate, but by 1955 he was bored and at a loose end. In one of his three books of reminiscences, Humphrey Lyttelton wrote of his father: 'the memories I have of GWL are mostly lighthearted if not actually frivolous . . . At meals he was by any nursery standards badly behaved.' If requested to pass something GWL would first ask 'Tunnicliffe or Denton?'—two cricketers, one famous for his slip catches and one for his work in the deep field. 'If you were lucky enough to nominate the deep fielder the object would be lobbed over gently. The wrong choice brought it thudding into your chest.' GWL had 'superb eyebrows, bristling reddish antennae set at a downward sloping angle, capable of beetling prodigiously but at their most eloquent when they began moving up his huge brow through degrees ranging from surprise to utter disbelief at the folly of mankind . . . Most of the enduring things I learnt from my father were by example rather than precept. His "serious talk" with me as I approached puberty lingers in my mind solely for its almost startling brevity . . . "Eschew evil" he boomed and then gave me a heavy paternal bang on the shoulder and left the room, humming to himself.'

Rupert Hart-Davis was, on the face of it, the son of a stockbroker married to the attractive sister of Duff Cooper (MP, wartime minister and ambassador, husband of Diana Cooper). But he revealed in his memoir of his mother, *The Arms of Time*, his gradually increasing suspicions that his real father was Gervase Beckett, a Yorkshire banker and MP. At Eton Rupert was in George Lyttelton's English 'extra studies' class – 'the only Eton master who had ever inspired me'. During his first term at Balliol College, Oxford, his beloved mother died. This left him so desolated that next term he found he could neither enjoy himself nor work, the only two reasons for being at university, so he left and became a student actor at Lilian Baylis's Old Vic Theatre. After two years and what was to be a brief marriage to Peggy Ashcroft, he realised he would only ever make a mediocre actor and so decided to try publishing, since he had a passion for books and reading. He worked first for Heinemann before moving to the Book Society and then, in 1933, to Jonathan Cape, described by one of his authors, Eric Linklater, as 'a publisher of outstanding genius with the heart of horse-coper'. In the same year Rupert married again, to Comfort Borden-Turner. Among the authors he brought to the firm were his schoolfriend Peter Fleming (*Brazilian Adventure, News from Tartary*), his uncle Duff Cooper (*Talleyrand*), William Plomer, Cecil Day Lewis, Neville Cardus and J. B. Morton (Beachcomber). During the war Rupert enlisted as a private in the Coldstream Guards before being made a Captain and Adjutant of the newly formed Sixth Battalion in 1941, and then Adjutant of the Training Battalion at Pirbright, which he in effect ran from 1943 to the war's end. Peter Fleming had inherited a 2,000-acre estate at Nettlebed near Henley, and the Hart-Davis family became tenants of Bromsden Farmhouse there from 1939 until 1985. It was at his desk in his library, converted from the farm's old dairy, that Rupert wrote his weekly letter to George who, weather permitting, wrote his reply from his summer-house in the garden at Grundisburgh.

Although he had introduced Field Marshal Lord Wavell's very successful poetry anthology, *Other Men's Flowers*, during the war, this did nothing to persuade Jonathan Cape to make Rupert an equal partner after it, so he left to set up his own firm with the novelist David Garnett and Edward Young, author of a famous wartime memoir, *One of Our Submarines*, and designer of the original Penguin paperback colophon. The new firm's colophon was a fox, in Rupert's words, 'partly because David Garnett had originally made his name with a book called *Lady into Fox* and partly because this animal might be said to represent both the author's and the bookseller's traditional view of the publisher'. Various friends including Peter Fleming, Eric Linklater and H. E. Bates invested money in the enterprise. The first book published by the firm, in February 1947, was *Fourteen Tales* by Henry James, the beginning of a long association with that author's books, letters and biographer, Leon Edel. Its first bestseller was Stephen Potter's *Gamesmanship*, a word that was soon in the dictionary. The Mariners' Library, of books about the sea, and the Reynard Library, anthologies of writing by single authors – Goldsmith, Carlyle, Johnson, Browning, etc. – were started. In 1950 *Elephant Bill*, nominally by Lt.-Col. J. H. Williams, but ghosted by David Garnett, became the second bestseller, and the firm moved to 36 Soho Square. The third was Heinrich Harrer's *Seven Years in Tibet*, which sold over 200,000 copies.

Other books and authors published were Leslie Hotson's Shakespeare studies, Gavin Maxwell's first book *Harpoon at a Venture*, about Hebridean shark fishing, Vincent Cronin, Ray Bradbury,

Patrick O'Brian, Maurice Druon the French historical novelist, and Gerald Durrell, whose animal books, with some help from Ralph Thompson's brilliant illustrations, became a string of bestsellers. In 1952 the firm needed more capital, and this came from two Americans, Herbert Agar and Milton Waldman. Then in 1957 another financial crisis was resolved by a takeover by Heinemann. This, and a third change of ownership in 1961, when it was bought by the American firm, Harcourt Brace, are described in the letters.

In 1952 Rupert's biography of Hugh Walpole had been published to great acclaim. This was only one among many activities, committees, pieces of disinterested literary midwifery and 'mild literary detection' that he threw himself into, but which had little or nothing to do with the firm, however much they enriched the world of books and the lives of others. His 'extra-curricular' life adds hugely to the interest of the letters but, as Philip Ziegler said in his review of the first volume of them in *The Times*, 'If he had devoted to making money half the energy he put into works of scholarship and the helping of his friends he would have retired a millionaire.' Rupert knew some of his commercial failings, writing to his third wife Ruth in 1951, 'I wasn't meant to be publisher but rather some dimmish man of letters, reading and researching a lot, writing a little. Starting the firm was fun, but holding it up for ever, like Atlas, is a dismal expectation.'

As David Garnett's son Richard, who joined the firm in 1949 and was production director and then editor, puts it, Rupert 'had a dislike of editing in typescript and would be all urgency to get the book off to the printer, but the moment it was in proof all his critical faculties would come into play. He would rewrite and rewrite – all improvements. Had he been obliged to do his editing on copy and taken a vow never to look at the proof, perhaps we might not have suffered so many takeovers.'

Harcourt Brace's infatuation with the firm did not last long, ending in 1962 when Rupert refused to publish Mary McCarthy's novel *The Group*. If George Lyttelton had still been alive he would have welcomed Rupert back as one who had strayed into supporting the publication of *Lady Chatterley's Lover* a year or two before, but had now seen the error of his ways. Thanks to the future Lord Goodman's skills as intermediary the firm was then taken on by the Granada Group, and Rupert retired from the scene. The days of the bookman were over, as was the primacy of the book, succumbing to the impact of new management and marketing ideas, and the new visual media. Literary appreciation such as George Lyttelton's was at a discount in the face of the new criticism, in which cultural relativism and deconstruction held sway.

Now that his and Comfort's three children were grown up, Rupert and she agreed to divorce; he was free to marry Ruth Simon, who had been responsible for jackets, art work and children's books at the firm. They went to live in North Yorkshire and Rupert was able to be a 'freelance literary bloke', as well as involving himself in the restoration and running of Marrick Priory Adventure Centre and Richmond's Georgian Theatre. Ruth died suddenly in 1967 and in 1968 Rupert married June Williams, an old friend who had worked for him in the early 1950s. He turned down the offer of £20,000 to write Somerset Maugham's biography, preferring to edit memoirs and diaries by friends such as Arthur Ransome, William Plomer and Siegfried Sassoon, and to judge the W. H. Smith Literary Awards each year. Financially he was helped by being left the royalties from Hugh Walpole's books and one third of the earnings from Arthur Ransome's. He also sold his library of 17,000 volumes to the University of Tulsa, Oklahoma, for £230,000 on condition that it remained in his possession until his death. Rupert died in December 1999, aged 92.

The guidelines behind the selecting and editing of these letters need touching upon. In his introduction to the second volume Rupert said that 'Eton and cricket have been pruned a little'. To these candidates for cuts have been added children, mutual admiration, lists of those at parties and dinners, though not the menus, and Rupert's cataloguing of his weekly social round, such as in December 1955:

> What else did I do last week? Visited Viola Meynell in hospital, dined with Madeline House and another of our Dickens team, attended a committee of the London Library, at which I was put on to a sub-committee to find a new Librarian (my friend Simon Nowell-Smith is retiring to devote himself to bibliography, and don't I envy him!), a dinner of the Lit Soc at which Tommy Lascelles was confirmed as President and myself (very reluctantly) as Secretary, *vice* Sparrow. I sat next to Sparrow and

Cuthbert Headlam, who nowadays is not the easiest person in the world to talk to, though no doubt he means no harm. On Wednesday I shirked a committee of the Royal Literary Fund. On Thursday I went to a cocktail party given by Stephen Potter—the usual screaming mob in a small hot room. I gulped down three glasses of champagne and hurried on to the Athenaeum to dine (as cosily as that forbidding citadel permits) with Wyndham Ketton-Cremer.

In his introduction to the final volume Rupert said, 'I know of no other published correspondence that is so completely antiphonal as this one.' Only a comparatively small number of letters have been omitted in their entirety and thus it is hoped that the remarkable continuity of the correspondence has largely survived. Dates indicate where such letters have gone. Since the entire correspondence is already in print, it has been felt unnecessary to use ellipses where cuts within letters have been made. In some cases one writer may give an answer to a question, asked by the other, that has been cut from an earlier letter. The hope is that the question is evident from the answer. Rupert sometimes flattered his readers by assuming more knowledge than most of them had, so a number of footnotes have been added, and initials spelled out. In some cases where a particularly outstanding passage from an author has been praised, it is given in a footnote.

As the original volumes appeared there was a certain amount of speculation over whether either of the correspondents had begun to have thoughts of eventual publication while writing the letters. Rupert remained indignant at the suggestion, though one suspects that the hope might have been seriously cherished by George, and that he was not entirely joking when he mentioned it in more than one letter. The fact that Rupert got June to start typing the correspondence and then mentioned this to Jock and Diana Murray when they came to lunch in October 1976 shows that by then he had realised its value and started to share George's hopes. We must be profoundly grateful that he did.

[Much thanks are due to Richard Garnett for the help he has given in the writing of this introduction.]

PROLOGUE

The Hon. George William Lyttelton, second son of the fifth Lord Lyttelton (who later became the eighth Viscount Cobham), was born at Hagley Hall in Worcestershire on 6 January 1883. His Eton career was strikingly successful: he reached Sixth Form, played twice against Harrow at Lord's, was Keeper of the Field and of the Oppidan Wall, and President of Pop. At Trinity, Cambridge, he gained a modest third in the Classical Tripos, and in 1908 he returned as a master to Eton, where his uncle Edward Lyttelton was Head Master.

In 1919 he married Pamela Adeane, by whom he had a son, Humphrey, and four daughters. In 1925 he got his own house, which he ran with gusto and success until 1944. Then, after one more year's teaching, he retired to Suffolk.

He taught mostly classics in the fifth form, but his great opportunity came when he persuaded the new Head Master Cyril Alington (with whom he collaborated in the admirable *Eton Poetry Book*, 1925) to allow him to start an optional course of English as 'extra studies' for senior specialists.

It was there that, in my last yeat at Eton (1925–26), I fell under his spell. His enthusiasm for teaching and for literature was infectious, his taste so sure, his jokes so amusing, that all his pupils on this course were stimulated to unusual efforts in an attempt to please him and to approach his high standards. Any boy who could recite two hundred consecutive lines of English verse to him was excused an early school: I achieved this exemption twice–with 'Love in the Valley' and 'The Hound of Heaven'.

After I left Eton his days dropped out of mine, until we met briefly in 1949, and thereafter occasionally exchanged letters. In 1950 I took him to a dinner of the Johnson Club in Dr Johnson's house in Gough Square; he was elected to the club and we met at its quarterly dinners. In April 1953 he read a lively paper on his eighteenth-century ancestor Lord Lyttelton, whose life was written by Johnson and to whom

Fielding dedicated *Tom Jones*. George was somewhat disconcerted when the occasion was for some reason changed from a dinner in Gough Square to a luncheon at Brown's Hotel:

> To feel hovering about us the spirit of Dr Johnson has, if one may say so, something inspiring about it, but what if we exchange it for that of Dr Buchman, whose headquarters are in Brown's Hotel? That is 'quite another thing', as George III used to reiterate, about almost everything, as far as I remember.

And then on 18 October 1955 we were fellow-guests at a dinner-party given by our dear friends Tim and Rosalie Nugent at their house in Chelsea Square. After a great deal of excellent food and drink George complained that he was lonely and bored of Suffolk, because there was no one to talk to: 'Nobody even writes to me,' he said. Flushed with wine I accepted the challenge.

'I'll write to you, George.'
'When will you start?'
'Next week-end.'
'Right. I'll answer in the middle of the week.'

Such was the origin of this correspondence, which continued un-broken until George died in 1962.

Perhaps, I now think, he had a faint hope that his letters might one day appear in print, but I was always so busy that the thought never occured to me. Nor would they have so appeared if it had not been for the perspicacity of Diana Murray and the foolhardy courage of her husband Jock, my lifelong friend and another old pupil of George's.

Editing one's own letters is a curious experience, and, when they are to appear on the same list as Byron's, is surely the height of pre-sumption. Luckly mine were written so long ago, and in what seems another life, that I can read them objectively, as though they had been written by someone else. I have resisted the temptation to improve them, and have confined my editing to the removal from both sides of the correspondence of libellous or hurtful passages, repetitions, padding, and references to weather and current affairs which no longer have any point. I have not indicated where the omissions occur. I have split up some of the longer paragraphs. Footnotes I have kept to what I hope is a helpful minimum.

In the first two letters I have retained the opening and signature, which are afterwards omitted, since they are almost always the same: any variation is printed. Similarly I have given our full home addresses in the first two letters and then abbreviated them. From Monday to Friday I lived in a flat above my publishing office at 36 Soho Square. Comfort was my wife; Bridget, Duff and Adam my children.

George was a large man with a huge head and a wide brow, which glistened with enthusiasm in conversation. Owing to some hip-trouble he walked with a stick. When this correspondence began he was seventy-two and I was forty-eight.

Marske-in-Swaledale　　　　　　　　　　　　RUPERT HART-DAVIS
February 1978

EXTRACT FROM THE EPILOGUE TO THE LAST VOLUME

Our published correspondence has been accused of 'elitism', snob-bery, name-dropping and old fashioned 'squareness', but happily the praise has far outweighed the denigration. I have had many hundreds of appreciative letters from all over the world, many love-letters from delightful old ladies, countless references to reading-lists compiled from our letters, and two separate strangers have written to say that our correspondence had changed their life.

As I have pointed out to many of our fans, my share in the corre-spondence was comparatively easy, since I was leading such an active life that all I had to do was to recount my week's doings, using him as the diary I never kept. But his task was far harder. Sitting when-ever possible in his beloved summer-house (the only time I tried it I just escaped *rigor mortis*) he had little straw for his magnificent bricks, since (except for reading) correcting exam-papers and attending examiners' conferences were almost his only occupations, until the Literary Society drew him to London once a month.

January 1983　　　　　　　　　　　　　　　R. H.-D.

*The original volumes were dedicated
by their editor, Rupert Hart-Davis,
with gratitude and affection to, or
to the dear memory of*

*PAMELA LYTTELTON
and to all her and George's
children*

DIANA HOOD, HUMPHREY LYTTELTON,
HELENA LAWRENCE, ROSE BOURNE
and MARY STEWART COX

JOCK AND DIANA MURRAY

ROGER AND SIBELL FULFORD

REGGIE AND JOYCE GRENFELL

TIM AND ROSALIE NUGENT

23 October 1955

My dear George

This not so much the first over, as a gentle limbering up, a few balls off the wicket to see whether the arm will still go over. You will probably find yourself sometimes cast as a mixture of psychiatrist and father-confessor, but you must be used to that. I shan't choose special subjects for you, as Horace Walpole did for each of his correspondents, but simply write whatever is in my mind or your letters suggest. Nor have I time to choose my words as I would for print, so you'll have to forgive many a lame and impotent conclusion.

If I had no family (bless them) or other ties and responsibilities, I should chuck publishing tomorrow, and live in a two-roomed cottage in the Yorkshire dales—don't ask me with whom, though one day you shall know—relying for my livelihood on free-lance literary work. I know exactly how little can be earned that way, but I have few expensive tastes (only books really), I could read all the great books which now I have only skimmed or forgotten or never read, and *then* I'd write you letters indeed! But that is a dream which will not be realised for many years, if ever. You must forgive all this egotism, but it's right that you should know whom you're writing to. I am in truth some sort of a research scholar *manqué*, but because I have made something of a name as a publisher and am good at getting on with people, it is assumed that I must *like* it, which frankly I do less and less.

The definition of genius: this I take to be nothing more or less than a super-normal degree of *energy*—physical, mental, spiritual, or in combination. Or can you at once produce a dozen indubitable geniuses to whom such a definition could not apply? 'Taking pains' to the nth degree seems to me to have nothing to do with the matter.

The other day John Sparrow[1] sent me his recent selection of Robert Bridges's poems: I have been reading them slowly, one at a time, and wondering why, with all their technical and verbal perfection, they are not more moving, not greater poems. Was it because his life was too sheltered? Or because the poems came more from the brain than

---

[1] Warden of All Souls College, Oxford.

the heart or guts? And yet quite a few of his *lines* stay in one's head, which is surely a good criterion. Goodbye till next week, when I shall expect a whale of a letter to answer.

Yours ever
Rupert

Finndale House
Grundisburgh
Woodbridge
Suffolk

27 October 1955
My dear Rupert

How neatly you touch the bullseye: 'I shall simply write whatever is in my mind, or your letters suggest'. Not that dear Maurice Headlam[1] does not do the former; but, alas, his mind is full of Irish politics of fifty years or more ago, of visits to old friends of whom I have never heard, of the novels of Charles Reade in small print, which, if you please, he sends me to read and return. Also a 'Dialogue of the Dead' between Kossuth, Garibaldi, and Michael Collins, composed by himself. The publisher of his *Irish Memories* refused it on the grounds (the tact of you publishers!) that it might stir up feelings better left at rest, leaving M.H. with the gratifying sense of having written something which Mr Lillyvick would have called 'absorbing, fairy-like, toomultuous'.[2]

As to research, who was it who described it as 'that state of resentful coma which scholars attempt to dignify by calling research' (not accurately quoted except for the first five words). Laski[3] produced it—mendaciously—as his own in a letter to Judge Holmes[4]. By the way how *immensely* good that correspondence is, don't you agree? Dr A.L. Goodhart once told me that practically nothing Laski said of what he had done (or read!) was true, but what does that matter? He had the root of the matter *qua* letter-writing in him, and so old Holmes often said. L. said of Horace Walpole 'You are glad he lived,

---

[1] Prominent civil servant. Brother of Cuthbert and Tuppy.

[2] *Nicholas Nickleby*, chapter XXV.

[3] Harold Laski (1893–1950). After teaching in the United States he became a highly influential Professor of political science at the London School of Economics.

[4] (1841–1935). Son of the essayist Oliver Wendell Holmes. Fought in the American Civil War. Appointed to the Supreme Court of the United States in 1902.

but very grateful that you didn't know him'. And after (as he said) sitting next to V. Woolf at lunch, 'Every phrase and gesture was studied. Now and again when she said something a little out of the ordinary she wrote it down herself in a notebook. *It was like watching someone organising her own immortality.*' Isn't that *beastly* good? Would *genius* be too big a word? Perhaps.

I think I agree with you about energy being the essence of it. Beethoven, Shakespeare, M. Angelo, Keats—yes, the impression I get from all of them is combined speed and intensity, which of course = energy. Which the expression 'taking pains' quite misses. There are so few signs of 'pains' about e.g. *Don Juan* that some quite unstupid people have been blind to its genius. When I was a young beak I praised it in my Extra Studies. A week later J.B.S. Haldane stopped after school and told me he had never enjoyed anything so much. The same day I was scolded for having set half College reading it. And I didn't at the time realise how right *I* had been and how wrong my stuffy old seniors! Do you realise that in those Extra Studies I had at different times Aldous Huxley, J. Haldane, C. Hollis, G. Orwell, C. Connolly, J. Lehmann, Alan Clutton-Brock, Peter Fleming, Noel Blakiston (I *think*), Alan Pryce-Jones, Rupert H-D.? There's glory for you!

Bridges? I entirely agree with you. Andrea del Sarto, do you think: 'All the play, the insight and the stretch—Out of me! Out of me!'[1] I have a dreadful suspicion sometimes that artists, if they are really to grow to full stature, mustn't have so much education. Hubert Parry is another example of brilliant promise ending in the merely accomplished and scholarly. 'Dreadful' is too big a word—insincere in fact, because I am no great believer in education—or indeed in democracy or a good many other things. I believe profoundly in what few others seem to nowadays, viz original sin. In fact my favourite text is Jeremiah's blunt assertion 'The heart is deceitful above all things and desperately wicked'. The truth of that seems to me positively glaring.

Well anyhow another thing which is also p.g. is that it is high time I stopped. You will be thinking how great the epistolary superiority

---

[1] From one of Browning's monologue poems, in which the Italian painter criticises his own work for lack of soul, in spite of his great technical abilities.

was of the boy whose letter home consisted of just 'S.O.S. L.S.D. R.S.V.P.' or the gamekeeper instructed to tell his employer when the woods had woodcock in them: 'Horned Sir. The kaks becum. Jarge.'

Bless you
Yours ever
G.W.L.

6 November 1955   *Bromsden Farm*

On Friday I went to Ronald Storrs'[1] funeral. The coffin glowed under K.C.M.G. banner of scarlet-and-white. I left the funeral remembering Ronald's telling me how he met my mother at a party in Venice in 1912, and how they quoted Meredith's poetry to each other in a gondola.

My next book, if I ever find time for it (what nonsense—one can always find or make time for something one is *determined* to do), will be about my mother, who was a lovely gifted tragic person.[2] She died aged 40 when I was 19, so the book will in fact also cover those years of my own life.

This must be the last sheet tonight, for I have a French novel to read—all about a dumb peasant and his bloody sheep—and a manuscript to prepare for the printer. Don't think for a moment that this delightful correspondence is solely for your benefit: it is pure self indulgence. You are the diary I have never kept, the excuse I have so long wanted for forming words on paper unconnected with duty or business.

9 November 1955   *Grundisburgh*

Did you ever get a letter from Monty James?[3] I once had a note from him inviting us to dinner—we *guessed* that the time was 8 and not 3, as it appeared to be, but all we could tell about the day was that it was not Wednesday. The late Bishop Brook of Ipswich maintained that all great men—Shakespeare, Napoleon, Brook, etc,—had illegible hands, and conveniently forgot, or more likely didn't know, that

---

[1] Middle East expert, governor of Jerusalem, Cyprus and Northern Rhodesia.

[2] *The Arms of Time*, 1979.

[3] M.R. James, Provost of Eton, author of *Ghost Stories of an Antiquary*, etc. G.W.L. had praised R.H.-D.'s handwriting.

Michael Angelo, Henry VIII, Elizabeth (when she chose), Lord Palmerston, all had conspicuously fine hands. But, though I hate to admit it, there is something in what he said—explained by some pundit, apropos, I think, of Napoleon's monstrous script, that where a brain is *very* quick, the hand just cannot keep up. An odd corollary to this is the undeniable fact that in a C or D division the stupidest boys did the best maps, the Collegers always the worst. I wonder why. 'Sir, you *may* wonder.'

What interesting forebears and relatives and connections you have. But some day you might like to hear of my uncle Albert.[1] He was *not* humdrum. He was a missionary. His face, his saintliness, and to a great extent, his clothes and his diet were those of John the Baptist. He was insatiably curious. When moving staircases came in he tried to stop one by holding on to one of the stationary knobs at the side. A moment later he picked himself up from the floor, quite satisfied by the proof that he could *not* stop it. Then he tried (about 60 odd) to go *up* the stairs that were coming *down*, and after a minute or so on what must have been exactly like a treadmill, found out that that too wouldn't do. You would have liked him.

13 November 1955   *Bromsden Farm*

I never saw Monty James's writing but doubt whether he can have been more illegible than Lady Colefax: the only hope of deciphering *her* invitations, someone said, was to pin them up on the wall and *run* past them! She had known everybody and remembered *nothing*.

I spent last Tuesday night at Cambridge. The Audit Feast at Christ's was quite impressive: 'scarlet and medals' the invitation-card said. I fought my way into my 25-year-old tails (it's the collar that almost strangles me) and was picked up by my host Graham Hough. At dinner I sat between him and Sir Hughe Knatchbull-Hugessen, an amiable little old man plastered with medals. Unprepared for such an honour, I could remember nothing about him except that when he was Ambassador in Turkey his valet stole and copied all his secret documents. This fascinating but delicate subject seemed better unbroached, so I confined myself to Shakespeare and the musical glasses, and we got along very well.

[1] The Hon. Albert Victor Lyttelton, priest (1844–1928).

I'm reading the new life of Kipling[1] with much interest and enjoyment. Now, *there* was a genius all right—just that energy we were discussing. I do hope you agree. I should say one of the great literary geniuses of the Anglo-Saxon race, and when time has winnowed away all the vulgarity, lack of taste, jingoism and cocksure brassiness, the residue will be read and enjoyed without end. I'm sure of it. But shall we ever know more of his secret thoughts and sources? I suppose not, for his wife and daughter have managed his posthumous fame as relentlessly as they did his living privacy. He had written almost all his best work by the time he was 40, at which age Scott hadn't begun his first novel—I know I'm drooling, but it's getting late and you won't mind.

Did you hear the story of the overworked law-student who confused arson with incest and ended by setting fire to his sister? I expect it's as old as the *Arabian Nights*, but I heard it only last week.

15/16 November 1955   *Grundisburgh*
I am almost the only admirer of Carlyle left. They tell me C's style turns their queasy stomachs, and they hate his 'philosophy'—as if that was his main quality.

I had a heated argument with some fellow-examiners at Oxford last year. One I silenced, i.e. reduced to speechless fury, by telling him his attitude towards literature was that of a lavatory attendant. Another I at least checked by asking him if he refused to read *The Jungle Book* because he disliked Kipling's imperialism.

I used to know *Captains Courageous* almost by heart, and still retain a good deal. My brother, who knew him well, told me it was R.K.'s favourite. Do you know his 'Proofs of Holy Writ'? It is not easily come by and is not in the 'definitive' collected works.[2] If you don't, I shall certainly send it for your perusal, and if you don't find it entrancingly brilliant, I shall go heavily as one that mourneth.

Look here, my dear Rupert, I do *not* like to hear of these headaches and insomnia (surely the worst of human ills, apart from the mere outrages like cancer, brain-tumour etc.).

[1] By Charles Carrington
[2] Published only in the *Strand Magazine*, April 1934, and in vol. XXX of the big Sussex Edition of Kipling's works. It is a dialogue between Shakespeare and Ben Jonson concerning a passage in *Isaiah*.

That is a lovely story of yours about the law-student—I can't send the ball back. But, suspecting your soundness about the higher clergy, I think you might like to hear that G. Meredith used to call the Archbishop 'The Mitred Cant'. And in the belief that you are much kinder about the lower clergy I am confident of your appreciating the information that Uncle Albert made a list of conversational openings; this list was found and among the earliest items was this: 'Are you aware that the heaviest eater in the zoo is the gnu?'

There was a peer in the train this morning, in my carriage. What a beautiful blend of splendour and absurdity it is that suitcase and hatbox and dispatch-box should all be merely marked with A. I don't know who he was, but I feel sure he expected us to know—as he will on the Judgment Day, and what a frosty look Peter will get if he *asks*!

20 November 1955   Bromsden Farm

Yes, I am much more tolerant of the minor clergy, quite ready to be 'preached to death by wild curates' any day, which reminds me, the Kipling biography proves, what we've really always known, that far the most important influence on R.K's writing was the Bible. If more people read or listened to it to-day the level of literary style would certainly be higher.

Other people's dreams are always tedious, but I shall tell you a recent one of mine nevertheless. When we were both twenty-two I married an enchanting actress called Peggy Ashcroft: it was a sad failure: we were much too young to know what we wanted, and actresses should never marry, especially young ones. Anyhow, after much agony we parted and were duly divorced. Nowadays Peggy and I lunch together perhaps once or twice a year in a Soho restaurant and have a lovely nostalgic-romantic talk of shared memories of long ago. She is a lovely person and the best actress living—did you see her Hedda Gabler? Some months ago, when I hadn't seen or consciously thought of her for months, I dreamed that we were lunching together as usual, and she asked me: 'Do you think you could ever be in love with me again as you were when we were young?' I answered: 'The lightning never strikes twice in the same place, but the sun shines on for ever'. Then I woke up. Next day I remembered the dream and wrote to tell P. of it. She was much pleased. I tremble to think what Freud would make of it, but it strikes me as beautiful. You needn't

7

fear a spate of dream-recital, for I scarcely every remember one. Do you?

23 November 1955   *Grundisburgh*
You must educate me gently and gradually in modern poetry. I found, not long ago, what *I* thought an excellent little poem by Day Lewis beginning 'Now the full-throated daffodils, Our trumpeters in gold . . .' and was told by a man, who prays, I think nightly, for the restoration of Ezra Pound's wits, that it was 'twee'.

I look forward eagerly to the Carlyle volume.[1] I hope J. Symons *has* included the passage in *Frederick* where T.C. likens the previous writers about him, who apparently copied unskilfully from each other, to two dogs who cautiously approach each other, 'investigate the parts of shame, and then depart with a satisfied air as from a problem solved'. I have not seen the passage for forty years, and probably misquote.

Old George Chitty[2] once consulted C. Miller[3] about his 'raves'. C.M. told him to tell him a fortnight later about his dreams. G.C. told him he could remember but one, and he didn't think it would help. C.M. heard it and agreed. It was very short—merely that he dreamt his cook had given birth to a zebra.

27 November 1955   *Bromsden Farm*
In principle I don't think any poem should need notes or laboured exegesis—or at any rate not until its first musical, magical impact has been made. Surely it is the *magic* that distinguishes poetry from verse or prose, and by its very nature magic cannot be analysed or explained. Still, it's interesting perhaps to see what added beauties or meanings the learned can extract for us.

'Proofs of Holy Writ' is terrifically good—brilliant, I should say— and I am most grateful to you for introducing me to it. It (do you remember Cobbett's 'When I see a number of "its" on the page, I tremble for the writer'?) It seems to me to throw rays of light on to the creative use of words by a genius—as exemplified in R.K. himself.

---

[1] A selection published in R.H.-D.'s Reynard Library Series in 1956.
[2] Eton master
[3] Eton doctor

He always referred to his own inspiration as his 'Daemon', and he makes Shakespeare do so here. The story reminds me of that wonderful one called 'Wireless', in which the consumptive chemist's assistant gets the Keats poem through the ether. Both are comments on how great poets work.

Sorry you wasted your time on that broadcast: I didn't hear it, but I gather that my remarks had almost all been cut (it was only 20 minutes out of 75). The thing itself began with a luncheon in a private room in the Howard Hotel—*assez lugubre* in all conscience. I sat between the BBC man who was arranging the broadcast and Lady Violet Bonham-Carter, whom I had never met before. A simple man of my acquaintance once met G.K. Chesterton and described him as 'quite all there and very spry'. I can't find better words to describe Lady V. We chattered amiably about her father [Asquith], the art of oratory, the future (God save the mark) of the Liberal Party, etc. With the brandy we were handed copies of the Questions, and there followed a long friendly wrangle as to who should answer which first. I was allotted two—'Are books too expensive?' (which I belaboured so stoutly that no one else dared utter) and 'Which are the two greatest poets of this century?' I said Yeats and Hardy, and eventually they almost all agreed with me. Do you? Hardy can only be included because (a) he *published* all his books of poems save one in the twentieth century, and (b) those uniquely wonderful love-poems, written after his first wife's death and harking back to their courtship, were composed in 1912–13. You must know them: if not I shall come and read them to you relentlessly. Of Yeats's greatness I have no doubt either. I once saw him in the Athenaeum, looking every inch the poet with flowing blue-white hair. Both he and Hardy grew in stature as poets all through their lives: so many sing their little lyrical song in youth, and then dry up or repeat themselves thinly.

Back to the Festival Hall, where we sat at little tables on the stage under bright lights. Away in the darkness were 3000 stodgy schoolchildren, who took some rousing. It was like appearing on the stage in a huge theatre without any rehearsal.

On Tuesday evening I journeyed to Putney (people never think their own home is far away) to dine with the Arthur Ransomes. My present concern is that he should finish his autobiography, for he has made me promise (as his literary executor) to finish it for him if he

9

dies too soon (he's only 71) and he has left all the most difficult bits to the last. (I am already literary executor for Hugh Walpole, Duff Cooper and Humphry House[1]—also in posse for William Plomer and others. It's a thankless and exacting task.) To continue my hideous week—On Wednesday evening I took the chair at the Book Exhibition for an author of mine called 'Elephant Bill' and dined him thereafter. On Thursday a dinner-party at the Priestleys' in Albany— nine people including Edith Evans and Rosamond Lehmann. All very agreeable, but when does one read or write, rest or think? J.B.P. was at his most amusing, all chips temporarily removed from his shoulder. He told of an American Rotarian who couldn't see half a grapefruit without getting to his feet and starting 'Ladies and Gentlemen . . .'

30 November 1955   *Grundisburgh*

You interest me about John Wain—clearly a good man. But I wonder why he should say anything so silly as that, apart from his knowledge of Latin, Housman was a very stupid man? And Auden said much the same of Tennyson, the only thing *he* knew about being hypochondria! Are you in a temper when reading as often as I am? Leavis on Lawrence, for instance. I haven't read much yet, and so far the atmosphere is that of a clever disgruntled undergraduate with his conceit, dogmatism, bad temper and sneers. Why should we all be bullied into admiring D.H.L.?

Surely the pessimism and gloom of the Audens and Co in the Thirties was a very poor, thin, *rootless* crop compared with Hardy's undramatic, unegotistical picture of the human situation as he saw it. And what sheer pleasure one gets out of a couplet like:

Numb as a vane that cankers on its point,
True to the wind that kissed ere canker came.[2]

That passion for after-dinner oratory is very odd. The Ipswich cricket club centenary dinner shewed how infectious it is. There were

---

[1] Duff Cooper, 1st Viscount Norwich, was R.H.-D.'s mother's brother. Humphry House was fellow of Wadham College, Oxford and an expert on Charles Dickens and the Victorian era.
[2] Hardy, 'She to Him'.

eleven speeches plus a soprano of tremendous manpower and a humorous raconteur. We sat down at 7.00 and rose at 12.15. I felt very Johnsonian about 'the paucity of human pleasures'. And there was no Lehmann, Evans, or Priestley in the company. One man told a cricket story that I first heard in 1899 and another a risqué one that was the signature tune of the penultimate class at Evelyn's Prep School in 1893.

4 December 1955   Bromsden Farm

I wonder you bother with Leavis on Lawrence. Leavis has his points; his writing is at least *alive*, which so much literary criticism isn't, but I much prefer the old-style critics who tried to get inside their authors, find out what they were driving at and interpret accordingly. Nowadays they attempt to force the authors into some preconceived theory of their own. With Leavis it usually takes the form of claiming that one, or possibly two, of the author's books are imperishable masterpieces, of immense 'importance', 'significance' and all the rest of it, while the rest of his *oeuvre* is beneath contempt.

Last Tuesday with pride and sorrow I watched my son Duff march off towards Germany with his battalion (1st Coldstream).[1] He looked enormous (the same size as me) and terribly young, and since tears always spring to my eyes at the first strains of a drum-and-fife band (as at a glimpse of the King or Queen), I was more moved even than I had expected to be. The band continued to play Auld Lang Syne on the platform until all the women were weeping. I left before the train went.

7 December 1955   Grundisburgh

[Rupert said he longed to know more of George's daily life and surroundings.] The diversions of Grundisburgh are not very numerous—no huntin', shootin' or fishin', no Morris dancing, nor Knurr and Spell. We could call on Mrs Pizzey, we could talk to Mrs Paternoster—oh no, I forgot, she is stone deaf. Charlie Balls has, alas, left the village. No coarse laughter from you, please. It is a very common name in Suffolk. There is always work of some kind in the garden—not much with the spade but with axe and saw. I hate the spade but love the axe. The fare is well enough and those who have tasted my wife's omelettes are convinced that even on the innermost

---

[1] He was doing his national service.

recesses of Abraham's bosom they would find nothing better. We have no resident staff. A good woman comes in the morning; the gardener we share with another, but, thanks be, he lives next door, so lights the stove every day. There is a rather spacious garden with a stream, a revolving summerhouse which is warm whenever the sun shines, even in January, and where I spend many hours, writing and reading. I get up rather loosely and breakfast at about 9.15. I never go to bed before 12 or to sleep before 1, though not going so far as Dr J. who said that anyone who went to bed before 12 was a scoundrel. I think it is perfectly true to say that (a) no one is entertained, and (b) no one is made to do anything he doesn't want to. Visitors have got on with their accounts, their income-tax returns, their school reports, their blank verse epics, their autobiographies.

Gosh yes, that *Titanic* poem![1] I remember the thing happening. I was dining with the Head Master and Mrs Warre came in, quivering slightly with age and dottiness, and said 'I am sorry to hear there has been a bad boating accident'—an odd but very characteristic way of describing the sinking of the largest ship in the world and the death of 1400 people.

I weep at all sorts of odd things, and a good many old men (who have not dried up) do, e.g. Winston, M.R. James etc. Do you remember how pleased E.V. Lucas was to find another man who, like himself, was chary of seeing the greatest of all jugglers, Cinquevalli, because he always made him cry? I know the feeling. It is something to do with seeing anything *perfectly* done, nothing at all to do with sadness. After all in old days Englishmen wept like anything, e.g. in Parliament when the Petition of Right was presented who was the great man who proposed to make a long speech beginning 'I protest . . .' and got no further than 'I p . . .' and after three attempts sat down?

11 December 1955   *Bromsden Farm*
I delight in your appreciation of Hardy's poems. We haven't mentioned *The Dynasts*. Did you hear the Third Programme broadcast of it? I firmly believe that the old boy, with true poetic prophecy, wrote it for broadcasting, though the thing was unknown at the time. He

---

[1] 'The Convergence of the Twain' by Thomas Hardy.

certainly wrote it for something, yet on the stage it is quite unactable, in the study almost (as a whole) unreadable. Those stage-directions, so tedious to read through, were *thrilling* when dramatically broadcast by several voices. Shutting one's eyes and having the work done for one, it was possible, at exactly the right speed and without the interference of print, to shift one's imagination from the whole of Europe to the field of Austerlitz. They cut it too, to great advantage. If ever they repeat it, you must listen to every moment. Particularly moving was the scene where Napoleon rides back, hopeless and alone, after Waterloo and is taunted by the spirits: some of it might be by Shakespeare:

> Great men are meteors that consume themselves
> To light the earth. This is my burnt-out hour.

I've no doubt the whole work is Hardy's masterpiece. Some fancy it as a film, but I'm sure such treatment would vulgarise most of the poetry out of it.

Heinemann are to buy all the shares of my company, at a very generous price. My original shareholders, poor lambs, will lose half their money (which they've long expected to do, for the shares were written down by half some three years ago), the later shareholders nothing. Heinemann will take over most of my travelling, overseas representation etc., but the choice and production of my books will remain completely mine. To the public there will be no observable change. Moreover I shall be able, for the first time, to draw a salary on which I can live. The power behind all this is a remarkable chap called Lionel Fraser, a banker who is chairman of the company [Thomas Tilling Ltd] which owns 40% of the shares of Heinemann (which is a public company). For some unaccountable reason Lionel thinks the world of me, and is determined that one day I shall be chairman of Heinemann. I've repeatedly told him I don't much fancy that kingly crown, but his backing is all-important. Immediately, as you can imagine, I feel as though the crushing weights were gradually being lifted from my shoulders.

14 December 1955   *Grundisburgh*
Rather a *de profundis* letter from me this week—in a very mild way. I am in the thick of exam-papers, sick to death of reading secondhand

tripe about Henry V, and Prospero, and Chaunticleer. Secondhand, because, except at the good schools, the candidates are merely repeating what their half-baked instructors have been telling them, many of whom I suspect are followers of the man Leavis. Who can it have been who told the boys of Bloxham, or the young papists at Birmingham Oratory, that, except for a few lines spoken by Caliban, there was no poetry in *The Tempest?*

And—a further proof of my degraded state of mind—I am writing in an arm-chair with a BIRO, of all disgusting implements. But enough of these trivial bunkers. Like John Wesley's friend who said, 'We all have our crosses' when his fire smoked.

Hardy's *Dynasts* I read through with intense enjoyment at Cambridge, and often *in* since, and one of these days shall re-read *in toto.* In the *Spectator* of Dec. 2 John Wain warns us against re-reading an author we enjoyed when young—e.g. Kipling or Housman. Utter rot! Rupert, you must take that young man in hand. His article isn't a work of criticism; it is a shudder of nerves—and so shrill, unbalanced, and *conceited,* for he tells us *ex cathedra* that this is what K. *is* and implies that we who don't agree are merely adolescent. Do tell him not to be such an *ass?* Because he is clearly very intelligent. Why has he not learnt that a little real humility sharpens the perceptions wonderfully and has other good effects too. What a strong tendency there is today to lay down the law about what one may or must, and may not and must not, admire. These brash young men will think that a change of fashion is an advance in wisdom!

I say, what ignoramuses politicians are. In the *D. Mail,* after Attlee's retirement, Desmond Donnelly gave as an instance of A's fondness for deflating exaggerated reputations his calling Mr Gladstone 'the W.G. Grace of politics'. The poor fool didn't realise this was the highest possible *praise.* Attlee was born in the same week as I was, and to any boy of that age the one and only hero was W.G. My father knew him well, and took my brother and me to shake his hand after a match at Worcester in 1897. He was very gracious in a sort of Newfoundland doglike way—more so than to another parent who had also presented his son to him. The first thing the old man said to the boy, his father standing by, was 'Well, young fellow, I hope yer a better fielder than yer father was; he was the worst I ever did see!'—and went off into a Gargantuan laugh. My father heard of this and said 'Oh yes, W.G. never forgave the wretched chap for missing a catch (off W.G.) which lost the match v Middlesex in—if you please—1870!' He had the memory and the patience, as well as the figure, of an elephant.

17 December 1955   *Bromsden Farm*
Last evening I was reading in a third-class carriage on my usual Friday train to Henley, when it suddenly ran off the rails. Mercifully we were moving very slowly and managed to pull up without injury or delay, but there were a few moments of incredulous terror. The carriage was full—an enormous woman, a very small boy, several tired business men, etc. At the vital moment they all woke and sat up silent, immobilised by the unexpected. I remember thinking 'The boy will be cushioned by the fat woman,' 'Are we on an embankment?' (It was pitch dark.) 'What can one hold on to?' (Nothing but glass each side, and the laden rack above.) 'This is what it feels like to be in a smash.' And then the train bumped to a halt, and everybody began to talk at once in the friendliest way, as they used to in the war. After a few moments we (and all the other passengers) opened the nearside door and helped the women and children down on to the track. We were only about half a mile short of Twyford station, towards which we trudged carrying our luggage (I had three bags full of books and MSS and my wife's Christmas present), tripping over sleepers and praying no other trains were due. Just before we got there, two porters arrived with lanterns. They forced us all into a tiny relief train, and we reached Henley only half an hour late.

c/o R.M.A. Bourne Esq
The Briary
Eton College
22 December 1955   *Windsor*
[Rupert had claimed to be one of the few people who had slept right through *Das Rheingold* on two chairs at the back of a box at Covent Garden.] Yes, of course, Wagner in bits—one must have them—and oddly, all the beginning of the *Rheingold* is a favourite of mine. And some of *Tristan*, but gosh! the tediousness of much. I remember a young man leaving in the middle of the last act, apologising loudly to the owners of the feet he trod on with 'You see I have got some

chaps coming to breakfast.' You must educate me up to Mahler. My musical knowledge is very rough and ready. I love the fairly obvious Beethovens because I love hearing 'desperate tides of the great world's anguish forced through the channels of a single heart,'[1] but I think of the symphonies I really like No 8 and the Pastoral best. Do you remember Ezra Pound's referring to him as 'the beastly Beethoven'? How one's toe itches sometimes!

Boxing Day 1955   *Bromsden Farm*
Last week in London was the usual pre-Christmas scrimmage. On Wednesday I caught the 11 o'clock train to Brighton with a dear friend and spent the rest of the day there, doing Christmas shopping. Brighton never fails to improve my health and spirits. I was a sickly child, always ill with this or that, and my mother inevitably took me to Brighton to recuperate: we must have stayed at *all* those big hotels along the front, and the combined sensations of spoiling and truancy persist to this day, quite apart from the air which I love. There are several good secondhand bookshops too, and a theatre, and the walk to Rottingdean, and the antique shops in the Lanes (now spoilt and expensive)—oh yes, I love it all.

One evening I dined with my old father at White's—mercifully two friends joined us and so prevented his usual complaining, wishing he was dead etc.—the most boring and unanswerable form of conversation. My plans for rereading an old favourite[2] during the holiday have been thwarted, chiefly by the piles of MSS which I had to bring with me. So far I have dealt with 50,000 words of an exploring expedition to Tibet in 1913 (the public doesn't seem to be as sick of this sort of subject as I am), a melodramatic novel set in the Welsh mountains, a travel book about Jugoslavia (who on earth wants to read about that?), and am in the middle of a selection of the letters written by the first Earl of Lytton (Owen Meredith) to his wife from Portugal in the 1860's. They have been put together by his daughter, Lady Emily Lutyens (a darling old creature whose book, *A Blessed Girl*, I published), but I doubt so far whether they're of sufficient general interest.

[1] From F.W.H. Myers' *St Paul.*
[2] 'Something short, sweet and long-forgotten – *Northanger Abbey* perhaps or *Old Mortality*' 17/12/55.

3 January 1956   *The Briary, Eton*
You remind me of old C.H. Blakiston[1] (only in *one* respect!).
Whatever village we passed on a field-day it always turned out that
C.H.B. once had an aunt there, or knew the vicar, or the *only* tailor
in S.E. England who made trousers that never wore out etc. Any
name in the literary, dramatic, political world I mention turns out to
be well known to you for years past.

Yes. *Nothing* is more boring than nine out of ten New Year parties.
We went to one once in Grundisburgh, and the hours passed on
leaden feet. At 10 the hostess played the piano, not very well. Dry cake
was passed round, so dry that my wife threw her bit into the fire—
unperceived, she hoped, but alas she suddenly caught the soulful but
reproachful eyes of her hostess looking at her from the looking-glass
above the piano.

8 January 1956   *Bromsden Farm*
1956 began for me with all the savagery of its beastly predecessor.
Do you remember that splendid opening of a poem by Sir John
Denham:

> All on a weeping Monday,
> With a fat Bulgarian Sloven?

I thought of it when I arrived at Soho Square last Monday to find
that my stout charwoman, who has 'done for me' these five and a half
years, had left a note saying she had flu, couldn't face the stairs any
more and must give up the job. On Thursday the darling old ex-
butler who has been coming one morning a week to keep my tattered
old clothes in some sort of order was taken to hospital and put in an
oxygen tent, where he died peacefully next morning, a victim of
smog, no doubt, though Lady Emily Lutyens (81), whom I saw on
Friday, says it's nothing to the fogs she knew as a girl. She was deliciously scornful of policemen wearing 'gas-masks' to direct the traffic.

18 January 1956   *Grundisburgh*
Your days' activities make me feel positively faint. Do you ever have
time to twiddle your thumbs—to ruminate? I expect your mind—in

---

[1] Eton master, later Headmaster of Lancing.

fact I know—moves very quickly. Mine moves like a hippo emerging from his wallow, with a good deal of mud clinging to him. And on Friday I address the Rotarians of Woodbridge. I think I shall tell them to fear God and keep His commandments, and then sit down. I am told they are not a very lively lot, but I suppose there could be no better instance of a contradiction in terms than 'a sprightly Rotarian'.

I notice, by the way, that you never write about politics. Acid references to Eden or Dulles, curses about the T.U.C. etc., are conspicuously absent from your bright and brimming page (in Henry James's not *very* taking phrase). Partly, I doubt not, for fear I might reply in kind. Have no fear. Old Maurice Headlam's long and barely legible letters are full of anger and lamentation about Asquith's handling of Ireland and the Liberal heresies of the early 1900's—it is like hearing the moaning of dinosaurs, so immensely long ago it all seems.

22 January 1956   *Bromsden Farm*
[G.W.L. had just re-read R.H-D's biography of the novelist Hugh Walpole, and asked which were his best books.] Hugh's best books, I should say, are *The Dark Forest, Mr Perrin and Mr Traill, The Old Ladies*, the *Jeremy* books, and as a curiosity *The Killer and the Slain.*

No, I seldom, alas, have time to ruminate or twiddle my thumbs, let alone stand and stare, and the lack of such amenity has a cumulatively crushing effect. My mind does in fact move very fast (on the surface, *bien entendu*, a sort of jet-skater), and that is its most effective quality, though it makes me intolerant of slowness and stupidity. I read about politics a bit, as we all must, but take little real interest, particularly since the disappearance of Winston, the last of the giants. Eden's toothy complacency, total lack of oratory, and record of indecision put him in the Atlee class (though I suspect *he* was much shrewder than he appeared). As for Dulles—God help us all! Do you remember his taking a revolver as a present to General Neguib?!

25 January 1956   *Grundisburgh*
I grow old, Master Shallow, though even *in articulo mortis* I believe I shall still remember that Attlee has two t's! But perhaps you put one

on purpose like one of Tennyson's Cambridge friends who always wrote oxford with a small o—mainly, as far as I recollect, because at Oxford they admired Byron more than Shelley. The modern Oxford don is not markedly full of 'sweetness and light', which M. Arnold (quite rightly) said was the *sine qua non* of all real civilisation. The Taylors, the Rowses, the Trevor-Ropers—they generally seem to be at someone's throat. Perhaps they always were. At Cambridge too they are pretty acid about each other.

And then the other book, the Henry James letters.[1] As always H.J. half fascinates, half infuriates me. No one, surely, ever displayed the infinite resources of word and phrase as he does. No nuance of feeling or fancy, no undertone of even the faintest audibility, is beyond the reach of his pen. But when he goes on and on and on, unravelling every tiny strand in—often—some quite commonplace network—well now—again the illumination is splendid and satisfying (as on Pater, p. 178). But too often there is a great peacock's-tail of verbiage—no, what *is* the right metaphor? Shall we say a rich overture of melodious chords leading to no particular tune. Sometimes the not very uncommon event of his being late with a reply produces a positive flood of apology, self-reproach, explanation, that is very wearisome. One oughtn't to read too many of his letters on end. After all, each *is* a work of art.

I envy you, going with the twelve-year-old to *Charley's Aunt*. I remember taking Humphrey to *Treasure Island*, in which his ecstatic enjoyment was only just not equalled by the horrid feeling that every scene brought the play's end nearer. I can remember my own delight at *C's Aunt* (also *aetat* 12). When the young man poured tea into the top hat, I felt that life had no more to offer.

29 January 1956   *Bromsden Farm*
About my beloved Henry James I can understand but not share your feelings. You're right about his infinite verbal resources—never a word used accidentally—but you miss, it seems to me, a lot of the humour in what you condemn. Those trails of words cover-ing nothing, or hiding his true opinion, spanning a vacuum, I find

[1] G.W.L. had been sent a copy of this selection by Leon Edel, by R.H.-D., who had just published it.

richly droll. Do you know this telegram of his, refusing an invitation: IMPOSSIBLE IMPOSSIBLE IMPOSSIBLE IF YOU KNEW WHAT IT COST ME TO SAY SO YOU CAN COUNT HOWEVER AT THE REGULAR RATES ASK MISS ROBINS TO SHARE YOUR REGRET I MEAN MINE. And did you ever read a lovelier letter of condolence than the one to Mrs R.L. Stevenson?[1] You're probably right about not reading too many on end, though I can take any number.

5 February 1956   *Bromsden Farm*
I used to see a lot of Beachcomber in London (he is an Old Harrovian called J.B. Morton) he was immensely gay and amusing. One day when we were walking down an extremely crowded Fleet Street, he suddenly went up to a pillar-box and shouted into the slot: 'YOU CAN COME OUT NOW!' I liked very much his poem on Tolstoy, of which the refrain ran:

> He ran away from home when he was ninety,
> And his golden hair was hanging down his back.

And he summed up the jargon-bosh of art- and music-critics beautifully by announcing: 'Wagner is the Puccini of music'. He always told me that the readers of the *Daily Express* were (often understandably) unable to distinguish between his funny column and the rest of the paper. In proof he told how one day, short of a paragraph and late with his copy, he filled up the space with these words: '*Stop Press.* At 3.55 pm yesterday there was a heavy fall of green Chartreuse over South Croydon.' Next morning he received *six* letters from six people

---

[1] To have lived in the light of that splendid life, that beautiful, bountiful thing – only to see it, from one moment to the other, converted into a fable as strange and romantic as one of his own, a thing that has been and has ended, is an anguish into which no one can enter fully and of which no one can drain the cup for you . . . For myself, how shall I tell you how much poorer and shabbier the whole world seems, and how one of the closest and strongest reasons for going on, for trying and doing, for planning and dreaming of the future, has dropped in an instant out of life. I was haunted indeed with a sense that I should never again see him – but it was one of the best things in life that he was there, or that one had him – at any rate one heard of him, and felt him and awaited him and counted him into everything one most loved and lived for. He lighted up one whole side of the globe, and was in himself one whole province of one's imagination.   December 1894

assuring him he was mistaken: they had all spent that afternoon in South Croydon and were positive that not so much as a drop of green Chartreuse had fallen! After that he gave up.

9 February 1956   *Grundisburgh*

Conybeare[1] always maintained that if you could sleep and eat, you had nothing really to complain of. I don't think that is wholly true, though he clearly believed it of himself. Often, when he played fives, his heart palpitated in a way that would have sent anyone else in a bee-line to the nearest specialist. He merely thumped his chest angrily, saying 'Go *on*, go *on*!' till his terrified heart didn't dare disobey. And, of course, even when he was still playing football, you could hear his ribs clattering like castanets as he pounded down the side-line. He cured a poisoned thumb by scrubbing it with a nail-brush till there was not only no poison left, but practically no thumb. A good man—would have been still better, if married. Not that that is true of everyone!

I have been reading *Oxford Apostles* by Geoffrey Faber during the week-end, and not finished yet. *Quite fascinating*! I can't put it down, even, or perhaps especially, because my feelings about Newman steadily mount to a sort of nausea—or would if he were not so completely remote. All that passionate almost hysterical feeling about Mother Church, that unintelligible conviction that evangelicals who regard Christ's words as more important than those of Aquinas are 'deep in error and sin'. What *leagues* away we are from Newman's belief in eternal punishment. The really horrible, unworthy, and only-to-you-mentionable thought comes into my mind, that the right treatment of the young Newman was that coarsely advocated by a Guards colonel, as to what should be done with a new, rather namby-pamby subaltern: 'Put him to the stud!' and p. to the s. he was with, no doubt, the manliest results; he may even be a colonel himself by now. And then dear Dr Pusey, on whom the effect of Mrs P's death was that he would not lace (button) up his boots or shave regularly, and got steadily fatter! He was all for flagellation but reluctantly eschewed it because it gave

---

[1] A.E. Conybeare, Eton master. R.H.-D. had reported that he felt well for the first time in months.

him bronchitis. There is really no limit to the pathetic absurdity of these great men.

12 *February 1956*   *Bromsden Farm*
You so often touch on questions of religion that I should perhaps tell you that I believe in none of it. I hope you won't be distressed, as I fear Jonah was when I told him. Original Sin, yes, but the Resurrection of the Body, etc, no. Don't think that I wouldn't like to believe: of course I would, and of course I realise that the lack of belief is at the bottom of most of our troubles to-day. Clearly one can go only a certain distance by intellectual ways—the final step must surely be an act of faith. I seldom go to church, but I like it when I do—the hymns and the wonderful words and the general *Gemütlichkeit*—but I simply don't believe a word of it. Not an Atheist, you know, but an old-fashioned Agnostic. One could hardly fail to be interested in a subject at once so fundamental and so fantastic, but I am generally too busy to spend much time on it. You must write an even longer letter, please, and tell me your own views.

15 *February 1956*   *Grundisburgh*
Religion—yet another matter on which we agree. Like P.G.W's Russian novelist on his colleagues, I spit me of the Virgin Birth, not merely as untrue, but as dehumanising Christ and making his life really pointless. Very crude and juvenile etc, I admit, and *think* of the great men of infinite wisdom and subtlety who have believed it! But I can't help that. As the Japanese student said 'A man must float on his own bladder', so there it is. George Herbert's 'But oh Eternity's too short to utter all Thy praise' throws a grim light on life after death—at any rate in heaven. And apropos of that I can't help thinking 'Oh ye ice and snow, praise ye the Lord' as absurd as any human utterance. My eccentric uncle Albert's substitution 'Oh ye strawberries and cream' (when the page was out of his prayer-book) was surely no more outlandish. Legend has added 'Oh ye bacon and eggs', but that is going rather too far.

And 'believe' is much too big a word to use about life after death. I vaguely feel, I occasionally hope, but that is all. That great man Judge Holmes surely hit the nail when he said 'I see sufficient reasons for doing my damndest without demanding to know the strategy or even the tactics of the campaign.' Was anyone *ever* influenced in his conduct by thoughts of the next world? I don't believe it. And how right you are about the outstanding beauty of some of the liturgy. I still feel hot anger at the memory of Jackie Chute altering 'indifferently' to 'impartially' in that wonderful prayer of Cranmer's in the Communion service 'Almighty and ever-living God'. You may (no I don't think so) say it was a venial substitution, and the rhythm was not gashed as those coxcombs (as W.E.G. called them) the Revisers did when they altered 'charity' to 'love' in *Corinthians*. But, gosh, the sermons! Bad ones put me in such a rage that my wife says church, which I attend pretty regularly for much the same reasons as you, obviously does me more harm than good. But it doesn't when I read—as anyone can who takes any trouble—to an entirely attentive audience the story of Absalom's death, Elijah in the wilderness, *Job* chapter 28, the last chapter of *Ecclesiastes* and many, many others.

19 February 1956   *Bromsden Farm*
Jelly's[1] funeral service was in every way suited to his spartan integrity (no comfortable chairs allowed in boys' rooms). Chapel was arctic, and the serried rows of beaks swaddled in scarves and overcoats looked scruffy but well-meaning. Some of the old guard looked like shrunken and frozen replicas of their old selves. Quite a decent sprinkling of old boys, and the west end of Chapel looked reasonably occupied. The service itself was utterly Jelly in its lack of concessions to the weaker spirits. The psalm was unsingable by the layman (one of those in which the caesura seems to shift disconcertingly), the hymn was unknown and very dull, the prayers inaudible. Only the Provost's clear, firm reading of the familiar words from *Corinthians* touched the imagination, but as the dear old fellow's coffin was carried out I thought sentimentally of the tens of thousands of times he must have attended Chapel, and was glad I had come down to bid him farewell.

23 February 1956   *Grundisburgh*
What, in the last resort, is there to be said for February? A positively whoreson month surely, and why did that admirable adjective ever

---

[1] E.L. Churchill, R.H.-D.'s Eton housemaster.

drop out of the language? Or, for the matter of that, the superb Chaucerian verb to 'swink'.[1] It wouldn't do in the welfare state of course, though no doubt good men do swink in the fields and coal-pits. The real idlers are to be found in the building world—as the excellent bricklayer who lives in our garden admits. He is a striking exception—loves doing his work well and quickly. He left his recent master because this wretch told him that a particular job must be 'made to last till Thursday'. My chap—an eccentric in 1956—held that, as it could easily be done by Tuesday, this order was dishonest. 'What laughable simplicity' was his mate's reaction. But he will come out on top on the Judgment Day—or would if there was one when 'the ungodly, filled with guilty fears, Behold His wrath prevailing'. Why so cross when He knew they would behave like that and in fact made them so that they were bound to?

As to heaven, why has nobody ever faced the fact that immortality *per se* is intolerable whatever we shall be doing in it, unless we have minds and bodies and tastes and faculties so different from anything we can imagine that it isn't worth talking about. There will probably be something, because 'this pomp of worlds, this pain of birth' looks, by and large, so very futile if it is all there is. And Judge Holmes didn't think there wasn't any strategy, only that he couldn't begin to see what it was. I am glad you liked his remark; I knew you would. He strikes one almost at once as a first-rate man—using that adjective sparely and only when it is deserved. You will also like him on George Moore, 'that delightful blackguard G.M. He simplifies the steps to copula-tion as Raphael does the mountain in the Transfiguration.' As 'dear Edward' Martyn said when asked about G.M's good qualities, 'He hadn't any'. But as a writer! I can't do *The Brook Kerith* and some others, but *Hail and Farewell* is a constant delight.

I like your vivid little picture of E.L.C's funeral. I wonder who chose the psalm and hymn. Musicians probably, who are mainly mad. I remember Claude Elliott [Head Master] showing me a list of hymns and asking me what I thought it was. I perused it and decided it was a list of the most popular hymns. No. It was the hymns the swell musicians wanted omitted from the new edition of A. and M. Practically all were retained. 'Scruffy but well-meaning' is *fine*. But it

---

[1] To toil.

cuts deeper than for this occasion, being in fact a pretty accurate epitome of the whole tribe of us at all times. But of course the times are scruffier. Ainger never washed up; Luxmoore never wheeled a pram; Broadbent never shovelled snow from his roof.[1] These things make for scruffiness.

26 February 1956   *Bromsden Farm*
I agree that without some sort of after-life this one is futile, but why shouldn't it be? Many of the most agreeable things are. I notice that when people can think of no other reason for the existence of heaven and hell, they usually fall back on the futility of everything without them, but I can't accept that as an argument. It's agreeable to hope, with Judge Holmes, that there is a strategy beyond our comprehension, but I can't see it as more than a pious hope. Which reminds me: do you know Belloc's unpublished ballade about Mrs Willie James, one of Edward VII's ladies? The *envoi* runs:

> Prince, Father Vaughan shall entertain the Pope,
> And you shall entertain the Jews at Tring,
> And I will entertain a pious hope,
> But Mrs James shall entertain the King.

1 March 1956   *Grundisburgh*
My uncle Edward, with towering and characteristic exaggeration used to say that a problem which had, since civilisation's dawn, baffled all the profoundest intellects of Christendom was—how to combine a full household attendance at family prayers with a hot breakfast. Well, without going quite so far as that, it is a constant puzzlement to me why the Russian leader should be always pronounced by our pedantic announcers as Kruschov if spelt 'chev', or conversely, why spelt 'chev' if pronounced 'chov'? A small matter you will say— quite rightly—but so is a very small stone in one's shoe.

Wasn't that an excellent review of your Carlyle book by Peter Quennell? One of the few who appear to realise the old crab-apple's purely literary magnificence; his portraiture is surely unsurpassable. I wonder if it would have been if he hadn't had all those gastric ulcers.

---

[1] Eton masters.

It is or used to be the fashion to overpraise *her* letters, which to me have an overdose of ill-health and domestic servants. It was only recently that I came across a trenchant verdict by someone that she could be a relentless bore with her protracted Scottish stories. A formidable pair they must have been with their united dyspepsia and insomnia and nerves.

Did *you* go through a stage when you thought 'We are the music-makers'[1] the finest poem in the language? I still think puppies must and ought to have a period when they roll in rich, soft mud, and at sixteen or so a boy should be enjoying lush, highly-coloured, 'vox-humana-with-tremolo' stuff. His literary muscles will be all the better for going through rather than round the exotic, scented jungle. To colleagues who said that florid writing in adolescent essays made them sick I used to say to be made sick was one of the things they were there for.

8 *March 1956*   *Grundisburgh*

I don't go all the way with dear Dr Leavis, who, I read, said some-where that there was no English poetry between Shakespeare and Hopkins. How *can* a man be such an ass as that? Where did I read that there is an excellent cheap and perceptive commentary on Hopkins? Please tell me, if you know. I am at present in the senile stage of not understanding modern poetry. I have *not* descended to the next stage, viz saying it is all rot, and hope I never shall.

How good Conan Doyle was at names. Jephro Rucastle and Colonel Lysander Stark have a fine villainous ring about them. But, Gosh, how thin some of those stories are. Even in the best, e.g. 'The Speckled Band', the house alterations of Dr Grimesby Roylott (another superb name) could hardly have helped rousing suspicion. But his women are simple souls mostly, even though one outwitted Sherlock himself.

Is Angus Wilson a good man? I see he reduces *The Forsyte Saga* to dust and ashes in last week's *New Statesman*. How jealous they all were, and still are, of Galsworthy's immense vogue. And the line they take is always so lofty that they miss the main point—that so many

---

[1] By Arthur O'Shaughnessy. R.H.-D. said he revelled in it and suspected the taste of anyone who didn't, in his or her youth.

of his characters do strike the ordinary reader as being live men and
women, and one reads on wanting to know how they got out of their
difficulties, and usually satisfied with the way they do it, and with G's
comments, and elucidations, and undertones throughout. And I'll
eat my hat if 'Indian Summer of a Forsyte' is not a beautiful and
moving bit of writing. But what *frightful* contempt our highbrow
critics pour on that view.

And I *will not* be bullied into reading Jane Austen over and over
again, as the David Cecils and others say one ought to and they do.
And I *will* say with my last breath that Miss Bates in *Emma* is a *shat-
tering* bore, Mr Knightley only just not a tremendous prig, and
Emma herself vain, conceited, and unamusing—and indeed crying
aloud for smacks on that area of her person which no doubt she
would rather have died than allude to.[1]

11 March 1956   *Bromsden Farm*

The interesting thing is that Hopkins' poetry (although not published till 1918 or much read before 1930, when it had an appalling
influence) was in fact written in the Victorian heyday, 1860–80. He
was a great original, but you're right in condemning Leavis's pronouncement as bosh. Why do you irritate yourself with Leavis at all?
I don't. I enjoy the Sherlock Holmes stories enormously still—not for
their plots but because of the delicious period atmosphere of hansom
cabs, fog, gaslight, muffins and all the rest of it. And for some of the
splendid dialogue—'Hand me my rattan, Watson.'

Angus Wilson is highly intelligent and a wonderfully good mimic.
Until recently he was in charge of the Reading Room at the B.M., but
has now retired to devote himself to literature. He's about forty. His
new novel, I'm told, has been chosen by the Book Society, so his retir-
ing gamble looks like coming off. I read *The Forsyte Saga* in 1929 when
I was driving through France and Spain with Peter Fleming, and
thought it very good indeed, though when I went on to read the
sequel, *A Modern Comedy*, I thought that G's touch grew less sure
with each succeeding generation. He knew his contemporaries and

---

[1] cf. 'I may have confided to you that, bar Miss Bates, I was bored by *Emma*. I
feel bound to test your friendship by this blasphemous admission.' (Mr Justice
Holmes to Sir Frederick Pollock, 27 September 1929.)

his immediate forebears, and he fell in love with his cousin's wife: that gave him the outline of the *F.S.* Later he had to rely on his creative imagination, which by itself wasn't powerful enough to mask his ignorance of his juniors: perhaps if he'd had children the later books would have rung truer.

My George Moore work goes busily on.[1] In most senses of the word he was quite illiterate—couldn't spell, punctuate or form letters, shied at the simplest proper name, was ignorant of the most elementary facts and books, etc—but behind it all, without pause, he was the 'dear addicted artist' (as your friend Auden said of Henry James) devoting his whole life to the production of literature, careless of all else. He re-wrote his books on every set of proofs and for every new edition: a great part of his income must have gone on printers' bills.

14 March 1956   *Grundisburgh*
The man Leavis, and why do I bother about him. I have just been at Cambridge, and things are even worse than I thought. Most of the young men teaching Eng. Lit. in our schools are disciples of his, and *all*American students think he is the cat's whiskers—the main reason, they tell me, being because, according to him, there are so few books worth reading, which, of course, is good news for students. And, my dear R., the real sin against the H.G. is *teaching the young to sneer, not* in saying 'Thou fool'.

I enjoyed my week-end [in Cambridge], as I always enjoy the converse of academic folk, its great merits (what John Morley said of Mark Pattison applies to several dons I know: 'the ineffable comfort, in his company, of being quite safe from an attack of platitude'), and its delightful and absurd occasional childishness.

Old George Trevelyan was in hall. He is rather deaf, and sat for the most part eyeing his plate with a sort of aloof and brooding ferocity—a look as of thunder asleep but ready. And once or twice it flashed and rumbled finely, e.g. at the recollection of the way in which *The Times* treated Abraham Lincoln at the beginning of the Civil War. Isn't that grand—unappeasable wrath at injustice however ancient? I believe if someone had recalled how Ulysses outwitted Ajax over the armour of Achilles we should have had another cloudburst.

---

[1] R.H.-D. was editing the letters he wrote to Lady Cunard.

Of course that passion for 'getting the thing down in the right words' gives George Moore the dignity of which, apart from it, I imagine no human character ever had less.

18 March 1956   *Bromsden Farm*

What can I tell you of last week? On Monday Peggy Ashcroft came to the flat for a drink. She is rehearsing for Enid Bagnold's new play *The Chalk Garden* and was gay and friendly. I can never quite get over the oddity of seeing someone you were once married to and now seldom see. I can *remember* exactly what I used to feel about her, but I don't feel it any more—just a deep and tender affection surrounded with memories. All rather moving and agreeable.

On Thursday I was taken to a cocktail party given by the literary editor of the *Observer*, a jam-packed gallimaufry in which I spoke *inter alia* to Arthur Koestler, Lord Montagu of Beaulieu and Gilbert Harding. The latter told me a delightful story. During the recent visit of the *Hamlet* company to Moscow, old Ernest Thesiger was missing for several hours, and the other actors feared for his safety. When he eventually returned unharmed he explained that he had been trying to buy some chalk with which to write on the wall of the Kremlin: BURGESS LOVES MACLEAN.

21 March 1956   *London*

I always rather hate London—so noisy, and crowded and inhuman. All those countless faces of the great army corps that streams out of Victoria at 9 every morning, practically indistinguishable from each other, being all the same colour, all expressionless, all knowing their day's work will be boring. Who was the young man in Kipling, who 'trod the ling like a buck in spring, And looked like a lance in rest'? Well, he was never in this crowd.

25 March 1956   *Bromsden Farm*

'Half the journalists', you say, 'and indeed book-writers don't know the difference between what is interesting and what is not'. Never in your long and valuable life, dear George, have you uttered words more profoundly true. Nor can they distinguish between the relevant and irrelevant, the amusing and the dull. But the gift of so distinguishing is surely just what we mean by 'taste', and ours is not, alas,

29

an age of taste. William Nicholson, the painter, once told me he met an old man in the train who confessed sadly: 'My trouble has always been that I can't tell one thing from another': an extreme case, no doubt, of the current malady. Sometimes as a publisher one is able to tidy writers up a little, removing their worst excesses, but many stubbornly persist in their idiocy.

I'm grappling with a typescript collection of unpublished letters by William Beckford. I published his Portuguese journal for the first time a few years ago, and I suppose I'll do these letters too, though I have never found B's personality even remotely attractive. That coy mixture of bric-à-brac, homosexuality and self-pity leaves me cold, though I must admit that he could write beautiful English.

This letter is the dullest I have ever written—to you or anyone else. Once long ago at Duff's house, I asked Belloc what he was writing. Rolling his French R's he replied: 'I am wr-riting a book about the Cr-rusades so *dull* that I can scarcely wr-rite it.'

29 March 1956   *Grundisburgh*
Whenever I have a free morning in London I haunt the Queen's Bench. Why? Because at least four times in six there is good entertainment, as Max Beerbohm found. What is the theatre or county cricket in comparison? A good cross-exam or even more a summing up gives me intense pleasure. But I hear less well than I did, or else the judges mumble more than they did, and I am often tempted to call out 'Speak up', thereby emulating the bravest man *I* ever heard of who, as Lord Russell of Killowen began his summing-up, said to him 'Make it snappy, old cock', and evoked a tornado of wrath which would have flattened a forest. I have in my time seen three murderers at close quarters, one being Brides-in-the-bath Smith, a very unattractive looking man, who from time to time hurled coarse and abusive words at counsel and witnesses. But as a man on trial for his life cannot, obviously, be committed for contempt, the judge merely reminded him mildly that he wasn't doing his case any good, and reduced him to mutterings, which, being close by, I understood were directed mainly to casting doubts on the legitimacy of the judge's birth, which even a layman like myself could see were irrelevant.

And now I am embarked on D.H. Lawrence's unliterary criticisms, undeterred by noting on one page his stating that Shelley's poetry was 'a million thousand' (sic) times more beautiful than Milton's, and by pages of, quite literally, intolerable babblings about pornography. I ask you, is anything in life or literature, past or present, in earth, heaven, or hell, anything more devastatingly tedious than D.H.L.'s interest in the human genitalia? But I should like to test some of his intense admirers thus—shew them a bit of poetry that he quotes and ask them 'Is he going to praise this to the skies or blast it with utter contempt?' I don't believe they would often be quite sure!

Easter Monday, 2 April 1956   *Bromsden Farm*
I agree that there should be a close season for D.H.L., but I am still interested in Shaw, not as a dramatist (one can scarcely sit through any of his plays today) but as a journalist; he was surely one of the best ever. I'm also interested in G.B.S. as a phenomenon in the world of letters, in which he knew everyone for so long.

4 April 1956   *Grundisburgh*
[R.H.-D. was coming to stay.] Let us remember, as Carlyle used to say, 'Have we not all eternity to rest (talk) in?' Though, since we are assured that all things will then be made plain, what the heck will there be to talk about? I refuse to believe that we shall be praising God *all* the time. After, say, King George IV, or Colonel Wigg M.P. or Mrs Aphra Behn have praised Him for two or three thousand years, won't the time *ever* come when, like Johnson with Hannah More, He says 'Pray consider what your flattery is worth before you are so lavish with it'?

As to Shaw, I mainly agree with you. His political, educational, philosophical theories, which always strike me as not more than emphatic half-truths, bore me a good deal, and of course that wearisome cocksureness; for surely in all who venture to explore man's predicaments in this world and the next, a certain basic *humility*, is a *sine qua non* to win the sympathy and understanding of any except those who like short cuts and certainties. 'To be uncertain is to be uncomfortable, but to be certain is to be ridiculous',[1] which I must have quoted to you before, but I do so again, partly to dispel *your* fear of repeating yourself, but mainly because it appeals to me strongly. But

[1] Goethe

Shaw's handling of the English language is a never-failing delight. Never was a verbal rapier wielded with such precision, swiftness and grace, nor was there ever a controversialist who met and blunted the rudest attacks with such perfect good temper (e.g. the row with Kingsmill). If I had to point to the best sentence he ever wrote, I should quote that little handful of words about Ellen Terry in old age.[1] Did he ever write anything else that really moves one—except perhaps the last speech of Brother Martin in *St Joan?*

I have to respond for Ipswich School to the Old Ipswichians next week. What on earth am I to say? The great name in their history is Cardinal Wolsey, who left it on record that he meant the school to be greater than Eton or Winchester. But how can that be mentioned without ironical thoughts intruding? A more profitable line is perhaps to draw a parallel between their early histories e.g. two headmasters, Nicholas Udall of Eton who was imprisoned for bagging the college plate (and possibly for vices which in Macaulay's words about Frederick 'history blushes to name') and an Ipswich H.M. who got into trouble for boxing a lady's ears. Udall afterwards became H.M. of Westminster, but the Ipswich man was never heard of again.

8 April 1956   *Bromsden Farm*
Next Saturday we all have to attend a wedding in London. This will entail hiring a complete outfit at Moss Bros, except for a beautiful grey topper of Duff Cooper's. When Diana Cooper was sadly giving his things away, she easily found recipients for everything except his hats, for he took a huge size. My head is even bigger, and one week-end at Chantilly she discovered this. I in fact wear a hat about twice a year, but she was relentlessly generous, and I returned to England, much to the suspicion of the customs men, with twenty-seven hats— black and grey toppers, a bowler, a *grey* bowler, a panama, a yachting cap, three deerstalkers, an opera hat and any amount of trilbys and Anthony Edens.

To-day, despite cold grey skies and intermittent rain, I made a start on the year's mowing, and feel worn out by the unaccustomed

[1] 'She became a legend in her old age; but of that I have nothing to say; for we did not meet, and, except for a few broken letters, did not write; and she never was old to me.'

exertion. Normally I take no exercise of any kind, except (whenever I can) swimming in the sea, which I adore. If you take exercise perpetually (as P. Fleming does) you can never stop, and it becomes a sort of religious ritual. Apart from disinclination, I haven't time. One of the depressing things about publishing today is that it takes seven or eight months to get a book out (it used to be much less) and therefore one can look forward too far. The period of gestation being so unduly delayed, one is heartily sick of most books before they see the light, and I know it's a mistake to take a book at all without *great* enthusiasm at the outset.

10-11 April 1956   *Grundisburgh*

This is a bad week—a constipation of committees, if the collective be allowed. I should greatly value your views on *direct grant* schools and their future, with special consideration of their advantages or the reverse over *state-aided* schools. On practically all these committees I move about in worlds not realised, but whenever I suggest resigning on the grounds of uselessness, the chairman enfolds my hand in a warm wet one of his own, and stresses fervidly (but unconvincingly) how incomputably valuable the presence is of a stout, elderly, inattentive layman who never says a word, and mostly does not know, or care, what the rest are talking about.

Peter Fleming had an excellent article recently as 'Strix' [in the *Spectator*], about the absence of *giants* in modern times. He could have mentioned—but didn't—old Warre. He had no eloquence, when he entered a room there was no one else in it, however full it was. When he left a schoolroom at Eton and—mistaking the cleaners' cupboard for the door—crashed into a medley of pots and pans, not a single boy smiled. But when I, in D5, pecked while stepping up to my desk, and sat in the w.p.b. it made their day—and their Sunday letter home.

Hats! I take size 8. My head was always in the swede rather than the grapefruit class, and the humorous fates saw fit to inflict me with a form of osteo-arthritis of which a main effect is a slow and steady growth of the occipital bones. And whenever I look in the glass or see a snapshot of myself, I am reminded of Petrarch's simple statement 'Nothing is more hideous than an old schoolmaster'.

I have never actually dealt with Moss Bros, though I once made a jolly good joke about them when a daughter asked if my tail-coat at her wedding came from them. 'No.' I said (like a flash, as they say) 'It comes from Moth Bros'.

Rooks have started building much too near the house, and wake me, shouting like auctioneers, at 6 a.m. My wife was told by some village wiseacre that a bonfire under the tree at dusk frightened them away for good. She lit one last night. *This* morning I was roused at 5.30 by the hoarse and hearty cachinnations of every rook in Suffolk, as they delightedly surveyed the lawn covered with the calcined débris of last night's bonfire.

21 April 1956   *Bromsden Farm*
I fear Max Bearbohm is dying: he is in a clinic at Rapallo, surrounded by devoted friends and just fading away. A whole tone of voice will perish with him. He was the perfect *petit maître* (in the literal sense), adorning all he touched.

29 April 1956   *Bromsden Farm*
I enjoyed every moment of my stay with you, and am looking forward to the next. Every single thing about the house and garden is so *right*, so welcoming and so peaceful. Pamela is an angel, with her lovely smile, her splendid cooking, and her charming acceptance of being read aloud to. I hope perhaps next time there'll be a sale for me to go to with her, for that is one of my pleasures which I hadn't confessed to you before.

I sent you the *Baldwin*: have you got G.M. Young's other books? You'd certainly love them and I have them all on my list (except his masterpiece, *Portrait of an Age*, which the Oxford Press wouldn't let go). Let me know if you'd like them. Did I tell you what G.M.Y. said of the O.U.P.? 'Being published by the Oxford University Press is rather like being married to a duchess: the honour is almost greater than the pleasure,' I could—and doubtless shall—write you a whole letter about G.M.Y. [see p. 37]

2 May 1956   *Grundisburgh*
Baldwin's career, his superb speeches, his abiding vision of what the word 'England' meant and means, his ceaseless striving to take a long view and not a short—all give point to a sentence in the *T.L.S.* review of Winston's history. 'The whole action of history seems to prove that

34

it is more dangerous to be intelligent than to be warlike. Culture is not only futile but, when combined with kindness, almost always actively fatal.' He is talking of kings of course, but if you think how much *wiser* a man Asquith was than Ll.G., or how superb Winston was in war but how unreliable in peace politics, one finds oneself bleakly facing the question 'Is it not true that it is easily possible for a man at the top to be too *good* to be successful?' And of course there was Mr Gladstone. What a fog one is in! The Creator really did make things too difficult. However I read in the *Sunday Times* that the earth is only one among at least a hundred *trillion* planets, and end up agreeing with Bishop Creighton who reassured an anxious seeker after the truth that it is 'almost impossible to exaggerate the complete unimportance of everything'.

What fine *bone* there is in so many of old Wordsworth's best things so that they last like the beauty of some women, untarnished by the passing years. I wish you had known John Bailey.[1] He could laugh at the solemn old egoist, but had boundless reverence for the central deep-rooted *core* of him, and often enlarged on his likeness to Milton—both so crabbed and unlikeable in ordinary externals, but inwardly of such majestic stature compared with the common run of great men. What has happened to that book of some months ago which set out to prove that the love of W. and Dorothy was incestuous? What lofty times we live in!

I see old Munnings is again protesting—on the right side, but I don't suppose the old ass helps much.[2] I recall Bishop Henson's rage when supported by Dean Welldon on some controversy with club-footed arguments—a rhinocerine gambolling wherever the ice was thinnest. As H. summed him up, he 'could neither speak with effect nor be silent with dignity.'

7 May 1956   *Keld, Yorkshire*
This cottage is perched on a green hill and is accessible only on foot, horse, tractor or jeep. The climb takes a good twenty minutes,

---

[1] John Cann Bailey (1864–1931), literary critic, married G.W.L.'s aunt the Hon. Sarah Lyttelton.
[2] Sir Alfred Munnings, President of the Royal Academy, regularly attacked modern art.

including pauses for breath, but when one gets here the sight is magical—ranges of hills, one behind another, on every side, all green with pasture up to the brown-and-purple line of the heather-clad fells (there is no arable land in this dale—Swaledale).

The cottage is tiny and completely primitive—one room up, one down, a tiny kitchen, a coalshed and an outside E.C. Water has to be fetched in buckets from a spring a few yards away. It's like camping out without the discomfort of tents and the weather. There is a tiny shop in the village, and a delightful farmer supplies eggs and milk. For more advanced shopping the town of Hawes (in Wensleydale) is only eight miles away, beyond the precipitous pass called Buttertubs. Almost the most miraculous thing about this hill (which is called Kisdon) is the *silence*. The only sounds are those of sheep, curlew (surely the most mournfully romantic of all bird-cries), plover, skylarks and grouse. Otherwise *nothing*, save when the wind whistles round the cottage, as it did last night. Like all the other houses in the dale, it is built of the local grey stone which goes beautifully with the green of the fields.

On Saturday, tell Pamela, I went to a sale in a village called Patrick Brompton, near Bedale, and bought a mass of miscellaneous objects, including a fine Victorian card-table (one that swivels and folds up) for 12/-. There were no china figures for her, nor wallclocks. Yesterday I read S.N. Behrman's book about Duveen, the picture dealer (I thought it might contain some reference to G. Moore and Lady Cunard, but it doesn't). I expect you read it when it came out: if not it's well worth getting from the library. What interests me so much is the sequence of events—the great Robber Barons of America, shrewd illiterates who made millions out of oil and railways and department stores and canned meat, easing their consciences by buying works of art, for which Duveen and Co charged them enormous prices. Then, to save death duties and at the same time win themselves immortality, they bequeathed all these masterpieces to the American nation, and now nobody cares how much Duveen rooked the old boys, since the results are so splendid.

One of the joys of reading W.W. is the way those lines of thundering magnificence suddenly crop up amid a lot of bathos. 'And mighty poets in their misery dead,' with the three fine lines before it, is all mixed up with that dreary leech-gatherer [see p. 110]. This country is tremendously Wordsworthian—much more so than the present-day Lakes, which are trodden down and exploited disgustingly.

I have just looked out of the window and noticed that the clouds have descended round the cottage, making it even more deliciously remote. Yesterday I heard a cuckoo down the dale, so in the nicest possible way, you see, I am in cloud-cuckoo land.

9 May 1956   *Grundisburgh*

Hawes, and Buttertubs, and Wensleydale—how full of strength and melody the names are. You won't be so foolish as many are on a country holiday, i.e. fill the whole day with exhausting walks. A wise passiveness is your line.

The Great Robber Barons: illiterate to a man, overwhelmed by their gold as an Indian village is by the jungle, frenziedly spending it on pictures of which they knew nothing. Rockefeller emerges as a really enlightened man compared, say, with Andrew Mellon; and Nuffield as a positive saint. (A dear little plebeian, who expressed extravagant happiness after a day's golf with a team of Tuppy Headlam's—i.e. beaks and dons, because 'I have had a whole day with a lot of friendly and intelligent men, and not one mentioned money. If you had any idea how rare an experience that is . . .')

15 May 1956   *Kisdon*

Yesterday I did in fact make a ¾ circumambulation of Kisdon (which is an island girt with rivers), about half-way up, scrambling over rocky outcrops and treading delightedly on thick mountain grass, studded with primroses, cowslips, anemones and dog-violets. Dry-stone walls take the place of hedges everywhere, winding inconsequently up the hillsides and dividing the green, green fields into every kind of shape. Made of the local stone, and matching the scattered farmhouses and byres, they blend perfectly with the natural scene, into which no trace of industrialism intrudes. An occasional tractor far away—otherwise this outlook cannot have changed for a century or two. The longer I stay here the less can I imagine why anyone chooses to live anywhere else.

I knew you'd enjoy G.M.Young and am most happy to have been the means of bringing him to you. No more of gratitude: it's pure self-indulgence on my part, since I want you to share in all the good and interesting things I've published, without having to bother with the failures and mistakes. G.M.Y. is tallish and thin, with a long thin pointed nose. Very little hair and that quite flat on his scalp, so that more than anything else he looks like a judge who has mislaid his wig and is feeling the cold. I think in fact he *does* feel the cold, probably has a bad circulation, and in winter wears an enormous astrakhan overcoat which he purchased in Tsarist Russia. He was educated at St Paul's and Balliol, and was then some sort of a Civil Servant (this part of his life is obscure and never mentioned) until he retired at about the age of fifty. Up to then he had not written a word, but had read (as you can see) enormously, and remembered everything in a Macaulay—Monty James way. Peter Davies published his *Gibbon* and *Charles I and Cromwell* in the early thirties, and then I wrote to him, suggesting a collection of essays etc. This produced *Daylight and Champaign* (which I brought out when I was at Cape's), and after the war, when I started up my own business, I reprinted these three books, and published the two further books of essays[1] and *Baldwin*. What I hadn't realised until *Baldwin* was that all the other books came largely out of his head, where their subject-matter had been brewing up for many years. *Baldwin* demanded a lot of *work*—going through papers, writing to people etc—and that he wouldn't or couldn't do. On top of that he found that his personal affection for S.B. was gradually turning to some sort of contempt, if not actual dislike—so it's no wonder the book wasn't first-rate. He tried to abandon it ¾ of the way through, but I brutally compelled him to finish it.

His private life was unusual. Where or how he lived when he was a Civil Servant I don't know, but possibly with his father, who lived at Blackheath and died there at the age of 99. Anyhow sometime in the late twenties G.M.Y. corresponded on some literary topic with Mona Wilson (sister of Sir Arnold W. etc), and she asked him down for the week-end to an attractive, old, but very uncomfortable house she owned at Pewsey, near Marlborough. To cut a long story short, he stayed there for twenty-five years, until M.W. died a year or two ago. There was, so far as I know, no just cause or impediment why they shouldn't have married, but they just didn't. I'm sure

---

[1] *Today and Yesterday* and *Last Essays*.

their relationship was entirely intellectual and companionable, without any sexual feelings—indeed I wonder whether either of them ever had much sex-life of any kind. Miss Wilson (as he always referred to her) was ten years older than he—a little hunchbacked old lady when I knew her, rapidly going blind (her cooking was terrible: since she couldn't *see* what she ate, the food was either raw or cindery). She smoked a little pipe, which he lovingly filled for her. The house was very dirty and untidy, full of books and papers, but they were charming together, and I loved visiting them. Once during the war I called unexpectedly about 3 p.m., and from the confusion following my knock it was clear that G.M. was still in bed. Eventually he arrived half-dressed and un-shaven but very welcoming. Eventually Miss Wilson got so blind, old and ill that she had to be moved to a home where she mercifully died. He moved into All Souls where, John Sparrow tells me, he complains all the time. Oh yes, every year he and Miss Wilson used to take a holiday at Lechlade, where G.M. used to row them violently about on the stripling Thames. I visited them there once and drove them to Burford, where we spent some time vainly looking for the tomb of John Meade Falkner.[1]

When I re-issued G.M.'s old books I started, as is my compulsive habit, to verify his quotations, and found they were all slightly wrong—see his essay called 'The Imp'. G.M. always assumes that one is his intellectual equal and makes no concessions in his conversation. This, though flattering, often carried matters well over my head until I knew him well enough to ask for explanations of all the allusions I couldn't understand. As Geoffrey Madan said, he is not a polymath but a pantomath.

Have been to two more sales. One of the auctioneers was a great wag: 'How mooch for this Gandhi table—dark legs and no drawers?' It was a bamboo table.

18 May 1956   *Grundisburgh*

Curiously few people are sensible about holidays; if not walking, they go sight-seeing and to picture-gallery after p.g. of all fatiguing activities. Many play golf, and one odd effect of that pursuit is that they

---

[1] It was there all the time. He was the author of *Moonfleet*.

return to work *manifestly* stupider than they were. It is, I think, the company of other golfers. Among my fortuitous but immensely precious circumstances I count almost the luckiest that when they began monkeying about with the game of bridge I couldn't be bothered to learn all the new stuff, so dropped out.

I shall have some fun in a fortnight's time when I address the Naval cadets at Greenwich roughly on the pleasures of reading, but on less Victorian lines than that suggests. At the moment I have in mind Conrad's account of the return of the *Narcissus*, John Fortescue on the Death of the Black Prince, Masefield's description of the storm in *Dauber*, Carlyle's account of Robespierre's end, Johnson's letter to Chesterfield, Meg Merrilies' 'Ride your ways, Ellangowan'.[1] What else? They are young men of action. I shall certainly tell them of your auctioneer, also of another who in selling a gallows described it in his catalogue as 'picturesque hanging wood'.

22 May 1956   *Keld*
At last the summer has come to these hills, and I am sitting behind the cottage, having just breakfasted there. The sun is truly *hot*, there is almost no wind (unusual up here) and larks are everywhere about me in the sky. I have fallen so deep into the gentle rhythms of this primitive life that a slice of lotus (or perhaps lot*os*) does for my sustenance, and it's a miracle that you're getting a letter at all.

Your Greenwich list is fine: what about adding a paragraph or two of Bunyan, about the trumpets sounding for him on the other side? When I was nineteen and my beloved mother died I was saved from death and destruction by *Pilgrim's Progress* which I carried about in a bag and chanted aloud to myself most comfortingly on every possible occasion. The only other thing in the bag was a huge bottle of liquid sleeping-draught, which eventually lost its cork and saturated Bunyan—but he had done his saving work by then.

25 May 1956   *Grundisburgh*
Biro again I am afraid. It makes one's youth seem very distant, when every boy in Trials found two quill pens in his place: and what a lovely crisp twittering, as of short-tempered but nice little birds, filled the

[1] Walter Scott, *Guy Mannering*.

40

room as we narrated *ventre-à-terre* the exploits of King Tiglath-Pileser, or listed the products of Asia Minor. When Wilfred Blunt[1] tried to interest a publisher in his book on the Italic Hand the man told him that this was the age of the typewriter, and no one but his (W.B's) aunts would read the book. But the good man was wrong, because the odd, largely excellent and partly priggish and precious, revival of the sweet Roman hand was just beginning, and is now in full swing. There is a society which meets and is lectured and magic-lanterned to from time to time. I attended one once and was at once reminded of a gathering of Baconians (of whom I was once one, though not in spirit) and, as then, felt very giggly. Why do the males of such societies run so much to Adam's apples, and wispy moustaches, and pince-nez, and the women to shiny noses and strangled contralto voices?

31 May 1956   *Grundisburgh*
I joined the Baconians from sheer curiosity. I left them because I thought they were so rude and silly and childish about all who continued to think Shakespeare was still S. And I still continue to think there is something very mysterious behind the whole story. And I incline to old Agate's theory that S. wrote the plays, but that Bacon had a persistent finger in them; he added—*more suo*—that S. was probably B's 'fancy-boy'!

3 June 1956   *Bromsden Farm*
To-day is my elder son's twentieth birthday, and the family has been briefly but happily reunited to drink his health in one of our last bottles of champagne. They were all very young and gay and handsome and happy, and they unknowingly provided one of those rare occasions when one can see in one glance that all the hideous sacrifices entailed in their education have not so far been wasted. I don't mean that I'm feeling pleased with myself, just a trifle reassured. Also yesterday I saw a spotted woodpecker in the garden for the first time—there are many green ones about.

Last week a splendid new manuscript turned up—two hundred letters from Max Beerbohm to Reggie Turner, covering the years

---

[1] Eton art master.

1892-1938. They're delicious, and you'll love them, though (like the George Moore ones) they'll need some editorial notes. One quotation I can't resist copying out for your private eye (for it's copyright etc etc):

> Did I tell you about Oscar at the restaurant? During the rehearsal he went to a place with my brother to have some lunch. He ordered a watercress sandwich: which in due course was brought to him: not a thin, diaphanous green thing such as he had meant but a very stout satisfying article of food. This he ate with assumed disgust (but evident relish) and when he paid the waiter, he said: 'Tell the cook of this restaurant with the compliments of Mr Oscar Wilde that these are the very worst sandwiches in the whole world and that, when I ask for a watercress sandwich, I do not mean a loaf with a field in the middle of it.'

6 June 1956   *Grundisburgh*

When *listening* to the ball-by-ball progress of a Test Match, there are such lengthy periods when nothing seems to happen. Watching on a good TV set might be altogether another matter, but the only set nearby is the Cranworths', and they are not very good at the knobs. The only cricket I ever saw on their TV was merely ghosts folk-dancing in a snowstorm. It didn't even come up to the Giants' Causeway, which old Samuel said was worth seeing, but not worth going to see. A nice distinction. The modern cricketer's fragility is a great puzzle. In days when they had no masseurs, thirteen men were taken on an Australian tour and though *one* usually drank too much, the rest played match after match without an ache or pain.

I was quite overwhelmed with the majesty of Greenwich, which I had never seen before. The first sight of it struck me more than any building I have seen, except perhaps the Acropolis, though for that my mental soil had of course been fully prepared. I know nothing of architecture, but surely Wren at his best is unsurpassable in the matter of proportion and dignity—without pomposity, like the best prose! The young naval officers were an excellent audience—deceptively quiet when I began, but like hounds on a scent when a joke or a good point appeared. I felt to the full the happiness of realising that they, and I, and John Milton were all of the same race.

My nephew [Viscount Cobham, see p. 207] lives here in a cheerful state of bankruptcy, and ancient aristocratic squalor. Through all the state-rooms, library, sitting-rooms, pass sightseers from the Black Country and Birmingham; gazing, with less expression than one would think possible on the human face, on the good lord, the mad lord, the bad lord, a Van Dyck or two, 'The Misers' by (in my day) Quentin Matsys but now said to be someone else whose name eludes me. For a time they were mysteriously stationary outside the house, where there is nothing special to see except the broken corner of a stone under the window where my Uncle Bob all but shot Mary Drew, and the spot where I fell off my bicycle in 1895. The coins thus extorted keep the wolf a yard or two from the door, audibly growling and visibly impatient, as if anxious to get the job done and move off elsewhere.

There is an unfathomable sadness brooding over the place, against which no doubt we may, indeed must, set the rounder cheeks and better clothes of the Hagley villagers, but no one ever suggested that the old order was in a particularly cheerful mood as it yielded place to the new.

I write to you from the depths of a most appalling task. I have an American authoress called Ruth McKenney, who normally writes funny books, of which I have published half-a-dozen with some success. About four years ago she and her husband (a delightful American of great wit and integrity) decided they must make some money by writing a long historical novel. They chose Napoleon's campaign in Egypt as background, and read a great deal of history. They wrote and rewrote the novel for months and months until, sometime last year, when it was 7/8 finished, Ruth cracked up under the strain and (not to put too fine a point upon it) went off her head. Her poor husband Richard asked me if I would read the manuscript, which was then 900 pages long, and encourage her to continue. Although I loathe historical novels I did this (it took weeks), correcting the grammar, punctuation and French as I went along, besides removing Americanisms, anachronisms and so on. As such things go it wasn't at all bad, and might well have been a winner, especially in America. However, my encouragement proved useless: Ruth got dottier and dottier, their money began to run out, Richard couldn't get a job here and she refused to go back to America (they were once Communists). Eventually, some months ago, Richard gave up and committed suicide (sleeping-draught) on her birthday—a classic psycho-analyst's pattern: her birth = his death. He was a darling man, and his death saddened and also infuriated me. It also brought Ruth more or less—and however temporarily—to her senses. She seized the manuscript and rewrote every word of it, putting back all the errors I had so carefully removed and doubling the length of it all, so that it now occupies 1800 pages of typescript (about 400,000 words). After Richard's death, as a gesture, I made an agreement to publish the bloody thing (though how that is economically possible I don't know) and now she is waiting expectantly for my opinion of it. Since I *may* after all publish it, I feel obliged to correct it all again—which does not make for speed. I began the fearful job yesterday and have only reached p. 177. Clearly it will take me weeks, and I have so many other things, more interesting and important, to do. I sit with it in my library, longing to read *any* of the books that surround me rather than this hideous work which has already killed one good man.

North Foreland Lodge
Sherfield-on-Loddon
Nr Basingstoke, Hants

27 June 1956

And if this isn't an impressive address I should like to know what is. I am in the head mistress's drawing-room; pianos are doing their duty relentlessly all round; floors squeak and rumble to the impact of toes, which, individually, may be light and fantastic, but collectively bear convincing witness to the school dietary. I had at lunch the largest helping of pressed beef, salad, and potatoes I have ever seen, followed by a kilderkin of custard. Later on the girls have tea at 3.50 and high tea at 6.30. I find that unalluring. My tête-à-tête spam with the head-mistress at 7.0 is better. But I am often reminded of Virginia Woolf's *A Room of One's Own*. However it is a lovely place and they all look happy. What else do you want? Moreover there are three bull-points here. They play no cricket, they play no hockey, and they don't have a speech-day.

I have just shaken hands with ninety-three girls and said good-night to each. I never realised how much one human hand could differ from another in texture, temperature, moisture, grip, size and general character.

1 July 1956   *Bromsden Farm*

I was sorry to read of Michael Arlen's death. He was another friend of my youth, always very friendly and charming. He looked awful, knew it, and described himself as 'the last of the Armenian atrocities'. He was an Oriental storyteller, like the author of the *Arabian Nights*, and his approach to writing was utterly realistic: directly he had made enough money (chiefly in America) he stopped writing altogether— and it was just as well, for his slender topical gift was already exhausted. Last week I was at two long meetings with four Coleridge scholars, drafting a manifesto which we hope will induce an American Foundation to cough up a grant big enough to finance a Collected Edition of S.T.C.'s works in twenty volumes! I know it's crazy to embark on such arduous and unprofitable tasks, but that's the way my fancy leads me. Tonight I must write a review of six detective stories:[1] your stubborn silence on this matter convinces me that you take the stern moral line of most who disapprove of this particular nonsense. Oh well, I suppose we can't agree about everything.

Château de St Firmin
Sunday morning 8 July 1956   *Vineuil, Oise*

Here I sit in my Uncle Duff's lovely little library, looking out over lawns to lake and trees, on the most beautiful summer's day ever. Also in the house are Isaiah Berlin and his newly wedded wife; Auberon Herbert who fought with the Polish army in the war and is now forever canvassing on behalf of that martyred but oh so boring race (Auberon is a Catholic: his sister is married to Evelyn Waugh); Norah Fahie who was Duff's secretary; my cousin Artemis, aged three, Duff and Diana's grand-daughter, and her English Nanny. Many others— Air Vice-Marshals, Rothschilds, all sorts—arrive for meals, and at the moment *all* the work of the house is being done by a Polish woman and a Chinese boy!

All this is so far removed from my usual round that it makes a wonderful change. Gossip with rich people in lovely surroundings on a

[1] R.H.-D. reviewed them regularly for *Time and Tide* under the pseudonym Norman Blood.

45

heavenly day might well pall after a little, but for a week-end it's amusing and even restful. You'd love this library and I'd love to go over it with you. No one else appreciates it now, which is rather sad, for Duff took such trouble with it. I long ago locked up some of the more pocketable rarities, like the three Keats first editions.

12 July 1956   *Grundisburgh*
I am much interested at the moment in the early life of H. James (published by you!) by L. Edel, 1953. Is the rest on the way? I have never heard you mention it. H.J.'s is a difficult character to grasp— all those layers of sensitive reactions, that mysterious back-ailment, which always recurred whenever brother William turned up! J.B. Priestley writes somewhere of J's characters seeming 'to have no employment beyond an obscure and suffocating kind of self-torture'. Surely H.J. himself? I cannot help being amused by the chapter about his obscure injury, and the swift and facile assurance of many critics that castration and/or impotence was what it obviously was.

How different our respective lots are—you go lunching with Rothschilds, talking to I. Berlin, delicately savouring the essence of an exquisite library, fighting with beasts at Ephesus in the shape of literary men—a life of overwork, strife, interest and variety. My afternoon will be spent in (1) buying a tin of putty (2) mending a wattle fence (3) discussing the lavatorial needs of the Woodbridge prep. school (4) pointing out to my banker that in the matter of legibility—the *first* duty of a bank-clerk—all his b-c's are at fault (5) writing a testimonial for an old pupil saying, roughly, that as he has failed to make good as a chartered accountant he is bound to be a good schoolmaster (6) passing the time of day with Mrs Pizzey (7) a little folding of the hands in sleep. And yet in a million or two years putty and I. Berlin will be of equal importance—Well, well!

15 July 1956   *Bromsden Farm*
High up in the Boulevard Beaumarchais, near the Bastille, I ran to earth the old Wilde fan. His flat was indeed murky as a fox's earth: every window, and most shutters, tightly fastened on a stifling Turkish-Bath afternoon. All the time I was there (about 1½ hours) sweat was trickling down inside my shirt. He is a short man of seventy-something, with a thick white beard, masses of white hair, and spectacles.

He received me dressed in trousers, a very *décolleté* pyjama-jacket and a dressing gown. At great length he described how he had been knocked down crossing the road, was now permanently lame, and moreover sometimes lost his memory in the middle of the lectures by which I imagine he earns his living. You can imagine the law-suit he is conducting against all and sundry. He told me that since 1903 he had collected every book, cutting, photograph and anecdote of Oscar, and he has shelves and cupboards and shelves and cupboards to prove his assiduity. Telling me he had written or translated more than 200 plays, he showed me glass cases full of puppets that belonged to D'Annunzio, also signed photographs of Sarah Bernhardt and goodness knows who. When I steered him back to Oscar in my halting French, he read me, with much emphasis and emotion, long extracts from his translation of *The Ballad of Reading Gaol* and the other poems. Then he produced two enormous files, which contained the programme of *every* production of *Salome* all over the world, together with photographs of lightly clad but hideous actresses in the name-part. At last I got him on to the letters, and he fished out a thick folder stuffed with copies of letters, all in his illegible old-Frenchman's hand, and all in French. After some discussion I promised to send him a list of what we've got, and he promised to re-copy and send me any of his that we lack, though I very much doubt how many of them are authentic. Beyond touching hands a little more than was necessary when handing me books to look at, he made no advances, and was I think genuinely pleased to have someone to talk and show his treasures to.

I came across this charming 'Italian saying'—'A priest is a man who is called Father by everyone except his own children who are obliged to call him Uncle.' Had you heard it before?

18 July 1956   *Grundisburgh*
It is such a mistake to damn a book one hasn't read (as Sir G. Sitwell told Osbert it was to expose oneself to the Germans entrenched forty yards distant). But as W. Cory stated, one of the faculties a good education develops is 'to express assent or dissent in graduated terms', and so few who write do that.[1] *You* do in that excellent review of

[1] See p. 62. William Johnson (1823–92), poet, Eton master from 1834 to 1872, when he changed his name to Cory.

Henry James's *Notebooks*, but, as you point out about H.J. himself, the times will not again allow the leisure or society essential for such artistry as his. Among the lights which Edward Grey saw going out one by one in 1914, this is surely one. We keep on coming back to Percy Lubbock's great dictum that civilisation, far from being established, has really only just begun.

What agonies old Henry J. must have suffered when his courtesy and friendship clashed with his artistic integrity, e.g. when Mrs Humphry Ward wanted to know what he thought of her book. Condemnation usually does emerge, but so swathed in affectionate and apologetic trappings as often to elude the author's partial and prejudiced eye. *His* eye which missed nothing must have often delighted in the spectacle of human vanity deceiving itself for the nth time. A final question. Was anyone—not a relative—ever completely at ease with H.J.? Men, I mean, not women? Percy L. rather hedged when I asked him. So did John Bailey, who practically said he was better to write to than to talk to. That habit you mention of stopping a story before the point was reached, because he had got all he wanted out of it, was rather daunting. I should have wilted.

P.S. H.J. and names—'*Peter Quint*' in *The Turn of the Screw* is a beautiful distillation of sheer poison. At Hagley there is a dark eerie corner on one passage, which for years has been known as 'Quint's Corner'. My nephew admits he always passes by it rather quickly.

22 July 1956   *Bromsden Farm*
Yesterday was my swan-song on the cricket field—the Fathers Match at my son's prep. school. I wasn't called upon to bat, bowled my own boy (1 for 0 in one over) and caught an inescapable catch. I felt pleasantly melancholy as I left the field.

26 July 1956   *Grundisburgh*
I have all day been reading the literary judgments of third-rate beaks at fourth-rate schools. These judgments are dictated to their pupils, who learn them more or less by heart, without more than half understanding them. The poor lambs were clearly bored with *The Antiquary*, but one and all babble of Scott's 'incomparable' mastery in 'describing scenery' of all tedious arts.

48

Your cricket swan-song was impressive—much more than mine years ago. I didn't bat or bowl; I bent to pick up a practically stationary ball at point, and a moment later was walking delicately, like Agag, back to the pavilion in the iron grip of lumbago.

I have just listened to a cello solo by Casals—perfectly celestial. The cello is a lovely thing—the Rembrandt of the orchestra, don't you think? I must stop. It is late and very hot. The room is full of moths, June-bugs, bees and I think a bat or two.

5 August 1956   *Yorkshire*
The scene here has changed little since May, save that some fields (I can see hundreds from this window, of every shape, all bounded by stone walls) are darker where the grass has become hay, and others are lighter where the hay has just been cut. The weather has been so bad that much of its seems likely to spoil, and yesterday's hot sunshine brought out tractors and horses and women with hayrakes. There is no arable land in this dale, just pasture for sheep and cattle, and the hay to feed them during the winter. Every prospect pleases, and man is miles away down the valley. This hill itself is carpeted now with wild thyme and meadow-sweet and other flowers in profusion. The plovers have left, the larks are silent; the grouse, apprehensive perhaps of the Twelfth, give an occasional honk; curlew fly past, their great curving beaks silhouetted against the blue sky.

Last week Edmund Blunden stayed with me in Soho Square, charming as ever with his quick perceptions and nervous sparrow-movements. He will be sixty in November, and when I asked him the other day whether he didn't sometimes forget how old he was (as I do) and momentarily imagine himself young again, he said 'Yes, and when I was young I hoped that one day I should be able to go into a post office to buy a stamp without feeling nervous and shy: now I realise that I never shall.' How lucky one is not to have been born with diffidence that must cause agony.

8 August 1956   *Grundisburgh*
For a brief spell Suez may have seemed no more to you than a name in a Kipling poem, but no doubt it is a very different story now. What a lot of people don't realise that imperial gestures are futile unless there is imperial strength and unity behind 'em.

I am getting a great deal of pleasure out of Frank Swinnerton's *Background with Chorus. Full* of amusing and interesting gossip, and I like him as he emerges from the page. I wonder why he disliked Walter Raleigh so much; nobody else did. I met W.R. at Eton—A.B. Ramsay's dinner-table, where he said he had never, till then, had as much whitebait—or perhaps sardines—as he had always wanted. He also said that he had only said one really witty thing in his life, when asked what he thought of some very poor claret, by a host who thought well of it. W.R.'s answer was 'Minds innocent and quiet take this for a *Hermitage*'.

Next week I shall write to you from Oxford where I shall be cooking the Cert marks. There are some forty or fifty awarders, divided very much as some wag once said the Cavalry Club members were—one half of them would give all they possessed to be able to make water, and the other as much to be able to stop. It is true that in colleges the lavatories can be a very long way off one's bedroom, but the case is better than it was only fifty years ago, when there was quite a walk under the open sky, and *either* university in February—!

I have just finished a frightful book about the Gestapo—and 'much it grieved my heart to think what man has made of man'.[1] It is a very sickening story, but it gave me one thing of value, viz Himmler's reference to Heydrich who, I suppose, was about as foul a creature as the vermin world has ever spawned. 'This good and radiant man.' Can you beat that? And talking of gems, and in the probably vain hope that you haven't yet read the book, Swinnerton gets Lloyd George in *two* words, comparing Asquith's mind with L.G.'s 'soiled quicksilver'; and he ends a fine portrait of old George Saintsbury[2] with the breath-taking facts that G.S. 'read *The Earthly Paradise* twenty times, and wished *The Faerie Queen* were longer'.

18 August 1956   *Oxford*
Today Marsden and I lunched with the Cowley fathers, of whom Beasley-Robinson[3] is one. Why are so many monks indistinguishable

---

[1] Wordsworth, 'Lines Written in Early Spring'.
[2] Literary historian and critic, Professor of English Literature, Edinburgh University, 1895–1915.
[3] Former Eton master.

from convicts? The close hair-crop certainly sets out in that direction, but it is the facial expression that completes the picture. I sat next to the Father Superior and disgraced myself by starting to talk immediately after the grace, and had to be checked by a wave of the hand while a reformed burglar read what I think was a chapter of scripture. After that he was most affable till a bell rang and they moved off like a parliament of rooks to tea or some form of worship. What a strange world they must live in! I couldn't stomach it for half a day, but they look contented enough, though without that inner radiance we hear of. Perhaps time and old age are needed for that.

Virginia Cowles's book is immensely readable; but what a grim picture of Victoria and Albert forcing the egregious Stockmar's education on the wretched Bertie [Edward VII]. My father never had the smallest respect for B. because when at Cambridge—living a mile or so away—B. was forced to play cricket, and the leading players were sent out to bowl at him. They did so, literally, and he used to fall down to avoid the ball. So my father reported, he being one of them. It is rather sad that almost everything that has come out about Victoria since her death makes her less admirable—so stubborn, narrow, and *selfish*. But there were great things about her. Do you remember the description of her (Strachey) entering a room with the Empress Eugénie—the loveliest woman in Europe, with the little round German widow—but there was no doubt which was the Queen, so superior is natural dignity to assumed. I wonder *what* she would have become with Albert alive for another quarter-century.

19 August 1956   *Bromsden Farm*
I wish I'd read some good books lately, so that I could dazzle you with quotations, but all my spare moments have been spent grubbing up material for George Moore footnotes, the erudition of which will astonish few. It took me ¾ of an hour in the basement of the London Library to find enough for a footnote about Cora, Lady Strafford, a thrice-married American. Before one of her marriages (perhaps the second—to Lord Strafford) she thought it would be a good thing to get a little sex-instruction, so she went over to Paris and took a few lessons from a leading cocotte. On her wedding night she was beginning to turn precept into practice when her bridegroom sternly quelled her by saying: 'Cora, *ladies don't move!*' I need

hardly say that this delectable anecdote is *not* in my footnote. The Oscar Wilde letters are going to demand a mass of annotation—just the sort of job I like, but *when* is it to be done?

How do you like this? 'French verse evokes an image of a carriage drawn by two horses both stepping beautifully; English verse of horses that can escape from their harness, spread their wings and take the air.' It's in a letter from George Moore to Gosse.

26 August 1956   *Bromsden Farm*

Frank Swinnerton is a pet: a small, ugly, bearded, ageless-looking man. He giggles and chuckles a lot in an infectious way, is a brilliant mimic, and is full of malicious anecdotes which he tells without any malice at all: indeed I don't think there is any in him. When I had finished my Walpole book I told F.S. that there were a number of faintly unflattering remarks about him in it, all made by Hugh, and asked whether he'd like to see proofs in case he objected. He said NO: he didn't mind what was said and would much prefer the *ipsissima verba* to any bowdlerised version. I see him at the committee meetings of the Royal Literary Fund, which I accuse him of not taking wholly seriously, since he occasionally introduces a laugh into that otherwise solemn assembly.

27 August 1956   *Grundisburgh*

Awarding is tedious work—as tedious as Dr J found the history of Birmingham—essentially because there is really not much objective certainty about the right mark for a short essay on the character of Brutus if the writer avoids mistakes of fact or spelling and grammar, and the chap who gets 92/200 fails while 94/200 passes. However we pass more who probably ought to fail than *vice versa*, and fear reproaches on the Judgment Day less than e.g. the marble-hearted mathematicians ought to.

I delighted in this book.[1] How beautifully he writes! But I gather that modern taste deprecates 'style' and uses the word 'elegant' only as a term of abuse. Who was the 'leading critic' who was dubious whether one 'wanted to spend three hours of life visiting Balliol in 1905'? And who or what is he leading except a drove of *asses*? He

[1] L.E. Jones (Jonah), *An Edwardian Youth*.

would be scandalised if anyone ran down *Ulysses* from a disbelief in the worthwhileness of spending a day in Dublin fifty years ago.

We were all rather sensible at Oxford and only one mathematician wanted to air and hear views about Suez and the T.U.C., the rest of us realising that there is nothing whatever new to say about either. Things will be as they will be, and though these world affairs are as loaded with dangers as the clouds with rain, it is all devilish interesting. Except in late Victorian times, up to about Jonah's time at Balliol perhaps, the world never has been comfortable since the French Revolution—and perhaps it was never meant to be. A rum affair altogether! I must go to lunch—with what is claimed to be the dreariest line in all verse ringing in my ears: 'The rain dripped ceaselessly down from the hat which I stole from a scarecrow'.

Hôtel de Paris
Hendaye Plage
10 September 1956   *Basses-Pyrénées*
This is a perfect family holiday place with a huge sandy beach and the Pyrenees on three sides. The Spanish frontier is a mile away and we have twice driven over to amuse the children, though Spain (except in its sunniest south) is grimly poverty-stricken and desolate. Photographs of Franco everywhere, and armed police every few miles. The mountains are beautiful, and on our first drive we picnicked high up in the Pass of Roncesvalles. All the family are enjoying it hugely: all burned brown, and my hair is bleached to what the children call greyish-white but I prefer to consider the last glimpses of the blondeness of what H.J. called 'my fermenting and passionate youth'.

27 September 1956   *Grundisburgh*
I have never really been to France—merely through it. I often have a suspicion that it, or at least the south of it, is the best country to live in. Away, of course, from all damned politics. But I don't really know anything about it. Though I know, I think, what Flecker meant when vituperating a certain (not *very* uncommon) English type of man, he burst out 'Go to France, bloody baby, and get educated'.

There must be a good many farmers who might echo what Mr Cayenne said on his deathbed ('I told him that God chastened those he loveth'. 'The devil take such love' was his awful answer). It was

M.R.J. who introduced me to *Annals of the Parish*.[1] Have I been a bore about it to you before? It is immensely good value and not nearly well enough known. No doubt Leavis thinks nothing of it.

29 September, 1956   *Bromsden Farm*
No, you've never mentioned *Annals of the Parish* before. Many years ago I picked up a charming little first edition, which I must now read, if ever I can find the time. In the late thirties I also picked up another Galt first edition for 1/6—*Ringan Gilhaize or the Covenanters* (3 vols, 1823). I've never read that either, but took it down this morning and was delighted by its opening sentence: 'It is a thing past all contesting, that, in the Reformation, there was a spirit of far greater carnality among the champions of the cause, than among those who in later times so courageously, under the Lord, upheld the unspotted banners of the Covenant'. If only a few novels of our day opened with such punch!

7 October 1956   *Bromsden Farm*
So stiff was I this morning that I thought the only remedy was more gardening, so I struggled on until I broke the scythe in two and honour was satisfied.

    P. Fleming looked in this morning, as he does most days when I'm here, bringing new paragraphs and a map for his book. He was a trifle *affairé* since he was expecting the Dalai Lama's brother to lunch! Before coming here he had walked for miles, cut down eight trees and read the Lesson at the Harvest Festival.

10-11 October 1956   *Grundisburgh*
And now I am in the middle of yet another H-D book—*Nanga Parbat* and the various attempts to climb it. I have just arrived at the almost daily holocaust in the 1934 expedition. I have always liked mountaineering books, being myself the worst imaginable climber with a head that begins dizzying half-way up a short ladder. The pictures always give me a thrill. I have many blind spots, and you will be horrified to hear I stuck in *The Towers of Trebizond*[2] about which the

---

[1] By John Galt.
[2] By Rose Macaulay.

reviews are unanimous in praise. But I found all the Aunt Dottery and comic parsons too much. I am quite ready to be told I am wrong.

How a' God's name did you *break* a scythe? All I have ever managed was to lose the wedge, and in very early days I did once reduce one to the likeness of a giant corkscrew. Now I refer with insufferable pedantry to the chine and the nebs and the tang etc, and make quite a good job of the actual operation, though I am still fairly ham-fisted at the honing, though slightly better than when the local expert, feeling my edge, said he wouldn't mind riding on it.

I am teaching a village boy of ten to read; he reads all the words separately, ignores commas *and* full stops, and always renders the indefinite article as 'hay'. However, they tell me he bids fair to become another Stanley Matthews, so what does literary progress matter?

21 October 1956   *Bromsden Farm*

Since I saw you my life has been overwhelmed by the Box-and-Cox appearances of my elder children—the boy on leave from Germany, the girl up from Wales to see him. He lost the keys of the flat, ransacked all my drawers trying to find a black tie, borrowed my bag and brought it back full of mud and water after playing the Wall Game— but to such a patriarch as you these irritations are only too well known. In my theatrical youth I once told a dear old cockney actor that the night before I had had too much to drink and been sick. A fond, nostalgic look came over his face, and he said 'Sick after drinking; it sounds like primroses to me, boy.'

On Friday night I appeared for 4½ minutes on Commercial Television. This involved spending 2½ hours in a studio in Aldwych, full of whisky and sandwiches and a strangely assorted company, myself arguing with the book-manager of the Army and Navy Stores about keyhole-memoirs of the Royal Family (Creepy-Crawfie and the rest), which I said should be prohibited by law! And for this evening's amusement they are going to pay me twenty guineas!

The *Sunday Times* have infuriated Fleming by sending all his articles from his book *Invasion 1940* to the Censor (whoever he may be). This personage has suggested that, instead of saying that if the Germans came we planned to use gas if necessary to stop them (as Winston told Peter was the case), Peter should say exactly the opposite! Naturally P. refused, so the whole passage is to be removed from the serialisation, though I have no intention of removing it from the book.

It is very odd how completely unable so many men are to put themselves in the place of their own audience—so very unlike the old Duke of Devonshire, who yawned during his own maiden speech because, as he told somebody, 'it was so damned dull'. It isn't a matter of brains at all. Dr Sheppard, once Provost of King's, is bursting with brains, but the blend of gush and childishness in his speeches is one of the most embarrassing things I know.

I entirely agree with you about all that Crawfie literature. But, human nature being what it is, how are those who run the Press ever going to forgo what is profitable and legal? If they knew their classics, they would only answer as Vespasian did when his prim son protested against him (somehow, I forget the details) taxing sewage. The old vulgarian laughed coarsely and retorted '*Pecunia non olet.*'[1] What have ninety years of popular education done to weaken commercial criteria? Less than nothing.

27 October 1956   *Bromsden Farm*
My delivery of Guy Chapman's lecture on 'The French Army and Politics' at King's College, London last Monday was, I think, a decided success.[2] I prefaced it with a bit of dialogue about what Silas Wegg should read to the Golden Dustman:

'Was you thinking at all of poetry?' Mr Wegg inquired, musing.
'Would it come dearer?' Mr Boffin asked.
'It would come dearer,' Mr Wegg returned. 'For when a person comes to grind off poetry night after night, it is but right he should expect to be paid for its weakening effect on his mind.'

Then I launched into the lecture with as much *élan*, punch, and *brio* as my lack of acquaintance with the script allowed. Knowing nothing of the subject, I probably read it better than Guy himself would have done, and he knows *all* about it! The audience (some fifty bodies 'of

[1] 'Money doesn't smell.'
[2] Guy was recovering from an operation.

repellent aspect, remotely connected with education', old and young, black and white, male and female) sat motionless—whether riveted or stunned I couldn't be sure. The many French names (particularly those whose spelling seemed peculiar) I enunciated with such confidence and in so French an accent that they added to the wretches' stupefaction.

I am still tidying up George Moore, and tomorrow I am to be received in audience by Sir Thomas Beecham, Bart. Since he supplanted G.M. as Lady Cunard's lover, he could clearly spill a bibful—but will he? I doubt it. Full report next week.

I have just listened to the News and learned of the death of my beloved friend of thirty years, Viola Meynell. In some ways it is a mercy, for she was suffering from progressive muscular atrophy, and had just reached the point where she could no longer walk or write, but I shall miss her a lot. I last saw her in August, when I drove over to see her in Sussex. Oh dear, I do hate people dying, don't you? V.M. wrote some lovely poems: here is one called Dusting:[1]

The dust comes secretly day after day,
Lies on my ledge and dulls my shining things.
But O this dust that I shall drive away
    Is flowers and kings,
Is Solomon's temple, poets, Nineveh.

She was a lovely person—and so I go sadly to bed.

Barbon Manor
1 November 1956   *Westmorland*
Your letter found me here yesterday—the home of Roger Fulford, all among the moors, and altogether very pleasant and comfortable. Today we had lunch by the roadside in a spot empty of all life except an obviously short-tempered and resentful bull in the field over the wall. We thought Roger's duffle coat—dyed reddish, which he says was the local Liberal colour—was annoying it, though I read somewhere lately that bulls are in fact colour-blind (another mare's tale gone west). So he took it off and in a 'monstrous little voice' tried to placate the bull with endearments—'Bullie, bullie, poor old bullie,'

---

[1] By kind permission of Mr Jacob Dallyn.

which so increased its rage and hatred that it bayed like the trombones in *Tannhäuser*, and pawed a great hole in the ground; so we retreated—a little too fast for dignity, but, we hoped, not fast enough to indicate fear.

The countryside is endlessly lovely—mile after mile of what Housman calls 'solitude of shepherds High in the folded hill,' and the sky produces different effects with extraordinary rapidity. We passed the abode of the famous old geologist Adam Sedgwick, a Cambridge eccentric. His bedmaker once sent his favourite chair to be re-seated. This was done in cane, and he was furious. He was always expecting sudden death and apostrophised her 'Woman, do you expect me to go into the presence of my Maker with my backside imprinted with small hexagons?'

Next week I go to tell the boys of Bromsgrove that education is not a mere passing of examinations; they must read for themselves and ruminate. The headmaster says he is going to insist on his masters being present, as they are the real Philistines of the community.

When I get to the Judgment Seat, I will see to it that all is in 'the Book where good deeds are entered'. But of course I may be knocking at a different door and seeing—rather ecstatically—through its bars Byron and Helen of Troy, and John Wilkes, and Oscar Wilde and other terribly attractive company.

I like that remark of T.S.E.'s that the critical attitude ends by preventing one *enjoying any book*—and that is the ultimate damnation of him who shall be nameless, whom you will soon call my King Charles's head.[1] Housman was at Bromsgrove and I shall put that in their pipes. If the science master is there I shall ask him if *his* backbone tingles and the flesh of his cheeks creeps if he thinks of a verse from the psalms as A.E.H.'s did.

I end with a little *trouvaille* from Roger's shelves—the last stanza of a hymn 'in use in a church near Cambridge' seventy years ago:

Milk of the breast that cannot cloy
He, like a nurse, will bring;
And when we see His promise nigh,
Oh how we'll suck and sing!

[1] F.R. Leavis.

The notes to, and dating of, Oscar's letters provide the greatest fun. Unlike G.M., Oscar has occasioned an enormous literature of comment, biography, criticism, bibliography etc—much of it written by chronic liars like Frank Harris and Lord Alfred Douglas.

Oh yes—my interview with Beecham was most civilised and agreeable, but produced little of value. He was courteously hospitable, giving me sherry and a good cigar. His flat in Weymouth Street is very grand, white-coated manservant and all. Lady B., a good thirty-five years younger than he and good-looking, was present all the time, so I could see there was no chance of any indiscretions about Lady Cunard. I fenced round the subject with incessant questions and found his memory excellent. He rolls well-chosen words off his tongue with relish and precision. He told me that George V went to the opera once a year—always to *La Bohème*. Once Beecham asked him if it was his favourite. 'Yes', said the King. 'That's most interesting, Sir. I'd be most interested to know why.' 'Because it's much the shortest', said His Majesty. An excellent reason indeed!

On Friday I went down to Sussex for Viola Meynell's funeral, travelling with Shane Leslie[1], who was grotesquely and most unsuitably dressed in a saffron-coloured kilt, with a bright green scarf round his shoulders. A bald head and thick tufts of hair on his cheek-bones (like Gow only more so) completed a figure from comic opera.

The Housman phrase comes from his 'The Merry Guide' which is my favourite. The other pictures in the poem struck home as we journeyed southward—the hanging woods and hamlets, and blowing realms of woodland with sunstruck vanes afield, and cloud-led shadows, and valley-guarded granges and silver waters wide. Yes, yes, I know I needn't have quoted them all, but the writing of them gives me physical and mental pleasure (you know that perfectly well, and will forgive).

Lord A.D. wrote some good poetry, and one must say that, even if put considerably off by his bland declaration that no one ever wrote better. A tragic life—and the physical alterations in him between the

[1] Anglo-American-Irish baronet and man of letters.

ages of twenty and sixty-five are simply those of Dorian Gray. I
suppose one cannot have so loathsome a father without paying for it.
I like the little interchange between old Agate and Douglas. J.A.
wrote 'Milton's poetry flames in the forehead of the morning sky.
Housman's twinkles in the Shropshire gloaming; yours, my dear A.,
glitters like Cartier's window at lunch-time.' To which A.D. replied
'are you not aware that seventeen of my best sonnets were written in
Wormwood Scrubs?'

Roger and I teaed at Dotheboys Hall last Friday (at Bowes). They
told us there was no doubt *it* is the building where Squeers's[1] proto-
type Shaw had his school. Dickens of course said S wasn't founded on
S but nobody believed him and Shaw was ruined. What an odd artist
Dickens was (if one at all). Squeers was first a sadist, then a figure of
comedy ('Natur' she's a rum 'un' etc), then a criminal. And D did
much the same with Pecksniff. The truth no doubt is that—like
Shakespeare—he didn't bother about probability or consistency, but
just let his fancy fly—and, by gum, what wings each one's fancy had!

22 November 1956   *Grundisburgh*
To the superannuated man of leisure a prospective committee is a
headache, an old boy dinner a heavy and a weary weight. This last is
due this evening. The absurd thing is that I always quite enjoy it when
it is once started, but that makes it no less of a hang-over. Anyway a
speech is always that, and I am expected to be funny. On the way up,
the train is about at Colchester when the conviction settles on me that
not only can I not think of anything remotely funny, but that there
isn't anything funny left for anyone to say and do. By Chelmsford a
ray of light dawns, viz that the audience will be mellow enough to
regard almost anything as funny, even if none have reached the stage
described by Sir Thomas More 'with his belly standing astrote like a
taber, and his noll totty with drink'.

25 November 1956   *Bromsden Farm*
Yesterday I drove to Oxford and spent four hours in Magdalen
library, checking and copying the Wilde letters there. Tom Boase, the
President, gave me an excellent lunch in the middle. At the end I had

---

[1] *Nicholas Nickleby.*

twenty minutes in Blackwell's before they shut, and picked up a few scraps of Wildeana—that job is the greatest fun, if only I had time to do it properly. 'We work in the dark—we do what we can—we give what we have. Our doubt is our passion and our passion is our task. The rest is the madness of art.' I expect you know where that comes from.[1] Like you, I copy out for the pleasure of doing it.

Last week was much occupied by Harold Nicolson's seventieth birthday present and dinner. John Sparrow started it, but very soon the whole of the organisation devolved (as they say) on me. Getting from his secretary a copy of his address-book, we circularised more than 350 of his friends. Eventually 253 of them contributed £1370! Getting the cheque to him on the right day, with an alphabetical list of donors was a great nuisance. I also circularised them all again, telling them the result.

Then the Duff Cooper Memorial Prize cropped up again in a big way. Constant telephone calls to Diana at Chantilly about getting Winston as prize-giver (which she did), a drive across London to look at Enid (Bagnold) Jones's drawing-room where the ceremony is to take place, much more telephoning to devoted ladies and cham-pagne-providers, drafting and sending out a press release, etc, making sure the cheque (£200) is ready—phew! Enid Jones lives next door to Winston, which is a help, since they say he's not good for much more than twenty minutes now. Her drawing room was built by Lutyens out of some old stables and is like an attractive stage set—at that moment another devoted lady rang me up here to say that Winston was going to speak only of Duff and would I get one of the judges who awarded the prize to say a few words about the *book*. Also, who is to marshal the press photographers? Unfortunately Hamish Hamilton (the publisher of the prize-winning book, Alan Moorehead's *Gallipoli*) is not on speaking terms with Randolph Churchill, who is now interfering actively—phew again!

29 November 1956   *Grundisburgh*
I caught a dreadful glimpse of myself at my dinner now and then behaving exactly like that emetic Mr Chips, but the opposite number to him would I suppose be someone like Cyril Connolly or Jack

[1] From Henry James's short story 'The Middle Years'.

61

Haldane, so what will you? Have you, by the way, read Hollis's *George Orwell* and if so, or even if not, can you tell me why he is so important? It is not fair to answer *1984* or *Animal Farm*, because he is regarded as very fine outside them and I can't quite see why. I like a good deal of his thinking aloud, but is it very profound or illuminating? I am rather on the fence about him, as about many things and people.

You don't tell me what the menu was at your dinner—I always like to know that. J.M. Barrie once said that the great merit of Phillips Oppenheim's books was the excellent eating in all of them. Another comment was that P.O. always tired of his book soon after the middle and then 'merely kicked it along to its end'. Tuppy had a complete set of P.O., which must have been as hard to collect as the whole of Trollope, of whom one has *never* read all.

P.S. Here is W. Cory on public school education—the last word, *me judice.*[1]

At school you are engaged not so much in acquiring knowledge as in making mental efforts under criticism. A certain amount of knowledge you can indeed with average faculties acquire so as to retain; nor need you regret the hours you spent on much that is forgotten, for the shadow of lost knowledge at least protects you from many illusions. But you go to a great school not so much for knowledge as for arts and habits; for the habit of attention, for the art of expression, for the art of assuming at a moment's notice a new intellectual position, for the art of entering quickly into another person's thoughts, for the habit of submitting to censure and refutation, for the art of indicating assent or dissent in graduated terms, for the habit of regarding minute points of accuracy, for the art of working out what is possible in a given time, for taste, for discrimination, for mental courage, and for mental soberness.

2 December 1956   *Bromsden Farm*

Orwell is of no importance from the literary point of view, but for some I daresay he has the fascination of litmus paper or a chameleon: he was (slightly to change the metaphor) a sort of barometer of the Thirties and early Forties, going through and writing about *all* the

[1] G.W.L. had quoted from it in his recent speech at Bromsgrove School.

experience of young left-wing intellectuals during those troubled years. If you and I cannot read him with pleasure, my dear George, let us be certain, even if ridiculous to boot.

I too always like to know what people had to eat: wasn't Galsworthy good at it? At Harold N's birthday dinner I ordered hot lobster with rice, roast pheasant and *soufflé surprise*, with sherry, meursault, claret and port or brandy. When I was a boy I too had an almost complete set of Phillips Oppenheim (over ninety vols),[1] but at some moment I grew ashamed of them and gave them away. I chiefly remember a proliferation of cocktails, usually described as 'amber coloured fluid'. I met him once on the Riviera and sat goggling at his feet. He was old, with a young and pretty 'secretary'.

The Duff Cooper Prize was duly awarded on Wednesday. My calling in Harold Nicolson to open the proceedings and mention Moorehead's book was immensely successful: he did it beautifully and briefly. Winston was terribly frail and tottery. Although his little speech was all written out, one couldn't feel sure he'd get through it without losing the thread. However, he did. (Beforehand he rather sweetly showed his script to Moorehead, to make sure he'd got his name right.) Moorehead replied in a few, very good, words, and then Winston, like an old hunter wanting more than a sniff of the chase, got up and said another sentence or two. It was all very moving and exactly right. Champagne flowed freely, and the old warrior drank some as he beamed round at his friends. Even in the grip of withering age he makes all our present rulers look like feeble pygmies. I couldn't stay as long as I'd have liked, since I had to rush home and change before dining with the Priestleys (scampi, partridge and delicious vanilla ice with lumps of ginger in it).

5 December 1956   *Grundisburgh*

Do you think that in seventy years someone will record as one of the aberrations of great critics that R.H.-D. thought nothing of Orwell? I don't think so; in fact what you say chimes in with my own doubts and suspicions. How a small and persistent clique can bolster up a writer's reputation. Landor's remark hits the nail firmly: 'We admire by tradition (or fashion) and criticise by caprice.'

[1] I now (1979) have 153.

'A Stoic' [by Galsworthy] has always been one of my favourites—Germane soup; filly de sole; sweetbread; cutlet soubees[1]; rum souffly, according to Meller, and old Heythorp added hors d'oeuvres (oysters as it turned out) and a savoury (cheese remmykin), and you remember 'cook's done a little spinach in cream with the soubees'. This from memory; I don't *think* it is inaccurate. Your Nicolson menu pleases me; was it a really *fat* pheasant? There is *nothing* so good. By the way Meller told old H. he had 'frapped' the champagne a little. What exactly does that mean?[2] I have never dared to ask anyone, because obviously one ought to know.

To-morrow I go to the King's Founder's Feast ('Doctors will wear scarlet; orders and decorations, medals or ribbons, will be worn'). Well that all sounds rather tremendous, but when I told them my tail coat had long been one with Nineveh and Tyre, they came down to earth and said half the company would be in tuxedos and quite a number in corduroys and jumpers. My speech is assembled, morticed, dovetailed, planed, polished and dried. Sometimes I think it will prosper, at others a swift and easy death is my only wish. Do *your* feelings on such occasions behave in so volatile a fashion? I take comfort from Roger's (I think) telling me that a Lord Mayor of London told him a few years ago that he had no nerves before a speech, and that he never prepared but said what came into his head, implying that his head could transmute anything into gold. He then, an hour later, made the worst speech R. had ever heard.

13 December 1956   *Grundisburgh*

The King's feast was immense fun. They were very welcoming. The Provost[3] seemed to me entirely charming; he is on the way to being an outstanding success, which, in the most censorious community in the world, i.e. dons, is a remarkable start.

I have just finished the [Lytton] Strachey-Woolf letters. Not fearfully good are they? Good things here and there of course, but Strachey is often trivial and V.W. often shows off, and on the whole one sees why many people spit at the name of Bloomsbury. Neither had any

---

[1] Soubise: onion sauce.
[2] Iced.
[3] Noel Annan.

humility, and I am more and more blowed if that isn't the *sine qua non* of all goodness and greatness. The trouble is that if you are very clever and don't believe in God, there is nobody and nothing in the presence of whom or which you can be humble. For instance, Milton and Carlyle, for all their arrogance, were fundamentally humble, don't you think? Here endeth the epistle of George the Apostle.

I am temporarily swamped in exam-papers. What *is* the point of examining on the *Midsummer N.D.*? The candidates have all been told by their palsied beaks that the plot and the character-drawing are masterly—the plot being absurd and the c-d perfunctory. Not *one* of those flatulent impostors has told his candidates that nothing in the play is of the smallest importance or merit except a great deal of celestial poetry—oh yes and of course Bottom.

16 December 1956   *Bromsden Farm*
My wife (her name, by the way, is Comfort—a New England name, which I believe she alone possesses in this country) is preparing an enormous joint of *spiced beef* for your and Pamela's visit. Apparently it has to be massaged with a different herb every day for a week—we'll hope for the best, and fall back on the Christmas ham if need be.

I'm not sure I agree that it's impossible to be humble in spirit unless you believe in God—in fact I'm sure I disagree, and if I weren't so proof-weary would quote examples to prove my point.

I'm longing to get on with Oscar Wilde, and all the detective work it involves. Recently, for example, I got hold of an undated letter (most of them are) to Clement Scott, the dramatic critic of the *Daily Telegraph*. The only clue was a phrase saying, roughly: 'I liked your Ode very much, and thought it much better than Lord T's.' No verse by C.S. in the London Library, but luckily I have two devoted friends who are often in the Reading Room of the British Museum, and I asked one of them to get out all books of verse by Clement Scott (he published several) and see how many odes he wrote, and when. There turned out to be one only—a valedictory ode on the retirement of the Bancrofts, which was recited by Irving from the stage of the Haymarket Theatre on 20 July 1885. As soon as I got down here I rushed to the big life of Tennyson, and found that his lines on the marriage of Princess Beatrice were published in *The Times* on 23 July 1885—which means that I can date that letter within a week or so. See what fun it is!

20 December 1956   *Grundisburgh*

We shan't be able to talk about humility over the spiced beef, but it is exciting to find you disagreeing about it. You will I am sure produce some cogent evidence, but I warn you that an 18-pounder I sooner or later shall bring into action is to maintain blandly, infuriatingly, irrefutably, that a great number of people think they don't believe in God, who, in fact, *do*!

3 January 1957   *Eton*

I thought of writing a 'thank-you' letter after that Sunday, but then the fear that *you* might think it a trifle gushing prevailed and I didn't—probably wrongly, as it was disobeying both Arthur Benson[1] and Dr Johnson, who said such impulses should always be followed. We did enjoy every moment of our visit enormously, and shall certainly pay another on a less grim day when the sunshine is external as well as internal. And I want to fix in my mind that study of yours where—*inter alia*—you write your letters to me.

5 January 1957   *Bromsden Farm*

It's fine to know that you and Pamela enjoyed your visit here and will come again—if we ever get petrol. Your reference to A.C.B. and Doctor Johnson reminds me of the stage-door-keeper at the Lyric Hammersmith in 1928–29. He was clearly a failed actor and looked like an aged pocket-Irving, small with long grey hair and a wonderfully histrionic face. I forget his name. Anyhow, he was always very nice to me, and at Christmas I gave him a present (I forget what). He wrote me the most charming letter, which I hope I've still got somewhere, in which he said: 'Always follow such generous impulses, dear lad'. He must be long dead. I expect you know the story of Winston in later years in the House of Commons. When a colleague tactfully told him that several of his fly-buttons were undone, he said: 'No matter. The dead bird does not leave the nest.'

Sunday evening, 6 January

The notes to Oscar absorb me. The trouble with footnotes (and this book will contain several hundred) is that they tend either to be bald,

[1] A.C. Benson, G.W.L.'s housemaster when he was a boy at Eton. Later Master of Magdalene College, Cambridge. See footnote on p. 190.

dull and severely factual, or (when one tires of that) to be full of fascinating but almost wholly irrelevant matter. For instance, I must have a note about the Roman Catholic church of St Aloysius in Oxford, which O.W. frequented as an undergraduate with R.C. leanings, and when I find that its architect was Joseph Aloysius Hansom, who also invented the Hansom cab, I can't resist putting that in.

13 January 1957   *Bromsden Farm*
The lecture at the Dickens Fellowship last Monday was a curious occasion. The Swedenborg Hall is a depressing *venue*—a grim room surrounded by long-dead, unknown and vilely painted Swedenborgians. Some sixty or so Dickensians turned up, mostly elderly and hard to rouse from apathy. My introductory remarks made up in booming clarity for what they lacked in sense and preparation, and then Kathleen Tillotson spoke for well over an hour. Dickens's revisions in the various editions of *Sketches by Boz* were her theme, and very ably she handled it, quoting many amusing passages previously known only to the readers of *Bell's Life in London* in the early 1830s. But my chair was hard, and being cruelly exposed on the rostrum I was compelled to sit up and appear to be listening intently. 'Any Questions' produced the usual pin-drop silence, which I ended by asking a few myself. All was mercifully over by 9.30 (we got there at 6.45) and since Mrs T. refused all offers of refreshment I walked gratefully home to Oscar.

At the Lit. Soc. on Tuesday I sat between Donald Somervell[1] and Harold Nicolson. The latter talked entertainingly about Swinburne's love of being beaten (if possible by muscular ladies), which he had learned from Gosse. Donald Somervell reminded me of Sydney Smith's saying: 'I had a wonderful dream last night. I dreamed there were thirty-nine Muses and only nine Articles.'

16 January 1957   *Grundisburgh*
Two parcels on the breakfast table this morning, viz my new suit of clothes and John Carter's book—the latter obviously promising a great deal of pleasure, the former very little, because the only time *my* suits ever look nice and new is before I have worn them even once. You, I suspect, if not exactly dressy in your garden, somehow manage

---

[1] Politician, judge, peer, Fellow of All Souls, Oxford.

to give your shabbiness an aristocratic air. I shall never live down the Southwold vet telling my daughter that he had given a message for her to 'your man', who in fact was her father sawing wood. Did the chap expect me to saw in spats?

Do you really tell me, Rupert, that you are not thrilled by lions and tigers and leopards and gorillas, or is it a relic of infantilism that I am? Jim Corbett's books are often looked into, and the page describing the appalling fury of the 'Bachelor of Powlgarh' tearing a tree to pieces about four yards away from J.C. flat on his face behind a prone trunk and eventually dragging himself away by his *toes*, still lying on his face, till he was out of earshot, and finding next day that the tiger, though silent for half-an-hour before J.C. dared to *stir*, *had* been there all the time—well that gives me more delicious shudders than any ghost story, or even Madame de la Rougierre in *Uncle Silas*.[1] A lion who carries in his mouth for four miles a dead buffalo, a gorilla who with *one* hand can pull seventeen men over in a tug-of-war, or, when vexed, grips a rifle-butt so tightly that it is *dented* by his fingerprints— well, as Faustus said, these things feed my soul.

Ervine's great book leaves me with a greatly enhanced admiration for G.B.S's character and much less for his intellect. His toughness and patience and cheerfulness all the first half of his life were surely quite outstanding, as were his generosity and good temper. But I do find his pontifications maddening; so many even of the better ones are no more than emphatic and well-phrased half-truths. Curious, by the way, that both Mrs Shaw and Mrs Chesterton were allergic to conjugal intercourse. Not Mrs H.G. Wells apparently, but then, as one of his extra-mural women said, his body smelt like honey— which I find faintly repellent.

Did they collect *everything* of Hilaire Belloc's, e.g. those tiny things about Lady Meyer etc and his inscriptions, some perhaps hardly printable, but I like:

I am a sundial, and I make a botch
Of what is done much better by a watch.

Tree-felling. Did I never tell you that it has always been a favour-ite exercise of mine, since the age of about fourteen, and even now I

---

[1] By Sheridan Le Fanu (1864).

will on the smallest provocation fill my discourse with words like 'kelf', and 'spurning' and 'helve'. My father was an expert with the axe, and indeed about trees altogether, and never could really forgive W.E.G. for being such a philistine about them; he only liked felling them and didn't do it very well. My father said you couldn't regard yourself as a really good axeman if you could not 'throw' a tree to within a foot of where you wanted, without a rope. As to the scythe, a Cumberland mower cuts a swathe ten feet wide. The normal mower is perfectly pleased with one of six feet. I do about five (when in form). The oldest mower in Grundisburgh is ninety-six.

Have you ever known anything but a 'pin-drop' silence when questions are asked for? At the Ascham Society meetings at Eton the same sequence was always in evidence. After a minute or two, Broadbent would utter a complicated sound composed in equal proportions of a snore, a belch, and a groan. Toddy Vaughan then gallantly saved the tottering situation with a question which proved, instantly and without a peradventure, that he had been unconscious throughout the paper. But what did it matter? In those spacious days the refreshment afterwards was toothsome, various, and unstinted.

I really must stop. Thank you for the Sydney Smith dream. Arthur Benson used to have marvellous dreams, full of wild fun and monstrous and irrational cruelties, e.g. himself about to be beheaded or one of his colleagues actually being hanged, inside a sort of cupboard, whence came a horrid noise of bumping and kicking.

19 January 1957   *Bromsden Farm*
Yes, the Nonesuch volume included all Belloc's printable verses, including many never printed before. I have often longed to assemble his unprintable ones, which are now available only in the memory of his friends. Did I tell you (I fear I did) of the time at luncheon at Duff's when he quoted his parody of A.E. Housman? It began:

When I was one-and-fifty
I found him at it still.
His eye was just as shifty,
He made me just as ill.

But how did it go on?

My military son has sent us a letter of twenty-three quarto pages, describing goose-shooting on the Baltic. After standing waist-deep in liquid and icy mud for four days he brought down *nine* geese and drove back to Dusseldorf exulting. I've never much cared for goose anyhow.

24 January 1957   *Grundisburgh*

The Ascham Society often entertained a visitor, but one might easily have found himself in for a grim evening, e.g. Broadbent on Beddoes, or old Chitty on Anselm, or Toddy Vaughan on Poggio which extended over two sittings. Arthur Benson was secretary then and there is a pencilled word 'closure?' in the minute-book when he consulted Luxmoore as to what was to be done. L., who had early school the next morning, sternly nodded. Ram told me that the paper began with so long a passage in Greek that the members, convinced that the whole paper was to be in Greek, fell into helpless laughter. However, after six minutes or so Toddy stopped, looked severely round and said 'So wrote Plato'.

I found some of Newman's *The Idea of a University* rather hard going, but at such times I remember Carlyle's contemptuous comparison of some man who decried Goethe to him, to one who 'complained of the sun because it would not light his cigar'. N. had an unchristian temper, and I suppose a good deal of the Socratic capacity for making the worse appear the better cause, but somehow he is one of those who are outside the reach of our superficial, *prima facie* judgments, and he often said things which hit one, if I may coarsely say so, plumb in the wind. And it is worth remembering, but I hesitate to say with what feelings, that D.H. Lawrence called 'Lead Kindly Light' and 'Abide with Me' 'sentimental messes' as compared with what he called 'healthy hymns', viz 'Fight the Good Fight', which is to put *Marmion* above the Nightingale ode.

I have just had a bit of luck—turned off a lot of muck from English stations and tried a foreign one and *at once* they began to play Bach's Air for the G. string, than which—to use the favourite ecstatic aposiopesis invented by Mrs Gladstone or her sister.

27 January 1957   *Bromsden Farm*

I attended a disastrous dinner of my bibliographical dining club at the Garrick. John Carter, who pretty well runs it, had run into Roger

Fulford and asked him to come as a guest. The general rule is that there are no guests, except on occasional Guest Nights or by general agreement. Roger was, I think, unaware of this, and the slight *gêne* caused by Carter's solecism would soon have evaporated, had not *two* members, quite separately, *arrived* heavily inebriated. Michael Sadleir, poor lamb, is I fear in constant pain from cancer or some such and drinks to dull the pain: most pardonable but not conducive to good conversation. The other, a bookseller you wouldn't know, was sullenly aggressive and in his studied but only partially coherent rudeness to one after another of his fellows a seething mass of Non-U inferiority was quickly apparent. I managed to insulate Roger between Carter and Sparrow, but the rest of the round table was hideous.

31 January 1957   *Grundisburgh*
Wordsworth must have been uniquely dried-up, stiff, dull, self-satisfied, arrogant, but at his poetic best—Who was it said 'He stumps along by your side, an old bore in a brown coat, and suddenly he goes up and you find that your companion is an angel', i.e. is at home in a region where Byron saw only George III and Southey having their legs pulled. I see the latest Byron book puts everything down to B having been a homosexual. But haven't we always known he was, remembering his own description of his feelings at school about Lord Clare? He must have been grand fun in company when not showing off, or on the defensive. Poor B., we must always remember he was a Harrovian.

7 February 1957   *Grundisburgh*
Don't get up till your temperature is what it should be.[1] Old Gladstone of course had a theory—rather like his thirty-two chewings of every mouthful —that to avert shock after a fall, one should remain some time *in situ.* So more than once passers-by were rewarded by the sight of a venerable statesman prone in the gutter, and returned home more than ever convinced that the G.O.M. was insane. But how dull it would be if great men had no foibles, like Barham writing *The Ingoldsby Legends* with a cat on each shoulder, or

---

[1] The result of a fall in the street.

71

Dumas putting on woollen socks whenever he had a love-scene to write, or Johnson touching every lamp-post he passed.

By the way I have just been re-reading Johnson's *Lives of the Poets*. How full they are of good things! Anything approaching the nonsensical always evoked some delightfully weighty irony. When someone timorously suggested that *The Beggar's Opera* would encourage crime they were put in their place with: 'Highwaymen and housebreakers seldom frequent the playhouse, or mingle in any elegant diversion; nor is it possible for anyone to imagine that he may rob with safety because he sees Macheath reprieved upon the stage.' That should do much to restore your temperature.

10 February 1957   *Bromsden Farm*

Yes, the *Lives of the Poets* are superb, and once again your words make me long for the leisure to reread such splendid stuff. 'By the common sense of readers uncorrupted with literary prejudices, after all the refinements of subtlety and the dogmatism of learning, must be finally decided all claim to poetical honours.' Them's my sentiments, and yours too, I know. My beloved Edmund Blunden knows chunks of this book (as of most others) by heart, and is fond of quoting, as though it applied to himself (I copy for the pleasure of it):

> His morals were pure, and his opinions pious: in a long continuance of poverty, and long habits of dissipation, it cannot be expected that any character should be exactly uniform. There is a degree of want by which the freedom of agency is almost destroyed; and long association with fortuitous companions will at last relax the strictures of truth, and abate the fervour of sincerity. That this man, wise and virtuous as he was, passed always unentangled through the snares of life, it would be prejudice and temerity to affirm; but it may be said that at least he preserved the source of action unpolluted, that his principles were never shaken, that his distinctions of right and wrong were never confounded, and that his faults had nothing of malignity or design, but proceeded from some unexpected pressure, or casual temptation.

That's the stuff! What an epitaph![1] And how cunningly I pretend to write you long letters which are mostly copied out of books!

[1] Johnson is writing of the poet William Collins.

I met Rose Macaulay in the London Library stacks, gropingly seeking the Theology section. 'You'll find yourself alone there,' I said. 'Yes', she answered; 'I always do.' And yet once I dare say that section was besieged by bearded scholars and earnest doubters.

14 February 1957   *Grundisburgh*

The passage you quote from Johnson would be a very good example to show the difference between the pompous and the powerful and precise—'long associations with fortuitous companions will at last relax the strictness of truth and abate the fervour of sincerity'. Every single word pulls its weight—which makes it all the more surprising that he wrote that Blackmore's prose was 'languid, sluggish, and life-less' and that Shenstone's landscape gardening might seem absurd to 'a surly and sullen' spectator. But perhaps the adjectives have shed some of their associations over the years.

In the train yesterday I was *thrilled* by *Moonraker* by Ian Fleming. Is he any relation to Peter F?[1] It is very well written, so perhaps he is. Are his other books good? The book I read on the going-up journey was *Paradise Lost*—the creation of the animals, Book VII. It is immense—'the river-horse and scaly crocodile,' 'the parsimonious emmet' etc. How right the Russian Moujik was who told Maurice Baring that he like *P.L.* because 'it makes me laugh and cry'.

17 February 1957   *Bromsden Farm*

I'm so happy at your joining the Lit. Soc.[2] It wasn't even necessary to rig the voting. I don't say I would have done so, but I very easily could have. As it was, you romped home top of the poll. The others elected were Alan Moorehead and John Piper. Last week's dinner brought Cuthbert Headlam to my side, with Ivor Brown on my other. After a few introductory prophecies of six weeks' hard frost Cuthbert mellowed considerably, and with a mixture of flattery and teasing I managed to keep him jolly until, when it was time for him to leave, he discovered we were thirteen, and refused to move until everybody rose together. Since half the members were out in the lavatory, this took some time to arrange, and in the meanwhile

[1] His brother
[2] The Literary Society, a dining club founded in 1807 by Wordsworth and others.

73

Cuthbert (looking himself like death slightly warmed up) told me of all the people he knew who had died through defying the superstition.

My daughter reports from Wales that the latest trade-name (among Evans the Hearse, Dai the Pub, etc) is the Hire Purchase agent, who is known as Trevor the Never. More hot news next week.

21 February 1957   *Grundisburgh*

Tommy Lascelles,[1] whether deliberately or not, achieved a masterstroke of tact in telling me that among the original members was poet-laureate Pye, of whom all I know is that he put into rhyme several episodes in my ancestor ('the good Lord')'s *History of Henry II*, and of course Byron's 'Better to err with Pope than shine with Pye'. T.L's mention of him had the effect on me that, according to Miss Reynolds, Goldsmith's bow had on everyone in the room—it put them at their ease, because at least they knew they couldn't possibly make a worse bow than *that*.

Well, the Collins passage I did notice with particular pleasure was: 'A man doubtful of his dinner, or trembling at a creditor, is not much disposed to abstract meditation or remote enquiries.' Good but not as good as yours.

24 February 1957   *Bromsden Farm*

You ask whether we disagree about anything. I think not, though I can't share your liking for books about large wild animals. Certainly I'm with you about Jane Austen, who has never been a great favourite of mine. But it's so long since I read her that I'd like to try again with the cold eye of middle age before finally jumping down on your side of the fence. I see what so many other people see in her, but myself (tell it not in Bloomsbury) if I want to refresh myself in that period I prefer Scott. My uncle Duff adored her novels, and in the last week of his life, when he knew (consciously or subconsciously) that he hadn't long to live, he came to Soho Square on Christmas Eve, and, saying 'I've brought you a Christmas present: I hope you haven't got it already,' he pulled two slim volumes out of each pocket of his great-

---

[1] Sir Alan Lascelles, President of the Lit. Soc., formerly Private Secretary to King George VI and Queen Elizabeth II.

coat. They were a first edition of *Northanger Abbey* and *Persuasion* (4 vols), in which he had written 'Old men forget but they are grateful when they remember'. I re-read *Persuasion* in this copy, and persuaded myself (almost) that I shared Duff's admiration for it. But in truth I don't think I did.

Last week I had a brush with the Cabinet Office, who suddenly demanded changes in Fleming's introduction to *Invasion 1940*. Since Peter was (and still is) inaccessible in America, I rang up Sir Norman Brook, the head of the place and a very nice man with whom I had tricky dealings over both G.M. Young's *Baldwin* and Duff's *Old Men Forget*. To him I made a strong *ad misericordiam* appeal, explaining (truthfully) that 30,000 copies of the book were already printed, the author couldn't be reached, and his suggested alterations would involve me in hideous expense and untold delay. Audibly shaken, he said he would reconsider the question, and on Friday evening I got a note withdrawing all his demands. Phew!

28 February 1957   *Grundisburgh*

Since my last, I have re-read *Mansfield Park*. It is much better than the insipid *Persuasion*. The Crawfords are interesting, and it is refreshing to find one of her snobbish dolls quite frankly committing adultery; but here again all the characters converse with exactly the same rounded amplitude which demands to be turned into Latin Prose. But some of the scenes and pictures are good. One sails along on smooth and shallow water under a mild blue sky.

I have with me—and am half through—*Lord Byron's Marriage*.[1] Immensely interesting. The highlight of it is of course the brilliant *Don Leon* poem of Colman's—very shocking and all that but as good as Pope *qua* skill.[2] I imagine Lady B. was fairly bloody, and her family and advisers worse. Odd that B. should never for a moment

---

[1] By G. Wilson Knight.

[2] George Colman was the leading dramatist and theatrical manager of his day, as well as being a good friend of Byron. *Don Leon* was written some time after Byron's death and, in Wilson Knight's words, 'purports to tell the inside story of Byron's homosexual propensities and concludes with him engaging in an abnormal sexual relationship with his own wife . . . For what it may be worth, we must note that Colman supports the view that Byron's wife was no unwilling partner in the act.'

have suspected that she and they might destroy his account of the whole affair, and so did not keep or safeguard a copy. Still, I suppose B. and marriage simply could not combine, whoever might have been his partner.

3 March 1957 — Bromsden Farm

Fleming is back from America, exhausted and with a heavy cold. He reports that Harold Caccia [British Ambassador] is doing splendidly in Washington, but is increasingly fed up with Dulles, and indeed with Eisenhower, who sees no-one except caddies and reads nothing but brief 'digests' of world news. He is, Peter says, now almost completely insulated from the world and its doings—which is pretty terrifying.

One of my few rules in life is never to refuse the offer of a book-case, since I never can have enough, and next Friday a *huge* one is being delivered at Soho Square, where there isn't a square foot for it: all would be well if I wasn't guarding Edmund Blunden's 7000 books there for him. They'll be with me at least till 1961.

6 March 1957 — Grundisburgh

I have just got from the Library the Holmes-Pollock[1] letters, as I greatly enjoyed the Holmes-Laski ones. *All* the good things I have noted so far come from old Holmes. I like: 'Whenever I read Shakespeare I am struck by the reflection how a few golden sentences will float a lot of quibble and drool for centuries, e.g. Beatrice and Benedick.' Not new of course but profoundly true, and crisply put. I am a poor Shakespearean, i.e. I am, like most, overwhelmed by the poetry, but so often bored by the absurd action of the play and the characters, and *always* by the wit. Holmes quotes with approval a Frenchman's answer when he was asked if a gentleman must know Greek and Latin: 'No, but he must have forgotten them'.

24 March 1957 — Bromsden Farm

I agree with Agate about French acting.[2] *Phèdre* last week was most beautiful and impressive, though I wished I'd had time to re-read and

---

[1] Sir Frederick Pollock, Bt (1845–1957). Professor of Jurisprudence at Oxford.
[2] He said it was in a different class from English.

absorb the play beforehand. Like Greek Tragedy, Racine should be known almost by heart, so that the subtleties of acting and phrasing can be relished.

Yesterday, in lovely hot sunshine, Comfort and I had our first trial of strength with the new motor-mower. Neither of us had ever operated one before, but we found it most satisfying and enjoyable, though we did more than we realised and are stiff and blistered today. Last night we dined gaily with the Osbert Lancasters, who live in Henley. Osbert and I went up to Oxford the same term in 1926, and he hasn't changed *at all.*

Don't you rather like this footnote: 'The remainder of this paragraph, which Coleridge wrote with his gout medicine instead of ink, has faded and is all but illegible'.

28 March 1957   *Grundisburgh*

I must say our end of the table [at the Johnson Club], under the— I am sure—approving eye of the Doctor, was very good fun. Malcolm Muggeridge: what riddles human beings are! That kindly, civilised, understanding man under the same hat as the spiky, unbalanced wrong-headed reviewer, pretending(?) that he prefers the *Mirror* and *Sketch* to *The Times,* the *Observer,* the *M. Guardian,* and that the taste for a nude bathing beauty and that for a *Times* Fourth Leader are on the same level. First thought on meeting him 'What an excellent chap!' First thought on reading his review 'What a Philistine!' But I suspect he enjoys trailing his coat. I liked him very much.

That paper I believe really to have been a definitely good one. But wasn't it dreadfully badly delivered? An intelligent Frenchman doesn't read *his* language like that—any more than a French orator would. Is it our native modesty? I sympathise with Arnold Bennett's exasperation when an Englishman sat like a graven image through Pavlova's swan dance till, near the end, a feather fell from her wing, on which the Englishman said 'Moulting'. No other word passed his lips.

I am in the summer-house surrounded by daffodils and my heart dances with them, and across the lawn is a cherry-tree in blossom, about which all I can say is what the historian of Solomon's reign said about the almug-tree, i.e. 'No such almug-trees were seen in the land' (which Monty James said was crossly interpolated by the scribe who was bored by the raptures being dictated to him). But of course every spring the earth's beauty is something new, never before seen. But how ludicrously brief it all is. Four or five days and the cherry blossom one morning is merely white compared with its first days, for which there is no word. Daffodils do last longer, though not so long as I want them to. Few things do.

31 March 1957   *Bromsden Farm*

Let us get one thing straightened out once and for all. I have been to far more dinners of the Johnson Club and the Lit. Soc. than you have, and I know, beyond, as they say, a peradventure, that it is *your* presence that makes these occasions *go*.

I adored your story of the Englishman watching Pavlova. I expect you saw her, but to me she is only a mythical bird, just as Nijinsky is a legendary faun. Actors—and even more dancers—can survive their last admirer only if they have been written about by a genius. Gordon Craig I consider a very phony genius, but his move-by-move description of Irving playing a scene from *The Bells* is immortal: do you know it?

An old and dear writer-friend of mine has sent me the typescript of a 350-page novel about a juvenile delinquent in an Italian quarter of New York. I have struggled past page 100 and must somehow finish. But what *am* I to say to him? This sort of thing is the most painful of publishing hazards. You couldn't say the book was *bad*: it's just *dull*, and who on earth wants to read such stuff?

4 April 1957   *Grundisburgh S.H.*
                                                            (summer-house)

I read your opening sentence to Pamela; she was undoubtedly pleased, but what wife of thirty-eight years' standing could ever see her husband as other than the humdrum old bore and egoist that he is?

Percy Lubbock is not at all well—bronchial, cardiac, etc, can do nothing, even walk upstairs, sees no one, writes no letters. And I suspect he is rather a rebellious patient, especially as his wish to live is not very strong. I have known him for sixty-two years, i.e. longer than any non-relative. Who was the good man I met recently who shared my opinion of *Earlham*, i.e. as a book of almost unique beauty? It is about the only thing of importance I am quite sure of—much surer, that is, than I am of the existence of God or that a point has position but no magnitude. Though I quite see what Desmond MacCarthy meant when he said it would have been even better if now and then Percy had just let his narrative scamper along in any old words.

11 April 1957   *Grundisburgh*

Tim and I had a good crack with H. Nicolson, who, *inter alia*, told us that Tennyson in his last years drank far too much and was often muzzy. Do you know at all who the 'small nervous Eton master' was who tried to talk to Tennyson in a high wind and came, no doubt, to a dead end, when T's first response was 'I don't know who you are, and I can't hear what you say'? It must have been before Toddy Vaughan's day. Pecker Rouse and Hoppy Daman were both mathematicians, and would have had nothing to say to him—or anyone else—outside sine and co-sine. Arthur Benson once told me that small collegers hated being fagged to Rouse's because, though you could avoid some, you couldn't avoid *all* the empty bottles that were thrown at anyone who came into the house—i.e. the level of Rouse civilisation was that of the mining districts 150 years ago. A bad beak does *a lot* of harm. I never really lied without a twinge until I was up to Rouse, when I learnt nothing about x and y but all about how to lie.

14 April 1957   *Bromsden Farm*

Today I have gardened in the sun—'sweated in the eye of Phoebus'—and only hope that all night I shall sleep in Elysium.[1] Also I opened the cricket season by bowling my youngest a few creaking overs in the meadow. Alas, at thirteen and three-quarters he already makes hay of my googly, which used to baffle him regularly.

On Wednesday I was one of sixteen at a stag dinner in the Garrick, given by Hamish Hamilton for the head of Harper's (American publishers). I was well placed between Fleming and Priestley, who was at his nicest and most amusing. J.B.P. said, of the

[1] *Henry V*, iv, ii.

Adams trial, that the most sinister words in the whole business were those used by the Doctor when he was set free: 'Now I must get back to work'.[1]

On Thursday evening I went with Elisabeth Beerbohm and two other friends to the first night of *Zuleika*, which is delightfully gay and tuneful, although the leading lady is quite without looks, charm or talent. With someone looking like your friend Marilyn Monroe it would run for ever. Most of Max's subtleties have been 'ironed out', but here and there a genuine line pops up:

'The owls have hooted, Miss Dobson; it's too late for love.'

I must read the book again. We were in a box, and Elisabeth spent most of the time singing and dancing the relevant 'numbers' in the shadows at the back. On Friday afternoon I took refuge in the Reading Room of the British Museum, where, among the rustle of black clergymen and wild-eyed researchers badly in need of a bath, I spent three hours looking up this and that scrap of peripheral Wilde information.

You must forgive so much of my letters for being literary—that's the way I am. What should I do without books? Turn jobbing gardener, perhaps, and rush home (as the Yorkshire Dales farmers do) to catch the latest instalment of The Archers?

17 April 1957   *Grundisburgh*

You are having the humbling experience of all fathers. But let me tell you when Pamela was teaching Humphrey divinity, and was emphasizing the incredible goodness of Christ, H., finding the wings of his imagination tiring in the void, asked 'Was he as good as Father?' When P., as is supposed, answered that he was even better, H. gave up and has been an agnostic ever since.

I started doing my income-tax return this morning, and my mind, till that is off it, is the mind of a Suffolk yokel, threatened with melancholia. Why do all the shares I sell—at a small loss—start booming next day? Among the sayings which the late Geoffrey Madan claimed to have culled from Chinese literature and which some thought he

---

[1] Dr John Bodkin Adams was accused of hastening the deaths of some of his elderly female patients.

composed himself there are three pleasing but grim items under 'The Three Illusions'.[1]

(1) To think investments secure.
(2) To imagine that the rich regard you as their equal.
(3) To suppose your virtues common to all and your vices peculiar to yourself.

Why does one's wife, when one says x is very dull, *always* assume that one's judgment is based on x not being at all *literary*. In vain I say I merely want him to be intelligent. I don't believe even the best wives understand more than a fraction of their husbands. Not that it matters that we are all 'in the sea of life enisled'.

22 April 1957   *Bromsden Farm*
I learn that the aged American poet Robert Frost is to visit England this year. Did you hear him reading some of his poems on the wireless the other day? I think very highly of them, and more than twenty years ago I prevailed upon him by letter to allow them to be published by Jonathan Cape, for whom I then worked (they still publish the poems, curse them). After much correspondence the affair was settled by a telegram reading:

THE POEMS ARE YOURS AND SO AM I FROST

I have never seen him, and had given up hope, for he is over eighty, but now perhaps I shall have my wish.

Have you looked at that book of poems called *Union Street*?[2] I did send it to you, didn't I? I think it has the real stuff in it, and I'm delighted to see that two critics have already said so—*Times* and *Sunday Times*. The poet is a Cornish *schoolmaster*, and funnily enough a delightful chap.

25 April 1957   *Grundisburgh*
Thank you very much for that little book of *first-rate* poetry. Who is Causley? and why have I never heard of him? He really *has* something to say and his own way of saying it. Pamela made me read *Under Milk*

---

[1] See *Geoffrey Madan's Notebooks*, ed. J.A. Gere and John Sparrow, 1981.
[2] By Charles Causley.

Wood recently, but I couldn't do much with it. Perhaps it demands to be heard. I gather many people love it. Do *you* read it with your pulses bounding? Is it well thought of in the Lit. Soc.? Does Sir Cuthbert know it by heart?

We have just bowed off the last of eleven grandchildren with attendant parents and nurses, and I revert from the role of Abraham to that of St Simeon, the summer-house being my pillar. I love them twittering and hopping and scampering and rolling about the place, daily missing homicide or suicide by a hair's-breadth, but there *is* a certain compensatory relief in finding the soap in its dish and not in the bath, and the ink in its pot and not on my cushion. I made the mistake of trying to read *Justine*[1] while the family played Racing Demon and uttered the screams and curses that appear to be part of the game—and I found that after twenty pages of *Justine* I had not the faintest idea what it, or he, or she was really at. And I have tried it again. No result! And they say it is superb.

28 *April 1957*   *Bromsden Farm*

So glad you like Causley's poems. Up to last week I had sold 140 copies—and then, after two good reviews, I sold 200 in one week and may have to reprint. (I printed only 1000). No one has heard of him before, and you are assisting, midwifely, at the birth of a poet. Wasn't that a splendid review of Peter's book in the *T.L.S.* Peter says that, on internal evidence, it must have been written by someone in M.I.14—and who am I to contradict him?

2 *May 1957*   *Grundisburgh*

I put it to you that one of the main defects of continental education—so much more *efficient* than English—is that so many are educated above their ability. They all learn at school to talk about levels of awareness and integrity and where to 'place' x and y, and the rest of the horrid jargon. It is odd how that sarcasm of eighty years ago of some German professor, who said he approved of English education because it was so good for the mind to be 'fallow till the age of nineteen' is much nearer to the truth than was supposed. Or it was till these scientists began laying down the law about their intolerable lore.

[1] By Lawrence Durrell.

82

I see too that some important ass has been saying that three years' training is essential for every teacher—when nobody really knows what education should be aiming at. When old Q.[1] came to Eton he told us how refreshing it was to find a staff which didn't profess to know exactly how English should be taught. Years ago I was a member of the English Association Committee, on which Professor Edith J. Morley held forth interminably, her face radiant and moist, on the theory and practice of English teaching, and old Bradley, walking away with John Bailey, murmured 'It is a pity, besides being rather strange, that poor Miss Morley herself cannot write a paragraph of tolerable English.'

Yes A. Douglas and F. Harris certainly—and of course Baron Corvo,—and A.W. Carr, captain of Notts, and Colonel Repington, and old Rogers the poet. There will be 'fine confused feeding' in the book. You really must think about it when you have finally polished off Wilde and Moore.[2]

Causley is by my bedside—with Shakespeare, *Earlham, Irish R.M.*, Ivor Brown's word-books and Humphry House, who very easily bears re-reading. I love re-reading. Each night from 10.30 to 12 I read Gibbon *out loud.* I read slowly, richly, not to say juicily; and like Prospero's isle the room is full of noises—little, dry, gentle noises. Some matter-of-fact man of blunt or gross perceptions might say it was the ashes cooling in the grate, but I know better. It is the little creatures of the night, moths and crickets and spiderlings, a mouse or two perhaps and small gnats in a wailful choir, come out to listen to the Gibbonian music—'Twenty-two acknowledged concubines and a library of 62,000 volumes attested the variety of his inclinations'—what sentient being, however humble, could resist that?

5 May 1957   *Bromsden Farm*
You ask whether reviews sell books. Single ones don't, but a concatenation of good ones at about the same time certainly does. Assuming that all literary-minded people read at least one daily, one weekly and one Sunday paper, a good review in all these within a week will probably stir them.

---

[1] Sir Arthur Quiller Couch.
[2] G.W.L. had suggested R.H.-D. should compile a 'Book of Shits'.

Where exactly does that superb sentence about the concubines come? Of whom was he speaking? On the 14th I have to speak at the annual dinner of the Antiquarian Booksellers Association, and I could surely quote Gibbon to them. I haven't thought what to say yet, but perhaps I'll begin by saying that when I was a child I thought 'antiquarian' meant 'very old', and it wasn't until I became a book-buyer that it really means 'very expensive'.

We didn't see the finish of the Lord's match, for we were there only on the Monday, but the sun shone incessantly, we saw Graveney bat, Trueman bowl, and Adam loved it all. Of the Lord's of my boyhood only the Pavilion, the Tavern and the Mound Stand remain.

9 May 1957   *Grundisburgh*
That Gibbon sentence describes the emperor Gordian whose 'manners were less pure, but his character was equally amiable with that of his father'. Then comes the sentence I quoted, which ends: 'and from the productions which he left behind him, it appears that the former as well as the latter were designed for use rather than for ostentation.'

It is disillusioning to one with my youthful loyalties to realise that the majestic MacLaren, with his 'superb crease-side manner', was an extremely stupid, prejudiced and pig-headed man, even in cricket matters. Plum Warner[1] always says he had the worst fault of a captain, viz pessimism about his team, expressed in their presence: 'Just look what they've given me—half of them creaking with old age, George Hirst fat as butter' etc etc. But let us remember that when Wainwright gave him a long-hop to leg to get his century off in a Gents and Players, he kicked it away and sternly ordered him to bowl his best.

But when I get onto cricket I drool like any old fathead in an M.C.C. tie (but just one more. A boy running h. for l. at Winchester cannoned head-down into E.R. Wilson on his way to school, looked up, and in horror gasped 'Good God,' to which E.R.W. gently replied 'But strictly incognito').

Will you please *swear* to tell me when I am a bore—not just when I strike a boring note, which all human beings do—but when the disease shews signs of taking hold. One's wife ought to, and some-

---

[1] Sir Pelham Warner, Cricketer, captain of England and Middlesex, president of the MCC, 1950.

times does, but probably realises that after a certain age the poor man's alternative will be total silence. (Who was it, by the way, who, seeing outside a fried-fish shop 'Cleanliness, economy, and civility, always hot and always ready', remarked 'The motto of the perfect wife'? Gibbon would have liked that.)

I think you omit the Grandstand which hasn't altered except for Father Time at the top. The first Eton v Harrow I saw was from a box above the Grandstand in 1895; a waiter had an apoplectic fit just outside. We—my brother and I—felt we were seeing life.

12 May 1957   *Bromsden Farm*
Today produced thunder, hail and torrents of rain. Mowing was impossible, and next week-end I shall stand breast-high in tears amid the alien weeds.[1] A bullfinch and P. Fleming have been the only visitors: thank goodness few 'drop in' unexpectedly here.

The trouble about the exact meaning of words is not only that they mean subtly different things to different people, but also that their meaning and undertones actually change with the passage of time and alteration in manners. And what are you to do about America, where the *sound* of words is differently interpreted? I remember a rather good Galsworthian play about the iniquity of cutting down the copse in front of some country house. It pleased in London, but on Broadway they thought cutting down the copse meant a reduction in the size of the police force, and were baffled.

15 May 1957   *Grundisburgh*
That 'copse' story is lovely. It is all wrong, I know, but I *cannot* ever take Americans quite seriously—I mean their tastes and judgments and values, though now and then one strikes an absolutely Class I man, e.g. the late Judge Wendell Holmes. I remember liking Steinbeck's first best-seller, but last week, seeing his name, I wasted half-a-crown on his *The Wayward Bus* to read in the train. Not a single character who was not either loathsome or silly. Is the whole of U.S.A. thinking of nothing but the female bosom?

Once at Eton I was aware that the young prigs in College had a tremendous down on the split infinitive, so I showed them the list of

---

[1] See Keats' 'Ode to a Nightingale'.

great writers who sometimes used it—including Dr Johnson. They were shaken—which is all one can ever do with a young K.S. But I approve of a dictum of Judge Holmes mentioned above, viz 'All right to end a sentence with a preposition, but not a paragraph. That should end with the blow of an axe.'

19 May 1957   *Bromsden Farm*
The Antiquarian Booksellers' 'do' lasted from 7.15 till 11.30. The first speaker was W.S. (Lefty) Lewis, the American millionaire who has cornered Horace Walpole and is producing (with a team of editors) an endless edition of his letters. He told one or two anecdotes of book-buying. Then came the President, who was fluent and quite amusing. By the time it came to my turn the company (about 180) was desperate with boredom and ready to laugh at anything. I started off with a brisk joke: they roared approval: and thereafter I had them captive. The Gibbon quotation stopped the show long enough for me to consult my scrappy notes so really I owe it all to you!

21 May 1957   *Grundisburgh*
How solidly uninteresting Browning could be in his letters! Of course every man is two men or more, but the poet and the diner-out ('Who was that too exuberant financier?' as a lady said) reached the limits of incongruity, surely. And is any great man so hard to get a clear notion of as Browning? I cannot imagine him walking, or talking, or smiling—and least of all in love with that bony little spaniel-wife, or father of that futile little bounder his son.

   I look forward to Lit. Soc. dinners with what can only be described by that horrible word 'gusto'. Is there better company to be found? Not in the Ipswich Country Club or even among the governors of Woodbridge School, though I rather *like* grocers and sanitary inspectors. As Walt Whitman said in praise of animals, they 'do not make me sick discussing their duty to God', and though on occasions they do sweat, they don't 'whine about their condition'.

26 May 1957   *Bromsden Farm*
Some Frenchman said '*On naît demi-dieu et l'on meurt épicier*', so perhaps we shall all come to it.

86

I dragged Eric Linklater unwillingly off to the Arts Theatre to see Genet's play *The Balcony*, which takes place in a brothel. The theatre was half-empty, and when the lights went down a scruffy, unshaven Central European came on to the stage and announced that Miss Something had been taken suddenly ill, there was no understudy, and the part would be read by Miss Somebody Else. Anyone who asked for their money back could have it. No one did. Needless to say the part was the chief one—the brothel-keeper's pet—and it was read by a nice homely girl from Bagshot, desperately trying to follow the dialogue in a script the size of the telephone book. When she had to help the other woman to dress she fell behind through having to put the book down. The other actors were all appallingly bad, and the play pretentious and windy—rather like the reverse of a Maeterlinck medal—instead of 'moonshine' they repeatedly said 'shit' and 'bugger'. We stuck it to half-time and then repaired to the Ivy for an excellent dinner. Next day, fresh as paint, I travelled to Bath and took part in a Brains Trust at Monkton Combe prep. school (which is in *lovely* country). George Cansdale, recently Head of the Zoo, brought along a python in a Gladstone bag, which delighted the boys. Tea-party, sherry-party, dinner-party, called at 6.45, and back to work.

29 May 1957   *Grundisburgh*
What rude things people say about grocers! I remember that French saying of yours being thundered at the Hagley congregation (in English) many years ago by the vast rector, who had the suitable name of Manley Power, but as far as I remember, the only effect was that the village grocer never darkened the door of the church again—like Neville Talbot, Bishop of Pretoria, girding at his flock for imagining God to be an angry old man with a beard—'like Mr Jones there', after which Mr J. joined the Anabaptists.

'The grocer who has made his pile—
Does he grow nicer?' 'No, Sir,
He alters not his ways nor style,
But grows a grosser grocer.'

Shakespeare or Milton, I forget which.

On Tuesday I gave a luncheon-party (six men) for the American poet Robert Frost, a wonderful old man of eighty. This was my first meeting with him. He was witty and charming and anecdotal and in every way delightful. After lunch I drove him back to the Connaught Hotel, where he wrote out a poem for me. We were in a large hotel sitting-room, and I suddenly realised that the only other people in it, at the far end, were my mother-in-law (to whom I hadn't spoken for three and a half years) and Adlai Stevenson (whose wife was my wife's first cousin, and whose books I publish). I decided that these two— in many ways the most interesting Americans alive—should meet, so I greeted my mother-in-law and got the two men talking very successfully.

That evening I dined with Elisabeth Beerbohm. Just as I was leaving who should arrive but Mr and Mrs Boris Karloff! I had imagined him dead long ago, but no. He is an Englishman (né Pratt) of perhaps sixty, well preserved and so dark that he must have more than a dash of the the tarbrush. I quickly discovered that his great interest is *cricket!* and we chattered happily of Surrey and the West Indies. He bemoaned the fact that he would have to miss one of the Tests to make a film. On Thursday I went to a champagne cocktail party at John Lehmann's. In the throng were T.S. Eliot with his new wife, thirty-eight years younger than he and very charming. They stood inseparably arm-in-arm in the most charming way, and the despairing lines of his face visibly softened as he talked of his new flat and his great happiness—very touching.

Did you hear of the would-be-psychiatrist who, when asked why he wanted to be one, said: 'I really wanted to be a sex-maniac, but I failed in my practical'?

Must I have another try at *Finnegans Wake* in my spasmodic efforts to 'keep up,' and not sink further into codgerdom? It is yours to command and mine to obey. But how happy I shall be if you say I needn't!

I must confess to you that my lavatory reading lately has been your Hugh Walpole. An essential for a book that is raised to this rare eminence is that one knows it and loves it already. Its influence is active and swift and benign, 'noble and nude and antique'. 'All occasions invite his mercies and all times are his seasons' was actually written by Donne of God, but it has other applications.[1] Who wrote that invocation, which begins:

Hail, Cloacina, goddess of this place
Whose devotees are all the human race . . .' and ends,
'Soft yet consistent let my offerings flow,
Not rudely fast nor obstinately slow.

I enjoyed two days at Oxford, where I had a good crack with my old pupil John Bayley of New College who writes novels and reviews and wholly unintelligible tomes about 'Romance', and is a very nice fellow. His wife Iris Murdoch was there, coruscating, but not offensively, with brains. I liked her, and promised to read her new novel, though I know that in three pages I shall be hailing the coast-guard.

I called on another don, who was closeted with four or five young men to whom he was expounding *The Anglo-Saxon Chronicle.* He and I chatted lightly for a few minutes, while they contemplated me with that derision that one sees on the faces of amiable camels when one throws them buns. At both Oxford and Cambridge some of the young men are growing beards, and to my mind and taste a young chin with hair is as indecent as a young skull without it. I had a boy in my house who wore a wig; one evening I visited him when he was about to sleep, and on the pillow was an object like a shell-less egg or a very young horsechestnut. It looked soft and damp—horrible.

11 June 1957   *Kisdon Lodge, Keld*
I have to-day re-read (after thirty-five years) and thoroughly enjoyed *The Prisoner of Zenda.* How well, in this book, Anthony Hope got on with the story. There's no padding anywhere. Tomorrow I shall devour *Rupert of Hentzau.* I bought a lot of Oscariana with me, but so far have read only *Both Sides of the Curtain,* an account by

---

[1] See p. 95.

Elizabeth Robins, the American Ibsen-actress and novelist, of her arrival in England in 1888, when Oscar was very kind to her. From her book I noted two plums (or anyhow sultanas) for your delectation. (1) When Mrs Kendal put on Ibsen's *Enemy of the People* she sought to soften the blow by introducing as curtain-raiser a recitation of G.R. Sims's *Ostler Joe*. How confused the audience must have been! (2) When Lady Ritchie was asked what Tennyson's reading aloud was like, she said 'melodious thunder'.

Now for your letter. You are hereby forever absolved from struggling with *Finnegans Wake*. When an American professor was sent for review a book called *A Key to F.W.*, he sent it back, saying 'What *F.W.* needs is not a key but a lock.'

13 June 1957   *Grundisburgh*

I went to the Lit. Soc. yesterday, and sat between Sir Cuthbert and Tim. Sir C. was most affable. He is a dry wine, but very far from flavourless. I enjoy that stern unbending Toryism; his old eye gleamed and smouldered when someone mentioned the *New Statesman*, and I feel pretty sure that if he found it in his house he would eject it with the tongs.

Peter Fleming took your place at the end of the table. What a particularly pleasant chap he is. And how bad, and at the same time compellingly readable, brother Ian's thrillers are! The pattern of all four that I have read is identical. Bond does not attract me, and that man with brains of ice and pitiless eye who organises the secret service in London seems to be a monument of ineptitude. Everything about Bond and his plans is known long before he arrives anywhere. But I cannot help reading on and there are rich satisfactions, e.g. when Mr Big is crunched by a shark. Very good about food; he always details what any meal consists of. The young women are rather oppressively and monotonously bedworthy, but then of course he isn't writing for septuagenarians.

To-morrow I go to present the prizes at Shrewsbury School and utter the inevitable platitudes, but I shall do a little cutting of the ground from under their feet by beginning with a quote from André Gide: '*Toutes choses sont dites déjà, mais comme personne n'écoute, il faut toujours recommencer.*' I recommend it to you as a very useful opening gambit (not necessarily in French!).

18 June 1957   *Grundisburgh*
(the day on which
Napoleon looked forward to
'une affaire d'un déjeuner.'[1]*)*

I knew there would be one of these insufferable heat-waves when
them above knew I was going to go by train from Ipswich to
Shrewsbury and make a speech in a school hall full to the brim with
millions of the freest pores in these islands. On Thursday I shall be
watching Ramadhin, and Weekes, and Worrell—and yawning when
Trueman bowls, or Bailey bats. (Do you realise that Trueman walks
thirty-five steps from the crease to the end of his run and that four
balls an over the batsman leaves alone?)

Charles Tennyson corroborated 'melodious thunder' for his grandfather's voice—and hinted—only hinted for he is very loyal—that it
must sometimes have been hard not to giggle at those readings; the
old man's 'o's and 'a's were so very hollow and long-drawn-out. And,
still on thunder, you know, of course, Haydon's superb 'feathered
silken thunder' for the sound of the peeresses in their robes rising
when George IV entered at his coronation.

I think I did meet at Shrewsbury about the only famous man you
don't know—though I may well be wrong about that. Father Trevor
Huddleston, who was to talk in the chapel on Sunday. An amiable
man. We did not talk about the South-African colour-problem, but
for some reason, obscure at the time, and now irrecoverable, about Sir
Ernest Oppenheimer, of whom I know as much as a cow does of a
clean shirt.

23 June 1957   *Kidson Lodge, Keld*

From A.E.W. Mason's account of George Alexander and the St
James's Theatre, I extracted this pleasing anecdote for you. The day
after the first night of Barrie's play *The Admirable Crichton*, Mason
ran into Squire Bancroft:

> I asked, having seen him at the performance, what he thought of
> the play. He was drying his hands on his towel in the lavatory of
> his club (? the Garrick) just before luncheon. He dried more slowly

---

[1] i.e. the Battle of Waterloo.

and shook his head with melancholy. 'It deals, my dear Mason, with the juxtaposition of the drawing-room and the servants' hall—always to me a very painful subject.'

27 *June 1957*   *Grundisburgh*
I much prefer Trueman as a bat to T. as a bowler. His three sixes off consecutive balls were worth seeing, and never shall I forget the lovely sound of 25,000 people roaring with laughter when Weekes fell head over heels into the crowd and disappeared.

For the last two days I have been among the girls—bumbling in and out of classrooms, listening to an anaemic, adenoidal lady with rheumy eyes declaiming the part of Lady Macbeth, watching Miss Biology Jones (this is how the H. Mistress distinguishes her from Miss Cello Jones, but the girls' affectionate name for her is 'Bilgy Rat') keeping sharp watch over the dissection of three crayfish. I took an ignorant but would-be intelligent interest in the three little virgins' work, but shied off just in time, as some little tension in the air told me that my questions were nearing those corporeal regions concerning which the crayfish, that prude of the piscine world, invariably purses his lips.

I found the snapshot of Khrushchev drinking soup in Finland disheartening. He looked so exactly like a pig. Of course soup *is* rather a severe test for anyone, with as many pitfalls to avoid as a golfer or an oarsman. How not to make a noise, or splash, or spill on the waistcoat, and of course if it is '*à la bonne femme*' the stuff is full of *strings*, very toothsome when they get to the mouth, but as hard to shepherd neatly as a flock of sheep.

7 *July 1957*   *Bromsden Farm*
The lovelier the holiday, the grimmer the return. My last day on the blessed moors (Saturday) was a happy one. I spent the afternoon (dull and raining) at an auction sale in the Temperance Hall of a neighbouring village, where I secured a gigantic writing-desk, stuffed with drawers and surmounted by a fine cupboard or bookcase, for £1.

Next day (Sunday) I sadly packed up the cottage and started off in steaming hot sunshine. All went well until, between Wetherby and Doncaster, the fan-belt broke, and the car nearly caught fire. By ringing up an extremely efficient A.A. man in Leeds I managed to get a new fan-belt brought from some garage, but this entailed a wait of one and a half hours. At Doncaster (a loathsome town at best) I ran into a cloudburst—visibility nil and water up to the axles. Thereafter all the elements took a turn—thick fog, two more distinct cloudbursts, incessant thunder and lightning. Eventually I limped exhausted into London just before midnight. My flat was stifling, and from the mountains on my desk it was clear that everyone I had ever heard of had written to me while I was away. The temperature was in the eighties all week, and ten yards outside my office-window gangs of half-naked men were riveting steel girders incessantly. Never has my hatred of London and publishing been so grim and concentrated.

11 July 1957   *Grundisburgh*

I am sorry to see judges have been doffing their wigs. They cannot realise that, in many of them, *all* the dignity they have resides in the wig, and that without it they are indistinguishable from sanitary inspectors. The great Justice Holmes was the only Yank I know who saw the point of our judicial wig, viz how it raises a probably quite commonplace official from humdrum humanity to an impersonal figure of justice.

I am just approaching my hard work of the year—marking exam-papers and subsequently cooking the marks. It is a dreary routine, but at least one does get *some* fun out of what they write on English Literature. Fancy having to mark a thousand Algebra papers—but the silver lining to *their* cloud is that they can mark twelve or fifteen an hour and we only about six for the same pay. The *Art* examiners mark forty-five to fifty per hour, i.e. a glance or two at that number of drawings of a pot—also for the same pay. Justice? Faugh!

I am re-reading FitzGerald's letters rapidly. They don't seem to me as good as they once did, or as they are usually supposed to be. Perhaps my taste has coarsened. It is interesting to find how absurdly bad he and Spedding and others found Irving's Hamlet, which C.E. Montague, Agate and Co all said was tremendous. Not very extraordinary perhaps. After all, Ruskin said *Aurora Leigh* was the greatest poem in the English language, and Coleridge said neither Gibbon nor Landor could write English, and that Tennyson had no idea of metre.

I once had a similar meeting with a fox to yours [with a deer]—a red-letter moment. I still recollect the piercing intelligence of his eye—all curiosity and vigilance and a general air of being equal to any occasion. I bet Chaunticleer would never have outwitted him as the Nonnes Preeste recorded, and as half the school population of England have been writing about this week—damn them! I am about half-way through my oakum-picking, but the worst is yet to come—mere essay-answers on five different books, and to separate the wheat from the chaff is a really infernal job. These exams are full of surprises. Can you tell me why the papers on *The Devil's Disciple* are mostly v. bad, while those on *The Riddle of the Sands* are mostly v. good? Because I can't. There are some good names—Grut, Seex, Allbless, Gbow, Jaglorn, Jellinek, Pedgrift, nicely sweetened yesterday by Flowerdew and Lillies.

I went with Diana Cooper to the Crypt of St Paul's to choose a place for Duff's memorial tablet. We were taken round by the Clerk of the Works (who would keep showing us where the bombs fell—and indeed I can't understand how the building stood it) and the accredited architect. We had the Crypt to ourselves, and since in the Cathedral over our heads two bishops were being lengthily enthroned by the A B of C, there was much fine singing coming down to us. I'd never before been in the Crypt and was much moved by it all—the majesty of Nelson's sepulchre, the massive ugliness of Wellington's. 'You've no idea,' said the Clerk of Works, 'how difficult it is to fit in the hot water pipes among all these graves.' The architect would love to move forward the altar in St Faith's Chapel, 'but,' pointing to a splendid tombstone on the floor, 'Bishop Creighton's in the way.' We chose quite a good place for Duff, round the corner from Nelson.

My first bout of drudgery nears its end. The girls are the worst infliction because they have imbibed *all* the right things to say and their regurgitations are relentlessly copious. They know all their five books by heart, and have that disgusting habit of quoting twelve lines to prove a point where two would be ample.

I have never been into St Paul's crypt; it sounds very impressive. Is Donne there?—a very tremendous man: 'If some King of the earth have so large an extent of dominion . . .' Do you know that sermon?[1] But I expect you have your favourites among them. I am not clever enough for much of his poetry, but, golly, he could write prose —as Housman said, a much more difficult job.

4 August 1957   *Bromsden Farm*
I imagine that this date means nothing to our children, but although I was only six in 1914 it tolls for me every year the death of the Golden Age, while September 3, which affected my life much more, passes almost unnoticed. I envy you and all those who had some grown-up years before the deluge, for the true *douceur de vivre* will not come again in our time.

Many of Donne's poems are wonderful, even if one doesn't fully understand them. Try declaiming in the nightwatches:

At the round earth's imagined corners, blow
Your trumpets, Angels, and arise, arise
From death, you numberless infinities
Of souls, and to your scattered bodies go.

Pull out all the stops, and the mice will marvel in the wainscot.

I dined with the Ray Bradburys[2] and another friend at the Mirabelle restaurant in Curzon Street, which is probably the most expensive in London. Admittedly we had a very good dinner, with two bottles of reasonable wine, but the bill for the four of us came to £16!! Even our American hosts were a little shaken.

[1] If some king of the earth have so large an extent of dominion, in north and south, as that he hath winter and summer together in his dominions, so large an extent, east and west, as that he hath day and night together in his dominions, much more hath God mercy and judgement together: He brought light out of darkness, not out of a lesser light; He can bring thy summer out of winter, though thou have no spring: though in the ways of fortune or understanding, or conscience, thou have been benighted till now, wintered and frozen, clouded and eclipsed, damped and benumbed, smothered and stupefied till now, – now God comes to thee, not as in the dawning of the day, nor as in the bud of the spring, but as the sun at noon to illustrate all shadows, as the sheaves in harvest to fill all penuries: all occasions invite His mercies, and all times are His seasons.

[2] American science fiction author.

7 August 1957   *Grundisburgh*

How right you are about pre-Aug. 4 1914. I can of course remember it very well, and equally of course that we didn't in the least realise at the time that it *was* a golden age. In fact I am pretty sure that the real golden age was before the Boer War. At the time of the Diamond Jubilee there literally wasn't a cloud in the sky, whereas from 1902 onwards there were continuous though not loud rumblings about the German menace—and a good many strikes too. I remember an evening at Hagley when Leo Maxse[1] shook us all to the core telling us all he *knew* about German plans, and how pleased he was after hearing that the Kaiser and Bülow had foamed with rage over one issue of the *National Review* and said that such a man as the editor oughtn't to be allowed to live. He also reported that the most encouraging news from Germany was that sodomy was about to be, not abolished, but legalised, as that must mean decadence pretty quick. How nice it would be if everything was as simple as that!

I suppose *you* have never handled a golden sovereign? A beautiful coin! It rang with a note like the song of a bird, as Homer says the string of Ulysses's bow did when he twanged it. And what a lot of things it bought—including a *ton and a half* of coke. But that way madness lies. Carlyle declared that three hundred years of trouble were needed for the human spirit to purge and rebuild itself after the first blast from heaven, i.e. the French Revolution. So we're not far past the middle of that. I think that dyspeptic old genius—who, with Ruskin, really *was* made unhappy by the awful gap between rich and poor a century ago—would not have been noticeably blither now.

13/14 August 1957   *Grundisburgh*

What a detestable month August can be! Today the garden is carpeted with thunderbolts, so to speak, and the thunder has that explosive suddenness and violence which led that lunatic (who ought to have been instantly set free) to exclaim 'God has shot himself'.

---

[1] Editor of the *National Review*. Francophile and Germanophobe, he turned down a lucrative position abroad in 1899 because he felt it his duty to warn Britain about the way Germany was going.

I have finished Aldington on Lawrence. You are surprised at my reading anything by the man who in a competition for the post of Europe's prize sh-t would surely win hands down. Well, I will tell you why I do so. I can hardly read ten consecutive pages of D.H.L. without being invaded by boredom raging like toothache. But apart from so many people saying so, I am sure he is a genius—and in descriptive bits he can touch almost any height. And you know, one of the chief dangers of senectitude is a contented nestling in tastes and opinions formed many years ago, and of necessity steadily narrowing, so I quite often have shots at writers like D.H.L. to whom I am on the way to being allergic. And besides that I find getting angry (not with living people) is rather a tonic. And again—I often used to tell boys about Tolstoy deciding that Shakespeare was absurd, and the universal admiration of him merely showed that the world was mad, and while you and I (I said to them) read one book half through and decide the author is bad, he formed his opinion after reading all Shakespeare *seven* times, and had a right to his opinion.

I gather from John Raymond and Co. that 'charm' is about the most damnable literary quality there is—'the logical and deathly end-product of the mandarin tradition' is his amiable reference to David Cecil's latest essays. What *is* the 'mandarin tradition'? It seems to me to be the pronouncements by the widely-read critics of the last generation on books they enjoyed and why they enjoyed them. Why all this rage? Half these angry young men, I suspect, in praising each other's stuff, are whistling to keep their spirits up.

18 August 1957   *Bromsden Farm*
This evening, contrary to my principles and practice, I attended a local cocktail party, at which I consumed two tumblers of what must have been very nearly neat whisky, so if this letter is illegible or incoherent, you must forget and forgive.

Your fear of senectitude and hardening of the literary arteries seems to me morbid. Never did I know anyone less likely to congeal. Therefore I see no need to mortify yourself with Aldington, Leavis and company. I have always found *Don Quixote* unreadable, but there's plenty else to wear out my eyesight. If you haven't even begun to ossify (mentally) at seventy-four, you never will, and I should, if I were you, read for pleasure only. What cheek—it must be the whisky!

22 August 1957   *Cambridge*

We have run up against some very loose and inefficient examiners—mostly women—whose marks have to be considerably doctored, and that delays us a good deal. However we get our own back by writing acid little reports on the bad examiners, and hope that they will be sacked before next year. The most depressing part of the whole business is the conviction that examination on set English books ought never to have been instituted. More than half the candidates merely retail what they have been told they ought to think. But this is all very shoppy. Let it cease.

Tuesday, 27 August 1957   *Villino Chiaro, Rapallo*[1]

The whole place is exquisite: the little *villino* (all on one floor) right on the road: above it a huge wide terrace, with a tiny work-room in the middle of it: above again and behind, the *casetta*, a three-storied guest-house, an old peasant's house, with the disused Roman road behind. Everywhere Max's books and drawings, all exactly as they were. The garden is full of figs and grapes and oranges and olives. I am sleeping in the *casetta* where Max recorded his broadcasts. E. has all the records and last night played me the George Moore one. She is spoiling me with wonderful food and loving care.

1 September 1957   *Grundisburgh*

A.E. Housman is one of those who somehow invite odd comment—some of it contemptuous, some patronising, some silly—e.g. John Wain, who says A.E.H. failed in Greats on purpose! It serves the old curmudgeon right really. No one has a right to be so arrogant and inhuman. But no one also has a right to say, as one ass did recently, that H. was less of a poet than Manilius[2] ('once in the wind of morning . . .' etc. Match me that in Manilius!). Critics are odd. Do you remember Walter Raleigh writing 'A wiser man than Macaulay, James Boswell'? Just trailing his coat, of course, for some reason.

I think I have had enough of Boswell *pro tem*. His absurdity is unvarying, and the unvarying grows tedious. And did anyone ever

---

[1] Max and Elisabeth Beerbohm's house.
[2] The second-rate Latin poet to the editing of whose works Housman devoted much of his life.

have venereal disease so often—and ultimately so luckily, for he was always cured. And the mystery of why so many people liked him and no one ever told him he was a B.F. Perhaps they did and he didn't mind. The Doctor of course did, but B. was full of family pride and a surely wouldn't have taken it from anyone else.

Pamela and I went last week to *Look Back in Anger* in Ipswich. I wish you would tell me why it has had such success. I gather it is regarded as tremendously original, but surely a young man ranting away at the world and its conventions and absence of 'enthusiasm' etc. is about as old as anything can be—only another form of Byronism.

Villa Lucie
Cagnes-sur-mer
Alpes Maritimes

2 September 1957

My two days at Rapallo were idyllic. Perfect weather and such cosseting as you wouldn't believe: Max's last years must have been blissful. We ate all our meals (except dinner) on a little terrace covered with ripening grapes: Max called it the Vining Room: and on my birthday Elisabeth greeted me with a large silver tray on which she had arranged fifty flowers in a garland surrounding the figures 50 in scarlet geranium-petals. It looked quite lovely and I was much touched. She gave me several books that had belonged to Max, including one with a superb drawing in it (which I will show you). The whole place is saturated with Max's personality—he lived there for forty-five years, with gaps during the wars.

My friends here have hired a tiny Renault, in which each morning I drive them to the beach—three miles away—for prolonged bathing and sunning. It is so long since I swam in the Mediterranean that I had forgotten how warm and clear and buoyant it is: one can keep afloat without movement. Most days I bathe again in the evening, after a considerable siesta. There are many books in the house, mostly French, German and Tauchnitz, including some Maughams, which I am re-reading with pleasure—*The Narrow Corner* (novel), *The Casuarina Tree* and *First Person Singular* (stories). Readability (extreme) is his great asset, for much of the prose is slipshod and many of the stories marred by a tiresome superiority and know-all cocksureness. I have also bought, and am enormously enjoying, Maurois's latest biography *Les Trois Dumas*. There isn't in fact much (all too little) about the mulatto general of Napoleon who sired the novelist, but *his* story is astonishing, and I have still to reach the *fils*, of *La Dame aux Camélias*.

At Rapallo it was the greatest fun looking through Max's books, with their manifold inscriptions, marginalia, drawings, and (best of all) his touching-up of illustrations, often so skilfully done as to be almost invisible, but always exactly to the point.

September 13 (Friday!) 1957   *Grundisburgh*

I am now reading, believe it or not, *The Pilgrim's Progress*, not exactly for fun, but I have to set a paper on it for next year—only two questions of the essay type, but it is fatal not to know something about a book set, and I have not read it for half-a-century. A plebiscite at Columbia University placed it *top* of the list of 'the most boring classics,' which I find hopeful, as nobody supposes that Columbia University can be anything but plumb wrong about anything. Wasn't Dulles an alumnus? Still, I must admit that after forty pages or so, I did have the best night's sleep I have had *in years* (American!). I should hate to find myself on the same side as Dulles.

15 September 1957   *Bromsden Farm*

Last week was mainly taken up with full mopping-up operations, but was brightened by the enclosed letter,[1] which my natural boastfulness prompts me to send you: please send it back for my archives. Of course I accepted, with a mixture of pride and trepidation. It's an appalling baby to have to hold just now, but if I can cope with it I can cope with anything.

While I was away, Peter hit on an idea for his next book—an account of the siege of the foreign Legations in Peking during the Boxer rebellion of 1900, together with the story of the relief expedition etc. I encouraged the plan, which please keep for the moment under your hat. Your praise of the Autumn List is particularly welcome, since the travellers complain that almost all the books in it are totally unsaleable except in the West End of London. Do they think I cater for Asia Minor?

[1] From Harold Nicolson, asking me to succeed him as Chairman of the London Library Committee.

I knew Ronnie Knox slightly during my short time at Oxford. He was then R.C. Chaplain to the University, and I remember a bare beautiful room in the Old Palace containing the minimum of furniture and a barrel of beer. Of him I remember little, save that he was friendly and unalarming. When I, or perhaps someone else, asked him if he knew the egregious ex-priest Montague Summers (then living in Oxford), R.A.K. said that Summers lived with a little boy and a huge dog. Plenty of people had seen Summers and the boy, and Summers and the dog, and the boy and the dog, but nobody had ever seen all three of them together.

20 September 1957   *Grundisburgh*

You will be derisively amused to hear that for the last two nights my evening book has been Colin Wilson's *Outsider* and my *bed*-book Trollope's *Prime Minister* which I hadn't read—a diet as it were of caviare and sago. And I find the sago far the more toothsome. Frankly I can't really see what *The Outsider* is all about, and my acquaintance with the young man's mentors—Sartre, Roquentin, Meursault, Krebs and Co is of the flimsiest possible. Household names to you I expect? Colin Wilson gives the impression of having read everything, but I gather from some of the reviews that, like the River Finn in my garden, the depth is not as great as it looks.

I say, Rupert, the London Library! Have you as it is *any* spare five minutes in the week—and at this moment when the poor old institution is under fire from those marble-hearted fiends of the Inland Revenue.[1] I beg you to *delegate* shamelessly from among your vast acquaintance. Lawyers no doubt are already active. Couldn't that admirable Somervell help? It couldn't surely take much to upset that sickening ass who said that the L.L. was a sanctum for the well-to-do, as it didn't bring Shakespeare to the costermongers. I have never belonged, as I never lived in London, but my grandfather was one of Carlyle's first associates in it. I once met old Hagberg Wright [its librarian], who struck me as the rudest man I had ever seen—till I met his brother Almroth who easily dead-heated.

---

[1] In 1957 the London Library, which had for eighty years been immune (as a charity) from paying rates, was suddenly informed by the Inland Revenue that it in the future would have to pay £5000 a year.

If you seriously think that only a nightly tussle with Colin Wilson's pretentious rot can prevent your sharing the tastes and outlook of that foul-mouthed old Philistine Munnings, I suppose I can only leave you to your unnecessary mortification. After one glance through *The Outsider* I decided it was both unreadable and not worth reading. You'd better buck up: his next book appears tomorrow!

On Wednesday I reluctantly agreed to dine with my father at the St James's Club—reluctantly because such evenings are generally a waste of silence and complaint. This one didn't begin too well, since we drank our sherry with a retired Civil Servant, who was slumped incoherently in a chair with a big glass. Just before we were due to go up to dinner your cousin Oliver[1] arrived, at his most amusing, and dined with us gaily. My father perked up considerably, ordered grouse and champagne, and laughed heartily at O's many good jokes and stories. Of the retired Civil Servant O. said: 'He has been fighting a losing battle with Haig & Haig [whisky] for years.'

Soon Diana Cooper will turn up, expecting me to have transformed her MS., and I haven't—oh dear! Already newspapers and magazines are bidding high for the serial rights, but there won't be any book to serialise if I don't invent some free time to do it in.

The only ways in which good editing and production get any reward in this world are (a) by creating, through good reviews, that intangible (which is said to be an asset until you try to cash in on it) called 'goodwill,' and (b) by tempting authors to try and get their books similarly handled. When new writers turn up out of the blue I always ask them why they've come to *me*, and they nearly always say it's because the books look so nice. Nevertheless, shoddily produced best-sellers butter more parsnips!

I have *no* inkling of why Colin Wilson's rot suddenly broke loose, and certainly nobody was more surprised than his publisher, who had expected a minuscule sale and perhaps some *succès d'estime*. I daresay some of the bright boys will be gunning for C.W.'s next book. I have

---

[1] First Viscount Chandos.

never read *The Prime Minister*, or indeed much of Trollope's mountainous *oeuvre*: I am keeping it until I am as unbuttoned as he is, but oh, when will that happy day arrive? I have just read a 400-page manuscript first novel about a rape in the suburbs of Philadelphia, and the awful thing is that it's very well done. As you say, no narrative is any good unless you want to know what's going to happen. That's why *Marius the Epicurean* and the later George Moore novels are no good: one couldn't, as they say, care less what is coming.

3 October 1957   *Grundisburgh*
I further risk your derision by telling you I am reading a book of L--v-s's. It is a form of masochism—a word of which I know the spelling, but not the pronunciation and am by no means secure of the meaning. Anyway I am indulging that odd human propensity to bite on an aching tooth. But I hasten to add, I am also humbly and admiringly reading Verlaine and shall probably interlard my conversation next Tuesday with French aphorisms, e.g. (though not from Verlaine) '*Le déluge n'a pas réussi; il reste un homme*', which I happened upon recently. It suits my misanthropic mood, which is invariably strong at the time of party conferences. But I am (at last!) going to take the hint given by your invariable silence on such topics, and say nothing about politics, knowing as good Johnsonians should,

> How small, of all that human hearts endure,
> That part which laws or kings can cause or cure.[1]

Not that the second line passes any more sweetly into the ear than Browning's 'Irks care the cropful bird' etc.

6 October 1957   *Bromsden Farm*
My daughter got leave from her rich employers in Upper New York State and spent last week-end most enjoyably with the Caccias in the Embassy at Washington. She was particularly impressed by the multitude of servants—a circumstance unknown to most young people of to-day. Which reminds me that in my childhood Sir Lionel Phillips, a South African millionaire friend of my father's, had *seventy* gardeners

---

[1] Johnson, 'Lines added to Goldsmith's *Traveller*'.

at his house in Hampshire. Somewhere I have a snapshot of myself, aged two, sitting on the lawn there, beside Robbie Ross [friend of Oscar Wilde].

Last week I was visited by an old Oxford friend (hitherto penniless) who told me he had just inherited £900 a year from his uncle. 'Hadn't he any children?' I asked. 'He had one daughter,' said my friend, 'but she was electrocuted by an electric iron at Beersheba.' He went on to tell me that this girl was a dipsomaniac who married a commercial traveller in whisky, and together they emigrated to Israel. Ironically enough, the only job the husband could get was in charge of the waterworks at Sodom! They saved his salary, and every three weeks went up into Jerusalem for a blind. Which only goes to show that truth is stranger . . . it's an ill wind . . . etc. Would you believe it?

9 October 1957   *67 Chelsea Square*
                                                                          SW3

I was particularly pleased to meet Edmund Blunden again. One gets in his company the same—what shall I call it?—easeful satisfaction that one used to get from Monty James. It comes—doesn't it?—when great kindliness of heart accompanies great distinction of mind. I remember M.R.J's cordial listening to a story which I knew he knew, and on another occasion to a man making assertions about the history of some cathedral which were so wrong that they *had* to be corrected, but how gently and beautifully M.R.J. did it. How unfailingly enjoyable these Lit. Soc. evenings are—the only fly in the amber being that so much excellent talk with A. and B. means that one can't have the same with C. and D.

And the evening ended in the glow of Peter's kindness in taking me to this very door. He and Bernard Fergusson insisted on waiting till they had actually seen the door open to my key—rather as debutantes were escorted home in Edwardian days with 100% protection of body and soul. Their belief that I am hardly to be trusted to look after myself in London is as benevolently obvious as it is justified. Cyril Alington once told me that in his study one morning he twice heard the same remark outside. It was 'Thank you; I think now I can manage for myself.' One was made by his father *aetat* 88, the other by his youngest son *aetat* 3. Both were being helped down the stairs.

16 October 1957   *Grundisburgh*

Of course it immensely pleases me to hear that the Lit. Soc. does not disapprove of your last candidate. All men love praise. Some pretend they don't. They lie—though of course there is that superb double-barrelled snub which the world's leading curmudgeon (Housman) spat at the scholars who commended him: 'You should be free to praise me if you did not praise each other'.

I didn't know Edmund Blunden lived in Hong Kong, but suspected he might dislike gatherings—like Henry James when John Bailey asked him if he would be Chairman of the English Assocn. Do, for your own pleasure, look up his letter (P. Lubbock's 2 vol Edition, Vol. II p. 279). He was having that painful bout of shingles at the time, and couldn't use a pen; he apologises for having to reply 'as I can and not at all as I would,' and then dictates a perfectly beautiful letter of courtesy, and humour, and understanding, and masterly English—the finest flower of civilisation, you might say. I once told Percy that this letter was my favourite; he agreed about its excellence.[1]

Poor luck yesterday. In the bus to Ipswich I noticed a small child of extravagant plainness, its face, like that of Sulla in Plutarch, resembling 'a dish of mulberries sprinkled with flour'. I was recalling that lovely remark of Groucho Marx when someone said he hated to see a small boy crossing the street, 'I hate him anyway.' This child sensed my feelings and retaliated suddenly by being sick—only just missing me, but in such cases a miss is as good etc. Shortly after the bus ran, rather wildly but with a good deal of splintering of glass, into a tree. Later on, after I had got out, I heard that a lady's shopping basket, into which she had thrown her cigarette, had caught fire.

19 October 1957   *Bromsden Farm*

The London Library occupies much of what I must call my thought. Did I tell you that what it needs is an *additional* £12,500 a year? Last

---

[1] An extract from the letter, declining the honour: 'I am a mere stony, ugly monster of *Dis*ociation and Detachment . . . I believe only in absolutely independent, individual and lonely virtue, and in the serenely unsociable (or if need be in a pinch sulky and sullen) practice of the same; the observation of a lifetime having convinced me that no fruit ripens but under that temporarily graceless rigour, and that the associational process for bringing it on is but a bright and hollow artifice, all vain and delusive.' For a further extract, see p. 315.

week I had an idea so simple that it can scarcely succeed: namely, that if I can persuade the English publishers to *give* their new books to the Library, instead of selling them as now, the Library will at once be £3500 a year better off. I feel fairly confident of cajoling *most* of the publishers. Then I plan to raise £100,000 in cash, which would bring in another £3500 a year. That would leave us £5500 short—which would be more than covered by an increase of two guineas in the subscription (there are 4000 paying members). As a first attack on the £100,000 I have applied to the Pilgrim Trust, which luckily meets in November. If they would give us a substantial sum in annual instalments, we might even get off paying rates, since one of the reasons for the failure of our first appeal was our inability to prove that we are supported 'wholly or in part by annual voluntary contributions'. I'm sure my only hope of persuading the publishers is to beard each important one in his office—about forty of them! There's a certain irony in trying to collect all this money when I'm at my wits' end to pay my sons' fees at Eton and Oxford.

23 October 1957 *Grundisburgh*

It always seems very odd to me that Agate should have so much admired Arnold Bennett's *Journals* and modestly hoped that the *Egos*[1] might be *almost* as good. The A.B.'s are full of entries like 'Long and interesting talk with F. Swinnerton,' and little or nothing more. I forget whether you knew A. Bennett. A good man, I always think, with all his limitations and blind spots. It was George Moore's *A Mummer's Wife* ('squalor and sordidness turned into poetry') that showed A.B. what could be done with the Potteries.

Bonfires, *yes*, superb; the smell, the noise, the spectacle.[2] One of the human tests surely—i.e. a man who does *not* love them must, in some way or another, be a poor creature. And what a sense of humour they have, viz just when the smoke is thickest and one is poking and prodding, the wind suddenly and momentarily changes and one retreats rapidly, but not rapidly enough, choking, eyes smarting, smut-bestrewn (which sounds like a line of Hopkins).

---

[1] The nine volumes of James Agate's diary covering the years 1932 to 1947.
[2] R.H.-D. had one the previous weekend.

I wish I knew some rich people. The richest man in Suffolk is Sir C. Fison, and if only the London Library dealt in chemical manure rather than in books, hopes might be bright. Shall I attempt with him a bold flight of fancy or analogy on the lines of books being manure for the mind? At the moment Ipswich is all bye-electing, and the air is thick with platitude, recrimination and mendacity, none of which, they tell me, changes a single vote, though Hailsham's oratory was the most popular. What rot it all is!

P.S. Can you imagine Mrs Sidney Webb ever enjoying a bonfire? Or Mrs Humphry Ward? Henry James would have, so long as he didn't have to build it.

27 October 1957   *Yorkshire*

I entirely agree about Arnold Bennett's journals, though our disappointment may be partly due to the prudish timidity of their editor, old Newman Flower. According to Hugh Walpole, N.F. was so appalled by much of what he found in the journals that he published only brief extracts, and those the safest. Perhaps we shall one day be given the whole works. I did know A.B. slightly, and liked him—most people did.

I dare say that the bonfire H.J. enjoyed most was the one at Lamb House, to which he consigned the great mass of letters he had received from everybody (it scarcely bears thinking of), retaining only a few choice exhibits. He seemed to think that his indiscriminate holocaust would also destroy all the letters *he* had written to everybody, but naturally they had all been kept; my friend Leon Edel has already examined more than seven thousand, and still they come.

On Thursday afternoon I attended a conference in the Chambers of the London Library's leading Counsel—none other than Mr Geoffrey Lawrence Q.C., the saviour of Dr Adams! He is a small neat man, with a quiet, well-modulated, exact voice, and (it seemed to me) unusual clarity of mind. We discussed our coming appeal before the Lands Tribunal (probably in January) and I rather enjoyed it.

With what joy and relief I drove off at dawn on Friday and got here at lunchtime. Since then the weather has steadily worsened, and the wind on this hilltop almost blows one over. But I have a roaring fire and an Aladdin lamp, and would like to stay here for months.

Sausage-rolls: they ought to be much better than they are; the pastry is always too dry, and the sausage lacking in flavour.[1] Someone should start a revival—a golf-club perhaps could become famous for its sausage-rolls—like Westward Ho for its curry, Rye for its buttered eggs, and somewhere I forget for its potted shrimps (Lytham-St Anne's?).

You will be contemptuous or cross, or both, when I tell you I have just read John Osborne's *The Entertainer*. My dear Rupert, I feel (almost) scared—like Douglas Jerrold in convalescence, reading *Sordello* [by Robert Browning] and terrified that, though physically mending, his mind had gone; he handed the book to a visiting friend, and when he saw him completely baffled, ejaculated 'Thank God' and sank back into refreshing sleep. *The E.* is utter, hopeless, outrageous rubbish, and yet T.C. Worsley in the *N.S.* uses words about it like 'brilliant', 'dazzling', 'gripping', 'masterly' etc. My only hope is that it looks and sounds quite different on the stage. In the study it is puerile. I suppose the enormous increase in the numbers of those who *can* read accounts for the popularity of so much rubbish; discrimination is still to come. They tell me the young flock to concerts, and Humphrey is always infuriated by the wild applause of every item, good bad and indifferent.

You didn't, I suppose, ask G. Lawrence about Dr Adams. I once asked the late Mr Justice Lewis about Greenwood, and he said it was quite certain Greenwood poisoned his wife (he was a junior for the prosecution) but got off because his daughter swore she had drunk from the relevant bottle of Burgundy. She disliked her father but wasn't going to have him hanged. I like to listen to judges, especially the sort of judge whom somebody once described as 'belonging to the great traditional line of judges. He was slow, he was courteous, he was wrong.' (Quoted by J. Agate, who added 'the exact opposite of me, who am rapid, rude, and right.')

Friday was Edmund Blunden's sixty-first birthday, and I invited some twenty of his family and admirers to a buffet lunch at Soho

---

[1] R.H.-D. had dined off them at the Royal Photographic Society the previous week.

Square (sausage rolls and all). It went with a swing and I'm sure pleased him. By the way, I've just discovered that he would dearly love to be a member of the M.C.C. Is there anything we can do, any string we can pull, to get him in? He plans to return finally to England in 1961, when he will be sixty-five. His cricket writings, in prose and verse, are, as you know, first-rate, and his knowledge and love of the game you have witnessed. Please give the matter your careful attention.

I see that all my efforts to wean you from deliberate mortification of the wits have failed: *The Entertainer* indeed! What a misnomer! All seem agreed that only Olivier's virtuosity keeps the play on, and I can see that he welcomed a change to shine in something so far from his normal playground.

I see that a new book (possibly the last) by one of my favourite living authors has just appeared: *Last Tales* by Isak Dinesen: order it from your library at once. And then her two earlier volumes, *Seven Gothic Tales* and *Winter's Tales*. Sometimes she writes under her own name, Baroness Blixen. She is an elderly Dane, reputed to take drugs—but a smashing good writer. My Uncle Duff thought that one of the stories in *Winter's Tales*, 'The Young Man with the Carnation', or words to that effect, was one of the best short stories ever written.

Poor old Dunsany[1]: I bet he's boring the wings off the angels with disquisitions on rock-salt and the semi-colon. I now feel rather smugly satisfied at having endured his last Lit. Soc. appearance (and incidentally touched him for a pound which he had owed me for more than a year).

7 November 1957   *Grundisburgh*

Of course Edmund Blunden ought to be a member of the M.C.C. and I have written this very day to Harry Altham (the Treasurer) to find out if there are any ways and means. I am not immensely optimistic, as they are pretty rigid about their rules and regulations, and the austere shade of Lord Harris[2] still broods morosely over the Committee Room. Some years ago there was an attempt to get Cardus

[1] Irish peer, author and member of the Literary Society, who had recently died.

[2] An early captain of England against Australia; populariser of the game in India when Governor of Bombay; for many years of great influence in the deliberations of the M.C.C.

in; I did what I could, but to no avail. But N.C. would, I suppose, be found by many much less likeable than E.B. Another difficulty is that many excellent cricketers are practically illiterate, and have no realisation of the obvious truth that it is the poetry of and in the game which keeps it alive. Tom Richardson had as little poetry in him as Achilles, but the sight of him bowling in 1896, or rather the mere thought of it, set N.C. writing stuff with the glow and quality of

> Stand in the trench, Achilles,
> Flame-capped, and shout for me.[1]

Isak Dinesen. I must confess that she is to me what the Holy Ghost was to the Corinthians. Why have I never heard of her? I shall order her stories at once.

9 November 1957   *Bromsden Farm*

Let us have a standing arrangement that on Lit. Soc. nights you will come to Soho Square at *six*, or as soon after as suits you. Press and pull every bell: they have just been mended and we must keep them in practice. Edmund Blunden is a firm Wordsworthian—and so am I. Inspired by your references I have just re-read the 'Extempore Effusion on the death of James Hogg': those three stanzas are superb. Many other great poets have written as many bad poems as W.W. (Tennyson for one), but has any other managed to hide away tremendous lines and stanzas in mediocre poems? What about:

> My former thoughts return'd: the fear that kills;
> The hope that is unwilling to be fed;
> Cold, pain, and labour, and all fleshly ills;
> And mighty Poets in their misery dead.

And then back to that egregious old leech-gatherer. Did the old gaffer realise that these matchless lines were any better than the lame verses that surround them?[2] I doubt it. I have never known a poet or writer who had any idea which was their best work: each poem or other work is inextricably bound up with the mood and circumstances of its creation.

---

[1] By Patrick Shaw-Stewart (killed in action 1917).
[2] From 'Resolution and Independence'.

14 November 1957   *Grundisburgh*

M.R. James loved to tell how some old King's don over a century ago had to give up his Fellowship when they found out he was married. Well he was only, so to speak, married in the sight of God, and was reported by a friend as saying '. . . and let me tell you, sir, that it's a damned lugubrious thing to be turned out of one's fellowship for fornication at the age of eighty-four.'

In your last letter you commented on what poor critics poets are of their own poetry. I would add 'and often of anyone's'. Are you familiar with *The Oxford Book of Modern Verse* chosen by Yeats? I don't know it well and in fact rather left it when I found his *wicked* omissions—including some of the best of his own early stuff. And what of Auden's *insufferable* comments on Tennyson, which so infuriated D. MacCarthy, and good Dame Sitwell's contempt for Emily Brontë's 'Cold in the Earth', which actually led to Q, in his senility, omitting it from the new *Oxford E.V.* (though I *believe* he left in 'Meet we no angels, Pansie?'—but I may be wrong). What does surprise me is how many of FitzG's alterations to Omar are *not* improvements, because his palate, though eclectic, was a fine one. And am I right in thinking Henry James's re-writings were often unfortunate?

I never go to London without finding all those *faces* deeply depressing. 'Zey are too many.'[1] A trainload in the rush-hour—silent, hurrying, mud-faced, wrapped either in private worries or in the evening-paper, but not *interested* in either, not really alive in any full sense—don't they devitalise you?

Give my regards to E.B. I never meet him without feeling a better, nicer, wiser man. I don't say even then that I am particularly good, nice, or wise, but, well, my uncle once heard a preacher enlarging on the miracle in the valley of Hinnom, and describing how when God breathed upon the skeletons they were 'elevated to the condition of corpses'. Consider me as having reached the corpse stage.

17 November 1957   *Bromsden Farm*

Did you realise that Eric Linklater was far from sober when he arrived at the Lit. Soc.? Not that liquor makes him tiresome—only

---

[1] Sarah Bernhardt's answer when asked what she thought of the Ten Commandments.

loud, vehement and repetitive. I think I told you his eldest daughter had lain unconscious for seven weeks after a road accident. Clearly E's arrival in London was the signal for tension to be released in alcohol. After leaving the Garrick he collected some friends from the Savile and spent most of the rest of the night in some frightful nightclub. Next morning he woke when the bar opened, spent three hours over lunch, and arrived at Soho Square at 4 p.m. very merry indeed. Somehow I propelled him to some nearby binders, where by means of astonishing will-power he managed to make a creditable shot at signing sixty copies of a limited edition of his new book. With great difficulty I found a taxi and sent him back to the Savile. Next morning he turned up, very sick and sorry, but bearing a letter from his wife to say that the child had at last spoken, and there was hope that her brain wasn't affected. You can work out the moral of this story if you're clever enough.

Yeat's *Oxford Book* cannot be taken seriously, except as a gloss on W.B.Y. Great writers are almost the worst critics, being egoists and usually interested only in their own work.

I have just read the latest novel of a man whom I consider one of the best living novelists—R.C. Hutchinson: have you read anything of his? If not, try this one: it is called *March the Ninth*, and though not his best is still jolly good. If you like it, then try *Shining Scabbard, One Light Burning*, and *The Unforgotten Prisoner*. He is an Englishman of roughly my age, and all his best books are about some European country to which he has never been: apparently his imagination has to be kindled by being far-flung. His long novel of the Russian Revolution, *Testament*, is astonishingly good, and he always writes beautifully. Here's another treat in store for you!

20 November 1957   *Grundisburgh*
There are five Dickens novels I love, but last week I re-read (after half a century) *Bleak House* and am now in *The O.C. Shop*, and I find his obvious and admitted defects outweighing the genius; and as for the humour—well now, do *you* go chuckling about Soho Square whenever you think of Mrs Jellyby, and Mrs Pardiggle, and Messrs Chadband and Turveydrop, and Mrs Jarley and Dick Swiveller? B. Darwin does, I am sure—just as *I* do about Pecksniff and Mrs Gamp and the Wellers and Mrs Nickleby etc. Why is this? Why do I, in my

bones, *know M. Chuzzlewit* (for all Macaulay called it 'dull and frivolous') to be *leagues* ahead of *Bleak H.*? Why do I love reading about
Mr Squeers and don't a bit want to go on reading about Quilp? These
are questions 'spirit-searching, light-abandoned', as one of the literary ladies said to Martin C.—and the worst is still to come, for little
Nell is still alive.

P.S. What does G.M. Young mean by 'the ribbon-development' of
George Moore's English? I am always coming across these brilliancies
and so often failing to see that their point is all that sharp. On the
other hand, almost everything G.K. Chesterton says of Mr Pickwick
gets me, so to speak, where it tickles. E.g. on that old suggestion that
the idea of Mr P. was really Seymour's.[1] 'To claim to have originated
an idea of Dickens is like claiming to have contributed a glass of water
to Niagara'.

One of the least attractive episodes of old Gladstone's career was
after his last Cabinet had said good-bye to him, practically all of them
in tears. He himself wasn't, and used to refer to them as 'that blub-
bering Cabinet'. I sometimes wonder whether George Meredith was
right in saying W.E.G. was a man of marvellous aptitudes but not a
great man. But who told me recently of A.J. Balfour in a company
who were all telling of the most frightening moments in their lives?
Battle, and fire and flood, crag and torrent, etc cropped up again and
again, A.J.B. knew nothing of any of these, but merely recorded Mr
G. looking at him in the House, *and his eyes widened.* But that brings
me to La Rochefoucauld: 'Why have we memory sufficient to retain
the minutest circumstances . . . and yet not enough to remember how
often we have related them to the same person?' I have a suspicion
that I heard the A.J.B. story with/from you.

24 November 1957   *Bromsden Farm*
Stay me with flagons, comfort me with apples! A glance at the
enclosed[2] will show you what I mean—but more of that later. I expect
you know that the Savile Club's present premises in Brook Street were

---

[1] The illustrator of the first numbers of *Pickwick*. His place was taken by 'Phiz' —
Hablot Browne—after he committed suicide.
[2] Two dinner menus. The quotation is from *The Song of Songs*.

formerly the home of 'Lulu' Harcourt. When Max was asked how he would describe the *décor*, he said: '*Lulu Quinze*'. And I'm certain I've already told you of J.B. Priestley's superb remark, 'The *Savage* Club is the place where dirty stories go when they die.'

Martin Chuzzlewit is my favourite too. The best description of George Moore's later prose compared it to one of the large French rivers—wide, placid, seemingly endless, no current, occasional felicities on the bank, shallow, and *just* moving. This applies to *The Brook Kerith, Héloise, Aphrodite in Aulis*, etc.

Last week was gruelling. Those two dinners alone, on consecutive nights, almost laid me out. The Trinity Hall evening was cosier, beginning at the High Table in their lovely little hall, and ending in the Combination Room with a horseshoe table and a little railway for the decanters. I was lucky to sit between the only two representatives of the humanities, my host Graham Storey[1] and Brooke Crutchley, the Printer to the Cambridge University Press. Later, when we were scattered among the Professor of Metallurgy and other such terrors, conversation became tougher. When at last I got to bed at 12.45, my hostess's hot water bottle had filled my bed with water. Luckily I know her very well and she was still up to produce a complete new set of bedding.

On Friday I lunched with Cecil Beaton at his exquisite house in Pelham Place (butler and all). The other guests were Nancy Cunard, Mrs Ian Fleming and W. Somerset Maugham, older and more lizard-like than ever. His stammer is as bad as ever, and he now clicks his fingers with annoyance when he can't get the word out, which adds to the confusion. When he came in, Cecil said: 'Willie, you look so sweet I shall kiss you'—which he did.

29 November 1957   *67 Chelsea Square*
In last week's *Spectator* the man Amis described 'St Agnes' Eve' as that 'sugary, erotic extravaganza'. It is not really much good setting up as a judge of poetry if *all* your five senses are blunted.

---

[1] R.H.-D.'s close friend Humphry House, who was to have edited the definitive edition of the letters of Charles Dickens, died in 1955. As his literary executor, R.H.-D. played a considerable part in the appointment of his successor as editor, Graham Storey, who has recently brought the project to a triumphant conclusion, in twelve volumes.

I have never really had a London club. *You* wouldn't regard my present one, the Royal Empire Society, as anything but an omnium-gatherum of hearty and earnest bores, who used to quote Kipling, and like to listen to addresses about Ghana and then refresh themselves with egg salad and blancmange. But it is very cheap and has quite good arm-chairs and is v. near Charing X.

It seems to me one of the odder anfractuosities of the human mind to want to kiss old Maugham, but one never knows.

Bishop Henson couldn't bear his Dean, Welldon, and once at Eton when odd old sayings were being discussed (e.g. 'right as a trivet', what *is* a trivet etc) when asked if he had ever seen pigs in clover, answered 'Well, no, not exactly—though I have seen the Dean of Durham in bed'. You would have enjoyed his company.

8 December 1957   *Bromsden Farm*

Despite Agatha Christie's phenomenal success of late in the theatre, I fear she won't leave a quarter of old W.S.M.'s haul. He made a great deal of his money in America (where the rewards are greater) and has mostly lived in France, paying no income tax of any kind.

Last Thursday I was taken to the first night of the Stratford *Tempest* at Drury Lane. Gielgud spoke beautifully, as always, and Caliban wasn't bad, but except for the flashes of poetry it's a boring play and I found my eyes closing more than once. In the audience I saw my former wife Peggy, looking very young and beautiful. Thank God I no longer have any ties with that intolerable profession the Theatre!

12 December 1957   *Grundisburgh*

When we were at 67 Chelsea Sq. I found a dozen Maughams on the shelf and read a lot of the plays and stories. Very efficient, very readable, but—well there is a vacuity somewhere, moral and spiritual very likely. (But on the whole one should try not to talk like a bishop!)

The critics were very enthusiastic about Gielgud's Prospero. I am immensely amused at your finding the play boring, because, to read at any rate, all the plays have always seemed to me bad *as plays*—though over and over again the poetry simply knocks one endways.

15 December 1957   *Bromsden Farm*

The Duff Cooper prize-giving went off beautifully on Monday.[1] The Queen Mother looked quite lovely in silver: her beauty and immediately irresistible charm are amazing. I explained the simple drill to her, and she was wide-eyed as a little girl who had never done such a thing before. After Durrell had been presented to her and they had taken up their positions, she whispered to him: 'I'm terrified. Are you?' which did much to calm his palpable fright. David Cecil made a tip-top speech, brief, poetical and entirely to the point. Then the Q.M. gave Durrell the prize and said some charming words about Duff, at which Diana's lovely eyes filled with tears. Then Durrell briefly said thank-you, and the ceremony was over.

On Thursday I presided at the London Library committee and delivered an interminable report on what had been done since the last meeting. As the meeting broke up Rose Macaulay burst in, looking like a wall-painting of a mummy, and said: 'Am I late? Do tell me all that has been said.' I was too exhausted to comply, and I fear she thought me churlish. The old pet is really quite useless on committees now, bless her.

19 December 1957   *Grundisburgh*

We will do the *28th* with great pleasure.[2] I remember we turn left at top of that long incline after leaving the Long Mile, but am rather vague after that—and snow will be falling, and darkness will cover the earth, and gross darkness the people. And I have always been one of those whose instinct for missing the way is unfailing. Pamela is better when by herself, but I invariably muddle her. So in the more derogatory sense the Holy Innocents' Day is the right one for us to be groping our way to you in darkest Oxfordshire.

Once when she visited Eton the senior beaks were presented to the King and Queen. H.K. Marsden was next to me. He had taught Maths to the K. at Osborne (or Dartmouth?). The Queen graciously told him that the King remembered him and mentioned it to her. All she got was the menacing reply: 'Then he must have been talking

---

[1] Awarded to Lawrence Durrell for his book *Bitter Lemons*.
[2] The Lytteltons were to lunch with the Hart-Davises.

during the service' (which they had attended) and of course the old dervish forgot to add 'Ma'am'.

Your power of work is really terrifying My processes are—to compare small with great—like those Housman said were his when he had to compose an address or inscription (in English: Latin he claimed was quite easy)—one day spent staring at a blank page and longing for death; a second one jotting down phrases and crossing them out, feeling rather sick—and so on. But in his case no one would guess at the hideous history behind the majestic pageant of his prose.

22 December 1957   *Bromsden Farm*
Shakespeare in modern dress is rubbish. Its advocates pretend that the process enables the audience to appreciate the words without being distracted by fancy dress, but in fact the effect is exactly contrary.

29 December 1957   *Bromsden Farm*
Looking through Emerson for an elusive quotation, I came on this excellent analysis of literary reputation. I expect you know it, but never mind:

> There is no luck in literary reputation. They who make up the final verdict upon every book are not the partial and noisy readers of the hour when it appears; but a court as of angels, a public not to be bribed, not to be entreated, and not to be overawed, decides upon every man's title to fame. Only those books come down which deserve to last . . . Blackmore, Kotzebue, or Pollok, may endure for a night, but Moses and Homer stand forever.

Isn't that splendid? Old Edward Garnett used to put the same sentiments into shorter space—'Everything finds its own level in the end'—but I am charmed by Emerson's rhythms.

                                                                          Royal Hotel
31 December 1957   *Cambridge*
That is fine Emerson—an oddly under-rated writer *me judice*. Perhaps there is too much bread to the butter. Do you remember his description of genius, 'that stellar and undiminishable something'. As near as anyone ever went I think? Old Samuel of course had the same

belief in the judgment of the public (when given time) as opposed to that of the intelligentsia, and 'Few things are more risible than literary fashions' hits a nail neatly and finally. Among my colleagues are nice sensible Oxonians who do not draw a very attractive picture of Bowra, A.J.P. Taylor, Rowse, Trevor-Roper or, in fact, any of the louder Oxford voices. I liked Bowra at that Johnson luncheon, but they say he now indulges relentlessly in monologue, which of course does not go down well in a community where all want to do the same. Rum places, universities. Gow told me that Housman attended one lecture of Jowett's,[1] but when the great man mispronounced one Greek word he attended no more. Nevertheless B.J. was a better man than A.E.H. The conversation of both was largely composed of usually unnecessary and uncalled-for snubs, but J. was much less conceited and thin-skinned and morose.

4 January 1958   *Bromsden Farm*

I was taken (for the second time, after almost a year) to the two-man review *At The Drop of a Hat*, which I enjoyed all over again.[2] They mostly use the same material, but include one or two topical songs: I rather liked this one of four lines:

> Russia is red, dilly, dilly,
> England is green.
> They've got the Moon, dilly, dilly,
> We've got the Queen.

Afterwards I had to put in an appearance at a New Year's Eve party in Chelsea, but managed to escape before the chimes rang out. Next day I travelled to Brighton in the afternoon, stayed with some friends, and after supper addressed the Hove Quill Club on Oscar Wilde's Letters. Some thirty stalwarts turned up, including (rather disconcertingly) a little girl of nine! I had prepared nothing, but simply let loose on them a hurricane of words, facts and quotations which kept going for three quarters of an hour. Next morning I caught an 8.30 train and reached the office just in time to give our assembled travellers a two-hour exhortation on the

---

[1] Master of Balliol College, Oxford
[2] Michael Flanders and Donald Swann.

Spring Books, and in the evening *five* hours on the proofs of Diana Cooper's book. And what a lot of licences seem to need renewing—thank heaven we have no dogs, menservants or crests on our carriages!

8 January 1958   *Finndale House*
I look forward to meeting T.S. Eliot [at the Literary Society]. Shall I ask Sir Malcolm Sargent if he knows he is known in the music world as 'Flash Harry'? Perhaps not—they are a jealous and backbiting lot, and anyway they can't deny that his tailcoat is the best-fitting in all London. Henry Wood's was a mere bag of ferrets in comparison. I shall see you beforehand and go through my usual hoop of ringing all bells and banging all knockers except the right ones at about 6 p.m.

You would, I know, greet any advice to go slower with the same contempt as Johnson, full of dropsy and melancholia and asthma, felt for the Frenchman who said '*Ah, Monsieur, vous étudiez trop*'.

I should like to have heard you on O. Wilde, unprepared, all bubbling out of you, fresh and inexhaustible. It was always said that the time to sit listening to Porson[1] was when he was quite sozzled and went on hour by hour 'hicupping Greek like a helot'. Only in one particular is the parallel inexact. I bet it was immensely worth hearing.

15 January 1958   *Grundisburgh*
I had a good chuckle with T.S.E. A very good man, I thought, with no affectations at all. Flash Harry too I liked; he looks extraordinarily young and fresh, which perhaps is not surprising as he said he *enjoyed* (like another I know?) being at work twenty-five hours in the day.

And I was delighted to meet Alan Pryce-Jones again—first time since he was up to me! I was glad to find he is adamant about anonymity in the *T.L.S.*—just as adamant as he was in the most benign manner about the plethora of foreign writers given all that space in his columns.[2]

---

[1] Richard Porson (1759–1808), Regius Professor of Greek at Cambridge.
[2] He was editor of the *Times Literary Supplement*.

Roger Fulford has discovered an occasion in the annals when Spencer Lyttelton and Lord Curzon were the only attendants. Very embarrassing for old Uncle S., who hated a tête-à-tête. He was a superbly handsome and vigorous man, but, well, when E.F. Benson asked him if he had ever kissed a girl, his answer was 'Once—on the brow'. A Victorian old bachelor but somehow not at all spinsterish.

19 January 1958   *Bromsden Farm*
Flash Harry (though clearly a bounder) is good company occasionally, and very friendly. Did I tell you how once at the beginning of a big dinner-party at Hamish Hamilton's I was approached by a very pretty girl whom I scarcely knew? 'Will you promise me something?' she asked earnestly, out of the blue. 'Anything,' I gallantly replied, strengthened by a powerful Martini. 'Promise me,' she said, 'that whatever happens I shan't have to go home alone in a taxi with Malcolm Sargent.' I duly promised, but later regretted my quixotry, since we had to wait till the small hours before Flash Harry gave up the chase, and then of course I had to escort the lady to South Kensington.

I have got Oscar out of prison now, basking in the summer sunshine of Dieppe in the brief lull before the poverty, squalor and degradation of his last three years. The story still has power to move me, and I think will always affect those who are susceptible of being purged by the pity and terror of a man's destiny.

23 January 1958   *Grundisburgh*
Shakespearean hunch: I am sure in my own mind that the adjective 'whoreson' came into *his* mind from some experience in Suffolk of a day like 22 January 1958; there is no other completely fitting epithet. I was in Ipswich and at precisely 12.21 midday fell headlong on the pavement—without, I may say, the smallest damage or even discomfort; I might have been a slalom champion in embryo. The only discomfort was caused by two citizens, who thought they were helping me, 'offering unneeded arms, performing dull farces of escort' (do you know those superbly absurd hexameters of Clough's *Bothie*?[1]). To-day the sun is here, but, like

---

[1] *of Tober-na-voulich*: 'A Long-Vacation Pastoral'.

Bet Flint vis-à-vis Mrs Williams's disapproval, the frost 'makes itself very easy about that.'[1]

I have just read Hesketh Pearson's *Gilbert*—a dreadfully tiresome man—huffy and irascible, and at the same time thinking much of his fame, and despising the achievement which created it. Very like Conan Doyle, who thought highly of *A Duet* and scorned Sherlock Holmes. Have you ever read Gilbert's plays? Frightfully feeble and soft and stilted. But the man who could pour out such lines as 'An affection à la Plato for a bashful young potato, or a not-too-French French bean'[2] shall surely remain immortal.

26 January 1958   *Bromsden Farm*

In one of his letters to Diana, written from the front in 1918, Duff praises Meredith's 'The Story of Chloe' as one of the best short stories in the language. I read it last night—with some difficulty, since it's almost impossible to see the story for the words, but there is one excellent chapter (where Chloe plans her suicide), and in some way the effect of the whole story is greater in retrospect than at the time. If you've got it, do try it and let me know what you think.

30 January 1958   *Grundisburgh*

What has happened to John Heygate?[3] His father was a colleague for some years—not an unamiable man, and immensely efficient in a philistine way. Mrs H. was a grim sardonic woman who knew all about football and rowing and had a sharp edge to her tongue. I treasure a remark of hers that the only thing Eton boys learnt thoroughly was the one thing Eton masters knew least about, i.e. good manners. Not bad.

Did you know M.D. Hill who died last week—as he told me a fortnight ago he was about to do, quite placidly. What had clearly happened to him is, I suppose, common at eighty-five, i.e. a complete

---

[1] 'I have known [said Dr Johnson] all the wits fom Mrs Montagu to Bet Flint!' 'Bet Flint!' cried Mrs Thrale; 'pray who is she?' 'Oh, a fine character, madam! She was habitually a slut and a drunkard, and occasionally a thief and a harlot . . . Mrs Williams,' he added, 'did not love Bet Flint, but Bet Flint made herself very easy about that.' (Fanny Burney's Diary, August 1778).

[2] Bunthorne in *Patience*.

[3] R.H.-D. had dined with Liza Heygate.

loss of interest in all that is going on—a sort of *uncoupling* of one's mind from world affairs, human interests, old habits etc. He was a blunt, matter-of-fact scientist but, *not* being a Wykehamist, had plenty of humour and could laugh even at himself. I liked him and we corresponded pretty regularly.

'The Tale of Chloe.' I read it at Cambridge, I think, and had it at Eton, where some boy borrowed and failed to return it. I remember nothing of it—except, wasn't there somebody in it called The Duchess of Dewlap? Will Meredith ever come back? The world his people lived in is so completely dead. But then so is Henry James's and he apparently is reviving.

My fall left no ill effects, though 'between the stirrup and the ground,' so to speak, I remembered Amsler's[1] saying that a very large percentage of big men over seventy died from the effects of a fall. But not yet!

P.S. When Heygate's won the football cup, the players were presented by Mrs H. with Bibles bound in the house-colours (blue and yellow).

2 February 1958   *Bromsden Farm*

I'm delighted to tell you that *Georgian Afternoon* [by L.E. Jones] is booming. We sold 550 copies last week (its first), and the booksellers had first to get rid of their pre-publication orders. Jonah is in high fettle, delighted with all his reviews and letters, and markedly less deaf! One of the places I saw him was at Ursula Ridley's. When I arrived, there were five women (very charming ones) and no men. I drank a whisky-and-water briskly, and when Ursie said 'Help yourself to another', I poured out a stiff whisky and filled up the tumbler with what I thought was iced water but turned out to be strongish Martini! Ursie wanted to throw it away, but I insisted on drinking it, and I can now tell you that a tumbler of Martini containing a large whisky is a great tongue loosener. I held the five women in thrall, and when Jonah and Evy arrived they must have wondered at my eloquence. Later this same drink, backed up by a glass or two of this and that, sustained me through dinner at White's with my father and the Duke of Argyll. The Duke is dullish and rather pompous, but in my

[1] Eton doctor.

ultra-uninhibited mood I remembered that he spent years trying to fish up a Spanish treasure-ship from the sands of Tobermory Bay, and so encouraged him to describe the whole enterprise.

5 February 1958   *Grundisburgh (summer-house!)*

I can remember about ten individual strokes that I saw made since 1897. One of Trumper's in 1905 stands out because it was unique, i.e. in none of the books, and never made before or since. Oddly enough one was a square *cut* by Rhodes, who later forbade the Harrow boys ever to cut (or 'coot') as it was unsafe. ('But, Wilfred, a cut's the greatest fun.' 'Cricket's not meant to be foon'—which ought to be in the *Oxford Book of Quotations*, being on the same level as Goering's 'Guns are better than butter'.)

I enjoyed your rake's progress from Martini to Martini—making glad the heart of both R.H-D. and His Grace of Argyll. Was he at Eton? If so, no doubt called Hamilton. *All* dukes at one time or another seem to be called Hamilton. (It is drenching at the moment, and the rain on my tarred felt roof makes a fine tattoo.)

Geoffrey Faber's *Jowett*: yes, indeed, but surely I told you how much I had enjoyed it and added some probably irrelevant comments about the resemblance between J. and Hitler, i.e. some genital inadequacy or oddity. But I expect it was towards the end of a letter, and very faint and few are those who get as far as that—as Macaulay said of those who were in at the death of the Blatant Beast (which, in cold fact, hasn't happened by the end of *The Faery Queen*. It must have been the only book which Macaulay didn't finish).

The P.M. [Macmillan] has just left N.Z., and my nephew, the Governor-General, found him very aloof and inattentive, but charitably supposes he may have been tired. But he does add how disappointing great public men are to meet—as Max Beerbohm once said, I believe. I haven't met many P.M's or ex-P.M.s. Eden was an icicle, Attlee amiable but wholly non-committal, Winston as Laski described him—'like a great actor playing a part'. Baldwin seemed more human at the top of Lord's pavilion during a Test Match, but he fell asleep long before any test could be applied. And years ago A.J. Balfour shed over all the company streams of that impersonal geniality which leaves one with the firm conviction that fundamentally he doesn't care a straw about anyone.

9 February 1958   *36 Soho Square*

On Friday morning I just had time to look through the post before catching the ten o'clock train and there was your faithful letter, bless you. I read it in the icy train. The snow started in mid-Channel, and my train was three quarters of an hour late in Paris. At Chantilly all the telephone lines were down—and still are. The only other guest was Loelia (née Ponsonby), last-but-one Duchess of Westminster. I spent most of yesterday going through the proofs with Diana. The house is centrally heated, and one can't get used to that in one day.

                                                          67 Chelsea Square
13 February 1958   *London S. W.3*

What a grandly perceptive eye Bishop Hensley Henson had—and the crispest possible style. I leave with you one thing of his which you will appreciate. It hits an old house-tutor full in the wind. His comment on 'that strange institution the public school': 'I cannot think that the conscientious and devoted governess method, sublime in its self-dedication and scrupulosity, can be altogether wholesome for the development of character.' Well, there you are; the old brute (whom I love) doesn't attack the system, as do others, at one of its *weak* points, but at what is usually thought its strong point.

   Still I did always try to follow that shrewd advice of C.M. Wells to A.B. Ramsay: 'Ram, I'll tell you a thing; don't see *too much* of your chaps.' It is *very* wise. And when one saw boys *drained* of individuality by too conscientious tutoring one realised it to the full.

16 February 1958   *Bromsden Farm*

I shall go to Charles Morgan's memorial service at St Margaret's on Thursday: it starts at noon, and at one I have to take the chair for a bookseller at a lunch-time meeting at the National Book League in Albemarle Street. A fast taxi will be needed, in which I shall reverse my double-sided jersey from black to scarlet, and whip on another tie, so as not to depress the assembled booklovers. There was a splendid row at last week's meeting of the Royal Literary Fund, during which the secretary and the treasurer accused each other of idleness and incompetence. If only all committee meetings were as lively!

Diana Cooper's first volume is now, thank goodness, passed for press,[1] and soon I shall have to start work on the second volume.

23 *February 1958*   *Bromsden Farm*
Charles Morgan's memorial service was well attended, and the choir (some dozen men) sang beautifully—the closing Nunc Dimittis was especially moving. But the service was torn in two, and its emotion dissipated, by what the programme announced as THE ORATION. Instead of a man with powerful lungs mounting the pulpit and roundly proclaiming Charles's virtues for all to hear, a chair was placed in the aisle between the choir, and to it was helped Dame Edith Sitwell, her bizarre beauty obscured by a fur coat and a huge black mushroom of a hat. Only her fingers, on which clustered emeralds the size of billiard balls, suggested her customary eccentricities. Having with difficulty extracted her spectacles and adjusted them, she began to read softly from a typescript, in which she several times lost her place. To me, scarcely a third of the way down the church, only an occasional word was audible: to the majority behind me, virtually nothing. Douglas Woodruff, who was sitting in front, told me next day that I hadn't missed much. The whole thing was a grotesque error of judgment.

By great luck I immediately got a taxi, in which I dexterously managed my quick change. The National Book League had mercifully saved me some sandwiches and a glass of whisky, and I just had time to knock them back before facing the audience of forty or so, mostly feminine and elderly. I introduced the bookseller, who was supposed to talk for thirty minutes, after which a discussion of the same length should follow. To my horror, after speaking jerkily for *six minutes*, the bookseller dried up and sat down. There was nothing for it but for me to resume, and to keep up some sort of noise until the audience joined in or the bookseller recovered. Somehow I did this, and at the end of the hour I had to apply the closure to what by then was a tolerably lively discussion. Phew!

26 *February 1958*   *Summer-house*
Roger spotted you at the memorial service, and maintains, *more suo*, that half of you was acutely observing who was or was not there, while

[1] *The Rainbow Comes and Goes.*

the other half was fervently and melodiously proclaiming the desire to fly to the bosom of Jesus. Do you remember Horace Walpole's brilliant description of 'the burlesque Duke of Newcastle' at George II's funeral—holding his spy-glass to his eye with one hand and mopping his tears with the other?[1] The sun is shining, a thickish snow is falling with a strong S.W. slant, though the wind is N.E. Sheer Lewis Carroll.

6 March 1958   *Grundisburgh*
[R.H.-D. had been reading *Sartor Resartus* by Thomas Carlyle, 'as clotted as Colin Wilson but much more rewarding.']
   I am delighted to hear you are re-reading *Sartor* which I shall at once do myself. It has superb things in it—the picture of London at night, the Alps ('a hundred and a hundred savage peaks') and the reduction to uttermost simplicity of such things as war ('What quarrel had these two men? Busy as the devil is, not the smallest', but they proceed to blow each other's brains out), and justice—Judge in red, man in the dock in blue. Red says to blue, 'You be hanged' and blue accepts it meekly and *is*. I don't quote—merely recollect from under-graduate days. It is odd to realise that so many professed lovers of literature fail to see, with all its blemishes, the enormous power (*yes*, and *fun*!) of Carlyle's writing.

9 March 1958   *Glyn Felin, Neath, Glamorgan*
I am staying with the octogenarian and stone-deaf (but nevertheless delightful) widow of a tin-plate magnate, who lives in this huge and arctic house with her un-married daughter. In the old days they had five indoor and five outdoor servants: to-day they spend most of their time clearing up after themselves and the one grudging woman who works for them. It is snowing hard, and I have visions of the rest of the Brains Trust being held up, and my having to hold the audience single-handed for upwards of an hour.
   I am enjoying *Sartor*, but my word, you have to dig out the

---

[1] He fell into a fit of crying the moment he came into the chapel, and flung himself back in a stall, the Archbishop hovering over him with a smelling bottle . . . Then returned the fear of catching cold; and the Duke of Cumberland, who was sinking with heat, felt himself weighed down, and turning round, found it was the Duke of Newcastle standing upon his train, to avoid the chill of the marble.

nuggets! All those capital letters, German words, and the number of lines beginning with inverted commas must deter the faint-hearted.

13 March 1958   *Grundisburgh (summer-house)*
I was interested to read in *Punch* that Anthony Powell always found H.G.W. unreadable. Odd—but I suppose to *his* generation W's spec-ulations and prophecies and impatient omniscience were all becom-ing rather tarnished. *My* generation simply battened on him—not so much, in my case at least, his prophecies etc as his humour and fre-quent penetration. Who was the man at some wedding breakfast who 'had just taken a mouthful that amounted to conversational suicide'?

How right you are about Sartor, I was always attracted by the thrawn old dyspeptic, his poor tummy fermenting with what he (mis-takenly) called 'an innocent spoonful of *porridge*' last thing at night. But, gosh, what marvellous pictures he had in his head. Do you remember the account of Robespierre's execution, ending 'Samson, thou canst not be too quick', with the dreadful reason why?[1]

I am pretty sure I shall dislike X, as I always do a writer who is hailed by the 'chorus of indolent reviewers' as 'having no nonsense about him'. One knows at once he is going to throw mud of some sort at better men than himself. And one is *not* prejudiced in favour of a man who describes *Middlemarch* as 'insincere humbug' because the author lived in what one's grandmother called sin with the 'little ape' Lewes. On the whole *M* is my favourite novel. Was it V. Woolf who said it was almost the only grown-up novel of nineteenth-century England?)

I spent a day or two ago among the March monthlies much im- or de-pressed by an article on 'Scriptistics', but immensely cheered by the name of its author, which, believe it or not, is Dr Virgil Wigwam.

---

[1] Just before he was arrested, Robespierre tried to kill himself, but only succeeded in shooting himself through the lower jaw, which was then bandaged with linen. (Samson was the executioner.) 'At the foot of the scaffold, they stretched him on the ground till his turn came. Lifted aloft, his eyes again opened; caught the bloody axe. Samson wrenched the coat off him; wrenched the dirty linen from his jaw, the jaw fell powerless, there burst from him a cry; – hideous to hear and see. Samson, thou canst not be too quick.'

My Welsh trip was on the whole agreeable, though the Brains Trust itself wasn't much cop. Some three hundred demented citizens had paid half-a-crown each, and they filled rather less than half the hall. The 'panel' consisted of Lionel Hale (in the chair), L.A.G. Strong, Lettice Cooper (a nice Yorkshire novelist), myself, and an ebullient Welsh schoolmaster (and, I gather, television star) called Gwyn Thomas. On him we had to depend for answers of some sort to such questions as: 'Do you consider that the flowering of Welsh literature can be partly explained by the fact that Wales escaped early from the domination of the Roman Catholic Church?' I managed to avoid the subsequent dinner. Lionel Hale told me next morning that all the Welshmen spoke until the Goddess Reason tottered on her throne, and he had no doubt that any two English doctors would have certified them all *in situ*.

Donald Somervell delighted me by telling me that when someone asked Renan whether he was turning Protestant, he replied: 'I have lost my faith, but not my reason'. William Plomer also, by his translating 'near-miss' to a Frenchman as *demi-vierge*.

I don't think Tony Powell is wholly representative of his generation in his attitude to Wells. I lapped up H.G.'s novels. *Mr Britling* was the first wholly adult modern novel I ever read, and I was as impressed with it as with my own advancement.

I am glad you are not an anti-H.G.W. H.J.'s admiration of his enormous richness and vitality was clearly deep and genuine, but I suppose with that up-bringing he could never get rid of all the chips on his shoulder. I should have liked to tell him what a grand bowler my father said his father was nearly a hundred years ago. Or did he regard bowling as G. Meredith regarded tailoring?

On Monday Humphrey defeated the Barnet Rural District Council over his 'cowshed'. The surveyor was fool enough to say his proposed house was 'anti-social', which slow full-pitch was duly despatched to the boundary by H's law-man saying that a house deliberately designed to enable him to trumpet away without annoying the neighbours was about as non-anti-social as anything could be. And the hanging-judge cordially agreed.

23 March 1958   *Bromsden Farm*

On Wednesday I went as a guest to the dinner of the International
P.E.N. at the Criterion Restaurant. I sat between the elderly wives of
the Estonian Minister and the French Chargé d'Affaires. They were
both very nice, but conversation was laboured until the Estonian
began in the greatest detail to tell me about her thrombosis. They
had just got her into the ambulance when the speeches began. A
French writer called André Chamson made a good speech (in
French) which included a moving tribute to Charles Morgan and
some good jokes. He said that wherever he goes he is asked the same
two questions: '*Qu'est ce que vous pensez de Françoise Sagan?*' and
'*Qu'est ce que vous pensez des Jeunes Gens Furieux?*' Then a ghastly
bearded Scottish Nationalist professor spoke for what seemed hours.
The Scotch *are* tiresome people, aren't they? Particularly when they're
trying to be funny. 'I'm sorry to disappoint the ladies by not coming
in my kilt—not that I've pawned it'—and so on interminably.

27 March 1958   *Grundisburgh*

We are soon in June when the dreariest of all ceremonies—school
prize-givings—are thick on the ground. Tell me what to say to the
boys of Bromsgrove, which will divert them from a career of crime
and the weekly perusal of *Reveille*.

Isn't there something in *Sartor* about how we 'haste stormfully
across the astonished earth'? Never for a moment did Carlyle forget
the mystery and the brevity and the incongruity of human life. A trait
which all writers ought to have—not necessarily *ever* to appear.

The Henry James biography Vol I [by Leon Edel] arrived just
before I left. In a minute I am going in to tea, then I shall open that
delicious parcel—and gloat. (Is there any greater pleasure?) I shall
start reading it the moment I have finished *Middlemarch*, of which
there are still 250 pages (out of 1200—one of the very few books that
really are long enough). According to old Saintsbury very few are.

30 March 1958   *Bromsden Farm*

You have unerringly put your finger on Carlyle's greatest quality—
that constant feeling of man in relation to the mysterious immensities
of the Universe—and one can forgive him a lot of his crotchetiness
on that account.

Stephen Potter once wrote of George Saintsbury: 'It is recorded that for eighteen years he *started the day* by reading a French novel (in preparation for his history of them)—an act so unnatural to man as almost in itself to amount to genius.' He also quotes G.S. as writing in his *History of Criticism*: 'Grillparzer's natural limitations appear to have been further tightened by his playwrightship and by the influence of Joseph Schreyvogel, a sort of Austrian Nisard, of whom I do not know so much.'

2 April 1958   *Grundisburgh*

And now comes H.G. Wells's byeblow[1] telling us that George Eliot was an impostor; he is reviewing her letters, in which he sees 'the slow perfection of a technique of self-deception that in the end equipped its possessor to become a perfect supplier of soft solder to *l'homme moyen sensuel*, the swamped and ignoble Tartufe (sic) of industrial society'. To which, as was once said, the only answer is 'resonant, monosyllabic, and plural'. For her great admirers were people like Mr Gladstone, Tennyson, Leslie Stephen, Birrell etc. It is true that old George Moore called her intellectuality 'studied brag', but that might have been expected. But what made Ruskin write 'that disgusting *Mill on the Floss*'? He may have been just about to go off his head—or have just gone. Of course one may well be derisive of all that solemnity, as of some sibyl receiving a string of worshippers, but I doubt if among them were to be found many *hommes moyen sensuels*.

I got from the library yesterday Lord Elton's biographical sketch of Bishop King of Lincoln—certainly the most saintlike man I ever saw: it was unmistakable. Nothing solemn about him, or hearty either. A young cleric, elected to serve on some committee, arrived late and frightened at its first meeting. Old King in the chair, an atmosphere of the heaviest solemnity, only one seat left, next to him. The youth stood appalled, but K. beckoned him to the chair next his, and as he sat down bent and whispered to him behind his hand 'We ain't so good as we look'. But probably these mild tales of clerical life bore you? It is very probable that you have never really come across a saint. Blunden has something of the look of one, I thought more than once.

[1] His son by Rebecca West, Anthony West.

Is that right off the target? Oh, but yes, you have, i.e. Mrs Alington; she certainly wasn't far off. That thing of Robert Birley's in *The Times* was first-rate.[1] The only thing lacking to a complete picture was her magnificent *wrath* at anything mean or vulgar. I remember a film in the School Hall in which the whole and sole point was that nearly everyone in it was drunk. She came out at the end, her face crimson and lowering, and standing on the steps in her bell-of-doom voice cried 'Damn,' and added a few blistering words about the results of long and expensive education. She had latterly every kind of ache and pain, and lameness and blindness, and never paid the smallest attention to any of them. She was the last of that generation, her eldest half-brother being my father, born in 1842.

Do you agree with Saintsbury's dictum that whenever you are offered fried sole, whatever may be the alternatives, fried sole should be your choice? I do rather, but C.M. Wells, though not antagonistic to this view, said that in his opinion cold ham was the only thing that deserved such a high place in the list. But he admitted that there must be nothing wrong with the feeding, the killing, the curing, the cooking, and the carving.

I know you like a juicy sentence. Here is what Meredith said in a letter of old Carlyle: 'Swim on his pages, take his poetry and fine grisly laughter, his manliness, together with some splendid teaching . . . I don't agree with Carlyle a bit, but I do enjoy him.' And 'He speaks from the deep springs of life . . . but when he would apply his eminent spiritual wisdom to the course of legislation, he is no more sagacious nor useful nor temperate than a flash of lightning in a grocer's shop.'

9 April 1958   *Grundisburgh*

So few recognise *power* when they come across it. They boggle at Carlyle's 'message' or his politics or religion. His father at family prayers read the story of Joseph and Potiphar's wife, closed the bible and said 'Aye, and thou wast a bitch, woman' in a loud angry voice as if she was sitting there.

I agree in resenting false teeth,[2] though I have long been in the

---

[1] She had recently died.
[2] R.H.-D. had admitted to a horror of them.

state of Miss Bobby Bennett's mother 'who imparted to me the surprising confidence that she had only two teeth in her head but thank
God, they met'.[1] It is tragically sad that E. Œ Somerville lost all her
love of the Irish at the end of her life. The rebels had burnt her
brother's house,[2] though the S. family had always been popular with
the neighbours and done a great deal for them. I should have liked
to tell her that my father, my sister and I *all* had *The Irish R.M.* at
our bedside.

13 April 1958   *Bromsden Farm*
By hugging the library fire I have managed to drag Oscar another
fifty footnotes towards completion. My present knowledge of the
Parisian underworld of letters in the late Nineties would fill an issue
of the *News of the World*, though all dates and facts are hard to pin
down. I have also read (or at any rate plodded glumly through)
Stephen Potter's new and allegedly funny manuscript. *Gamesmanship*
made me laugh a lot, and its two successors were just good enough
(all three still sell prodigiously), but the world has moved (death-
wards, you may say) in the last ten years, and Potter hasn't budged
an inch. In truth the joke is played out, but he won't face the fact.
This manuscript consists of a bunch of marginal articles written
during the past six years and slung together with the minimum of
care. What am I to say to him? Some dreary compromise, I
suppose—what a bore!
    I never met Miss Somerville either, but I corresponded with her,
and won her approval by playing up to her belief that Miss Ross was
still collaborating with her *d'outre tombe*. I fancy Miss S. was a great
spiritualist in her latter days.
    Last week, walking to the London Library, I passed the little dead-
end called Apple Tree Yard, between Jermyn Street and St James's
Square. William Nicholson had a fine studio there for many years and
I was often a visitor. His great delight was to give one lunch in a tiny
dark harness-room (the whole place had been a stable)—either herrings or lobsters, both of which were obtained from an adjacent

[1] In *Some Experiences of an Irish R.M.* by E. Œ. Somerville and Martin Ross.
[2] G.W.L. is in error here: they rather shot dead her brother Boyle, a retired
Admiral, when he answered his front door, in 1936.

fishmonger's with the splendidly eighteenth-century name of Dash & Bellamy. The shop is still there, but its name has marched downhill with the Common Man.

Don't you love names of pith and character? Our Henley butcher (though long run by others) retains its original name, Gabriel Machin, and the pleasure of writing it helps to alleviate the boredom and irritation of the monthly cheques. I had always been struck by the extraordinary names Henry James gave his characters—did ever a novel have such an off-putting start as 'She waited, Kate Croy'?

17 April 1958   *Grundisburgh*
[R.H.-D. said he'd never been to a sheepdog trial, and would much like to, just once.]

Yes of course you must go to one sheep-dog trial, but if you are with s-d *fans* remember to have a pressing engagement in, at longest, an hour. Then you will enjoy it. It is the third hour which gets one down. Best of all of course is to come accidentally across a fell-side shepherd on, say Helvellyn, giving orders to his dog on Skiddaw.

The Alingtons some years ago found a man at their gate knocked out by a motor-car. Lavinia their doctor-daughter had him brought in and put on a sofa, and then came and told her parents 'Believe it or not, but his name is Gotobed'. Yet I have a feeling that it is not as rare as one might think—like Lord Emsworth's pig-man 'Wellbeloved'. I am pleased that a leading scientist who once stridently declared 'the spark-gap to-day is mightier than the pen' should be called Hogben. That vast tome of his called *Science for the Million* contains obiter dicta such as 'Time will come when Johnson will be remembered, *if at all, for his ineptitudes*'! I am sure he is a man to whom one can safely apply the adjective 'rebarbative', a word I have never used before and doubt if I ever shall again, any more than I have and shall the word 'ambivalent' which is compulsory in almost any *New Statesman* review.

23 April 1958   *Grundisburgh*
Is this the workaday world, or is it some species of fairyland? You will wonder at the question till I tell you a series of facts. Last *Thursday* Pamela was rung up by the B.B.C. and told Humphrey was to be the victim in the 'This is your Life' programme on *Monday*. Would she

or I come and take part? No. Could his old nurse or governess? Both dead. His old tutor? Abroad, address not known. His friends? Well, yes, we told them the names we could think of. His sisters? One possibly from Eton, but alas the one who knew him best, Mary, was in Malaya, so of course couldn't come. Oh couldn't she! We'll fly her over, and back. And so they did for her seven or eight minutes with H. We saw the half-hour; it was quite amusing. The best thing in it was H's face when he heard Mary's voice outside. M. says the flight must cost them about £350, and others were flown in from all over England. Does it make sense to you? Didn't Macaulay take a year to get to India?[1] The number of people who watch TV is staggering. I went in to Ipswich yesterday, and *everyone* I met, except two, had seen the show, and reproached me for not being in it. It is obvious that it will soon be regarded as a *duty* to appear if asked. Also that in ten years or less a house without a TV will be as out of date as one without a water-closet.

After Edel's biography of Henry James I embark on Gordon Ray's Thackeray volumes, once again trying to find out why I dislike T. as a man. Is it (in the words of that very far from stupid man Hugh Kingsmill) because of his 'claret and Ecclesiastes melancholy, and nervous insistence on his gentlemanliness'? Something of the kind, I think. I used to love *Esmond*, but I remember P. Lubbock once saying that 'after a time you began to see how it was done' and that spoilt it.

27 April 1958   *Bromsden Farm*
I've just spent a whole hour listening to a broadcast of an interview with Harry Truman. I've always had an immense admiration for him, which this talk only enhanced. He seems to me a wonderful argument for the American political system at its best. A little haberdasher from Missouri who had to decide to drop the first atom bomb, to intervene in Korea, to run the Berlin air-lift, to fire General MacArthur—a man of immense courage, honesty and common sense. I only wish he was still there!

Bob Boothby, whom I dined with the other night, told me he'd just seen Monty, newly returned from the U.S.A., who said that Eisenhower is firing on one cylinder and can't string two consecutive

---

[1] No. Four months.

sentences together: it really is appalling. Boothby also said that Winston was so decrepit when he went to the House last week that they can't believe he'll last very long. This was at White's, where my usually somewhat glum dinner with my old father was turned into a feast of fun by Bob's presence.

30 April 1958   *Grundisburgh*
I agree with you (as so nearly, and I hope not boringly, always) about Truman, who met great seas of derision, pity, patronage, advice, and detailed denigration with unvarying calm, and, without any roaring or lashing of tail, was clearly as brave as a lion, and perfectly clear too about what he meant to do. But I am merely dotting your eyes! (i's).

I want you to say if *you* are a Thackeray fan. Somehow I don't expect you are. I continue to dislike him, but rather less. I mean the man. His early stuff remains intolerably unfunny and foully mushy in places. All that resolute jocularity is very trying, don't you find? Yet the old chap had guts and never threw up the sponge. But too often he makes me hot all over, and I hate heat. (Gosh, what a day—exactly the right temperature, a world of daffodils and bird-song all round me, all the green of exactly the right tint, etc etc.)

I must go to supper. There will be haddock cooked in—I think—cream, as Pamela knows how to do it, and a French cheese by no means to be cursorily dismissed. To end, I shall eat a ginger-nut (with my coffee) which must come from Huntley & Palmer and no one else. Then I shall read some more Thackeray with some little bouts of senile sleep—and a Wodehouse short story in bed.

P.S. And bed will not be before midnight.

Saturday, 3 May 1958   *Bromsden Farm*
I don't know whether I'm a Thackeray fan or not: certainly I'm not strongly agin him. I loved *Vanity Fair* in youth, and *Pendennis* later, and *Esmond* sometime, but I never liked that arch way of taking the reader aside, and treating the characters for the moment as puppets. Some of his journalism is good: I remember 'The Second Funeral of Napoleon', but I never cared for *The Rose and the Ring*, which my father always thrust down our throats. How I should love an opportunity of re-reading W.M.T.'s complete *oeuvre*: how long, oh Lord, how long?

135

The Briary
8 May 1958   *Eton College*
It is the *man* Thackeray I cannot get to like—hardly any of his letters
seem to me at all interesting, and their humour is such fourth-form
Victorian (why does he always call his horse his *'oss*—and does 'duty'
spelt 'jewty' split *your* sides?). But *V.F., P.,* and *E.* I grant you are *good*
but for the button-holing. I expect Dickens was a good deal of a
twirp, John Forster clearly was dreadful.[1]

What fun memorial services of beloved relatives are, when there
is no tragedy about the passing—and how dear old Hester Alington
would have relished the very general pleasure at the meeting of old
friends after singing her requiem in Lower Chapel. Some of my con-
tempories do look every bit as decayed and scruffy as no doubt I
look to them. One is frequently reminded of that remark of some
old old peasant-woman in Synge that 'Old age is a poor untidy
thing' and of course Winston's reference to 'the surly advance of
decrepitude'.

15 May 1958   *Grundisburgh*
I read *The Stricken Deer*[2] at the Hoods'. Of all unnecessary sources of
insanity, is there any more absurd than the fear of everlasting Hellfire?
Odd that our ancestors never for a moment realised what utter condemnation the theory establishes of the character of the Creator. Also
that eternal torture is impossible. One would get used to it, or go so
entirely mad as to be unconscious of it.

But I have no reason to suppose you are at all interested in
eternal punishment. Probably you might even refer to the figure of
God in a religious picture as Roger Fry did when lecturing to students,viz as 'this important mass'—one of the nice things in Plomer's
book.

I never asked about your session at the dentist. Most unimagina-
tive and unsympathetic of me. Fifty years ago I experienced *all* the
sensations possible at the dentist's—from the clear, clean flame-like
agony of a nerve extracted without *any* anaesthetic to the degraded
humiliations of a stump *gouged* out with a sharp spike.

---

[1] Dickens' friend and biographer.
[2] Lord David Cecil's biography of the poet William Cowper.

Sunday night
Next week looks like being a hellish rush: into an already crammed
engagement-book are bursting Elisabeth Beerbohm and (separately,
bien entendu) Alistair Cooke. They will both expect time and attention—oh for June 6 and my lodge in the wilderness! Unlike you I am
not at heart a social or gregarious person. The fact that I am tolerably
good at coping with people is misleading. I much prefer near-soli-
tude, at any rate for long periods. Maybe too much of it would drive
me back to the world of men, but I've never had enough leisure to
test the theory, and see little chance of it for years to come. So, on
with the dance, let joy be unconfined.

One night last week I gave a dinner at the Garrick for Kathleen
Coburn, the Coleridge expert, and two other friends. Afterwards we
took a taxi to K.C.'s flat for more talk. I told the driver '26 Brunswick
Square,' and he said in a cultured voice: 'Let me see, which one is
that? I always get confused between those Hanoverian squares.' And
sure enough, he took us to Mecklenburgh Square. I thought his
remark a curious *trait de moeurs*:
In Yorkshire, despite the 'Telly', I shall find simpler folk:

bright and fierce and fickle is the South,
And dark and true and tender is the North.[1]

21 May 1958   *Grundisburgh*
The Strachey book[2] has interesting things, but is on the whole heavy-
ish going, with much repetition.

L.S. (who somehow was rather repellent, physically) is like those
people (I know several) whom one always rather dislikes when they
are not there. One does, so to speak, outgrow much of *Eminent
Victorians*, but last night I took up *Elizabeth and Essex* and by gum!
anyone who sneers at his style is surely a fool. The real flaw in S. is not
that he had no religion, but he had no understanding at all of anyone
who had; he didn't know what it, or they, meant. How hard it is to
tell the truth, and how few do it. I treasure Housman's sentence

---

[1] Tennyson, *The Princess*.
[2] *Lytton Strachey: his Mind and Art* by C.R. Sanders (1957).

(omitted from his famous lecture at the last moment): 'Not only is it difficult to know the truth about anything, but to tell the truth when one knows it, to find words that will not obscure or pervert it, is in my experience an exhausting effort.'

You call me 'social and gregarious'. I grant you I never draw breath when in company, but I repudiate 'gregarious'. I flatly refuse almost all cocktail parties and recently the Lady Albemarle who lives not far off told someone she understood I was a *recluse*. Long may she think so.

Your taxi-driver! The re-grouping of the classes? I heard last week that a markedly 'wet' old boy of mine, whom I had never heard from or of since he left thirty years ago, is now the station-master at Swindon, i.e. the most important junction in S. England! What on earth does one know of anyone?

Whit Monday, 26 May 1958   *Bromsden Farm*

I am trusting—and hoping indeed—that you didn't see my TV nonsense yesterday. My mouth became, and remained, as dry as a sanddune. (James Fisher, who has done it hundreds of times, told me afterwards that his is always the same.) On the whole the questions weren't too bad—part literary, part ornithological, part general—and the chief difficulty is in having to give an *immediate* answer. 'Yeats wrote "Too great a sacrifice can make a stone of the heart". What is the Brains Trust's opinion of this?' 'What books would you recommend as a picture of the 1920s?' 'Why are no great hymns written nowadays?' And so on. After brief reflection one could cook up some sort of an answer, but out of the blue, under all those hot lights, it's hard—until, I suppose, one has done it a number of times. Comfort said I looked very nervous to begin with—as indeed I felt. Goodness knows what the other *three million* viewers made of it all! Mercifully the number is so large as to be almost unimaginable. Anyhow I retired the richer by forty-five guineas, and shall certainly do it again if I am asked—which I very much doubt.[1]

Incidentally, how would you define the difference between pride and vanity? And is humility the opposite or absence of both? You see what effect the Brains Trust is having on me!

[1] I never was.

G.K. Chesterton, Shaw, Alington, William Temple are the only men
I can think of who could answer immediately and convincingly, but
one only heard *them* after they had had much practice. It is interesting to know that Rebecca West (much the cleverest woman in
England) is a flop on any Brains Trust—just as the omniscient Lecky
after five minutes' agonised thought in that paper-game (all the
famous people you can think of whose names begin with H.) is said
to have produced Hengist and Horsa and no more. Your only question I could have answered at all is the one about hymns (why no
great ones today?) the answer being that the demand is less, and the
existing supplies are ample. Though 'O Valiant Hearts' is as good as
any—and many streets better than e.g. 'There is a fountain filled
with blood, Drawn from Emmanuel's veins' which M.D. Hill used
to say made him feel physically sick (besides being manifestly
untrue).

I was staying with friends at Oxford and we had one excellent
evening when John Sparrow dined. What good value he is—and, as
no doubt you know, he loves the Lit. Soc. Why hasn't he written
more? Perhaps the All Souls Wardenship fills his time—but there is
nothing of which a Cambridge man knows less than of All Souls.

I put it to you that e.g. Milton, like all Puritans according to
Macaulay, had invincible pride before men and utter humility before
God, that there is no evidence that he was proud about his poetry,
but plenty that he was vain about his blindness *not* spoiling his looks;
that J. Caesar wasn't a bit proud of straddling the world like a colos-
sus but *was* vain of his looks, and liked the senate's permission to wear
the laurel-wreath on his bald head more than all his other honours;
that Dizzy was invulnerable to censure or abuse, but it demanded the
greatest tact to dissuade him from inflicting his abominable French
on the Berlin Conference. But you know lots more.

The Glorious First of June has proved wet and dull. The laburnums
droop like yellow tears, and the cuckoo calls through a waterfall.
Surely my Yorkshire mountain-top will be kinder.

All the known 'viewers' agree that the television cameras treated me
to a benevolent elongation, so that instead of Holbein's Henry VIII,

which they expected, they were served up an old Cavalry Colonel painted by El Greco.

I am devoted to Sparrow, but his idleness is not due to the duties of his Wardenship, which are almost nonexistent. He suffers (don't we all?) from a delightful congenital idleness, which this post (the plum of all academic jobs in the country) has gently fostered. Almost ever since I have known him (we met as undergraduates in 1926) he has been meditating and preparing a book on Mark Pattison. Did you know that he was a boy-prodigy? He edited Donne's *Devotions* for Cambridge, also Cowley and Bishop King for the Nonesuch Press, soon after he left Winchester.

Framlingham Chase

Norwich

4 June 1958

Have you ever stayed at a 'Chase'? Do you know what a 'Chase' is? (I don't.) One seems somehow in a Scott-Lever[1]-Trollope atmosphere, and there is even something of Mrs Knox's[2] establishment about it—you remember, a miserable soup in a marvellous old silver tureen followed by a perfect salmon on a cracked kitchen dish. When it comes to writing-paper and envelopes, a good deal of thoughtful research is necessary, and as for pens—. But it is all very delightful and hospitable, and after all those who originally dwelt in Chases had no truck with pens and paper. Communication with all and sundry was via varlets and scurvy knaves astride of palfreys or stots perhaps of comely grey, pricking over moor and fen. From where I am writing, I can see cedars of Lebanon that are said to have been planted in the reign of Queen Bess. They make me feel a mere ephemerid, a grasshopper (I speak of the soul rather than of the body). It was Bismarck who always said he preferred trees to men, and in the heart of a Chase like this one sees why—with a great deal of sympathy.

John Sparrow. What you say is most interesting. That exhaustion of the precocious happens more often than it should to Wykehamists because frankly they do work their best scholars too hard. They win everything at Oxford and peter out by thirty.

[1] Charles Lever, Irish novelist (1806–1872).
[2] A character in *Some Experiences of an Irish R.M.*

I took up last week the letters of T.E. Lawrence—which clearly should have been edited by you. You would have eliminated much of that endless jaw about the *Seven Pillars* and his ultimately repellent utterances about its entire worthlessness, which never strike me, at least, as quite sincere. I don't wonder that many of far less venomous spirit than Aldington have been allergic to him, but I expect you have noticed that, like G.B.S., everyone loved him who knew him in person and not only on paper. He had a very wayward literary judgment; has anyone else found *The Odyssey* artificial and third-rate?

Kisdon Lodge
Keld

9 June 1958
The worst of living deliciously in lotos-land is that it is always afternoon—in the words of the harassed theatrical landlady, 'Half-past four, and not a po emptied.' I haven't shaved or seen a newspaper since last Thursday, but locusts are plentiful and it looks like a good year for wild honey. Each time I come here I am overwhelmed all over again, first by the beauty of the surroundings, and then by the majestic *silence*. Except for an occasional moor-bird's cry or bleat of distant sheep, there is simple *no sound* from dawn to dusk, and I sit entranced with wonder at this simple fact. You remember the lines about silence coming like a poultice to heal the wounds of sound: well, that is just my state, poulticed, grateful, but not in any way very active.

Kisdon Lodge
Keld

17 June 1958
[Donald Somervell had told R.H.-D. 'several anecdotes he'd told me before, including one I'd told him, but made up for it by quoting verbatim a footnote by Gibbon'.]
I hadn't time before I left London to look up Gibbon on the Giraffe, but will do so as soon as I get back. Meanwhile my faulty memory of Donald Somervell's excellent one is that the footnote starts: 'The tallest, gentlest and most useless of the larger mammals. *Camelopardus Maximus*. Little seen in Europe since the Revival of Learning . . .' That last phrase is superb, with its picture of herds of giraffes retreating from a platoon of greybearded scholars.

20 June 1958   *Grundisburgh*

I suppose you *must* read all through Alfred Douglas for O.W's sake. I always think of him as a pitiful figure, the seamed haggard face dominated by that dreadful white and bulbous nose (a really white nose I put it to you is worse than a red one, which, however ugly, is at least suggestive of one-time bonhomie and conviviality, however abused and prolonged). Though are not some of his sonnets very good and (of course) much underrated? At one time he said his life's object was:

> To fight with form, to wrestle and to rage
> Till at the last upon the conquered page
> The shadows of created Beauty fall.

I have just been at the Abbey School Malvern telling the Sixth Form about reading—my gist being largely that they should ignore all damning criticism of old or established authors but not the laudatory, and nearly all of both concerning contemporaries. And that few utterances written or spoken are more fatuous then 'Nobody can afford to miss . . .' and 'Nobody reads X (e.g. Tennyson, Browning, Meredith, Moore) now'.

Why *do* you do these things?[1] From now on you must cultivate the habit of some medieval monastery, where the monks, when summoned by the Abbot to consider and discuss some new proposal, all fell asleep and only woke up when he paused, to say '*Namus, namus*' (i.e. 'we're agin it', short for *Damnamus*) and then fell asleep again.

                                        Kisdon Lodge
23 June 1958   *Keld*

The sale last Wednesday was great fun. It took place in a meadow in a little village near Thirsk (about fifty miles away) on the hottest and sunniest day of my holiday. By great good luck I secured a lovely grandfather clock for £1 (tell Pamela), made in Thirsk and I imagine always housed in the neighbourhood.

---

[1] R.H.-D. had become chairman of a committee to create a fund 'for the advancement and maintenance of literature, authors and the theatre', the money to come from a royalty on all out-of-copyright books. It was later christened the Phoenix Trust.

I hate leaving this beautiful place, the silence, the wonderful air, the ticking grandfather and warm Aladdin lamp, the earth closet, the water fetched in buckets from a spring in the next field, with a high stone wall to climb in between.

29 June 1958   *Bromsden Farm*
The London Library's rating-appeal comes on tomorrow morning at 10.30 before the Lands Tribunal in Hanover Square. Both T.S. Eliot and I have to give evidence, though in fact everything depends on the persuasive oratory of our counsel, Mr Geoffrey Lawrence QC.

I have now finished with the works of Alfred Douglas.

> To clutch life's hair, and thrust one naked phrase
> Like a lean knife between the ribs of Time.

are certainly remarkable lines. His tragedy was much longer and less dramatic than Oscar's.

As long as I manage to avoid Henley Regatta I shall be content. For a fortnight the town is intolerable, with all possible prices raised—for regulars as well as visitors—you know, all those fat men in tiny pink caps. Why in rowing alone do the old hands have to turn up in fancy dress?

2 July 1958   *Grundisburgh*
I wish I could be optimistic about the result [of the Tribunal], but I have, like everybody else, become so used, in any and every such case, to see the worse cause vanquish the better that I am full of apprehension. And there is no greater offender than the law, since almost every judge rather sheepishly defends a manifestly unjust law by saying he has no power except to administer it. The oases of civilisation are daily more beset by the sandstorms of barbarism. As I told one of my girls' schools last week, schools are once again, as in the middle-ages monasteries were, the last desperate strongholds of 'sweetness and light,' and warned them that when they go out into the world, they will find most of the standards they have learnt derided or ignored or even actively attacked.

P.S. I see a scientist has said that beer, milk, tea, fried food, early marriage and celibacy all help cancer. And scientists expect us not to think them B.F.'s! *Zu Dienstag.*

The Tribunal was exhausting but fun. It lasted four full days of legal time (10.30-4 with an hour off for lunch) and we probably shan't get the decision for at least a month. Our counsel, Geoffrey Lawrence Q.C., was superb, both in his pleading and in his treatment of witnesses. The two opposing counsel seemed like cart-horses matched with a thoroughbred. Lawrence made me the first witness, hoping that I might be able to knock the shine off the ball before Eliot came in. Somehow I scrambled through, but to read the verbatim shorthand account next day was highly chastening. 'Tell me, Mr Hart-Davis', said the rating authority's counsel, 'what is the touchstone by which you distinguish literature from other written matter?' 'How would you define a man of letters?' etc. It was definitely less nerve-racking than the TV Brains Trust, but one always had the feeling that every question concealed a trap. Eliot was terribly nervous, but warmed to his work and finished in fine fettle, rather sorry that he wasn't asked more. Clearly the judge was entirely on our side, and it is simply a question of the law.

Very hot in the train yesterday, and unfortunately, as I was wearing braces, I could not doff my jacket. Why is it all right to reveal any garment and practically the whole human frame, but never braces? Very odd. *My* braces, at least, have nothing provocative or suggestive about them. Perhaps that elderly man, who finds women with one or no legs more erotically exciting than any others, could throw some light on the matter.

I have frequently since seeing you pondered that question they put to you, viz How you distinguish 'literature' from other written matter. I think Housman would have said it was as unanswerable as he said was great poetry—as a rat to a dog. You know it when you meet it, but define it? No.

Lawyers' emphasis on *fact* often obscures *truth*, as it did when Edith Thompson was condemned, when that rather dreadful man Mr Justice Shearman actually interrupted her counsel's address to the jury to underline that they must think of nothing but the facts, and not try to weigh their possible meanings. Has any *good* judge worn a moustache as he did? Or run the hundred yards for Oxford? Sprinters always try to beat the pistol, therefore are essentially unscrupulous and unreliable. I hate judges when they moralise and tell the jury they are sure they view the fact that the woman in the dock slept with some man 'with the utmost detestation and horror'. I prefer the perfectly true comment of—who was it?—who when some teetotal ass said he would rather commit adultery than drink a glass of port said 'So would we all, my dear L., so would we all.'

P.S. I thought your secretary charming!

13 July 1958   *Bromsden Farm*

Before I forget it, the Gibbon reference is Vol I, Chap IV: the marginal heading reads:

'Commodus displays his skill in the amphitheatre'. Donald had slightly improved the footnote, which in fact reads thus:
Commodus killed a camelopardalis or Giraffe (Dion. I. lxxii.p. 1211.), the tallest, the most gentle, and the most useless of the large quadrupeds. This singular animal, a native only of the interior parts of Africa, has not been seen in Europe since the revival of letters; and though M. de Buffon (Hist. Naturelle, tom xiii) has endeavoured to describe, he has not ventured to delineate, the Giraffe.

She whom you praised is not my secretary, but my assistant, right hand and great joy these twelve years past. You shall see and hear more of her in due time. Needless to say, your success with her was instantaneous and immense.

St Swithin [15 July] 1958   *Grundisburgh*

I didn't know O.W. was fond of Matthew Arnold's poetry. My *bête noire* is 'who prop, thou ask'st, in these bad days, my mind?' which challenges Browning's 'Irks care the cropful bird' in 'Rabbi Ben Ezra'. *Per contra* 'Thyrsis' and 'The Scholar Gypsy' are utterly lovely, and why the hell, when I *could* learn, didn't I learn them by heart? And I hope never to read Sohrab's death without that tingle behind the eyeballs, because then I shall be dead in any sense that matters. I rather wish he hadn't given us that simile of Rustum eyeing S. much as a rich lady in bed eyes the 'slavey' (1890) who comes to lay her fire, because surely it diminishes instead of heightening the incident, like the comparison I came across not long ago of the sound of the sea to the swish of feminine skirts, which is to me a good many poles away from

> Black leagues of forest roaring like the sea
> And far lands dim with rain

describing (I think) the view from Luther's Wartburg.

Your *ten* to lunch gives me a headache. On your rest-day too! But how like you are to Florence Nightingale: 'Rest! Rest! Have we not all eternity to rest in?' But is rest restful if you never wake? Socrates said nothing was more enjoyable than dreamless sleep. But not, surely, till you wake up? One often agrees with Macaulay, who thought many of S's dialectical victories were too easy.

20 July 1958   *Bromsden Farm*

I always leave Sunday evening, the last of my weekend, free for writing to you, and if anything intervenes there is no time left. This time it was my daughter's second *crise de nerfs*. She has been perfectly happy while her young man has been home on leave, but this evening, as his departure approached, she became very emotional and overwrought. After Comfort had driven him off to Reading, the poor child broke down, and I had to spend an hour trying to comfort and calm her. Just as her mother did twenty-five years ago, she worries terribly about dying and not believing in God. I tried to persuade her that most people go through something of the same sort, and that when she is happily married and having children she'll be too busy to spend time brooding.

24 July 1958   *Grundisburgh*

Foolish grown-ups always talk as if the sorrows of the young are light and transient, and of course to hindsight they may be, but they are devilish heavy at the time, for the young can't see the silver lining— indeed have insufficient experience to know that there always is one, and *time* weighs so crushingly at that age: 'the years like great black oxen tread the world'.[1] The best advice of all is my old friend Charles

---

[1] W.B. Yeats, *The Countless Cathleen*.

Fisher's to a hesitating bridge-player: 'Play the card next your thumb.'
It is much better advice for life than for bridge.

I often find it hard to see why people *should* believe in God, as I
once said to Hester Alington. Her answer was that He certainly did
make it very difficult, and at such moments one *mustn't worry* but go
desperately on—Charles Fisher's line in fact. Much harm—especially
to the young—is done by pious folk who pretend that it is all clear
and easy and comfy—but as our common friend Carlyle said 'With
stupidity and sound digestion a man may front much'.

My *internal* pessimism is black and immovable—not mere funk,
because I should not greatly mind if I passed away tomorrow, but at
the strong possibility that Macbeth was perfectly right in calling life
a tale told by an idiot etc. What, except luck, is to prevent three
hundred years of painfully acquired civilisation from going up in
smoke? But this is vain talk, because a genuine pessimist wouldn't
enjoy as I do 'books, and my food, and summer rain'.[1]

You will be pleased to hear that the Wykehamist entries for the
Tennyson paper did contemptibly, and so I said in my report.

27 July 1958   *Bromsden Farm*
The London Library Annual General Meeting was attended by 150
or more members. T.S.E. led off mellifluously and then we swapped
chairs, and for almost an hour and a half I stood up answering questions—an exhausting process, and for the first time in my life I had
recourse to the water on the table. However, all went well in the end,
all resolutions were carried, and the subscription was raised from six
guineas to ten. The rating verdict is to be delivered next Tuesday at
2.30: I shall attend the court to hear it.

31 July 1958   *Grundisburgh*
I am black with sympathetic rage[2], though I suspect you expected it.
In these squalid times when financial interests are opposing those that
are clearly civilised, the former always win, one of the proofs that we
are in for a new Dark Age.

---

[1] Stevenson, 'The Celestial Surgeon'.
[2] At the failure of the London Library appeal.

The signal-fires of warning
They blaze, but none regard;
And on through night to morning
The world runs ruinward.[1]

But no more of that; I suspect that you are just as impatient of my gloom as my family are. And Cassandra was murdered, and no doubt Jeremiah was too, though history is silent on the matter.

I am nearly through now, and have not committed suicide yet— even after perusing the script of Miss Betjeman (daughter of John?) who wrote *forty-eight* sides on her five answers, not solely through that cerebral diarrhoea which she shares with nearly all schoolgirls in the G.C.E., but from having so enormous a handwriting.

C.M. Wells, when primed with Hermitage, will tell you of his best innings, viz nine runs on a ruined and crumbling pitch, in the dark, against Richardson and Lockwood—and of course no protector. 'I needn't have had a bat; I was hit all over from chin to heel, but I didn't get out that night. I was bowled first ball next day.' By Tom Richardson, whose genial way it was to say as his victim passed him pavilion-wards: 'Best one I've bowled this year, sir.' All old cricketers of any aesthetic sense will tell you that Tom R bowling in 1894–8 was the finest sight in the world. And he committed suicide—like Shrewsbury, Stoddart, Albert Trott, A.E. Relf and many others. I wonder why. 'Sir, you *may* wonder.' As so often, Dr Johnson provides the only answer.

It is the shadow over so many of my summers—the sight of ruined or spoilt harvest, hay or corn. Nature is a tremendous ass, besides being quite inartistic as O.W. said.

It is a gorgeous day here, and shortly I leave the summer-house for lunch, where I shall have beans and bacon (the *de rigueur* dish at all Worcestershire *archery* meetings in the early Nineties. Have you kept up your archery, as Roger Ascham insisted?) and raspberries and cream, and anyone who wants a better lunch than that can whistle for it—he won't get it.

4 August 1958   *Bromsden Farm*
Last night I finished the typescript of Peter's new book, *The Siege at Peking*, which he unexpectedly brought on Saturday, eager for an

[1] A.E. Housman, *More Poems*, XLIII.

immediate (and reassuring) verdict. This I was luckily able to give, for I found the story absorbing and excellently told.

We all went to the Lands Tribunal to hear the old fool[1] deliver his judgment, which he read from a typescript, haltingly and with a thick but soft brogue which made hearing difficult. This appeal has cost the Library well over £2000, and I can't think there's much point in our spending even more to hear the same miserable points of law argued before three judges in the Court of Appeal: however we are to have a meeting with Lawrence next week, at which all will be decided. I think the next move is a public appeal for money (letter in *The Times*): apart from the legal costs, we now owe the Revenue some £12,000 of arrears, incurred while our appeals have dragged along.

Of course I like broad beans: in fact I like almost all food except various branches of offal—and I might even like them if I didn't know what they were. I love liver and kidneys, so why should I be repelled by the thought of heart, head, brains and trotters? I particularly like spinach in all its manifestations.[2]

16 August 1958   *Bromsden Farm*
I had another meeting with Geoffrey Lawrence, at which we decided to carry the London Library's case on to the Court of Appeal. I'm sure this is the right thing to do, for reasons too complicated for enclosure here, but to be told you when we meet.

And now, as promised, and very much for your eye alone, I shall briefly tell you about my darling Ruth. She is a little older than I am, her maiden name was Ware, and she was brought up in Herefordshire, where her father was a choleric and impoverished man of leisure who captained the county in the Minor Counties championship. When she was nineteen she went up to London and got a job with a Jewish printer called Oliver Simon, a very good and successful typographer and printer of fine editions. He fell in love with her, proposed, and out of a mixture of being flattered and feeling grownup she accepted him. She was never in the least in love with him: he had a fearful inferiority complex and a nervous grin: his

[1] See last sentence in R.H.-D.'s letter on p. 144.
[2] In his next G.W.L. said, 'You are not, I hope, repelled by sweetbreads.' R.H.-D. said he loved them and wondered 'who brilliantly coined that name to obscure the physiological truth.'

mother was a Rothenstein (sister of Will the painter) and they all came from Bradford. They had two children, who are charming. The marriage staggered on unhappily.

I must now switch to Comfort. She is one of the (I suspect) many women whose sex instincts are in fact wholly directed to the production of children, and when their quiver is full they want no more (as they say in the courts) intercourse. So it was with her: when we married in 1933 she was passionate and gay, but after Adam's conception in 1942 she had had enough. I bore this enforced chastity uneasily for four years: if I had been a person who could flit from flower to flower, that might have provided a solution: but I am not: sex to me is indissolubly linked with love. And then in 1946 I met Ruth, and we fell in love like steel-filings rushing to a magnet. It was touch and go whether we didn't elope immediately, but somehow we held on, for our families' sake. I told Comfort about it, and she took it wonderfully, saying she was rather relieved on the sexual side, but hoped I wouldn't break up the family. I said I wouldn't. Ruth told her husband, who preferred to play the ostrich and go on pretending he knew nothing. Soon after this I got Ruth into my business, where she has been my prop and right hand ever since. For twelve years now we have been lovers in every sense, always blissfully happy together, with a complete unity of interests and of stillness. We are together in the office, in my flat whenever possible, and best of all in Yorkshire. We first visited that neighbourhood in 1947, and have been thereabouts every year since, but it wasn't till 1954 that we found the ruined cottage which we have restored and christened Kisdon Lodge. It had had sheep in it for fifty years, so in its new incarnation it is our creation, our child—the one place we can be quite alone.

I would have told you all this years ago, but first I thought you might be shocked, and then the opportunity never seemed to come. Two years ago Ruth's husband died, which made her life much easier. Now her children have left home, and one is married.

Sometimes we wonder whether our love has been fostered by all our difficulties, and then we think that perhaps it must be very strong to surmount so much. What the end will be I don't know, but on Tuesday we set off for another blessed fortnight. I wrote most of *Hugh Walpole* in Yorkshire, with R. typing each page as I finished it, and criticising brilliantly. Comfort is so used to the set-up that it is seldom mentioned. Sometimes she is unhappy, I fear, but I can find no better solution.

20 August 1958   University Arms Hotel
I am much honoured and touched by the story you tell in your last. It is, you know, something like an idyll—like the Book of Ruth! I mean of course objectively, because to you it is much more than that. Nothing was ever truer than *Amor vincit omnia* (as Chaucer's Prioress, in whose company I have been for a week, wore on her brooch) and both *Amor* and *vincit* have a score of meanings, from the depths to the heights— as indeed *omnia* does too. There really is something triumphant in what you tell me and in the way you have handled an immeasurably difficult situation—made so by the Immanent Will, which so often and so dis- astrously allows the union between this man and that woman, which seemed so promising, to be harmed, and it may be ruined, by deep and unforeseen and unmendable discrepancies. Shocked!! I can't think you really thought I might be that. (Though I dislike those—often young women—who proclaim that they are 'unshockable'.) But I only by what strikes me forcibly as vulgar or mean or cruel, none of which ele- ments remotely enter the love-story of Rupert and Ruth. Please let me meet her again some day soon—by which date you will (probably) have been able to convince her that I am less old and hidebound and slow- witted than I look:—or at least that all the good wishes my heart holds for you shall always include her too.

I have to be very tactful and reticent these days, as you will under- stand when I tell you that the livelier of my colleagues thinks *The Dynasts* 'dull stuff', *The Irish R.M.* moderately funny, Carlyle and Meredith intolerable, H. James an old humbug, has never heard of *Earlham*—and hates porridge. Another, when D.H. Lawrence is den- igrated, behaves rather like Dr Arnold when St Paul was by someone put above St John. 'He burst into tears and begged that the subject might never again be mentioned in his presence'—so Arthur Benson tells it.

                                              Kisdon Lodge
25 August 1958   Keld
You've no idea what pleasure your letter gave us both. I knew you'd see the point, but you did so in a particularly wholehearted and

delightful way. Bless you. I fancy the period during which I thought you might be shocked must have been brief, and after that I hesitated for fear of appearing unnecessarily disloyal to Comfort. She is a wholly *good* person—no vice in her at all, unselfish, uncomplaining, hardworking, but also now utterly unsentimental, with her deeper feelings so submerged as to be unguessable. Mercifully this teaching occupies and to a certain extent satisfies her. Enough of that.

I can't remember how much I've told you about the cottage. It consists of two rooms, one above the other, each with a tiny room opening off it. The bedroom is wide and low, with a miraculous view. The sitting-room contains two comfortable arm-chairs, four other chairs, a wide kitchen table, and a superb desk-bookcase-chest-of-drawers (£1 at a sale). A splendid old range-fire downstairs, and a little coal one upstairs, which we light every night, for the luxury and pure pleasure of it. The tiny downstairs room is a combined pantry-kitchen-larder, in which we had a sink installed. All the water we fetch in buckets from a spring in the next field. We wash in a basin by the fire.

When we have to go shopping—usually to Hawes in Wensleydale, eight miles away over a steep pass—we pack all our purchases into haversacks and carry them up the hill. It's a precipitous twenty minute climb up a rough track: only a tractor or a jeep can manage it on wheels.

27 August 1958   *Grundisburgh*
I inherit an abiding pessimism from my father. And somehow his defence, viz that if you always expect the worst, all the surprises you get in life are pleasant ones, like all other philosophical theories, ought to be more reassuring than it is. One or two things said by old James Forsyte always remind me of him, e.g. J.F.'s gloom about his cellar after his death: his excellent claret 'would be spoilt or drunk, he shouldn't wonder'. Surely that 'or drunk' is a delicious touch. Not that my father ever took his wine seriously—or anybody else's. I never remember the Hagley claret having the chill taken off it, and I am sure he meant eulogy when he said of our extravagantly insipid port that 'it would do nobody any harm'. Like so many of that generation he got his wine from some old friend on the verge of bankruptcy.

At Cambridge I won a bet of a million pounds. A dogmatic exam-colleague, with whom I saw the *Titanic* film, said that the tune of

'Nearer My God to Thee' was by Sullivan. I said it wasn't, and when he said 'What will you bet!' I said 'A million pounds', being really quite sure, but not really wanting to take the pound off him that I know he would have bet (an excellent but cocksure fellow). Of course it is by Dykes, as so many of those honeyed tunes are which we all pretend to be superior to, but really enjoy.

Kisdon Lodge
Keld

31 August 1958

I am sitting on the flag-stones outside the cottage door in the *sun*, which has shone deliciously yesterday and today. Sunday or no Sunday, I can see farmers and their wives and families haymaking in a dozen fields far away—but you want the view described.

Swaledale is a broad green valley running pretty well east and west for some thirty miles, from Richmond to Keld, which is the end of Swaledale proper, or rather its beginning, for it is here that the River Swale first takes shape and name, fed by many mountain streams and waterfalls of great beauty. As one drives up the dale from Richmond the scenery grows gradually wilder, and here there are only very green grass fields up to where the brown-green of the fells begins towards the top of the surrounding hills. The cottage is high on one side of this wide green valley, 1600 feet above the road, on which even the twice-daily bus and an occasional lorry 'show scarce so gross as beetles'.[1] Behind us, one big field away, the fell begins. We can see as many as a dozen scattered farms, all built of the same local stone as the field-dividing walls. Cattle and sheep are the farmers' livelihood. The sheep are on the fells except in the depth of winter. A proportion of each farmer's fields is permanent pasture, and the rest kept for the hay on which the animals live in the winter. The only change ever in the look of the fields is their turning various shades of yellow-green as the hay ripens and is cut. The word 'fields' needs qualifying, since few of them are flat and many precipitous: their contours and varieties on the opposite hillside are a constant source of joy, particularly when the evening shadows deepen the ghylls and hollows with mystery and beauty. We are some way above the tree-line, and all the hilltops which stretch one beyond another

---

[1] *King Lear*, Act IV, Scene 6.

in all four directions are bare and noble. Some way below us, straight down, there is a charming wood of ash and birch and hazel, but that is invisible from here. The tiny village of Keld can just be seen to our right at the bottom. Straight ahead the furthest range to be seen (about four miles away) is in Westmorland, near Kirkby Stephen.

As it is Sunday, Ruth is frying us some sausages, bacon, tomatoes and potatoes for lunch. Usually we have a cold lunch, and always boiled eggs for our supper. The farmer's wife bakes us endless delicious cakes etc.

Here are two of Oscar's jokes, from the time when he was reviewing books for the *Pall Mall Gazette*:

Andiatoroctè is the title of a volume of poems by the Rev. Clarence Walworth, of Albany, N.Y. It is a word borrowed from the Indians, and should, we think, be returned to them as soon as possible.

K.E.V.'s little volume is a series of poems on the Saints. Each poem is preceded by a brief biography of the Saint it celebrates— which is a very necessary precaution, as few of them ever existed . . . Such lines as those on St Stephen may be said to add another horror to martyrdom. Still it is a thoroughly well-intentioned book and eminently suitable for invalids.

Ruth has arranged lovely bouquets of wildflowers all over the cottage—she always does—and they will have to be sadly committed to the flames before we leave. I've had a cheerful letter from Comfort in Scotland, where the weather seems to have been better than here.

4 September 1958   *Grundisburgh*

You have never told me whether you read in bed. Probably not, as you must always be exhausted by 12.0. But let me tell you that as a bedside book W.W. Jacobs's omnibus volumes (there are two) are unsurpassed. Each story is of the right length, and you fall asleep chuckling, which is better than any barbiturate.

I don't believe Sonia C's story[1] of that game with King Edward— sliding bread and butter pieces, butter downwards, down his trousers—not once but often. I mean, he may have been a fool about many things, but surely not about trousers?

[1] From *Edwardian Daughter* (1958) by Sonia Cubbitt, née Keppel.

Here everything is drenched and dripping, and our lawn is rather like
William Plomer's. He wrote the other day from his Sussex bungalow:
'Our lawnette, when stepped upon, closes over the ankles with a noise
like gargling, and squirts jets of water up one's leg.' Comfort says the
kitchen garden is full of interesting pond-life, never seen there
before—but we have masses of ripe and ripening *strawberries*!

Did I tell you that on one of our last Yorkshire days we picked a
jam-jar-full of wild raspberries just down the hill? Lots of harebells
still, and wild geranium, loosestrife, ragwort etc, with heather, bil-
berries and rowan berries—oh I am so homesick for it all, and shall
remain so until next June.

Oh yes—our drive to the sea was a great success. We reached
Morecambe about 1. pm, the high tide was slapping the orange-peel
up against the foot of the promenade, and we immediately saw that
bathing there was not for us. So we bought a picnic lunch and drove
on another twenty miles to Grange-over-Sands, on the other side of
the bay. It's a wholly charming little place, like a bit of Cheltenham
set down between hills and sea. We had a delicious swim off some
rocks, ate our lunch, and drove home *via* Kendal, where we had tea
and visited the tiny secondhand bookshop, then through Sedbergh
and Wensleydale, beautiful beyond words.

I was at Grange once with Tuppy Headlam and recollect nothing
beyond that he had a row—as nearly always—with the station-
master, and that a man asked if he might watch us playing billiards
on the hotel table; I made a break of six and he departed, obviously
murmuring *Nunc dimittis.*

I am humbly but testily re-reading *Emma.* I can only conclude that
the 'Janeites' are all mad. I am half-way through, and send you an
interim report, viz that the conversations in the book fall mainly
under two heads, i.e. Mrs Dale,[1] and passages to be put into Latin
Prose. Mr Woodhouse ('Oh my dear, *deliciously* amusing!') hits
exactly the same note every time he comes in, and the boringness of
Miss Bates is positively overwhelming. No more o' that i' God's name.

[1] *Mrs Dale's Diary* was a long-running radio serial.

By dint of talking very firmly—and very *loud*—for half an hour, I managed to persuade the London Library committee (of which fewer than half turned up) to endorse my plan for carrying our appeal to the Court of Appeal. Roger, Harold Nicolson and old John Hugh-Smith had previously agreed to oppose me, but Roger and Harold allowed themselves to be persuaded, and no doubt Hugh-Smith would have been too, had he not been too deaf to catch a word that anyone said. This left him in a puzzled minority of one, wondering what had happened to his allies.

The family holidays here are just ending and P. and I return to our normal Darby and Joan existence. Last Sunday we filled three pews in the parish church, which made a considerable sensation among the worshippers.

John Hugh-Smith is a rum old bird. I have known him since 1892 at prep school, and he was in Arthur Benson's house at Eton, and at Trinity. We always quarrelled, and are now bosoms, when we meet, i.e. about every five years. He was at Diana's pre-wedding party last year, his chest so heavily equipped with gadgets as to resemble the engine-room of a submarine; but he paid little attention to it and heard practically nothing that was said to him—or else, which is equally likely, heard it but paid no attention. He is a relative of Pamela's and greeted her with the breezy question 'Are all you girls still alive?', the youngest of the girls being over fifty. Luckily they all are alive; not that he would have turned a hair whatever the answer, which I don't think he waited for. I remember him asking Arthur Benson at Boys' Dinner 'Sir, would you take orders if you were in the running for the headmastership?' to which the reply was 'My dear John, that is the kind of question that should never be asked.' Was J.H-S. abashed? He was not.

Those lists which each spring and autumn reach you looking so fresh, and occasionally tempting, are always a source of the utmost mortification. Each time I am *sure* that there will be *no* books for the next list: then at the last moment I manage to scrape together a sufficiency, but by the time I have written or rewritten those frightful 'blurbs' I am so sick of them all that I can barely stand hearing them mentioned. Some weeks pass, and then the finished article always surprises me by being much less awful than I remembered.

Tiresome though it may be, I can't resist telling you that on Friday Comfort picked *three hundred* ripe strawberries (she got so bored with it that she counted them to keep herself amused).

On Friday evening I stayed up to attend the annual dinner of the book-publishers' 'travellers', where I was the guest of my London representative. The dinner itself was very good, but the proceedings lasted from 6.15 till 10.45, and there were 450 men with all the chairs and tables very close together. Two powerful singers performed and there were speeches. One of the chaps at my table asked me if I knew what the Leaning Tower of Pisa said to Big Ben—'I've got the inclination if you've got the time'.

24/25 September 1958   *Grundisburgh*
I am interested that Comfort finds counting a palliative of boredom—because that is the only way I can get through doing four hundred strokes of the hand-pump which empties the flooded cellar. There is an electric pump, but in Suffolk whenever there is a thunderstorm all electricity is cut off and the pump doesn't work. I find the best method is to count *one* 10 times, two ditto and so on. I used to recite *Paradise Lost*, but it slowed down the pumping.

When I have finished setting papers I shall embark, six hundred words apiece, on George Herbert, Herrick, Heywood, Surrey and Hakluyt for Routh.[1] I shall enjoy doing 'em, but I don't suppose they will be up to much.

28 September 1958   *Bromsden Farm*
R and I attended T.S.E.'s birthday party, at 6 p.m. Only twelve people, with champagne and birthday-cake, and all his presents laid out on a table. I lit the cake and told him he must blow all the candles out with one breath, which he meekly knelt down and did. I instigated Epstein[2] (who was nothing loth) to propose his health, and

---

[1] An Eton master compiling a small dictionary of national biography.
[2] Sir Jacob Epstein, sculptor

when we had all drunk it, T.S.E. said, very simply and with evident truth: 'This is the happiest birthday I've ever had.' Both Ruth and I have come to love him dearly: he is so affectionate, simple and modest, and in private his sense of humour is fine. We gave him a little old silver snuff box and a specially bound copy (all leather and gilt edges) of the Symposium[1] about him.

Yesterday (Saturday) I drove seventy miles to an enchanting little church at Fisherton-de-la-Mere, near Salisbury, for the memorial service to my lifetime friend Edie Nicholson (widow of the painter). It was at 3.15, and realising that Siegfried Sassoon lives only five miles away, I boldly invited myself to lunch with him. (Although we have corresponded for many years, and have numberless mutual friends, particularly E. Blunden, we had never met before.) He lives quite alone with a housekeeper in a huge and lovely Georgian house, set in a vast park, nobly timbered and surrounded by miles of wall. The spreading lawns are all long grass, except for an area next to the house. The drive is overgrown and inaccessible, so I had to leave my car by some long stables and approach the house through a shrubbery. Inside, one huge room opening into another, one after the other, all with fine books and pictures. In the hall S.S.'s bat and pads proudly displayed, for though well over seventy he still makes some runs. He is thin, tallish, good looking with a large but not noticeably Jewish nose: a tonsure-sized bald patch covered by profuse and only slightly grey hair from in front. Dressed in flannel trousers, dark blue blazer and loosish collar. Although he complained of lumbago, he rushed about speedily. He was neurotically nervous to begin with, and didn't look at me for almost an hour. He gave me a glass of sherry, said he never drank in the middle of the day, and asked whether I could manage half a bottle of claret. I said yes, and he bustled off to the cellar and returned with a half-bottle of Beycheville 1933—terrifically good—with which I washed down some fine roast duck. We talked nineteen to the dozen, about Oscar and Max (whom he knew well: he has six or seven drawings), Edmund B., Nicholson, Gosse etc. Gosse, he told me, though perfectly normal in every other way, had what can only be described as a passion for S.S.'s uncle Hamo Thornycroft, the sculptor. When someone asked Lytton Strachey whether Gosse was homosexual, L.S. said—wait for it—'No,

[1] Published by R.H.-D.

but he's Hamo-sexual', which I thought rather good. Eventually I had to tear myself away, for fear of missing the memorial service altogether. I truly believe S.S. enjoyed the visit as much as I did—which was immensely. At any rate he begged me to return as soon as possible, for as long as possible, but goodness knows when I'll have the time. He confessed to being terribly lonely, especially in the winter.

Do let me see your potted biographies when they're done. I once asked G.M. Young how to pronounce Hakluyt. He said: 'Hacklewit, of course: it's an old Devon name'. So there!

Peter flew up to Scotland the other day to shoot with Gavin Astor and the P.M. [Macmillan]. He said the air was black with grouse, and the P.M. shot well. Their best day was 160 brace.

1 October 1958   *Grundisburgh*

As to T.S.E., I have never been a fan, my line about his poetry always having been that of the old Scotch peasant-woman who, after praising a sermon, and being asked if she had understood it, replied 'Wad I hae the presoomption?' And the fans (like J. Austen's) irritate me when they ecstasize over the '*poetry*' of some line in e.g. *The Cocktail Party* like 'She will be coming later'. But don't let that make you think for a moment that I don't know he is a great man. The trouble is no doubt—and many must feel it besides me—that if one's tastes were mainly formed before 1914, one is bound to be, as regards modern writing, in a fine chaotic bewilderment in 1958.

Your account of Siegfried S. is very interesting—and sad too. *Why* is he so lonely?

I am re-reading *Hamlet*, full of the views about him of Rebecca West and Señor Madariaga, which I doubt not you know. They completely upset the age-old view of him as a gentle weak-willed visionary. Surely the actual evidence for their view is very strong, and how does the Bradleys' and Dover Wilsons' belief in his lovableness and high-mindedness square with 'I'll lug the guts' etc? It is all very strange. I wonder old Agate didn't spot it. He would have welcomed the idea that Ophelia was no innocent.

P.S. I did old Agate an injustice. He did see the ugly side of *Hamlet*, and complained that it was often so much cut about that it didn't emerge.

Siegfried has always been neurotic and homosexual: the first war shattered him beyond recall. In middle life he married Hester Gatty and had a son called George. The marriage held together precariously for some years, and then Hester left. Siegfried was pathologically affected by this, and for some time refused to speak to even his oldest friends unless they promised never to see or communicate with Hester again. E. Blunden for one refused to comply (he didn't particularly want to see her, but was sorry for her and refused to be dictated to). After some years S. took him back into favour. Now Hester lives in Scotland, George is a married scientist with no literary interests, and Siegfried is an ageing ghost in a huge disintegrating frame. When occasionally he stirs outside it and meets congenial people he enjoys it enormously, but for the most part his neurosis makes him play the hermit, writing occasional poetry and prose. He has always been well enough off.

When I was a student at the Old Vic Ernest Milton played Hamlet, not perhaps according to the latest views of today, but in a frankly *sinister* way (nothing lovable or sunny about it), which seemed to fit the words very well. I always love seeing parts played in totally different ways. Sybil Thorndike played St Joan (as Shaw meant) as a bumptious North Country lass: Madame Pitoeff as a tortured mouse. This altered the whole emphasis of the play but didn't spoil it—which proves the play's worth, to my mind.

Mark the date, for this morning we removed the nets from the strawberry-beds, which are still covered with fruit and *flowers*. I write this not in vaunting vein but as a scientific Selbornian fact. A good bonfire is going in the orchard, but the B.B.C. prophesies rain, and no doubt this idiotic moon-rocket will further disturb the already chaotic atmosphere.

Siegfried has now asked me to be one of his literary executors, along with E. Blunden and G. Keynes. Apparently he has voluminous diaries, which he thinks I'm just the chap to edit! Might be most amusing.[1]

---

[1] R.H.-D. duly did so, in three volumes.

23 October 1958   *Grundisburgh*

I like 'Grim-Grin'.[1] The French always know exactly where the nail's head is. '*J'aime Berlin*' for Chamberlain when kow-towing to Hitler, and their faulting the education of the P. of W. and the late King as having 'too much Hansell (their tutor) and not enough Gretel'. Hansell, I believe, was the worthiest, and stupidest, and primmest of prep-school beaks.

Did I tell you that I went to two horror films in London to see if their blurbs were right in promising that my hair would behave like quills upon the fretful porpentine? Alas, at one I fell asleep, and my only reaction on a close view of the faceless man was to think how nice it would be if far more people *were* faceless. I forget exactly why he was, but perhaps the fact that he was buried with Pompeii, when Vesuvius erupted, is a satisfactory explanation.

26 October 1958   *Bromsden Farm*

The only point of Frank Harris's so-called autobiography[2] was its persistent obscenity, all of which was removed for the London edition, leaving only his lies and slipshod prose. I could have told you not to waste your money on it, but perhaps you hoped that, like the horror films, it might stand your hair on end. I can't help applauding your questing spirit, even when it leads you to sleep uncomfortably in the London Pavilion rather than peacefully at home.

30 October 1958   *Grundisburgh*

Local affairs are rather pressing at the moment. Yesterday I had, as President of the Ipswich Gilbert and Sullivan Society, to welcome the Mayor and escort him to his seat to see and hear *The Gondoliers*. I am sure now that I never wish to see another G. and S. opera. To *hear* eight or ten tunes out of each, yes, but the humour is all evaporated by now out of all those songs one really knows by heart. The incurably Victorian prose dialogue is dead. Some say the tunes are too, but they are not to me, and not for another decade shall I leave off singing e.g. 'Take a pair of sparkling eyes' in my bath.

I say these young Oxonions! Why are rowing-men always quarrel-

---

[1] R.H.-D. had reported this to be what the French called Graham Greene.
[2] G.W.L. had been disappointed by it.

ling? Perhaps because nobody *really* knows how to row, how to teach one man to row, and *a fortiori* how to teach eight men. Tuppy once picked up a little manual of rowing in Spottiswoode's, and was delighted by the first sentence he saw, in heavy print: 'Remember the oar is put into the water with the feet.' I treasure an exhortation I once heard of Jelly Churchill's describing some movement of the hands: 'It is like passing someone a plate of hot foup (you remember his lisp). It is hot, so you want to get rid of it quickly, and it is foup, so you don't want to fpill it.' Bobby Bourne says it is an excellently vivid and apt simile for that particular movement. The towing-path at Eton was full of human nature. Marsden, his eyes on his crew, bicycling into and out of the river, wet through but making no pause in his objurgations. Brinton, furlongs distant (he couldn't bicycle), crying in the wailing tones of some sea-bird 'Try to row well; try to row well'. I once told Havvy[1] that all coaching consisted of was to shout in a furious voice, 'Three, you're late'. After an interval while his laughter was quenched in asthma, he said 'You might well do worse. Three always *is* late'.

2 *November 1958*   *Bromsden Farm*
I have never in my life witnessed a Gilbert and Sullivan opera. Some day I suppose I must, just in case they proved to be my favourite fare. If such an opportunity arose, which would you advise me to tackle first?

I am condemned to be the Guest of Honour at the annual gathering of the Robert Louis Stevenson Society, in some temperance building off the Tottenham Court Road. I'm told the attendance will be scanty, and mostly old ladies, but one or two will know *everything* about R.L.S., and who am I to invade their idolatry?

5 *November 1958*   *Grundisburgh*
Gilbert and Sullivan. No, I think you were of the generation which began to turn up its nose at the operettas. Humphrey, who likes any amount of good stuff that is not jazz or modern, can't bear them; he was the first I ever heard who definitely said it was possible for music to have *too much tune*. If you ever do come across G. and S. I would

---

[1] R.S. de Haviland, former Eton master.

recommend as your first *Iolanthe* (2) *Patience* (or even first for an Oscar Wilde expert) (3) *Mikado*. These, *me judice*, have the best tunes and G's best wit.

There was an element of comedy about the Grundisburgh [clerical] Brains Trust. There were rather too many questions but in the end only two were left out. Both had been sent in by our Rector! He rather stuffily wanted to know why, and I answered with truth and nothing but the truth that they were not on my paper, leaving him under the impression that somehow the slip on which he wrote them had gone astray. The flaw of all such affairs is that there are no atheists, or even agnostics, in the audience. I always hope to hear asked—Why are so many churchy people conspicuously uncharitable, censorious and narrow-minded? and How is it that, as we see so often, it is perfectly possible for a man to be upright, just, charitable, magnanimous etc without any religion at all, e.g. old Judge Holmes?

Saturday night, 8 November 1958   *Bromsden Farm*
I didn't come down here till this morning, having been delayed in London by the Robert Louis Stevenson Society. The whole evening was richly comic, and at the same time rather touching. I enclose the programme, so that you can briefly survey the full horror. It took place in two small rooms of some sort of students' club connected with London University. There were twenty-eight people present, mostly elderly ladies and old men with deaf-aids. I and the President (a nice Yorkshire novelist called Lettice Cooper) had comfortable chairs behind a table, but most of the audience were on hard wooden collapsibles. Soon after the President had begun her introductory remarks a late-coming old lady slipped in and sat on one of these, which collapsed completely, precipitating her onto the floor. She was patched up, and the fun went on. The two musicians were determined ladies of uncertain age with short grey hair. Miss Somebody, in particularly attacked the piano with gusto, as if to make sure she got full value out of each note. Never has a previous announcement of composer and piece been more necessary. The young lady from Samoa was rather beautiful in a husky Polynesian way, with long black shining pigtails, and a pink chrysanthemum over one ear. Forewarned of her approach, I greeted her with some lines of verse

written by R.L.S. for an earlier Samoan beauty. My half-hour of random jaw and readings from letters (Oscar and Henry James) seemed adequate—at least they took it in silence, and no one else fell off their chair. At the end I had to ask these poor old creatures to stand for a minute in solemn silence to the Immortal Memory, after which Miss Reeves sang 'Under the wide and starry sky' rather well, and we adjourned for sausage-rolls, sandwiches, cake, coffee and fruit— all good and plentiful, but difficult to handle standing up and besieged by old ladies longing to explain their or their families' long-connection with R.L.S. Then Miss Somebody got going again, and I thought of

> The Abbé Liszt
> Hit the piano with his fist.[1]

Then Miss Reeves sang 'Home, Sweet Home', almost everyone made a speech, thanking everyone else, and I walked home exhausted. It lasted two and a half hours (outrunning the programme) and they were all as nice as could be.

Sunday noon

On Monday Comfort came to London for *her* half-term holiday. We dined excellently at the Garrick with my sister (oysters, roast pheasant, ice-cream) and went to T.S.E.'s play *The Elder Statesman*. I was prepared for the worst, but it bettered expectation. I don't think the old pet will ever be a dramatist, and the flat pseudo-verse in which these plays are written destroys naturalism without putting anything practical in its place. This play is tolerably acted, and there are a few good scenes and remarks, but that's all. On Monday the stalls were more than half empty, so I fear the play's days are numbered.

My friend Michael Howard, who is Lecturer in Military History at King's College, London, has just sent me the manuscript of his long-awaited history of the Franco-Prussian War. It is enormously bulky, and he wants my detailed opinion of it, being prepared, he says, to rewrite it entirely if I so advise!

---

[1] From E.C. Bentley's *Biography for Beginners* (1905).

13 November 1958

I hesitate to interrupt your meditations about obscenity which I see you have been in the middle of.[1] 'Something will come of this', said Mr Tappertit, 'I hope it mayn't be human gore'.[2] That ridiculous existing law about 'those whose minds are open to such influences' has had too long a run; I am always surprised to see how respectfully lawyers and others treat it. Because all the expression I have quoted really means is 'the entire human race'. But lawyers are strange creatures. When some perfectly understandable case comes up, e.g. a man has run off with a married woman, some asinine old judge will always say that he knows the jury one and all regard the man with the utmost horror. Bilge, my dear Rupert. I remember that old bore Lord Phillimore judging a case where a barge had run into a pier, and it came up that the mate had seen what was going to happen, but had kept his mouth shut (the reason being that he was not on 'speakers' with his captain). Old P. could not understand it, and eventually asked the mate—a morose and inarticulate man—'But, witness, could you not have said to him "You goose, you goose, can you not see that a collision is imminent?"' Phillimore was an ultra-refined old scholar. What was that epigram about Nature making 'a brace of Phillimores' when she wanted to make two bores, and ending 'But Nature herself would yield the ghost, if asked to make a Phillimost.'

We had Agnews and Cadogans to dinner yesterday: Geoffrey Agnew most affable, but, alas, my old fag and friend Alec Cadogan![3] Well I suppose the diplomatic iron has entered his soul, and all conversational topics are handled as if the other participants were Gromyko and Molotov. It may not be all Gromyko's fault because the Lady Theodosia C. (straight out of Trollope) might dry up the genial current of anyone's soul. She never drew breath.

We lunched with the Homes[4] (she was Elizabeth Alington) at the House of Lords. The dowager Duchess of Devonshire was of the

[1] R.H.-D. was a member of the committee, chaired by A.P. Herbert, trying to get the law on obscenity reformed.

[2] *Barnaby Rudge*, chapter 4.

[3] Agnew was head of the Bond Street art dealers of that name while Cadogan had been Permanent Under Secretary of State for Foreign Affairs from 1938 to 1946.

[4] He was later Conservative Prime Minister.

party ('Mowcher' Cecil) one of the nicest creatures in the world. They were all very funny about the recently-made peeresses; of one all one old peer could find to say after long contemplation was that she had a very good neck for an axe.

16 November 1958   Bromsden Farm
I must admire your daughter's [Diana Hood's] crested writing-paper. Is the bird a *Hooded* Crow? And why is it leaning on the admiral's anchor? Presumably to get its second wind (*ventis secundis*), though I can't make out why this is in the ablative plural—or isn't it? Did I ever tell you of the flustered Coldstream guardsman who was asked by the R.S.M. what the regimental motto was. '*Nulli secundus*, sir.' 'And what does it mean?' 'Better than nothing, sir.' He was despatched to the guardroom at the double.

Wednesday night I was obliged to sit up playing bridge[1] with the Gollanczes till 1. am, and was not at my best for darling old Rose Macaulay's memorial service on Thursday morning. Betjeman, unusually neat in a tail-coat, read the lesson very well—from *The Wisdom of Solomon.* Can you explain the meaning of 'run to and fro like sparks among the stubble'? And is it not rather hard on the beloved dead that we should pray for light perpetual to shine on them? Russian prisons contain few worse tortures.

However, the whole service was good and fitting, though it contained rather too much unaccompanied choral singing for my taste. Outside afterwards Betjeman rather spoiled his effect by wearing a battered brown round pork-pie hat, which combined with the tail-coat to give an effect of the Crazy Gang.

Tomorrow I have to lunch with several hundred chartered accountants—can you imagine?

19 November 1958   67 Chelsea Square
Are family crests generally intelligible? The crow and anchor above seem to me on the same level of incongruity as the goat and compasses or the dog and duck. And you may well ask—Why '*ventis secundis*'. There cannot be more than one fortunate wind at a time.

---

[1] Earlier R.H.-D. had said he played 'only in self-defence – in the Mess, with my mother-in-law and so on.'

I like 'Nulli secundus', the pendant to which is perhaps 'pax in bello' which some genius of fourteen translated as 'freedom from indigestion'. Old Inge had a good collection of such howlers, and made a pretty penny out of printing extracts from his commonplace book in the *Evening Standard*. I remember a good one—not a howler—viz that the great Field Marshal von Moltke was only seen to laugh twice in his life, once when they told him his mother-in-law was dead, and once when he heard that the Swedes regarded Stockholm as a fortress. Grim!

23 November 1958   *Bromsden Farm*
To-day we planted a hundred daffodils and narcissi in the orchard, in the distant hope that Spring will one day return. The myth of Prosperine must surely have originated in one of these northern fog-bound lands, and not in the perpetual sunshine of Greece.

My old friend William Plomer told me he is writing the libretto for Benjamin Britten's new opera—all about a tortured boy in mediaeval Japan.[1] Anywhere for a lark, I suppose.

27 November 1958   *Grundisburgh*
Our family crest is a Moor's head and the motto is '*Ung Dieu, ung Roy*', *ung* being, they tell me, old French for '*un*'. The resources of the English language are inadequate to depict the entire irrelevance of both. My great-great-grandfather was Governor of Jamaica; I had a great uncle who was very possibly eaten by cannibals. I know of no other connection with the colour-bar. As for the motto, it is a fine defiant gesture to nothing in particular, like many another: isn't yours a shout from some heroic last ditch? It has more blood in it than ours, and has also that pleasant English trait which Chesterton noted as part of Joe Chamberlain's appeal, i.e. the impression of a superb rear-guard fight against enormous odds, when he really had all the big battalions behind him.

Talking of Joe C. I am immersed in the strange Dilke story—surely one of the oddest ever. To begin with, was there ever a drabber, duller-looking Don Juan in the whole history of romance? And what a mask those great beards were. Though one knows that when Browning did

---

[1] This, transposed to medieval England, became *Curlew River*.

167

shave his off, Mrs B. exclaimed 'It must be grown again this minute'. And I think it was FitzGerald who somewhere found fault with Tennyson's mouth.

30 November 1958   *Bromsden Farm*

Perhaps one could write an essay showing that the greatest womanisers have always been ugly—Casanova certainly was, but Byron must have been handsome before he got too fat (doubtless his lameness was a great attraction).

Our silver wedding party went off much better than I had expected. Preliminary glasses of champagne were drunk before my father tottered in for dinner, and by putting the girls (Comfort, Bridget and my two nieces) beside him in relays, I managed to keep him in good humour throughout. We ate smoked salmon, roast pheasant and ice-meringue with hot chestnut sauce. My brother-in-law proposed our health graciously, and the bill came to more than £30. Luckily next day I earned £21 by speaking for forty minutes to some seventy members of the Book Society.

The celebration made my darling Ruth very unhappy. Although it had no significance, and changed nothing, it's easy to see how the reaffirmation of the tie that prevents my marrying her upset her. I think she's all right now, but her misery made me feel miserable too. As I have quoted before, 'He who lives more lives than one . . .'

                                          3 Wyndham House

4 December 1958   *Sloane Square*

Yes, Casanova, John Wilkes, H.G. Wells—all ugly men. George Moore? but how far *was* he a Don Juan, for didn't some lady say he was one who 'told but didn't kiss'? A few of the Byron pictures hint at charm, which all said was overwhelming, and he said himself that it was always the women who made the first advances to him and not *vice versa*. Who knows the truth? It will be most annoying if after all there isn't a next world where we may get the answers to all such problems.

7 December 1958   *Bromsden Farm*

This afternoon I interrupted my labours on Diana's proofs to spend three solid hours going through Peter's with him, so you will understand if my usual epistolary waffle degenerates into proof-corrector's symbols. So many thousands of hours have I spent on such thankless work that I can scarcely read *any* book without whipping out my pencil and marking the solecisms, tautologies and plain errors.

Had I applied this treatment to Somerset Maugham's latest, the margins would have been black with glosses. However, at luncheon on Thursday he was at his mellowest. He hates women, and their presence always brings out his adder's tongue: on Thursday there was nobody except himself, his male secretary, John Sparrow and myself. He always has the same suite at the Dorchester on the fourth floor, overlooking the park, and the huge sitting-room is furnished with his own books, pictures, Epstein's bust of him, etc—all of which the hotel stores when he is away. Luncheon is served there by a bevy of waiters. We had Martinis, a sort of Scotch egg cooked with cheese, a tremendously good and authentic mixed grill, fresh peaches and ice-cream, washed down by copious Hock, with brandy and coffee to follow. All excellent, and of course I never stopped talking.

10 December 1958   *Grundisburgh*
You are in Henry James's predicament—who, whenever he read a novel by another, rewrote it in his mind throughout. I do the same with many a sermon I hear—generally in the way of supplying an obvious and relevant quotation. Clerical ignorance of literature seems very common now. Our man here—he came only eight months ago—goes to another extreme. Last Sunday he referred to Karl Barth and the Orphic myth, without any explanation of either.

Who by the way is J.G. Cozzens who, according to Colin Wilson in a monthly magazine, is 'in every way a much greater writer than Max Beerbohm'? 'In every way' is surely a little excessive.

Exam-papers have been coming in a steady dribble. I am just finishing the Shakespeare papers. And I declare to you, Rupert Hart-Davis, that *except for some of the poetry* greater drivel than *The Merchant of Venice* has rarely been written. I mean all the *gup* about its drama and characterisation etc. I feel sure S. meant Shylock to be a figure of hatred and derision, and was so bad a dramatist that he just didn't see that to make all the men-Christians sh-ts, and Jessica a heartless little bitch, and to give Shylock a gift of magnificent speech simply didn't make sense, but was bound to arouse admiration and sympathy. I don't believe he cared twopence about his plots or characters; he *did* care about words, and had the most overwhelming command of them that ever was.

Soho Square: never have a lift. Don't have that jagged tooth under your stair-rail removed or that hidden step on the top flight made visible, I *like* these things. And when I arrive panting and—only temporarily—speechless, let me always find you and Ruth *exactly* the same as ever. I may die there, as Housman always hoped to after scaling the stairs to his rooms in Whewell's Court [at Trinity College, Cambridge]. I *should* like that, but it might bore you.

Château de St Firmin
Vineuil
14 December 1958   *Oise*

You ask about J. G. Cozzens. He is a pretentious American novelist of extreme volubility. His latest tome (*By Love Possessed*) has been widely acclaimed as the 'Great American Novel', so long awaited. Like those endlessly ponderous novels by Theodore Dreiser, *B.L.P.* consists of long discourses on business, sociology etc, interspersed with lubricious sex-scenes, to keep the reader going. You have been warned! Mr Cozzens is not worthy to sharpen Max's pencils.

I assure you, my dear George, that to a man who once spent several weeks holding a spear (pike or halberd) at the back of the stage on which *The Merchant of Venice* was regularly performed—to such a wretch you need say nothing of the play's shortcomings. Those interminable casket scenes—oh heaven! I'm sure you're right, and Shylock took control of his creator.

Last Monday Ruth and I journeyed to Stratford-atte-Bow (no distance on the underground: only three stops after Liverpool Street) and there paid our first visit to the Theatre Royal. It is an exquisite eighteenth-century theatre, quite unspoilt: even the bar is contemporary. The play was *The Hostage* by Brendan Behan, the Borstal boy—an extremely amusing charade with songs and tragic interludes, set in a Dublin tenement and impossible to describe. Very Irish, very fast, very gay. Some good jokes: 'What is an Anglo-Irishman?' 'A Protestant with a horse'. We enjoyed it no end.

18 December 1958   *Grundisburgh*

Were you, in fairly early youth, allowed to choose your favourite
dishes on your birthday? A good old Victorian habit. How loftily you
will smile on hearing that my choice was mince and egg and what is
called summer pudding—bread soaked in some kind of fruit-juice,
with of course lashings of cream. One day they sent up custard
instead of cream; I never thought the same of grown-ups for years
afterwards, and doubt if I don't still feel the same now (we had mince
and egg and rice-pudding at lunch today—both first-rate!).

20 December 1958   *Bromsden Farm*

I discovered at the Gare du Nord that my seat was in the Pullman to
which lunch is brought, so of course I succumbed and ate my way
deliciously through hors d'oeuvres, a whole fried sole, superb veal,
petit suisse, ice and coffee, washed down by a half-bottle of excellent
wine. A brandy-and-soda on the boat, followed by tea on the English
train, kept me going to London. Next day I was taken by an American
friend to the terrific new musical, *West Side Story*. It is *Romeo and Juliet*
transposed to juvenile delinquents in New York, and the music is loud
enough to blow one's head open. The dancing is superb, and the
whole thing most effective. We were in the sixth row of the stalls, and
next to us was a party containing the P.M. and the U.S. Ambassador,
with their wives. When the P.M. came back to his seat after the interval, the whole house cheered him. He was clearly delighted.

On Thursday, after much fuss and many arrangements, the Duff
Cooper Prize was presented to Betjeman by Princess Margaret, to
whom I completely lost my heart. My dear George, she is exquisitely
beautiful, very small and neat and shapely, with a lovely skin and staggering blue eyes. I shook hands with her coming and going, and
couldn't take my eyes off her in between. All her photographs belie
her. Much champagne was drunk, and Diana was pleased.

4 January 1959   *Bromsden Farm*

I am halfway through a borrowed copy of *Lolita* and must finish by
Wednesday, when the Herbert Committee meets to consider it and
Mr R. A. Butler.[1] I fear that between the two of them our poor old

---

[1] Home Secretary.

Bill may founder. So far I should say *Lolita's* literary value was negligible, and its pornographic level high. It is about *nothing* but a middle-aged man's lust for a twelve-year old girl (who had already lost her virginity to the farmer's boy and is quite ready for her elderly lover). No detail is omitted, all told with relish, and in so far as the book might well suggest to children that sex begins at eleven, I think it should not appear.

8 January 1959   *Grundisburgh*
Why does one find every winter fouler than the last? And how often the *laudator temporis acti*[1] is right. Perhaps not for wage-earners, though they don't seem all that happy. We get back to Faust, who could never be got to admit contentment whatever they gave him. And you remember the shoe-black passage in *Sartor*.[2] Did you, by the way, notice how *one* of the two possible theories about how the world began (in the final Reith lecture), i.e. that there is *no* beginning or end, takes us straight to Henry Vaughan's:

I saw Eternity the other night
Like a great ring of pure and endless light.

Science limps after the poets for all the massive conceit with which it stiffens its votaries.

10 January 1959   *Bromsden Farm*
Elisabeth Beerbohm was angelic to me, and one side of her sharply divided nature was warm and cherishing. I grieve for her, and for her

---

[1] The praiser of past times.
[2] Will the whole Finance Ministers and Upholsterers and Confectioners of modern Europe undertake, in joint-stock company, to make one Shoeblack HAPPY? They cannot accomplish it, above an hour or two: for the Shoeblack also has a Soul quite other than his Stomach; and would require, if you consider it, for his permanent satisfaction and saturation, simply this allotment, no more, and no less: *God's infinite Universe altogether to himself,* therein to enjoy infinitely, and fill every wish as fast as it rose. Oceans of Hochheimer, a Throat like that of Ophiuchus: speak not of them; to the infinite Shoeblack they are as nothing. No sooner is your ocean filled, than he grumbles that it might have been of better vintage. Try him with half a Universe, of an Omnipotence, he sets to quarrelling with the proprietor of the other half, and declares himself the most maltreated of men. Always there is a black spot in our sunshine: it is even, as I said, the *Shadow of Ourselves.*
Carlyle, *Sartor Resartus,* book 2, chapter ix)

macabre end. Apparently the doctor says she must have died instantly—from a heart attack in her bath—but wasn't found for something like a week!

Goodness knows what will now happen to all the Maxiana, the copyrights etc. On Monday I shall ring up Max's lawyers and find out whether they have Elisabeth's will. As I think I told you, I have long had in mind as many as five or six more Max books, which may now become possible if there are reasonable executors.[1]

Adam, believe it or not, is *making* a wireless set out of a thousand particles of metal! I am astounded that a child of mine should be capable of doing such a thing: my own mechanical skill *just* enables me to switch a set on and off. But I suppose it's no more extraordinary than that *your* son should be the world's leading jazz trumpeter. Certainly the inborn belief that one's children will be recognisable chips off the old block dies hard.

15 January 1959   *Grundisburgh*
I am expecting great fun with Havelock Ellis,[2] moving about in surely a very strange world. E.g. on pp 20, 21 I somehow miss the full beauty that H.E. sees in all that maternal micturition. And yet he *was* a Victorian.

I see my cousin Molly Stanley is dead—one of those really staggering heroines. Fifty years ago she was permanently paralysed below the waist by a hunting accident (her first remark when she became conscious was 'Do take my foot away from my neck, it looks so silly'). She survived, crippled, for half a century, had a family and was never depressed or impatient or out of pain. There must be *something* after death for human beings like that.

18 January 1959   *Bromsden Farm*
On Friday my telephone-girl (who is very pretty but almost half-witted) got my Paddington taxi ten minutes too soon. I was still

---

[1] In the end R.H.-D. produced seven: *Letters to Reggie Turner* (1964), *More Theatres* (1969), *Last Theatres* (1970), *A Peep into the Past and other prose pieces* (1972), *A Catalogue of the Caricatures* (1972), *Siegfried Sassoon's Letters to Max Beerbohm, with a Few Answers* (1986), and *Letters of Max Beerbohm* (1988).

[2] The biography, by Arthur Calder-Marshall, of the pioneering investigator of human sexuality.

signing letters, so told her to make love to the driver till I was ready. She asked him in, and on the way to the station he described the scene with true Cockney wit:

'She said: "The boss says I'm to make love to you till he's ready," but I said: "I'm too old for all that. What I used to do all night now takes me all night to do."'

Here he paused, then said musingly:

'I should say she's a simple girl—the sort you could send out for a pint of pigeon's milk.'

23 January 1959   *Grundisburgh*
As a rival to the business of looking in a dark room for a black hat which isn't there, I confidently put up marking a closely written answer of three sides to a question on a 500-page book which one read over fifty years ago. And what old Pardon[1] once described as 'touching the confines of lunacy' (the actions of the selection committee of 1909) would equally apply to the well-meaning organisers having obliterated all the marks and underlinings of the original examiners (and sometimes a line or two of the answer as well).

We once had a man-cook, retired seaman, who described our half-witted boot-boy as 'put in with the bread and taken out with cakes'.

I have just re-read *Jane Eyre*, *Oliver Twist*, *The Warden* and *Cranford*. I will not read *Hard Times* or *Redgauntlet*.

26 January 1959   *Bromsden Farm*
Adam and I both hugely enjoyed the Old Vic *Macbeth*. An actor called Michael Hordern played Macbeth better than I have ever seen him played before (Gielgud was a disaster in the part), the others were adequate, the production was good, and every one of the matchless words clearly audible. Beatrix Lehmann's Lady Macbeth was not a success, except in the sleep-walking scene which she did beautifully. Earlier she trembled on the edge of comic parody, but it's a terribly difficult part for any actress.

I will allow you to leave *Hard Times* on the shelf, but I beg you to

---

[1] Sydney Pardon, writer on cricket.

reconsider your harsh decision about *Redgauntlet*.[1] It is almost my favourite of all that noble band, and I think perhaps you have forgotten it. Or have you only an edition in very small print? If so I shall be tempted to forget my principles and lend you my first edition, in which the words on each page are so few and so well set out that they practically read themselves. The early nineteenth century was the peak-time for novel-printing, and most later novelists (e.g. Dickens and Thackeray) suffered from huge, crowded, eye-straining pages. The only things worse than too-long lines are very short ones printed in double-column like a newspaper.

30 January 1959   *Grundisburgh*

He nothing common did or mean
Upon that memorable scene,
But with his keener eye
The axe's edge did try.[2]

No doubt you have already drunk to the memory of the royal martyr?

Macbeth. You make my mouth water. Of course Gielgud wouldn't do; whoever cast him for it must have been a fool. Do you know the enclosed sentence of Masefield's? Anyway you won't mind being reminded of it.

Let your Macbeth be chosen for the nervy, fiery beauty of his power. He must have tense intelligence, a swift leaping, lovely body, and a voice able to exalt and to blast. Let him not play the earlier scenes like a moody traitor, but like Lucifer, star of the morning. Let him not play the later scenes like a hangman who has taken to drink, but like an angel who has fallen.

[John Masefield, *A Macbeth Production*, 1945]

As to Lady M., who ever really played her right throughout? I never saw the great Ellen Terry, but I cannot believe she did, for all her magnificence. The first thing she was was *lovable*—surely the last Lady M was? To avoid caricature, hasn't the actress got to do that hardest of all things, viz. *under*play verbally and vocally, and at the

---

[1] By Sir Walter Scott.
[2] Andrew Marvell, 'An Horatian Ode upon Cromwell's return from Ireland'. King Charles I was beheaded on 30 January 1649.

same time give an appalling impression of malevolent strength and determination behind every word, and who the devil can do that? Agate always maintained that Macbeth was a far harder part than Lear, the blend of murderer and poet being beyond human scope. I wonder.

I read *one* chapter of *Redgauntlet* which answered one of the questions in an exam-paper, thought it excellent and made a note of R. for my next bedside book. I had so totally forgotten it that I am not even sure I *did* read it, and I was vaguely classing it with *Castle Dangerous* etc. when I foolishly condemned it to you (G.K. Chesterton: 'We all have a profound and manly dislike for the book we have not read').

1 February 1959   *Bromsden Farm*
When Oscar saw Irving and Ellen Terry at the Lyceum in 1888 he wrote: 'Judging from the banquet, Lady Macbeth seems an economical housekeeper and evidently patronises local industries for her husband's clothes and the servants' liveries, but she takes care to do all her own shopping in Byzantium.' Can't you *see* the whole production?

4 February 1959
(Thomas Carlyle died 4 February 1881)   *Grundisburgh*
Be *very* careful now; the east wind is abroad in the land like Bright's angel of death[1] and there is that familiar February phenomenon of the thermometer saying the temperature is 40° and the tips of one's ears and nose saying it is 20°.

I have had a nice little local *row!* Asked to contribute to a leaving present for a Woodbridge parson—unwillingly sent cheque for £1— not acknowledged—wrote fortnight after to ask had it arrived—no answer—wrote to protest about discourtesy—organiser offended— and asked didn't I know that cheques need not be acknowledged now-adays—wrote glacially commenting on organisers regarding a contribution to a gift in same light as payment of tradesman's bill. No

[1] 'The angel of death has been abroad throughout the land; you may almost hear the beating of his wings.' Speech in the House of Commons, February 1855, by John Bright, appealing for peace in the Crimean War.

answer. The organiser said he was not in the habit of being discourteous. I ought to have answered as Gussie Fink-Nottle did when old Tom Travers said he had never talked nonsense. 'Then, for a beginner, you do it dashed well.'[1]

12 February 1959 (birthday of Abraham Lincoln)   *Grundisburgh*
After good-nighting you [at the Lit. Soc.], Roger, Betjeman and I drifted into a neighbouring pub where hoi polloi were in force. We were the only men wearing hats and they came in for a good deal of derision—J.B's rightly, for it was almost non-existent in depth, and sat on the noble brow like the crest of a waxwing (do you have them in Oxon? One appeared in the garden here a week ago). But a sozzled Canadian made a dead set at me, on the ground mainly that I didn't know the right way of wearing a Hamburg, as he called it. So I had to ask him to show me the right way. He put it on and was not the first man to find that his head went very little of the way towards filling it. He returned it, hiccuping that I had the largest head not only in England but in France too. It was all very inconsequential and odd. Tommy Lascelles would not have been amused.

There was a very plain elderly lady in my carriage who smeared and powdered herself *twice* between Liverpool Street and Colchester. She gazed long at her handiwork in her glass and, like the Creator at the end of the sixth day, saw that it was good. I could have told her different, as Sir W. Robertson[2] used to say to the cabinet.

Do you see eye to eye with those who say *all* things are sent for our good? Our rector is one of them. H.G. Wells has a fine indictment of this optimism in *The Undying Fire*. He makes it very hard to maintain one's affection for the liver-fluke, which, in the delicious words of Mrs Cadogan[3], 'plays tallywack and tandem' with one's liver.

Pamela is sitting at the rector's feet listening to his lenten address—not because she wants to, but to swell his meagre audience. Last night

---

[1] P.G. Wodehouse, *Right Ho, Jeeves*, chapter 17.
[2] The first Field Marshal to have started in the ranks. Chief of the Imperial General Staff in the First World War.
[3] The housekeeper in *The Experiences of an Irish R.M.*

she attended the Youth Club, merely because the good woman who runs it said no adult ever came. To-morrow we both go to hear a lecture on leprosy for a more mundane reason, viz. I have a morbid interest in leprosy (another of God's ultimate blessings?) ever since reading about Damien.[1]

15 February 1959   *Bromsden Farm*

Your unedifying visit to the pub reminds me of the Chinese proverb: 'The Dragon in Shallow Waters became the Butt of Shrimps.'

How was your lecture on leprosy? In my salad-days I took part in a three-hour variety performance at the leper colony in Essex (the only one in this country, I believe). We had fully rehearsed a three-act comedy (two men, two women) called *The Mollusc*, but at the last minute the mother of one of the girls refused to let her go, for fear of catching leprosy. So we collected another couple of chaps (including a pianist) and did our best. We were housed and fed (for the evening) in a bungalow so drenched with disinfectant that one could scarcely get one's breath, and we performed in a decent-sized hall with a proper stage at one end. If our planned programme had gone through we should have been protected from seeing our audience by footlights. As it was, all the lights were on, and although it was encouraging to see the lepers' pleasure, their appearance was most distressing. I remember in particular a grizzled old sea-captain and a little girl of nine or so.

I sent Ruth a Valentine on Thursday—the first I have ever dispatched. She was much pleased. She is my prop and joy.

19 February 1959   *Grundisburgh*

How pithy Chinese sayings always are! Geoffrey Madan unearthed a good many, but there was a strong suspicion among his friends that he invented quite a lot of them. I like 'A man with a red nose may not drink, but nobody thinks so' and 'Better the chill blast of winter than the hot breath of a pursuing elephant'.

The leprosy lecture was dreadfully tame—no 'butt-ends' of

[1] Father Joseph Damien, a Belgian missionary (1840–1889), spent his last sixteen years tending the lepers on Molokai Island in the South Pacific and eventually died of leprosy.

178

humanity, only a few men who had a few what looked like water-blisters of the most domestic variety. I am afraid Gehazi leaving Elisha's presence 'a leper white as snow' is mere rhetoric. The whiteness of a leper is like that of a white elephant, i.e. a lot of greyish scruffiness looking like patches of dust.

Tell me something brilliant to say about Herrick, on whom I am writing for Dick Routh's Junior National Biography. He wrote over twelve hundred lyrics. Too many, some immensely bad. But then he suddenly produces 'Here a little child I stand, Heaving up my either hand' which is simply and easily delicious. He seems to have paid about as much attention to the Civil War etc as Jane Austen did to the Napoleonic.

22 February 1959   *Bromsden Farm*
I go further than you, and assume that *all* 'Chinese proverbs' originated in the western world. I'm particularly fond of 'Ask the young: they know everything.' When I was young I took this literally, and gracefully accepted it as a tribute to the clear-eyed omniscience of youth. Now that I have grown-up children I see that the saying is wholly ironical.

Laurence Housman[1] was a tiresome old cissy and he made a frightful hash of A.E.H.'s remains. I always think A.E.H. himself was largely to blame: he had the greatest contempt for L.H. and his works, and yet left him to decide what unpublished material should be printed. Most of L.H.'s many books are dim and dated, but some of his little plays have life in them, and in one called *Echo in Paris* he wonderfully recaptured (so responsible witnesses affirm) Oscar's conversation in 1899-1900.

26 February 1959   *Grundisburgh*
From inscriptions on the Great Wall of China

  (1) The Three Good Things:
    (a) Certainty held in Reserve.
    (b) Unexpected Praise from an Artist.
    (c) Discovery of Nobility in Oneself.

---

[1] Brother of A.E. Housman, recently dead.

(2) The Three Bad Things:
  (a) Unworthiness crowned.
  (b) Unconscious Infraction of the Laws of Behaviour.
  (c) Friendly Condescension of the Imperfectly Educated.

Plausible inventions if spurious?

The omniscience of the young—yes. Old Henry Jackson told us he had heard W.H. Thompson, the Master of Trinity, at a College meeting say to a young Fellow: 'We are none of us infallible, not even the youngest', which if you ever come across you will always find ascribed to Jowett. It puzzles me that W.H.T., the grimmest, and Aldis Wright, the second grimmest of men should both have been great friends of FitzGerald, surely the ungrimmest of men. I like to remember that some spirited undergraduates once pushed a sheep into A.W.'s room at Trinity. The sheep was all against it, and there was a good deal of scuffling before entry was effected. A.W. was sitting on a hard straight-backed chair with his top-hat on (he was said to wear it in bed) and there followed this faultlessly simple dialogue: 'What's this, what's this?' 'A sheep, sir,' and the door banged. Did you know that no smell has such stamina as a sheep's, especially if it is frightened? Old Aldis's room was uninhabitable for days. A ridiculous old pedant.

A.E.H. and Laurence Housman must have been vinegar and oil. Affable guests at Trinity frequently ruined their chances of a pleasant dinner by congratulating A. on something that in fact was the work of L. On such occasions A. spoke no word for the rest of the evening. No one ever mistook him for Old King Cole.

You did not, I hope, miss the mention of that vicar who wants flogging back in the penal code for young delinquents. His parish, believe it or not, is Much Birch near Hereford. How delighted the boys at Eton were when Jackie Chute, whom they liked (rightly) but thought a bit of an ass (also rightly), became rector of Piddlehinton.

Where is that tremendous epitaph on the grave of a child that died as soon as it was born?

When th' archangels trump shall blow,
And souls to bodies join,
Many will wish their lives below
Had been as short as mine.

1 March 1959   *Bromsden Farm*

I have often vowed never again to publish any book that I can't read in
the original—i.e. in French or English. The people whose opinions one
is forced to follow on other languages are often would-be translators in
need of work and money, so that one can't wholly trust them. But then
I remember that far my biggest seller was a German book—*Seven Years
in Tibet*—and then I weaken and let through some horror. I have spent
all today and yesterday reading the translation of a 750-page German
autobiography, for which I have already paid the translator £600.[1] It's
rather a good and interesting book, but far, *far* too long, and will clearly
have to be so expensive that no-one will buy it—oh dear, it has quite
flattened me out.

I loved your Great Wall of China sayings: did you make them up?
The first one reminds me of Yeats's lines:

Be secret and exult,
Because of all things known
This is most difficult.

5 March 1959   *London*

Those Chinese sayings are from Geoffrey Madan's collection.[2] I don't
think he invented them, but wouldn't have put it past him. Next week
I will send you another little handful. He had a sharp eye for anything
in any way apt, culled from any quarter, e.g. an Underground notice
'Stand on the right and let the rest pass you'—as good as many axioms
from the New Testament.

My lumbago is on the way out; but I now have a slight pain in the
place occupied, I believe, by my liver. I suspect cirrhosis. Watch the
paper for bulletins. But Amsler[3] once said in his blunt way 'You're like
all perfectly healthy men; your skin itches a little after a midge-bite,
and you think you've got leprosy.'

8 March 1959   *Bromsden Farm*

Idiotically I have only just realised (or remembered) that you were
part-editor of *An Eton Poetry Book*. It came out during my last year at

[1] *The Owl of Minerva* by Gustav Regler (1959).
[2] *Livre Sans Nom*, five anonymous pamphlets (1929–1933).
[3] Eton doctor.

Eton, I bought it immediately, learnt most of it by heart and have treasured it ever since.

What you say of literary fashion is partly true in this country, and wholly so in America. Once when I was there, the two books which were in everyone's drawing-room (mostly unopened) were *The Waves* by Virginia Woolf and a book called *How to Win Friends and Influence People*. It seemed to me inconceivable that *anyone* could enjoy them *both*, and I'm sure they were simply social assets. However, it doesn't much matter if a good book is bought for the wrong reasons. The author has earned royalties, and the chances are that eventually many of the copies will fall into appreciative hands. The great tragedy is when a first-rate book doesn't sell at all, for then there are no copies to fall into anyone's hands. The only thing in favour of 'remaindering' unsold books is that the copies are at least circulating rather than rotting in the publisher's warehouse.

Peter Green (a very intelligent young man) sent me a proof of his life of Kenneth Grahame, which I am half-way through. K.G. I find both pathetic and distasteful: I'd be amused to know your reaction.

12 March 1959   *Grundisburgh*

How kind you are about the *Eton Poetry Book*. It is, I think, out of print now, and never had very much of a sale. Macmillan's didn't do much about it and always maintained that its title was against it, but Cyril Alington insisted on it. It is true the relevance of it is not very clear. My copy always opens at 'Little Orphan Annie' which I tried to eliminate, but Cyril was mysteriously keen on it. One or two reviews rightly derided it, but mostly such reviews as the book got were quite cordial. One infuriated me. I did practically all of the stuff about the poems and poets, and some ass regretted that readers should be 'told what to think about them'. As no doubt you (and everyone else with eyes) saw, the main gist was to record what *had* been thought or said about them, very often inviting readers to differ, e.g Coleridge (was it?) saying that Blanco White's sonnet was 'the finest and most grandly conceived'—I think I quote right—'in the language'. Surely very high among rules for critics is 'Never use superlatives'.

The Mercers' Hall where we [the Governing Bodies Association] lunched was rebuilt last year and must have cost an astronomical sum—so vast that the insurance policy on it forbids any smoking.

And at the general meeting after a lunch at which Lucullus would have opened his eyes (and, of course, his mouth) I always look forward to 'abstract my mind and think of Tom Thumb' and enjoying a Monte Cristo cigar out of my opulent son-in-law's Xmas box.[1]

Kenneth Grahame. I shall read his life. A pitiable man apparently, but who can say those three books are anything but delicious, one would say the work of a serene and delightful man. I always liked *The Golden Age* and *Dream Days* better than *The Wind in the Willows*, for e.g. 'The Reluctant Dragon' tale, with the talk between St George and the Dragon before the fight—St G. indicating a spot on the vast body which he could safely prod with his spear, and the dragon demurring, as it was a ticklish place and it would never do if he laughed during the battle.

15 March 1959   *36 Soho Square*

Geoffrey Keynes met me at Cambridge[2] and drove me out to his house at Brinkley (about thirteen miles). It's a pleasant Jane Austenish house with three acres of garden. They (G. and Mrs G., who was a Darwin, sister of Sir Charles and of Gwen Raverat, cousin of Bernard, grand-daughter of *The Origin of Species*) gave me a huge dinner, after which we sat in G's incredible library and he showed me rarity after rarity: goodness knows what his books are worth. I got to bed exhausted at midnight. On Saturday Geoffrey took me for a walk by the Backs, over King's Bridge where the crocuses carpeted the ground in full bloom. We penetrated the dim religious light of King's Chapel, and G. thoroughly enjoyed showing me everything. Did you know that Maynard Keynes, by wise speculation, doubled King's income and then left them all his books and pictures as well as half a million in cash? Geoffrey had to sign a cheque for £243,000 in favour of the Revenue for death duties!

19 March 1959   *Grundisburgh*

I am back again in the armchair and inflicting upon you—now what would Henry James have called the Biro? Of course you

---

[1] 'When Charles Fox said something to me once about Catiline's Conspiracy, I withdrew my attention and thought about Tom Thumb.' (Doctor Johnson)

[2] R.H.-D. had been invited to a dinner at King's College.

remember H.J.'s apologies for his typewriter—never called a typewriter but such things as 'this graceless mechanism', 'this bleak legibility' etc.

Did you know Maynard Keynes? Very courteous and kind, and with a mind of frankly terrifying swiftness in ordinary talk.[1] What talk I had with him, you will be surprised to hear, was never about finance. His death, like Temple's, was infuriatingly untimely. Did King's Chapel impress you? Surely yes. Gow told me that Lovell of Queen's, Oxford, some sort of expert on buildings, and clearly looking at architecture as Leavis looks at literature, on entering King's Chapel, looked at the roof and murmured 'Bestial'.

Another handful of Chinese sayings:

The Three Rare Things (Sights of the Kingfisher)
1) Clear memory of Romantic conversation.
2) The meeting of Great Equals.
3) Unremarked abbreviation of Pious Exercises.*
*(This beats me, but it has a mysterious charm)

The Three Foolish Things (Spring Lambs)
1) Deep sleep in an Unknown House.
2) Setting to sea in a Borrowed Junk.
3) Not to lag behind when the Elephant approaches a New Bridge.

P.S. I am deep in *Redgauntlet.* Very good but I do sometimes murmur 'Get *on*, get *on*, old dear.'

22 *March 1959*   *Bromsden Farm*
Last week was somewhat interrupted by my journeying on Wednesday to Manchester to be the guest of honour at the annual dinner of the Manchester Society of Book-Collectors. I had relied on the four-hour train-journey to compose my speech, but a resolutely affable chemical engineer from Macclesfield insisted on talking most of the way, and I arrived with only a few notes scribbled on a small piece of paper. It was very hot in the upper room at the Old Nag's Head and I had *two* stout table-legs where my knees should have been. I was between the President, an H.M.I. who recently published

---

[1] Virginia Woolf likened him to 'quicksilver on a sloping board'.

a bibliography of Chesterton, and his wife, who won my heart by immediately saying she hated Manchester and hankered for her home in the south. The dinner was plain but adequate, my speech neither, but once again I got away with the Emperor Gordian—God bless you!

Odd! Whenever I get a letter from you in which you say you are practically down and out, smothered with work and fatigue, I know that it is going to be a particularly good one. Kipling's 'Recessional' was retrieved from the waste-paper basket wherein he had chucked it as not up to much.

I am glad the Emperor Gordian came in useful again. My brother who is always speechifying to audiences interested in iron and steel, and extolling the advantages of cooperation, also has a winner (I think I found it in some digest in a dentist's waiting-room). An advertisement: 'Communist with own knife and fork would like to meet Communist with own steak-and-kidney pie.' And he often uses Walter Hagen's remark on the *first* tee of the *first* round of the open championship 'Well, boys, who's going to be second?' And then did actually proceed to win it.

I send you the menu of C.M. Wells's birthday dinner *(aetat* eighty-eight, and he looks about fifty-six). The Burgundy he took two sips of and said 'A little disappointing'. Wells in 1901 had Woodcock on his MCC side v Eton. I made 22 against him—nearly all through the slips. I played at his first delivery as it plopped into the wicket-keeper's hands. Wells reminded me that as his side came onto the field, Woodcock, knowing that schoolboys had never seen anyone nearly as fast, said to him, 'Shall I slip 'em down, sir?' and got the reply 'What do you mean? Bowl your ordinary stuff.'

I only hope I shall be enjoying Burgundy at eighty-eight. My father at eighty confines himself to whisky and kümmel in very large and frequent doses.

I have been finishing *Heroes and Hero-Worship*, begun many months ago, and have specially enjoyed all the stuff about Cromwell at the end. I think it will have to be *The French Revolution* next. I'm also enjoying the new biography of Ethel Smyth.[1] Her friend the Empress Eugénie [of France] invariably referred to the Franco-Prussian War and the overthrow of the Second Empire simply as '*les événements*', which is almost Dickensian in its charm.

Monday morning

The sun is shining, but black clouds loom. I have been lingering deliciously over my coffee, toast and marmalade, unable to put down *The French Revolution*. What a magnificent opening, with every stop pulled out and sounding. I care not whether the history is exact and rejoice in the book as literature—surely the greatest piece of sustained rhetoric in the language. When did you last read it? I can't wait to go on, but the garden is calling, and I am in the middle of relaying a brick path—a soothing therapeutic task which I enjoy. Occasionally Fleming rides by on a foaming horse, otherwise nothing intrudes on the rustic solitude.

1 April 1959   *Grundisburgh*

I knew you would appreciate the C.M.W. menu. He always had three gastronomic *bêtes noires*, i.e. sherry or cocktail, soup, and sweet. I agree with him to a great extent—though I have come across some very affable soups in my day. And at lunch, of course, a currant-and-raspberry tart, a blackberry fool, a jam omelette, a treacle-pudding—well dash it all. Before we go a step further, I must know whether you are with me so far. There are others too. Which would you choose for your last lunch before execution?

I am delighted by your liking for Carlyle. So many find him rebarbative and don't recognise power when they meet it (*'Une des plus grandes preuves de médiocrité, c'est de ne pas savoir reconnaître la supériorité là où elle se trouve'*—another of Geoffrey Madan's, written apparently by one J.B. Say, whoever he may have been).[2] Scene after scene in *The F.R.* will—literally—raise your pulse and your rate of breathing.

5 April 1959   *Bromsden Farm*

I can't decide what sweet I'd choose for my last meal—probably apple tart in the end, though I'm very partial to rich concoctions of chestnut purée.

[1] By Christopher St John (1959). She was a composer.
[2] Jean Baptiste Say (1767–1832), French political economist.

Tonight I must review five thrillers, and read (much of it for the third time, and it doesn't grow on me) the latest manuscript of three quarters of the first volume of Stephen Potter's autobiography. Before condemning the vanity of authors (as I do every day) one should reflect that it is pretty well all they have to sustain them in their lonely task, and that it is present in the great no less than in the minor scribes.

9 April 1959   *Grundisburgh*

Cold apple-tart I hope, and then I am with you. George Wyndham practically sacked his cook if she ever sent it up hot. But the practical Pamela says that it is very rare to find cold pastry that is not heavy on the tummy, and she may be right.

You will have passed by now the lovely 'O evening sun of July'[1] in *The French Revolution,* but you have some tremendous things to come. FitzGerald, whose favourite poet was Crabbe, and clearly found it uncomfortable to be roused, wrote in a letter of 'Carlyle's canvas waves', but surely the authentic sea is audible in the great passages. F. had a good deal of the old woman about him (not perhaps in *l'affaire* Posh[2]!)—easily shocked, e.g. by Hardy, George Eliot, and even Browning; and I gather the real Omar had a fine oriental salacity in many lines, expurgated by F.

11 April 1959   *Bromsden Farm*

G.M. Young's assumption of knowledge in his reader I find almost as flattering as irritating. Sometimes I tried to make him explain an allusion for the benefit of the weaker vessels, but he invariably refused incredulously. Nowadays when most writing is directed at

[1] O evening sun of July [14th, 1789], how, at this hour, thy beams fall slant on reapers amid peaceful woody fields; on old women spinning in cottages; on ships far out in the silent main; on Balls at the Orangerie of Versailles, where high-rouged Dames of the Palace are even now dancing with double-jacketed Hussar-Officers; – and also on this roaring Hell-porch of a Hotel-de-Ville! Babel Tower, with the confusion of tongues, were not Bedlam added with the conflagration of thoughts, was no type of it . . . It was the Titans warring with Olympus; and they, scarcely crediting it, have *conquered* . . . blaze of triumph on a dark ground of terror: all outward, all inward things fallen into one general work of madness!

[2] Nickname of Joseph Fletcher, a Lowestoft fisherman to whom FitzGerald was much attached.

the semi-literate I respond to some sort of a challenge, though I shall never get anywhere near the standard of Macaulay's school-boy.[1]

St George's Day [23 April] 1959   *Grundisburgh*
My meeting at Cambridge over the G.C.E. went off all right, though a young bearded highbrow from the north objected to my saying that answers on poetry produced dictated judgments and second-hand raptures (which of course is luminously true, as Gore used to say). How common in matters educational, religious or political is high-minded cant! The young beardie maintained that it is not hard to teach the young how to enjoy poetry. Nor is it—if a teacher is *first-rate*. And how many first-rate teachers are there? I have met four in thirty-seven years—and none of them taught Eng. Lit., which is the hardest subject.

24 April 1959   *Bromsden Farm*
Delighted with your letter to-day. Still bedridden [with flu], feverish, unable to read, write or think. Perhaps jaundice now plays a part. If I could find the wall I'd turn my face to it like Mrs Dombey. Will write when I can.

28 April 1959   *Grundisburgh*
You would, I think, be incredulous and amused to know how much I hate your being ill. I feel quite inclined to act as old Carlyle did—i.e. sent a bottle of Mrs C's medicine to an ailing friend, having no idea what it was supposed to cure, or what the friend had.

The ink keeps on drying on this letter, because I am in the summer-house, there is a cherry-tree on my left front, an almond (or is it a prunus?) on my right ditto, and as you know, 'fifty years are little room'[2] to get the full benison of things in bloom; while the sun is out, what *is* there to do but just look?

I liked Diana Cooper's book, though not so much as the first volume chiefly because there are fewer letters from Duff. There are

---

[1] 'Every schoolboy knows who imprisoned Montezuma, and who strangled Atahualpa.' From Macaulay's essay on Lord Clive; Cortes and Pizarro the answers.

[2] A.E. Housman, *A Shropshire Lad*, ii.

some good portraits in it, and Conrad Russell's letters are good value.[1] He used to come to Tuppy's from time to time, and I loved his slow calm wisdom and humour. Tuppy took him once to dine with a bachelor colony, i.e. Chute, R.A. Young, and Sam Slater. Each came in separately and Conrad afterwards said there should have been some sort of warning, as a guest might easily have a weak heart. They were about as ugly a trio as you can imagine.

4 May 1959   *Grundisburgh*
This is far beyond a joke, even for Nature who loves over-doing things (e.g. drought, rainfall etc). Jaundice is one of her worst ploys— on and on, and human beings share the same pedestal of repulsiveness with steamed fish, which was for days all they allowed me. Not that one wants *anything* much. All summed up in that great sonnet's line 'With what I most enjoy contented least'.[2]

Do you remember old Johnson's reply to Boswell's complaint that he did not write: 'Do not fancy that an intermission of writing is a decay of kindness. No man is always in a disposition to write; nor has any man at all times something to say.' What even his penetration did not reach to was the man who has nothing to say, but none the less writes, a less common breed perhaps than those who talk without anything to say, but equally calling for suppression. This is of course the age of jaw, and how it darkens counsel.

I have just heard from someone who has recently seen Percy Lubbock. He is almost quite blind and longing to be off; but he has a nice young intelligent boy who is a good reader: Henry James and also, inexplicably, Arthur Benson—some of his biographical sketches, no doubt. Not surely *The Upton Letters* etc which, in that nice French phrase, do not permit themselves to be read now. In fact their vogue was gone before he died in 1925. And I imagine E.F's novels and R.H's are as dead as A.C.B's. A very odd brotherhood, so clever, and humorous and self-conscious and ultimately rather futile. The old father must have been a terror, with his

---

[1] Diana Cooper's second volume of memoirs was entitled *The Light of Common Day*. A volume of Conrad Russell's other letters, edited by Georgiana Blakiston, was published in 1987.
[2] Shakespeare, Sonnet 29.

temper and insomnia, and intolerance and lack of humour, and religion.[1]

I have just, by the way, finished Ethel Smyth's Life. Rather too much about her music and the fuss she kicked up about it, but that doesn't matter, and in all else the excessive old termagant is good fun to read about. The sequence in nearly all her personal contacts recurs regularly—*Schwärmerei*, rage and disagreement, estrangement.

I have just written brief biographies of Lydgate and Malory. L. is abysmal, M. is sometimes on the *Iliad* level. Why don't you bring out an abbreviated *Morte D'Arthur*? Perhaps it has been done. Do you know the 'Chapel Perilous' chapter? or 'Balin and Balan' or Lancelot's fight with 'Turquine'? The man—very likely without knowing it—was an *artist*.

10 May 1959   Bromsden Farm

Alas, I am still in bed (three weeks yesterday) and still not fully *compos mentis*. Trying to concentrate for more than a minute or two makes me sweat and feel dizzy. But it's all getting better, and I am far less suicidal.

Comfort said 'Why don't you read some of your beloved Scott?' But I could face nothing: even a glance through *The Times* reduced me almost to tears (the effort, I mean, not the contents). Now I have got as far as Dorothy Sayers, whose works I am *very slowly* re-reading with much pleasure.

Comfort has to be away teaching most of each weekday, and since there's no one else here she sent an S.O.S. to Ruth, who has been here for the inside of the past two weeks, and returns again this evening. The two of them get on well, so I am wonderfully looked after.

13 May 1959   Grundisburgh

How immensely encouraging and civilised is what you tell me about Comfort and Ruth happily meeting—the kind of thing that renews one's faith in human nature, which is constantly in need of renewal in a world of politicians and press magnates. (You will not, please, omit to give R. my love.) I found Trollope was the first reading I

---

[1] Both A.C. and E.F. Benson have undergone something of a revival; A.C. because of David Newsome's biography, *On the Edge of Paradise*, and E.F. because of the televising of his Mapp and Lucia novels. Their father, Edward White Benson, was Archbishop of Canterbury.

could face without feeling sick. Tuppy once said a Trollope novel was the best reading in the train, because, *inter alia*, if the wind did blow over a few pages while you took a nap, it didn't matter; you just went on. What was the story about a man who couldn't stop reading a scabrous novel, but at the same time disapproved of it so strongly that he tore out each page when finished and threw it out of the carriage window? The sort of thing Pepys or Boswell might have done.

21 May 1959   *Grundisburgh*
[R.H.-D. reported that his son Duff made '65 not out in twenty minutes. He was dropped in the deep eight times (four times by the same chap), and two of the drops ricocheted over for sixes.']
    I like your tale of Duff's innings on the loveliest cricket-ground in the world—Worcester College. My nephew Charles once hit a ball so far into a neighbouring wood there that it was no good attempting to find it, and no attempt was made. A man *did* go and look for a later hit, and after five minutes a party went out to look for *him*. There is something majestic about being missed eight times—the sort of thing that used to happen whenever I watched my Junior house side—when they were in the field. Tuppy wouldn't, couldn't, watch his. He once told us why not. A and B were batting, C bowling. A hit a catch to short-leg (D) and didn't call, so B ran and arrived at A's ground. D missed the catch, but picked up and threw the ball—to the wrong end, where A and B were. B started back to his ground; the wicket-keeper (E) threw the ball to the bowler who broke the wicket when B was still yards away. But he couldn't be given out because there was no umpire, which nobody had noticed. Tuppy was quite right—nothing is more degradingly futile than really bad cricket, to play or to watch.
    Do you know the story about the girl who had the question 'Where are elephants found?' She had no idea, so wrote: 'Elephants are enormous and highly intelligent animals and are very seldom lost.'
    Love to Ruth. Some things however well known and established must none the less always be expressed. Taking divine and other blessings for granted is one of humanity's worst stupidities.

29 May 1959   *Bromsden Farm*
Physically I feel fine (and am so sunburnt that no one will believe I've been ill), but mentally I'm still fairly woolly, and good for only the

shortest spells of reading or writing. I have no doubt that this long and enforced rest-cure was badly needed.

Yesterday Diana Cooper signed copies of her book at Hatchard's, and five hundred copies were sold! Apparently Evelyn Waugh escorted her there, extremely tipsy, and bullied everyone who came into the shop to buy a copy and get it signed!

3 June 1959   *Grundisburgh*
I suspect a heat-wave, as there invariably is when I go a long train-journey with a heavy suitcase. Ivor Brown and I go tomorrow to Malvern. He sends me a mysterious postcard saying he will probably be joining my train at Evesham—where, if I remember rightly, it doesn't stop. I used—*aetat* thirteen—sometimes to watch the expresses thunder past Slough, and—I think—the South Wales expresses do ditto past Hagley, and merely swelled with pride when my father stopped our train from Eton at Hagley, which normally it ignored. He was a director of the G.W.R. and had a gold token on his watch-chain which enabled him to travel first-class, free, all over England.

8 June 1959   *Kisdon Lodge, Keld*
We were in the cottage by 3 p.m., having been driven up the hill with our luggage by the farmer's son in his jeep. His wife had already swept and aired everything and lit a magnificent fire, so we settled in immediately. That night we slept eleven hours, and last night the same. The climate here is quite different from anywhere else. Ever since we arrived a gale has been blowing, with intermittent sun, and we are glad of a fire in the sitting-room all day. We also have a delicious one in the bedroom in the evening. The place is alive with curlews and larks and on the last stage of our drive, coming up the pass from Wensleydale, we saw our first blackcock—great excitement.

10 June 1959   *Grundisburgh*
Where did I recently read a demure reference to the undoubted truth that the only Kings of England that were certifiable were the two with whom Eton is most closely connected?[1]

---

[1] Henry VI, who founded the school, and George III, whose birthday was the Fourth of June, which became the biggest day of celebration in the Eton calendar.

The book I had with me on all these journeys (Bromsgrove at the week-end) was your uncle Duff Cooper's *Talleyrand*. Has it ever been fully appreciated? It seems to me beautifully done. How did he thread his way through the hideous tangles of French Revolution intrigues? T. seems to me a really great man in many ways—so far-sighted and sure in all his counsel, which the little cad of a megalomaniac [Bonaparte]—so like Adolf H. in many ways—after a time ignored.

On Monday my old pupil John Bayley and his wife Iris Murdoch came to dinner. I liked the tousled, heelless, ladder-stockinged little lady—crackling with intelligence but nothing at all of a prig; her only defect as a dinner-neighbour was a too low and rapid utterance. My daughters of course say their father is as deaf as a haddock, but it wasn't only that, as the other guests agreed about her inaudibility.

What I find annoying is that so little of A.E. Housman's admirable prose survived. The pedantic old churl didn't choose to leave behind him anything not perfect, and, despising the judgment of his fellow-men, he was unmoved by their praise. All he said about such things as his superb address when George V visited Cambridge was 'It may have a certain amount of form and finish and perhaps a fake air of ease, but there is an awful history behind it.'[1]

15 June 1959   *Kisdon Lodge, Keld*
Take yesterday for instance—a heavenly day with fourteen hours of continuous sunshine from a clear blue sky. We got up at 8 (an hour earlier than usual) and breakfasted behind the cottage on the eastern side. Two upright garden-chairs and a pretty portable table. Invariably our breakfast consists of cornflakes (which I never touch elsewhere) with brown sugar and fresh farmer's milk, bread, butter, marmalade and tea. Then I smoke one of the four pipes to which I ration myself

[1] [Your reign] has witnessed unexampled acceleration in the progress of man's acquaintance with the physical universe, his mastery of the forces of nature, and his skill in their application to the process of industry and to the arts of life . . . Your Majesty's subjects, who have looked abroad upon the fall of states, the dissolution of systems, and a continent parcelled out anew, enjoy beneath your sceptre the retrospect of a period acquainted indeed with anxieties even within the body politic and perplexed by the emergence of new and difficult problems, but harmoniously combining stability with progress and rich in its contribution of benefits to the health and welfare of the community.
Reprinted in *A.E. Housman, Selected Prose*, edited by John Carter (1961).

each day—large ones, you know, stuffed with strong flake tobacco (Erinmore and Condor Sliced) which I smoke only here. Then, yesterday, we sat all the morning reading, sunbathing, and watching a pair of curlews keeping guard over four mobile babies in the grass. Lunch, also alfresco, consisted of a delicious veal, ham and egg pie which my sister had sent from some special place in Nottingham, with salad, followed by white peaches (from a tin) washed down with lemonade. By mid-afternoon the sun had moved over, so we shifted chairs and table to the front of the cottage, where we can contemplate the extravagantly beautiful view. Tea, out there, is all of the farmer's wife's baking—fruit-cake, shortbread and ginger-biscuits, all first-class. About seven we came in, lit the fire, and at 8 had our accustomed supper of boiled eggs, lemon-curd tart, bread and jam, fruit and Wensleydale cheese, with more tea. Then we draw up our armchairs to the fire and, with the Aladdin lamps on the table behind us, read and gossip till bedtime. Ruth is always longing to cook elaborate meals, but I won't let her (though she's a wonderful cook) because I want her to have a proper holiday. I relent only on some Sundays, when we have hot meat and occasionally sausages.

I agree about *Talleyrand*: for a first book it's an astonishing performance. I brought it to Jonathan Cape soon after I arrived there, and its great success did me a lot of good.

18 June 1959   *Grundisburgh*
Have you dipped into the new volume of the *Dictionary of National Biography*? It is much less impersonal than the old ones, and Leslie Stephen's[1] motto 'No Flowers' is fairly often ignored. So far it has not had a very good press. There was a silly slating by R.H.S. Crossman in last week's *New Statesman*—so smug and cocksure and Wykehamist—complaining that craftsmen and socialists in industry were inadequately treated. Is the *D.N.B.* meant to be a history of the times? He admits that there have been very few outstanding socialists. I cannot see that Maxton and Ellen Wilkinson are very poorly handled. What, after all, did they *do*?

Gow hates Henry James, particularly *The Turn of the Screw*, which he calls an 'obscene' book. And one can't call him exactly prim. I

---

[1] The *D.N.B.*'s first editor.

suspect it frightened him, as it well might. The book that terrified *me* sixty years ago was *Dracula* and I believe still would; and I didn't much want to read *Uncle Silas*[1] in bed. I once read at Eton a ghost story called 'Thurnley Abbey' to a lot of boys in a room lit by one candle. Some were very pallid when the lights went on.[2]

Eighty-three in the shade! 'Rich and deep was the day, gathering its power, bending its great energy to ripen the teeming garden' (*Earlham*, of course).

22 June 1959   *Kisdon Lodge, Keld*
On Saturday night our farmer cut the hay in the fields before and behind us, so now instead of waving flowers and grasses we are surrounded by the delicious smell of new-mown hay, freshened this morning by some heavy rain which fell in the night.

Have I never before mentioned crossword puzzles? I'm sure I must have, for they are almost the only things I am (through long practice) extremely good at. I began doing them when I was at Eton, which is also when *they* began, and have done *The Times* one pretty well ever since (it used to be difficult to get hold of when I was a private soldier in barracks in the Blitz). Normally in Soho Square Ruth and I do *The Times* one in ten minutes or so during our morning coffee. I also do the *New Statesman* and *Spectator* (have won thirty shillings' worth of book tokens this year so far), the *Observer* (Ximenes) and the *Sunday Times* (Mephisto), but the best of all is the *Listener*, which is often most ingenious and amusing (occasionally it becomes mathematical and I retire). Luckily Ruth shares this passion, as she does everything else. We both love jigsaws too, but they take up too much time and space.

On Saturday, a perfect summer's day, we drove twenty-three miles across the moors to Barnard Castle, where we shopped. Then on to a sale in the Temperance Hall of a nearby village. We stayed only for the china and oddments, which took one and a half hours, and bought three plates, part of a charming tea-set, an engaging toast-rack and two lovely coloured lithographs in maple-wood frames—all needed and suitable here—for a total cost of 14/9.

---

[1] By Sheridan Le Fanu (1814–1873). Published in 1864.
[2] By Perceval Landon (1869–1927). Published in his *Raw Edges* (1908) and reprinted in *The Supernatural Omnibus*, ed. Montague Summers (1931).

I haven't shaved for over a fortnight, but alas the growth is slow, and I still look more unshaven than bearded. What there is is a pepper-and-salt mess, though Ruth sweetly says it's getting golden in the sunshine. I long to see what the finished effect is like, but in another week it will all have to come off. Have you ever grown a beard? It's delightful not having to shave I find.

25 June 1959   *Grundisburgh*

I returned this morning from my girls' school, where every year I behave for two days exactly like that hearty old horror Mr Chips. The headmistress has a touch of genius. She once got a lot of small girls to write down anything they thought or wondered about the head-mistress's ways, and more than one apparently asked 'Why, when short skirts are the fashion, does Miss X always wear long ones?' She laughed delightedly and said: 'But don't you realise that I have such hideous ankles'—i.e. she has like Monty James so much natural dignity that she never has to stand on it. The assistant mistresses are always the slightly disheartening element in a girls' school. Why must so many of them be so *anaemic*?

I return to a garden the colour of the Sahara, or at least the Gobi desert—and in Hampshire yesterday there was half-an-inch of rain and all the madder-browns were emerald-green in twelve minutes. What does 'madder' mean? and, if it comes to that, why crimson *lake*, burnt *siena*, and yellow *ochre*? As far as I remember, crimson lake had the nicest taste, and gamboge—why *gamboge*?—the nastiest, perhaps because so much yellow comes from arsenic. Couldn't you *bottle* some of your new-mown-hay fragrance and send it here?

Granny Gow would *not* do at Kisdon, though you would enjoy his dry flavour in the right surrounding.[1] After all, even Housman produced a silvery laugh after punishing the Trinity port laid down in Edward FitzGerald's time.

My respect for you and Ruth, which might have been thought incapable of increase, approaches the region of awe at what you tell me of your crossword powers. It is tremendous. I can't believe it is only practice. There is native genius in it somewhere. Ximenes! A friend staying here once took fourteen minutes to get *one* word—and

[1] He had been staying with G.W.L.

196

that turned out to be wrong. Will you do the *Times* one in my presence one day?

I notice a suspicious silence about *How Green was my Valley*. How well I know that state of affairs. Have I praised it too much? That fatal treatment has kept me off any number of books, e.g. Damon Runyon and Thurber. I grew a beard in Greece in 1912. It was *red* and far from popular. No one ever said anything as nice about it as Ruth did about yours.

29 June 1959   *Kisdon Lodge, Keld*

I am full steam ahead with Oscar, and by Wednesday he will be printer-worthy. There are still a great many missing notes, dates etc, which I hope to gather while the type is being set up—and it's possible that a few new letters may turn up—but the major work is done, and the relief enormous. While we've been here I've transferred thousands of corrections (on 850 letters and 1600 footnotes) to the top (printer's) copy, so now we have a complete duplicate of everything.

I wish you could see the great stretches of green which sweep away from us on every side, topped by the heather-covered fells. No Gobi-colour here. (By the way, Peter Fleming told me long ago that the word Gobi means Desert, so Gobi Desert is a tautology: I love pointing out such pedantries to one who enjoys them.)

We went to another sale last Thursday—an enchanting one out of doors in a little village. We bought (for a total of 24/9) a coloured china rolling-pin, a very pretty candlestick, two sweeping-brushes, a double saucepan, a first-class Aladdin lamp with shade (one of ours was a bit dicky), and a lovely glass plate engraved with dates etc of the 1887 Jubilee. This last will probably come to Soho Square and be proudly shown to you.

Ruth is now settled by the fire with a book from the cottage library—*Hetty Wesley* by Q. We have a fine run of Nelson's admirable seven-pennies—much better print and binding than our vaunted Penguins. My reading has lately been all Oscar, except for a chapter or two of *The French Revolution* at bedtime. I am still only just over half-way through, and Dogleech Marat is scarcely on the scene.[1]

---

[1] A slip: Carlyle actually likened Marat to a horseleech.

On the table is an exquisite bowl of wild roses, which R. picked yesterday in the rain. Both the last two nights we have slept for *ten* hours! I send all these details so that you can a little picture the scene. As I finish each section of Oscar, R. reads it through to see what I have missed; she also types many new notes, which I cut out and stick into the bulging folders. Write to me, as Oscar says, when you have something better to do.

2 July 1959   *Grundisburgh*

I remember the 1887 Jubilee *(aetat* four), or rather I remember two things about it (a) that I contributed a spadeful to the planting of the Hagley Jubilee oak, and (b) that I was shortly afterwards sick—thus contradicting the common fancy that one always remembers pleasant and forgets unpleasant things; for I have no recollection of the delectable comestibles that had that lamentable result.

Christopher Hollis came here to give away the Woodbridge prizes. He did it very well in a crackling voice, though stressing rather unnecessarily at one point that all his audience, old and young, were born in sin. I don't think Woodbridge parents hold any such view.

I hope you didn't miss that review (some good man, but gosh! my memory in 1959!) in which a good deal of praise of the E. Marsh book was tempered by a remark that it compared unfavourably with the Life of Hugh Walpole. This is not *nearly* well enough known. However, you can say with Landor: 'I shall dine late but . . .'[1]

I remember reading *Hetty Wesley* years ago and have a vague memory of an iron upbringing—e.g. flogged for crying after a flogging, surely a good example of the vicious circle. The 'dog-leech' episode I remember as wonderfully vivid, in his 'slipper-bath' whatever that may be.[2] How sporadic and local your uncle shows the 'Terror' to have been, daily life in most places going on much as usual.

---

[1] '. . . the dining-room will be well lighted, the guests few and select.' To which more than a century later W.B. Yeats added, in 'To a Young Beauty':
   And I may dine at journey's end
   With Landor and with Donne.
[2] The murder of Marat in his bath by Charlotte Corday in July 1793.

Perhaps all revolutions are like that. Marat I imagine as largely lunatic. Does Belloc write of him at all—as he did, splendidly, about Robespierre—'a man all convictions and emptiness, too passionless to change, too iterant to be an artist, too tenacious to enliven folly with dramatic art, or to save it by flashes of its relation to wisdom.' (I wish I was *quite* sure what he means by 'iterant').

5 *July 1959*   *Bromsden Farm*
Soho Square, which nine years ago was delightfully quiet at night, is now pandemonium until 1 a.m. at earliest. Fleming's book [*The Siege of Peking*] is selling splendidly, but we shall run out of stock if the printers' strike goes on more than another fortnight. Briginshaw and his union NATSOPA (which, by the way, my daughter was forced to join when she went to the *Farmers' Weekly*) are easily the worst of the lot. That union contains all the *un*skilled workers in the various trades—hewers of paper and drawers of ink—and they are constantly trying to get as much money as the skilled men. The only advantage of the strike is that no proofs can arrive to demand my attention, and in a few days my desk should be clear.

Oh yes—among the massed correspondence here I found a rebate note saying the Inland Revenue owe me £193!! Another Eton half assured. I go from hand to mouth.

9 *July 1959*   *Grundisburgh*
I am writing a life of Shakespeare in 1500 words for Dick Routh's wildly improbable biographical dictionary. I don't find it very easy. Until I began to poke about I hadn't realised how very few facts about him are really known. The point I have arrived at combines the convictions that W.S. of Stratford couldn't have written the plays, and that no one else could have.

I much enjoyed Peter Fleming's book. He gives the whole Boxer affair the right tone of fundamental absurdity punctuated with horror. I love the explanation of the rebels always firing high as they thought the higher the rifles' sights were set, the more potent the shot. I hope the six hundred millions of them are equally childish now. There are grim possibilities about a people who don't value individual life waking up to the truth that collectively they can overwhelm the rest of the world.

On Thursday I lunched with T.S. Eliot to discuss the London Library, whose A.G.M. is on Tuesday. He was suffering a little from shortness of breath, but was most genial and charming. He explained gravely and sadly that his false teeth didn't allow him to eat his favourite raspberries in public. I have always preferred older people to those of my own age or younger, and I dread the time when I am left the oldest.

15 July 1959 *Grundisburgh*

You know, my dear Rupert, the Swan of Avon frankly maddens me at times. I have had to look into *Much Ado* again. Do *you* find Beatrice the last word in charm? I don't believe it. I am sure Ruth never tricks and twirls the language about like that! It is S. the *poet* who appeals to me; the dramatist is so wildly silly sometimes—simply could not be bothered; e.g. in *As You Like It* Orlando not recognising Rosalind in the forest, and the fantastic pairing off of Oliver and Celia. Apropos of the former, some great detective once said that anyone could disguise his or her face, but the voice was very difficult and the walk still more so. It was this last, wasn't it, that dished Miss Le Neve on that ship. Or was it her shape, for I believe the captain said much the same of her as Sainte-Beuve said of George Sand, viz 'She had a great soul and a perfectly enormous bottom'? I always felt sorry for Crippen; he had tremendous courage and the day before his death wrote a very good letter to Miss Le N.

P.S. I have rheumatism in the left wrist and am shortly to have electric treatment from a man called Prodger—a name straight out of H.G. Wells or Dickens.

23 July 1959 *Grundisburgh*

I was just hoping that the work this morning would go on wings, when I came upon thirty papers on *Eothen*[1] done by young women who knew the book by heart and rewrote most of it with astounding speed and disheartening illegibility.

---

[1] *Eothen, or Traces of Travel brought home from the East* (1844) by A.W. Kinglake (1809–1891).

I don't like your still being on the waggon. All wrong. How long, O Lord, how long? The body 'that handful of supple earth and long white stones with seawater running in its veins' may be a thing to marvel at, but it goes wrong too easily and too often. Prodger's ante-room is a 'sair sicht'. I am easily the most lissom mover.

I was stung on the lip last week by a wasp in my port, lunching at the Cranworths'—ten minutes after old Lowther—Speaker's son— had been stung by a different one in *his* port. A completely unique incident. For the next twelve hours I resembled the late Ernest Bevin.

26 July 1959   *Bromsden Farm*
I've just found a slim volume of Nineties verse called *Vox Otiosi* by David Plinlimmon. And how well the title would suit a thousand other books!

Last Monday Ruth and I were taken to John Gielgud's Shakespeare recital, which proved to be an evening of rare pleasure. Wearing a dinner-jacket on an empty stage surrounded by red curtains, he recited and acted many of the loveliest speeches, interspersing them with Sonnets, and with extremely apt comments of his own on what was coming next. It was wonderful to hear a whole evening of S's supreme poetry, without any of the boredom and nonsense that so often intervene. He spoke all exquisitely, so that one heard and under-stood every syllable. I wish you could have heard it. Afterwards we supped with the great man at the Ivy. He was in excellent form and most amusing. When I commented on his admirable restraint in Romeo's balcony and death scenes, he said: 'You've no idea how much easier it is without a Juliet. When there's a beautiful girl above you on a balcony, or lying on a tomb with candles round her, naturally the audience look at her the whole time, and Romeo has to pull out all the stops to get any attention.'

30 July 1959   *Grundisburgh*
Prodger's efforts are so far as unavailing as the tears and sighs of the ungodly, filled with guilty fears, who behold His wrath prevailing— an awfully silly line surely? If God is omnipotent he could have easily made them less ungodly, and if omniscient why that outburst of angry rage? Really Hymns A. and M. *are*! But Prodger is quietly confident; he has the air of a sworn tormentor of old who knew that

if his thumb-screw didn't make much impression his rack certainly would. My doctor hinted the other day that at seventy-six one must not expect aches and pains to vanish as they used to, and that I am very lucky, especially as internally my heart is like a rainbow shell that paddles in a halcyon sea.[1] I don't know where the 'handful of supple earth' comes from. I happened on it as *quoted* by Rider Haggard. It is less contemptuous than Webster's 'a box of worm-seede at best'.[2]

6 August 1959   *Grundisburgh*
How infinitely I prefer Rosalind to Beatrice[3]—or in fact any other Shakespearean lady. Beatrice no doubt would have been fun to sit next to at dinner, but every day, no thank you. Cleopatra for half the twenty-four hours. Do you remember the lady in the Bülow memoirs who might have married Isvolsky the Russian foreign secretary; after he had reached that eminence, she said, regarding what she had missed: '*Je le regrette tous les jours; je m'en félicite toutes les nuits.*' It is *ad rem* to mention that Isvolsky resembled one of the plainer species of toad (*bufo disgustans*).

The cornfields here look superb, every haulm standing beautifully at attention, so different from last year when every field was as tousled as a third-former's head.

University Arms Hotel
13 August 1959   *Cambridge*
We have just ended the first day's work, in the usual state of complete inability to see *how* we can possibly finish in a week. Did you know that practically all the schools in England begin with B. or C. or W.—and all of them send in several thousand candidates. And of course it becomes clearer every year that *examination* on set English books is absurd, meaningless and demoralising to all concerned—the cheque that comes at the end is the only sound and sensible thing about it.

I have brought a Trollope to read in the intervals, viz *Can You*

---

[1] Christina Rossetti, 'A Birthday'.
[2] *The Duchess of Malfi*, act iv, scene 2.
[3] From *As You Like It* and *Much Ado*.

Forgive Her? What fantastic titles he did light on. But *how* good they are—*real* people and you really want to know what is going to happen to them. *Miles* better than AUSTEN (Hush!)

16 August 1959   *Kisdon Lodge*
[His wife and sons having gone away, to separate destinations, R.H-D. took the chance to retreat to Swaledale for the second time this year.]

Trollope's titles are excellent, but so were others of the time. I particularly like *What will he Do with it?* and *Red as a Rose is She.* To my mind these are almost as good as *Have With You to Saffron Walden,*[1] surely the best ever.

When we first came here we discovered, deep under the turf which came right up to the cottage door, a fine set of huge flagstones forming a little terrace in front, and on either side a path to coalshed and E.C. Well, today we found a lot more, buried even deeper, which complete and enlarge the path to the coalshed. We had tremendous fun digging them out in the sunshine, and I can see that the re-arrangement and levelling of them will take us ages.

At night I am *still* Carlyle-ing, and have now passed Charlotte Corday. Ruth is reading Henry James by day and a detective story in the evenings. We had sausages, fried potatoes and beans for lunch, followed by apple pie and stewed blackberries. An occasional grouse, hare or curlew passes by: there is a water shortage in all the Dale villages, but our spring trickles on, and all the fields are incredibly *green*. The brown tops of the fells are now purple with heather. All the hill-farmers are so used to taking three months to get their hay in, because the weather is never right, that this year, when every field was harvested by mid-July, they don't know what to do with themselves in August: a few days' beating for the local shoots perhaps.

21 August 1959   *Grundisburgh*
How little many people have read, whose job one would have thought needed a good deal more—e.g. an English Lit. examiner of fifty or so, who was reading *Howards End,* 'the first one of Forster's I have ever read'. He teaches Eng. Lit. too, at some not wholly dim

---

[1] By Bulwer Lytton; Rhoda Broughton; Thomas Nashe.

school. That would not happen in Germany surely? Fancy not knowing Carlyle's description of Coleridge at Highgate![1]

Do you include in your good titles *Is He Popenjoy?*[2] which I can't quite swallow, though I seem to remember it as excellent reading.

24 August 1959   *Kisdon Lodge*

[G.W.L. had asked R.H.-D. to recommend some Simenon novels, having been disappointed by *Maigret in Montmartre*.]

Today a gale is raging, and by ill luck this is the evening on which we arranged to climb down the hill and sup with our benevolent farmer and his family.

Simenon is excellent at his best, but he has written so much that, although I've read most of them, I can't now remember which is which. You may well have struck an inferior one. I should try some more—perhaps non-Maigret ones, for M. is, as you say, not wildly exciting. Simenon's greatest gift is that of conjuring up the feel and atmosphere of French seaports and small towns in the minimum of words and almost without adjectives. Maupassant had this gift, but S. is even more successful at it.

10.45 p.m. We have just staggered up the hill, blown out by endless home-made cakes etc. Luckily we borrowed a powerful flashlight from our hosts, for the night is pitch-black, with the gale still blowing.

At long last I have finished *The French Revolution*, and I somehow doubt whether, for all its splendid flashes, I shall ever read it again. When I get home I shall start on *Past and Present*: searching for Oscar's quotations is certainly enlarging my scope, and I don't need much excuse to launch out into well-worn but by-me-neglected paths.

---

[1] Coleridge sat down on the brow of Highgate Hill, in those years, looking down on London and its smoke-tumult, like a sage escaped from the inanity of life's battle; attracting towards him the thoughts of innumerable brave souls still engaged there. His express contributions to poetry, philosophy, or any specific province of human literature or enlightenment, had been small and sadly intermittent; but he had, especially among young enquiring men, a higher than literary, a kind of prophetic or magician character . . . The practical intellects of the world did not much heed him, or carelessly reckoned him a metaphysical dreamer: but to the rising spirits of the young generation he had this dusky sublime character; and sat there as a kind of *Magus*, girt in mystery and enigma . . .

[2] By Anthony Trollope

Often we don't breakfast till 10. Lingering over breakfast is the office-worker's first step to liberation. Do you remember Birrell's remark: 'Chippendale, the cabinet-maker, is more potent than Garrick, the actor. The vivacity of the latter no longer charms (save in Boswell); the chairs of the former still render rest impossible in a hundred homes.' I copy it out irrelevantly because I have just come across it quoted by Oscar and enjoyed it. Now it is time to light our candles and go up to bed. The wind is raging outside: otherwise there is no sound save the quiet tick of the grandfather clock.

27 August 1959   *Grundisburgh*

Good! The old rhythm [of the letters] is re-established—systole and diastole don't they call it? I don't know exactly what they/it mean(s), and strongly sympathise with the embryo science-student who wrote that in all human affairs could be observed a regular movement of sisterly and disasterly. How G.K. Chesterton would have loved that and brilliantly demonstrated the profound truth of the remark—just as he did of the apparently faulty definition that an optimist was a man who looked after one's eyes and the pessimist one's feet.

I am in the summer-house—after a month during which it was far too hot. And of course this would be the day on which Pamela is turning me out of it and entertaining; and all the afternoon and evening the garden will be full of shapeless old women, led by a vivacious nonagenarian named Mrs Shadrach Gray. She used to darn my socks and when I questioned her charge of one penny per sock as being absurdly small, she replied firmly that it was what she charged in 1897 and why should she change?

Of course you won't read *The French Revolution* again—but you will sometimes dip into it in search of some half-remembered gem of phraseology or characterisation. You will like the past part of *Past and Present* and put Abbot Samson among your heroes.

The Ipswich Library, pursuing its policy of acquiring the most expensive and least readable literature, has just got three obese volumes of Theodore Dreiser's letters. I browsed on them for half-an-hour yesterday with very little pleasure or profit. A dullish dog surely? He wrote in 1941 that he would prefer to see the Germans established in England rather than the continuance in power of aristocratic foxhunters. In brief he was pontificating without sense or point.

The garden swarms with offspring and I contemplate them as Macbeth did the descendants of Banquo, though considerably less horrified.[1] Pamela of course is in her element, ceaselessly busy, and obviously enjoying every moment. Millions of good wishes for your birthday. Let me tell you fifty-two is just about the prime of life in many more ways than not. Of course if you still want to high-jump or waltz all night it isn't, but for calm enjoyment of the passing show, for freedom of taste, and indifference to fashion, it is the right age.

30 August 1959   *Bromsden Farm*

Systole and diastole were repeatedly used by Carlyle to describe the action of the guillotine, so I suppose it will do to describe the ebb and flow of our correspondence—ah well, the tide's out here, as the talkative lady in *Juno and the Paycock* declared, holding out her empty glass. I recall Cardus describing how Beecham once rang him up from Leeds (or somewhere even more distant) and discoursed for half an hour, apropos of nothing, on English music from Purcell to Delius. Knowing B's dislike of Elgar, Cardus at last interjected 'What about Elgar?' To which Beecham: 'What about him? Is he ill?'

I'm sure Mrs Carlyle must have been hell, but the old boy can't have been too easy. Have you ever visited their house in Chelsea? It's a museum containing all their furniture and many relics—austere, uncomfortable and very interesting. The nicest great-man's-house I've seen was Napoleon's Malmaison, where the library is a gem.

Theodore Dreiser's books are enough to stop me in my tracks, never mind his letters—that slovenly turgid style describing endless business deals, with a seduction every hundred pages as light relief.

2 September 1959   *Grundisburgh*

I am trying to set a paper on *Julius Caesar* in which no question is repeated that was set in any of the *four* papers in the last five or six years. And it is really not possible, as whoever thinks there are more than sixteen questions that can be asked on the play is like the cricket enthusiast who claimed that Trumper had seven different ways of dealing with a yorker. I think I shall try a quotation from old Agate, viz that Brutus is 'a magnanimous ass', but it won't pass

---

[1] 'What, will the line stretch out to the crack of doom?' (*Macbeth*, act iv, scene i).

the revisers —I tried it on before. J.A.'s calling Richard II 'a muff' was objected to on the grounds that many candidates would not know what a muff was. It is true that the number of candidates who don't understand plain English steadily increases. 'Reading'[1] was once set as one of the essay subjects, and produced several answers all about biscuits.

6 September 1959   *Bromsden Farm*
Last Tuesday my old father (age 81) drove to the Grand Hotel, Eastbourne, for a fortnight's holiday. He was accompanied by a twenty-four-year-old waitress called Iris, posing as his niece. Until recently he took such about with him for dalliance, but now it's simply, I fancy, for companionship, though how a cultivated man can long endure the conversation of an illiterate Cockney girl is rather baffling. Anyhow, the very first night the old boy fell over in the bathroom and (it appears) pulled a muscle, or something of the sort. He spent the next three days in bed in the hotel, and on Friday I heard that he was being moved to a nursing home. Iris then left for home, and as my sister is away in Scotland I thought I ought to visit the old fellow. So yesterday morning I left here at 9.15 in our old Morris station-waggon and drove the hundred miles to Eastbourne. The roads were crammed with sea-going traffic, and the journey took me three and a half hours. Several times I thought I must be behind a funeral, and eventually I found I was! The nursing home is a Catholic one, run by Irish nuns, and since he is a violent Agnostic I was amused to find him surrounded by holy pictures and statues of the Virgin. I took him some flowers and books, and was reassured by his comparative comfort and the bottles of whisky with which he had come armed. I stayed an hour with him, ate an excellent tea, and drove home.

9 September 1959   *Grundisburgh*
I hope you saw that my admirable nephew after visiting Stevenson's grave in Samoa offered £50 to have the misquote 'home from *the* sea' put right on his headstone?[2] I call that a good gesture, but I have no

---

[1] The location of Huntley and Palmer's biscuit factory.

[2] Charles John Lyttelton, tenth Viscount Cobham (1909–1977), Captain of Worcestershire cricket side 1936–1939, Governor-General of New Zealand 1957–1962. 'Home is the sailor, home from sea, And the hunter home from the hill.'

doubt that one of the sillier socialists, like that ass among the apostles, will grumble that it wasn't put into the poor-box.

13 September 1959   Bromsden Farm
I have just agreed to open the Francis Thompson centenary exhibition at Preston on October 29, and am brushing up my memory of that remarkable poem 'The Hound of Heaven' parts of which (as much as you would let me) I once recited to you so as to escape Early School. Luckily I still think *very* highly of F.T., so should be able to fill thirty unforgiving minutes of jaw about him.

I'm ashamed to tell you that Oscar *still* hasn't gone to the printer: more and more letters and facts keep cropping up, and it seems silly to run up unnecessary bills for proof-corrections if I can do them now. And I have very little time. The other day Shane Leslie told me that one of Oscar's boys was caricatured in Michael Arlen's *The Green Hat*, so I re-read it (the first time since it appeared when I was at Eton) and was astonished to find how readable and interesting it was. The plot is ridiculous and much of the dialogue fantastic, but the book has a definite quality beyond the curiosity of a period piece. I remember in 1930 asking Somerset Maugham what he thought of Arlen's books, and he said 'The first thing to remember is that he's an Armenian, an Oriental'. I now see that he was right: this book is like something by the author of *The Arabian Nights* set down in London and Paris of the 1920s.

16 September 1959   Grundisburgh
I had forgotten that your Early School exemption choice was the Hound. A very good one too. And you have never forgotten it—which of course was my *raison d'être*. Luckily the authorities never found out, or I should have been scuppered. They would have asked for a ruling, and of course the whole arrangement was *ultra vires*. I never did any action of the entire rightness of which I am more certain.

20 September 1959   Bromsden Farm
Adam went back to Eton on Wednesday, and yesterday I drove over to take the three things he had forgotten—his portable wireless, his *braces* and the funds (some £3 in a small tobacco tin) of the Eton College Chess Club, of which he is (however unsuitably) treasurer.

Peter Fleming is flying north tonight for three more days of grouse-shooting. Shooting is like a religion to him—something solemn and ritual, which can scarcely be joked about. When I occasionally suggest that it's a very expensive form of self-indulgence he is pained and shocked. Are all shooting-fans like that? I see no reason why people shouldn't do it (or hunting) if they like, but I can't quite swallow all their stuff about its being good for the birds and foxes. Or are you so ancestrally deep in the *mystique* that you think me iconoclastic?

23 September 1959   *Grundisburgh*

You will be amused to hear that my nephew's gesture apropos of Stevenson's tombstone *did* produce a letter of protest in a New Zealand paper on the grounds that there were many causes worthier of £50, and the inscription as it stood did adequate justice to its subject. Charles hasn't stopped foaming at the mouth since he saw the letter. I have replied by pointing out that, though not at first sight strongly resembling Mary Magdalene, he is being misjudged exactly in the same way as she was over that spikenard. I remember a young Socialist years ago condemning Shakespeare as valueless because 'he wrote nothing about the class-war'.

I giggle over what Adam left behind—as cheering evidence that boys don't alter. Braces and the Chess Club money are supremely right. Was it in your day that the Hon. Sec. of the Shakespeare Society took the minute-book with him to Cambridge, and Luxmoore had eventually to get the Cambridge police to extract it from him?

I didn't know Peter was a gun-fanatic. I never was. There is a very good scene in a book of R.H. Benson's, *The Conventionalists*, describing the awful solemnity with which the 'veterans of the smoking-room' discuss the 'problem of the second barrel'. The host presides, with great tact and geniality while chiefly engaged in 'smoking a cigar as well as it could be smoked'.

27 September 1959   *Bromsden Farm*

An incredibly addle-witted society woman called Mrs Claude Beddington published a rubbishy book of memoirs, full of wind, famous names and split infinitives. In the middle of it she irrelevantly printed four excellent letters from Oscar to someone called 'Harry', written in 1885. Seeing Mrs C.B.'s name in the telephone book, I wrote to her (she must be very old) asking if she had the original letters, and whether she could now tell me who Harry was. No answer, so I rang up. She proved to be a vitriolic old tartar: 'I certainly shan't tell you who he was, no matter how often you ask me!' She then wrote me an abusive letter, accusing me of 'stirring up muck' to make money, which seemed a little hard since after all she printed these letters first. Nettled by the old bitch, I determined to find out Harry's name without her. The only clues in the letters were that he had been a Bluecoat Boy and was up at Cambridge in November 1885. I wrote to Christ's Hospital asking for a list of Old Blues who were at Cambridge in November '85, and had Harry or Henry as Christian name. Back came the answer: 'There was only one—H.C. Marillier (1865-1951)'. This was a great stroke of luck and a glance at *Who Was Who* showed that he was clearly my man. But I still wanted the originals, so while I was busy Ruth went down to Somerset House and looked at his will. He left everything to his second wife, and the will was witnessed by 'Ernest H. Pooley, Barrister'. This rang a bell, and sure enough I found in *Who's Who* that Sir Ernest Pooley married in 1953 the widow of H.C. Marillier!

All this happened last week, and on Friday I wrote to Lady Pooley, asking whether she had the original letters, and if there were more (Mrs Beddington in our telephone duel told me that 'Harry' had a suit-case full!). I can't wait to get her answer.

Mrs Beddington seemed to think that to have received a letter from Oscar would brand anyone as a pervert down the ages. Harry, she told me, was '200% normal' (sounds terrifyingly unbalanced, doesn't it?) and twice married. 'Why do you worry then?' said I.

1 October 1959   *Grundisburgh*

The majestic splendours of September's passing equalled or even surpassed its incomparable prime. Lord's at 4.30 yesterday afternoon was not a cricket-ground of this world, though the committee-room was earthly enough. Poor old Plum really does 'mop and mow' now. Does the passage of time really insist on a jaw that wags and wags, and that eyelids shall be rimmed with geranium-red? I am not sure they were not more sensible in medieval times when the holy maul was kept behind the church-door with which to brain the senile when they were beyond a joke.

Mrs Beddington—I remember Roger Fulford being as indignant as he can be (which is nothing much!) at old Queen Mary and George VI objecting to his mentioning that Q. Victoria's dress on a certain occasion was too low. ('Why lug this in?' H.M. pencilled in the margin.) It had already appeared unobjected-to in print: Greville, I guess.

I came back from Cambridge yesterday where I was for one night at a hotel in a garden bordering the river. There was a largish badelynge of ducks which one guest out of every three fed with bread. The ducks were clearly socialist ducks. Whenever one got a larger bit than the rest a dozen at once pursued her and tried to bag it. The possessor eluded them and won but only by dint of bolting the morsel, so in the end it did no good to anyone. I enjoyed the air of meek triumph which it assumed the moment after victory. You could *hear* it saying 'Sucks to you' (there is a pun somewhere here).

Do you think my Extra Studies had somehow a homosexual influence? So many of my audience have gone that way. But it is of course well on the way, judging by our novelists, to becoming a *virtue*. Our philosophers appear to be agreed that there are no absolutes in morals, so the vice of one century may be the virtue of another.

4 October 1959   *Bromsden Farm*
On Tuesday I got a charming answer from Lady Pooley (*çi-devant* Mrs Marillier) saying she had *no* O.W. letters and remembered her late husband (Harry) saying he had never had them back from Mrs Beddington! Accordingly I wrote to Mrs B, saying I now knew who Harry was, and that his widow believed Mrs B still had the letters, and wouldn't she have another look for them.

The Trustees of Carlyle's House in Chelsea (Harold Nicolson is one) have asked the London Library to lend them for an indefinite period Carlyle's sofa and armchair, which for many years have stood in an obscure corner of the Library, unlabelled; indeed I doubt if half-a-dozen members even know they're there. Committee-members leave their hats and coats on them: that's all. My strong feeling is that they should go to Cheyne Row, where they will be seen and known (perhaps even admired) for what they are.[1]

---

[1] They now are there.

I copied out an incredible paragraph from the egregious Mrs Beddington's memoirs.[1]

7 October 1959   *Grundisburgh*

Last week I attended a committee-meeting of the Governing Bodies Association, and was bewildered by the ease and confidence with which portentous knights like Sir Griffith Williams and Sir William Cleary threaded their way among the intricacies of the English educational system. They really do know the difference between a direct-grant and a grant-aided school which to the normal man is as much a mystery as the difference between a Republican and a Democrat in the U.S.A. However *Who's Who* reveals that they have been in or about the Board of Education most of their lives, where I suppose such knowledge is essential. I now understand the slightly frosty look on the jowly visage of Sir Griffith when I said a certain action of the minister's apropos of Woodbridge School was 'bogus'. It is not impossible that he formulated it. My suspicion that I had put my foot in it was aroused by the impish grin on the Archbishop's face.[2] I like his boyishness, though many no doubt would say archbishops should not be boyish. But it is an effective and lubricatory element of his admirable chairmanship.

Last night I began *Dr Zhivago*, but rather doubt if I shall persevere. I am *not* good at the Russians—'fluid puddings' as Henry James called their great novels. I don't understand *why* they say and do the things they do. I expect you took it in your stride and put it at the top of twentieth-century fiction.

11 October 1959   *Bromsden Farm*

At 10.30 tomorrow the Court of Appeal will begin its hearing of the London Library's rating-appeal, and I must be there to listen. After keeping us waiting fifteen months for a date, they finally gave us four

---

[1] 'Mrs Cornwallis-West's daughter, Shelagh, had married Lady Grosvenor's son, the present Duke of Westminster, and George Wyndham's brother, Guy, was the husband of Mrs Cornwall-West's sister, Minnie; thus Mrs Cornwallis-West was the mother-in-law of Lady Grosvenor's son as well as the sister-in-law of Lady Grosvenor's husband.'

(Mrs Claude Beddington, *All That I have Met*, 1929, p. 171.)

[2] Geoffrey Fisher, of Canterbury.

days' warning. T.S. Eliot was (still is) on his way to America, but I managed to telephone to him in his cabin before the *Queen Mary* sailed, and he angelically said I could put his name to any letter I thought suitable for *The Times*. If we lose our appeal, it seems sensible to try and float our public appeal for money on the wave of sympathy which we shall surely receive, so there probably won't be time to send a draft letter to the U.S.A. for T.S.E.'s approval.[1]

Did you hear of the parson who began his sermon: 'As God said— and rightly—. . .' It grows on one. I have never attempted *Dr Zhivago*, and doubt whether I ever shall —so there!

22 October 1959   *Grundisburgh*

It is a warming thought to reflect what an amount of great and continuing happiness *you* have poured into my senescent years—letters, Lit. Soc., books, *Ruth*—isn't that a pretty good cornucopia? This very morning two lovely fat books, obviously bursting with good qualities. No return that I can make for these rich benevolences looks anything—*is* anything—but derisory in comparison. As Pamela said at breakfast, the luck of finding such generosity in the book-world just when reading is one's chief pleasure is simply fantastic.

Agate's view was that there are two truths to everything—factual and artistic, the first being what *did* happen and the second what *ought* to have happened, or alternatively what Achilles actually did, and what Homer recorded his doing. Agate's great example of this theory was Cardus's superb description of Tom Richardson at Old Trafford in 1896—T.R. standing dazed, like some great animal, by the failure of his heroic effort—the factual truth being that when the winning hit was made he was legging it to the pavilion and had downed his quart before anyone else had got there.

Geoffrey Lawrence sounds a good man. Why are barristers usually spirited and interesting chaps and solicitors exactly the opposite?[2] I don't think mine will abscond—yet, anyway. My brother is hot on their trail. The head of the firm is straight out of Dickens or Wells. He bites his thumb, not as a sign of contempt but to give him an air

---

[1] The Library already owed the Inland Revenue upwards of £20,000.

[2] Lawrence, the London Library's Counsel in its Appeal, had waived his fee, while G.W.L.'s solicitors were guilty of sitting on £4500 of his.

of deep thought; he makes notes about what one is saying on his blotting-paper, and once, I know, there was certainly no lead in his pencil (may I remind you of the Staffordshire squire who begat an heir when over seventy and mocked at the disappointed heir-apparent for 'thinking I had no lead in my pencil'. Hush!).

Solicitors are always getting wrong exactly what we pay them—rather heavily—*not* to get wrong, e.g. wills. My uncle Bob was a solicitor—and far the stupidest of all the eight brothers. He did all the family business and cost them thousands through his blundering. Still, I recollect with gratitude an item on the bill he sent my cousin: 'To conversation on telephone about Captain X's pension, and agreeing that it would be a small one: £1. 6. 8.' Which brings me to the saddest and shortest biography ever written. Look up II *Chronicles* xxxvi, 9, because if I merely quote you won't believe me.[1] You will be interested; so will Ruth (and I suspect, that like me, it will move her just a *little* way in the direction of tears!). What *could* the poor imp have done? I suppose he catapulted the postman's dog or something of the sort. It must be admitted that the same king in the *Book of Kings* is given *eighteen* years, but no one has thought of correcting *Chronicles*, and there it remains.

25 October 1959   *Bromsden Farm*
Yesterday we drove to the Cotswolds to lunch with Comfort's stepmother, and afterwards I spent a delightful hour with Katie Lewis. She is 81, daughter of the first Sir George Lewis, the solicitor, and the only person I know who actually knew Oscar. True, she was only a child, but her memory is excellent, and since she seems to have known everybody since, she is splendid company. Her parents were close friends of the Burne-Joneses, and her house is full of his pictures, as well as others, including a fine Rossetti drawing of Mrs William Morris. On the way we stopped for half-an-hour in Oxford and I snapped up a few secondhand books at Blackwell's.

I'm just finishing the manuscript of a book I shall certainly publish. It's the first volume of the autobiography of John Morris, who

---

[1] 'Jehoiachin was eight years old when he began to reign, and he reigned three months and ten days in Jerusalem: and he did that which was evil in the sight of the Lord.'

recently retired from being Head of the Third Programme. It's an unusual book and he an unusual man. A contemplative recluse-type, he spent most of his life as an officer in the Indian Army (Gurkhas) and was on the first Everest expedition (1922). He is—or was— homosexual, and he treats this subject explicitly, with quiet dignity and good sense. I think it will interest you. It's called *Hired to Kill*— from Swift: 'A *Soldier* is a *Yahoo* hired to kill in cold Blood as many of his own species, who have never offended him, as he possibly can.'

29 October 1959   *Grundisburgh*

What a pity the horse-whip is out of fashion. Did you ever know it used? I did—on an (eventually) eminent civil servant who jilted an old-fashioned and hot-tempered man's sister. I still meet him at Lord's sometimes. He is riddled with arthritis and couldn't horse-whip a mouse now.

You must have had a good spell with Sir George Lewis's daughter who 'saw Shelley plain', so to speak. Wasn't O.W. great fun with children, or did I imagine that? My hat, there will be good reading in your book when it comes. *Will* it come? Remember, as warning, the Balzac story in which an artist spent so long perfecting his picture that it ended as an almost complete blur, save for one tiny foot of breath-taking loveliness.[1]

Have you ever picked up a real bargain at Blackwell's or Foyle's? John Bailey haunted the Charing Cross Road for years, but had no luck, till one day in Paris he picked up a book of poems with on the fly-leaf 'William Wordsworth from his friend Robert Southey'. I don't know what happened to it.

Did you ever read Taine[2] on Swift with his 'terrible wan eyes'? Taine is very vivid—superb on the Elizabethans, but completely mystified by the English admiration of Dr Johnson. He would be. The leading miller of Ipswich recently announced in the Club that 'Dr Johnson was a bore—not that I ever read Boswell of course'. Yes the horse-whip ought certainly to be revived.

---

[1] In Balzac's *Chef-d'Oeuvre Inconnu* there is no loveliness left. '*Je ne vois là* [*dit Poussin*] *que des couleurs confusément amassées et contenues par une multitude de lignes bizarres qui forment une muraille de peinture.*'

[2] Hippolyte Taine (1828–93), French philosopher and art historian.

I'd adore to see your arthritic old friend trying to horsewhip a mouse, after limbering up by breaking a few butterflies on the wheel.

Oscar was indeed excellent with children, but then he was excellent with everyone, and all fell beneath his spell—even as I have fallen, sixty years after his death. Yes, the book will definitely appear, though I still can't say exactly when.

My best bargain at Foyle's was a copy of Edward FitzGerald's (anonymous) *Readings in Crabbe*, inscribed by him to a friend. I got it for sixpence. In the old days on the Farringdon Road barrows (which nowadays I have no time to visit) I was always finding for sixpence or a shilling books worth several pounds, and I can still remember the first edition (four vols, one shilling each) of *Middlemarch*, which I had to leave because I could carry no more. Next day, not unnaturally, they had gone.

On Wednesday, armed with sandwiches and coffee provided by Ruth, I travelled to Preston: the train was exactly an hour late. I stayed at the Victoria & Station Hotel (which must clearly take second place to the Hotel of the Immaculate Conception & the Post Office at Lourdes) and next day was lunched heavily by the (female) mayor and a mass of aldermen. Afterwards I spoke for half an hour in the Public Library to an audience of two hundred or so. Since my talk was almost purely literary, and most of them were utterly illiterate, little pleasure was enjoyed, except by the Library staff, who had arranged the Francis Thompson manuscripts and books most intelligently. (F.T. was born in Preston in 1859.) Sadly clutching a ham roll and a bar of chocolate I travelled back to London in a state of exhaustion.

I can tell from my own feelings pretty well how angry you must be feeling about this Philistine triumph as the nice contemptuous little leader in *The Times* puts it. Shall you appeal to the House of Lords, or are they bound to say the same? I see by the way that the rating of Lord's is probably going the same way as the London Library's. The M.C.C. want it to be £3500, the rating brigand £9000 odd, fortified no doubt by someone's suggestion (roughly) that a single-wicket match between Marilyn Monroe and Diana Dors would fill the stands.

Books do seem to be increasingly read; they cannot all be drivel. A

fan of Ian Fleming's said I *must* read his last one, and I did, but—!
I. F.'s recipe is cards, wines and dishes (as costly as possible), torture,
a seasoning of breasts and thighs, and a series of ludicrous strokes of
luck and escapes by that very unattractive Bond from impasses in
which his chief, who may have eyes of chilled steel and jaw of ditto,
but certainly has a brain of cotton-wool, is always landing him. Can
one really shoot a man in the back while playing baccarat in a crowded
casino, without anyone hearing or suspecting till the murderer has
vanished? What does P.F. think of I.F.'s books?

7 November 1959   *Bromsden Farm*

The final scene in the Court of Appeal was on the drab side: since one
can appeal only on points of law, the verdict is purely legal, without
occasion for sympathy or shame. Although our two main (and vital)
points were disallowed, so that a further appeal to the House of Lords
is pointless, two minor points were given in our favour, and may well
be a great help to other bodies in similar plight.

After the verdict I asked an usher if there was a room in which I
could have a brief consultation with the Librarian, our solicitor, etc.
He said 'You can go in here, and ushered us into THE LORD CHIEF
JUSTICE OF ENGLAND'S COURT (as was proclaimed by the entrance).
In these impressive surroundings we licked our wounds and decided
to put in motion the appeal for money. I hope that the leading article
on the book-page of next Thursday's *Times* will be devoted to the
Library, and the *Guardian* rang me up yesterday about a piece they
are preparing. The great thing is to get as much publicity as we can
as quickly as possible.

I'm sure I warned you that Ian Fleming's last book was pretty poor:
Peter is the soul of fraternal loyalty in these matters.

Yesterday morning I discovered, after months of patient tracking,
that a Pall Mall bookseller has got nine excellent Wilde letters (which
ironically enough, I sold in Hugh Walpole's library at Christie's in
1945. Then they fetched £50, and now the bookseller wants £1000 for
them). I went along to see him and he let me read the letters: at least
two of them are first-rate, and somehow I *must* get them for my book
(the bookseller would rather sell them as 'unpublished' and so is
unwilling to let me copy them). I have already written to an American
millionaire (who bought some other letters so that I could see them)

and am hoping I can find a purchaser somewhere. How this book does grow!

I am told that *Queen Mary* and *Lolita* (blest pair of sirens) are carrying all before them in the bookshops, and we petty men must walk under their huge sales and peep about to find ourselves dishonourable graves.[1]

12 November 1959   *As from Grundisburgh*

Again an excellent evening—though less good as lacking the hour beforehand. The old acid drop[2] was in pretty good fettle on the whole, though he wasn't going to admit approval of much. He said, *inter alia*, that I was very deaf (untrue), that the Lit. Soc. now mainly consisted, as far as he could see, of novelists whom nobody read (untrue), that, yes, Donald Somervell was a nice enough chap—but he saved his face by adding 'he was a very bad Attorney General' (probably untrue, and I thought of the equally sour Housman, when told that X said he was the best Latinist in Europe: 'That is not true, and if it were, X would not know it'). The flavour of Tommy Lascelles' conversation on the other side had the additional freshness of contrast—a nutty claret after quinine. And what a nice fellow Alan Moorehead is. I like to meet a chap who really does take the fall in the hippopotamus population to heart.

What a foul city you live in! To breathe this afternoon is to inhale vaporised pennies—old ones. Everyone was delayed in getting to the Abbey School G.B. meeting and I had to take the chair. Like all school G.B. meetings the main topic was finance, but one item of the agenda was the rather incongruous one, for what sum should we sell the stuffed head of a bison which we mysteriously acquired with a recently bought house? I did what I could to keep them dallying with this, and just when short-term mortgages were looming, thank God the Chairman arrived and the bison was indefinitely consigned to limbo.

Do I know your *bêtes noires*? I think I should. Mine are parsnips, artichokes, Brussels sprouts, ginger, boiled mutton, macaroni, sago, skate, pike, and whale—not only because Dr Summerskill recommended it, though that could surely be held ample reason. And I

---

[1] See *Julius Caesar*, I, ii, 134. R.H.-D. substituted 'sales' for 'legs'.
[2] Cuthbert Headlam.

218

wanted to ask you about *Lolita*. Need I read it? *Dr Zhivago* smothered me before half-way.

I turn steadily into Mr Pooter. Yesterday evening I bent to light a spill and a shout of ribald laughter announced that the seat of my trousers had a rent in it, one of those silent unannounced rents that come to thirty-year-old trouser-seats just before they give up the ghost. Has it ever happened to you? I inherit it. My mother used to send my father's oldest clothes to jumble bazaars in Worcestershire. My father used to visit the sale and buy them all back.

I shall not read about dear Queen Mary, who (oddly?) does not interest me, any more than her second-rate son (eldest) did. She and the bearded saint, as Roger called him, must have been very indifferent parents. But much may be forgiven him [George V] for (a) when asked what film he would like to see when convalescing, answering 'Anything except that damned Mouse' and (b) when the footman, bringing in the early morning royal tea, tripped and fell with his load and heard from the pillow 'That's right; break up the whole bloody palace'. The old autocratic touch.

14 November 1959   *Bromsden Farm*
My *coup* of the week was to persuade Winston (through his wife) to write to *The Times* about the London Library. I expect you saw his letter this morning. I only hope it brings in a few more cheques: so far we've had upwards of £3500, and there's a long way to go.

It's really high time Cuthbert was mercifully put away: he's a misery to himself and a ghastly nuisance to everyone else. When he left he was still complaining that 'the whole atmosphere of the club has changed' (if he hates it, why not resign?), and when he claimed to have lost his hat and coat (with the strong implication that they had been deliberately stolen) I slipped quietly out into the night. Before dinner Cuthbert asked Brand: 'What claim has the Duke of Devonshire to belong to the *Literary* Society?' To which Brand mildly replied: 'About as much as I have', which temporarily shut the old curmudgeon up.

You're clearly much fussier about your food than I am. I positively like all your *bêtes noires*, except pike and whale, which I've never consciously eaten and certainly don't yearn for. I think the only things I positively dislike are brains, tripe, black pudding, trotters, hearts and a few other varieties of so-called edible offal. I always avoid fish with lots of little bones.

I'm sure you *will* read *Lolita*, but you will be bored and disgusted.

18 November 1959   *Grundisburgh*
Will, won't, the Government do something about these exorbitant rates? I see Dr Barnardo's Homes are being squeezed now. Damn all jacks-in-office. Also backbenchers who worry mainly about flogging and TV. The coming years are going to be a great test of Macmillan, who must wage ceaseless war against his own Philistines in Parliament and Press. What *would* old Carlyle have said about the squalor and selfishness and stupidity of 1959, seeing how fiercely he attacked those of a hundred years ago? Ruskin's summing-up always strikes me as good. 'What can you say of Thomas Carlyle but that he was born in the clouds and struck by lightning?' Like Johnson it must have been fun to listen to his talk, provided that you carefully refrained from crossing swords.

22 November 1959   *Bromsden Farm*
On Monday I duly delivered my speech after Jonathan Cape's eightieth birthday dinner: there were no others, so I can safely say mine was the speech of the evening. Anyhow it seemed to please the old buzzard and his assembled friends, and thank God it's over. On Tuesday I heard that Hugh Walpole's sister Dorothy had died suddenly of a heart attack in Edinburgh, where at the age of seventy-two she was still practising as a doctor. I am one of her executors, so on Thursday afternoon I travelled north (comfortably reading in a first-class Pullman) and stayed the night with my co-executor, a nice intelligent fortyish Edinburgh lawyer (W.S.). Dorothy, bless her, left me £1000, which will safely cover the rest of Adam's Eton bills, and so relieve me of a perpetual headache. Also, when Robin, the surviving brother, dies, all Hugh's copyrights and royalties (if there still are any) are to belong to me. Dorothy was deeply religious (their father, you remember, was Bishop of Edinburgh) and on Friday I attended *three* services (all in the rain)— one at the little church she went to, one at the crematorium, and one at the burial of the ashes in a charming country churchyard at Dalmahoy, where the parents are buried. A delightful old Scotch canon conducted all three, reading and speaking beautifully, and the

Bishop of Edinburgh gave a goodish address at the first one. He ended with this prayer, which I had never heard before:

Go forth upon thy journey from this world, O Christian soul,
In the name of God the Father Almighty who created thee,
In the name of Jesus Christ who suffered for thee,
In the name of the Holy Ghost who strengtheneth thee,
In communion with the blessed Saints, and aided by Angels and
    Archangels and all the armies of the heavenly host.
May thy portion this day be in peace, and thy dwelling the
    heavenly Jerusalem.

Very beautiful, don't you think? I later copied it from the Scottish Prayer Book, where it appears under 'The Visitation of the Sick', though the Canon told me it is seldom so used, since its recitation doesn't exactly encourage the sick person.

25 November 1959   *Grundisburgh*

I cannot believe you wouldn't enjoy Froude's *Life* [of Carlyle], though I cannot remember meeting anyone who finds such rich enjoyment in it as I always have. They just never mention it. There is of course too much groaning and grousing, which is not easy to skip, though desirable, because brilliant flashes may lighten the darkness at any moment, and no one could relish them more than you will. You keep on coming across things like the juryman who stuck out against the other eleven, his head 'all cheeks, jaw, and no brow, of shape some-what like a great ball of putty dropped from a height'.

I was sorry to see G.M. Young's death, though I didn't know him except through those *first-rate* little books that were about the first of your fairy-gifts to me. A big batch of extracts from his observations on men and things found their way into my commonplace book and from that to my Governor-General nephew in N.Z. who uses them in his speeches (which recently were called in a N.Z. paper the best ever made by a N.Z. Governor-General!).

Very busy today. New car arrived, and Pamela was shown the ropes. She will have to get used, by trial and error, to the brake and the accelerator having changed places, which no doubt is as it should be, but error might be costly. Then P. had to cook lunch for our Bishop against time. At 1.20 no Bishop. I rang him up, and in words stifled by compunction and the bread and cheese of his own lunch he explained that his secretary for the first time in donkey's years had made a muddle. Extending forgiveness to a Bishop is a luxurious experience. Have you ever had it? And on the top of it I ate his lordship's lunch, so all ended on a happy note.

I have been reading in bed Evelyn Waugh's life of R.A. Knox with ambiguous feelings—as one has, or I do, in reading about Newman. Does God want all that endless heart-searching about Him and how to worship Him? I am a thousand miles away from understanding what those profound minds are at in their ceaseless meditations on such matters.

There is a lovely blunder in the index. Was Bishop G.A. Selwyn laughed into oblivion before your Eton day?[1] He used to be rammed down our throats by visiting preachers as the perfect model all Etonians should copy? Well, he is mentioned in the pages dealing with R.A.K.'s schooldays. The index has 'G.A. Selwyn (eighteenth-century wit)'. They mixed him up with the other George Augustus who was sacked from Oxford for blasphemy, and spent his time attending executions, visiting morgues and being mildly (and generally indecently) witty.[2] How R.A.K. himself would have enjoyed this supremely rich gaffe!

28 November 1959   Bromsden Farm

On Tuesday the trouble began. We were slowly preparing the press-release of the Phoenix Trust[3] to be put out early in December, when the Evening Standard (goodness knows how) got the whole story. I refused to tell them anything, but on Wednesday they printed two long and accurate paragraphs about the scheme, and immediately the other papers were round me like a swarm of hornets. To avoid antagonising them all I was forced to rush out an official statement in a couple of hours. Almost all the other Trustees were unobtainable, so I had to get the statement into final form, duplicated, and sent round by hand with covering letters to seven newspapers and press agencies.

[1] Old Etonian, Bishop of New Zealand and then of Lichfield. Selwyn College, Cambridge founded in his memory.

[2] He also held the sinecures of 'Clerk of the Irons and Surveyor of the Meltings of the Mint'.

[3] See p. 142.

I daresay you saw it in Thursday's *Times*. That afternoon, while I was being interviewed by a young lady from the *Sunday Times*, the secretary of the Pilgrim Trust (Lord Kilmaine) rang up in a towering rage to say I had no business to say the Phoenix Trust had been 'founded and endowed' by the 'Pilgrim', since all they had done was to lend their name, give us £500 and nominate a Trustee. He calmed down a little when I pointed out that the offending words were the ones from his own Charter which he had read out to me as the Pilgrim T's authority for helping us, but I had to agree to send out a correction, again by hand, to the same seven places. Next morning (Friday) appeared that savagely malicious leader pouring scorn and ridicule on the new Trust. It seems, don't you agree?, an extraordinary thing for *The Times* so to attack a philanthropic scheme directly it's announced, and I can only imagine that the article was inspired, if not written, by some tight-fisted and self-important person (probably a publisher) who fears his pocket may be endangered. I felt the article must be answered, and I drafted a letter, which I hope they will print on Monday. A.P. Herbert was most helpful with telephonic advice. Meanwhile I had to stay up last night to appear (or rather be audible) for eight minutes on the Home Service, talking about the Phoenix Trust. I don't suppose you heard it. Pretty dull, I fear: I only hope comprehensible. The worst thing about such jobs is the time they take: for those eight minutes I was in Broadcasting House for just on two and a half hours! And in the middle of everything I got a cable to say that the wealthy Bollingen Foundation of New York has agreed to finance a multi-volume complete edition of Coleridge's works, for which I've been scheming for several years.

Just now I took down Cobbett's *English Grammar* for fun. He writes: 'This work has been published to the amount of *fifty-five thousand copies*, without ever having been mentioned by the old shuffling bribed sots, called Reviewers.' That's the stuff! I must read him again.

5 December 1959   *Bromsden Farm*

R.A. Butler was very sympathetic to the London Library when I saw him last week at lunch at the Birkenheads'. We discussed the Dilke case[1], and when he admitted that Joe Chamberlain probably did

[1] See p. 167.

nothing to prevent D's disgrace and disappearance, I said: 'It's a dirty game, politics'. 'Yes', he answered simply; 'You see, it's for power.' He struck me as immensely self-satisfied, but fundamentally right-minded.

12 December 1959   *Bromsden Farm*

The best news is (1) Adam has won the Chess Cup—not only the biggest in the school, but apparently bringing with it a fiver in cash! (2) I think I have succeeded in wheedling £1000 for the London Library out of the B.B.C.! But mum is very much the word until the news is official. Privately they asked whether we would mind publicity about the gift. I said on the contrary: it might stimulate other donors. That would bring the total to £6500. Meanwhile the Christie's sale goes forward, and Henry Moore has promised to give a small bronze, which should bring in a few hundred pounds. Soon I must tackle goodness knows how many other possible benefactors.

On Wednesday evening I took the Librarian of the London Library to dine in the House of Commons with Leslie Hale, the Labour M.P. who is going to organise a deputation of the thirty-six M.P.s who are members of the Library. He's a vigorous, frank and engaging fellow—a country solicitor from Leicestershire, who has the reputation of speaking faster than any other M.P. Unfortunately our host had ordered a mass of wine (sherry, white, red), and it was all opened and decanted, so I simply had to ignore my post-jaundice tee-totalism and drink it. A nasty headache all next day seems to prove that I should still keep off it.

After dinner we spent a very dull hour listening to Mr Maudling fluently spouting about Unemployment to a largely empty chamber. Fancy spending one's working life there—ugh!

I was most touched by Roger's kind words at the London Library. Most of the committee are like lumps of driftwood, moving slug-gishly with the current, so R's intervention was as unexpected as it was encouraging, bless him.

Diana Cooper has sent me most of her third volume—in the roughest form—and I shall have to spend some of the Christmas holiday trying to get it into preliminary shape. Next week she is coming over for the presentation of the Duff Cooper Prize, which this year is being given by the Duchess of Kent to Paddy Leigh Fermor for his book *Mani*, a large tome about southern Greece. Ruth and I have had to arrange everything and send out all the invitations. Diana's list was written in pencil, all names spelt wrong and no addresses.

She tells me that last week-end at Petworth she gave the P.M. a memorandum about the London Library (I'd love to have seen it) and he seemed most sympathetic and interested—as I'm sure he is. One can't have too many irons in this particular fire.

All the same, I wish I was with Ruth in Kisdon Lodge, reading another chapter of *How Green* by the open range! June seems a long way away.

It is not many miles to Mantua?
No further than the end of this mad world.

I bet you don't know where that comes from!

17 December 1959   *Grundisburgh*
This weak utterance comes to you so to speak *de profundis*, but simply because I have to deal with a large batch of scripts by a monstrous regiment of young women. The questions are on 'Narrative Poems of To-day' and to every question the young women write, in that horrid looping, swooping hand so many of them affect, voluminously, never quite on or off the point, enthusiastically, insipidly. The after-effects are what you get from immersion in a very large bath, quite full of luke-warm water, and I recall Arnold Bennett's recipe for the right treatment of Mrs Humphry Ward's heroines, i.e. that they should be gathered in a besieged city about to fall, all armed with revolvers to protect them from the cruel and licentious soldiery, that the city falls, the soldiers burst in—and all the revolvers turn out to be unloaded.

Please congratulate Adam from me on his Chess Cup. I was in the final, *aetat* eleven, at my prep-school, lost, and burst into tears. How often one is *very* unhappy at the age of ten. And on the whole what hateful places prep-schools, anyhow, were, especially if situated, as mine was, among the brickfields near Uxbridge.

20 December 1959   *Bromsden Farm*
The best news is that the B.B.C.'s cheque for £1000 reached the London Library last week, with a very nice letter from Sir Ian Jacob. This I hope

to use as a lever to prise open the coffers of ITV. Also, to my great surprise, the *New Statesman* responded to my appeal with a cheque for £250! The Library has now received £7000 in all, and I am pressing on. The Phoenix Trust will just have to wait. Like the man pursued by the Hound of Heaven, I feel 'trellised with intertwining charities'.

The presentation of the Duff Cooper Prize went off well. Evelyn Waugh (who has promised a manuscript for the Christie sale) is now very fat, glassy-eyed, and carries an ear-trumpet! I told him it suited him and he should never be without it.

Those two lines about Mantua were written by Maurice Baring, and you're supposed to think they come from *Romeo and Juliet*— which indeed they might.

I still haven't got a single Christmas present, so my next few days will be busy. I shall think of you in the midst of your progeny, taking credit for all the individual presents that Pamela has so cleverly bought.

New Year's Eve 1959   *Cambridge*
Last night we went to a film—*Great Expectations*. Excellent. All the setting and scenery etc were masterly. Mrs Gargery was made too savage. She didn't merely give Pip a cut or two with 'Tickler' but *thrashed* him, thereby making one despise Joe, who stood by doing nothing. Joe irritates me in fact in both book and film.

Yesterday I was given a lovely Penguin, *Yet More Comic and Curious Verse*, An excellent volume—full of things I had never seen or heard of, though of course you have. You won't mind being reminded of the couplet:

> God in his wisdom made the fly,
> And then forgot to tell us why.

Last night I was smoking one of Alexander's cigars, and the slightly bibulous attendant exclaimed 'Lummy, here come the millionaires'. Just the effect we were aiming at!

4 January 1960   *36 Soho Square*
I expect you saw Raymond Mortimer on Hotson[1] in the *Sunday Times*. J.B. Priestley in *Reynolds News* (but who reads it?) was much

---

[1] *Shakespeare's Wooden O* by Leslie Hotson (1960), in which he sought to prove that the London theatres of Shakespeare's time were literally 'in the round'.

more forthcoming and pronounced himself entirely converted. I shall eagerly await your opinion. As always, vested interests will be massing on the other side: if Hotson could be proved right, all their damned text-books would have to be rewritten. We ran into John Wain today, just married again and very cheerful—no sign of the Angry Young Man about him except that he wore no tie.

6 January 1960 (77th birthday)   *The Timbralls*
Eton

My three days at Cambridge were oddly busy, partly because what you regard as my masochistic instincts made me go to another film. My God! It was called *Expresso Bongo*,[1] all din and glitter and semi-nudity, and acrobatic dancing, and prestissimo dialogue, mostly to me inaudible, but, they told me, crackling with wit and satire—which made it particularly unfortunate that all the w. and s. I did hear was insipid beyond words. I felt 150 years old. My colleagues—intelligent young-middle-aged men—were as pleased with it as Mr Peter Magnus said his friends were when he signed himself 'Afternoon'.[2] Have you or has Ruth seen it? If either of you didn't think it dreadful rubbish, I shall give up trying to keep up.

At Cambridge I always find Trollope best for bedtime reading, after reading third-rate manuscripts all day. And shall I be lynched if I say how awfully bad *The Warden* seems to me? All its issues go below its surface—the whole business of John Bold and Eleanor left in the air, and he does not succeed in persuading me, at least, that the Archdeacon is not essentially a man of four letters, which he appears to want to do. I forget whether you are a Trollope fan—or share perhaps Gosse's distaste for 'the listless amble' of Trollope's style? I wonder if anyone in England has *all* his novels. I have read scores, it seems, but am always coming across the names of many I haven't. No secondhand bookshop ever has any beyond the Barchester lot. Odd.[3]

Do you ever do things quite wrong, misquote etc, as I am always doing, e.g. in a crib supplied to examiners in the G.C.E. Because here is the perfect defence: 'What is obvious is not always known, what is

[1] The film of a musical play by Wolf Mankowitz (1958).
[2] In *Pickwick Papers*, chapter xxii: a play upon his initials.
[3] Enthusiasm for Trollope suddenly sprouted in the late 1980s and there have since been four complete editions of his forty-seven novels.

known is not always present. Sudden fits of inadvertency will surprise vigilance; slight avocations will seduce attention, and casual eclipses of the mind will darken learning.' Isn't it perfect? Johnson of course.

Expresso Bongo indeed! It'll be strip-tease next, mark my words. I certainly haven't seen E.B., nor has Ruth: we call for sterner stuff. I am not a Trollope fan, but only perhaps through lack of leisure. I mean, I'm all *for* him but haven't read many. Certainly I'm not in any way *anti*, and the professional hardheadedness of his writing habits, which so scandalised the readers of his *excellent Autobiography*, endears him to me.

Yesterday I, as they say, 'took delivery' of a new car—a Morris station-waggon, like our old one but seven years more up-to-date. Heinemann's have bought it for me, and we are all delighted with it. Never before have we enjoyed a car with a *heater* in it.

Yesterday morning I took Diana Cooper to the crypt of St Paul's for a private view of Duff's memorial tablet (carved by Reynolds Stone), which is to be unveiled later this year. All the cathedral's heating is in the crypt, which is always warm and to me full of beauty and romance—with Nelson and Wellington sleeping out eternity side by side in vast hideous sarcophagi—though Wellington's battle-flags are wonderfully romantic and threadbare.

Did I ever mention my friend Christopher Devlin? He is a Jesuit priest, brother of Patrick Devlin the judge and William Devlin the actor, and a charming person. He helped me a lot with the Gerard Manley Hopkins papers which were left unfinished when Humphry House died, and soon afterwards he (C.D.) was sent out to South Africa as a missionary. At first he hated it but gradually became reconciled. I have sent him books and occasional letters. Just before Christmas I got a scrawled note to say he was being flown home for a serious operation. Poor creature, he had cancer of the rectum: can you imagine anything more agonising? He had the operation just after Christmas and is apparently going on all right. His sister-in-law (the judge's wife) rang up to say he could have visitors, so I'm going to see him on Monday. I suppose one ought to be grateful every moment that one is well and without pain, but one never thinks of such things until someone one knows is involved. I suppose

Christopher will somehow reconcile this appalling event with God's infinite mercy, but it will take some doing.

14 January 1960   *Grundisburgh*

My Johnson sentence for you was from the magnificent preface to his Dictionary. Was ever a defence so complete—and every noun and adjective and verb is exactly the right one. I remember a large majestic youth called Keele giving it at the Fourth of June speeches on J's bicentenary, and the sight of Augustine Birrell's rich enjoyment of it in the audience. Keele spoke it beautifully, and I can still hear the final sentence: 'I therefore dismiss it with frigid tranquillity, having nothing to fear or to hope from censure or from praise.' Keele was killed in the first war. He was a fine chap.

Tell me of your visit to Devlin. What awful things Fate can and daily does do. A cousin, whose memorial service I attended last week, had had several years of absolute immobility from arthritis, and for the last year had been stoneblind. 'Fatherlike he tends and spares us!'

I have a pain in the chest—probably some form of dyspepsia. My family cheerfully suggest angina pectoris. How scored off they would feel if they turned out right! Was it not Walter de la Mare who said what splendid names for heroine and villain Lady Angina Pectoris and Sir Rheumatoid Arthritis would be?

16 January 1960   *Bromsden Farm*

I'm sure you'd be wise to put in central heating: I'd do it here if I had the money. As it is I hug the library fire, whence I can watch the nuthatch bullying the tits on the bird-table.

Last week began with my visit to poor Christopher Devlin: it took me three hours, though I was with him for only twenty minutes. He is in a Catholic hospital at Cheam—an endlessly sprawling and flat section of what I believe is now called Subtopia. I took him some flowers and books, and I think he was pleased to see me, though he was clearly in pain: I shall try to go again next week.

On Wednesday there were 101 diners in the festal lights of Christ Church hall, but I spoke only to my host, Michael Innes, a very shy Canon on my other side, and Masterman, the Provost of Worcester. I saw at once that, as regards the menu, it was all or nothing, so I went doggedly through the seven courses and six wines, all excellent (list enclosed), and was no whit the worse. M. Innes is a most civilised and amusing chap: he has written all those thrillers to educate his five children. I think the two best are *Lament for a Maker* and *The Journeying Boy*. At about eleven I walked back through the snow to All Souls, where I found the Warden [John Sparrow] sound asleep by his study fire in the Lodging. He woke refreshed and kept me up till one, showing me all his latest book-acquisitions. The house is thoroughly comfortable, with a cherishing old manservant. I hadn't had a bath run for me since I left the army in 1945.

Have you ever read anything so drearily turgid as Eden's memoirs? They're like chunks of the day-before-yesterday's newspapers written by a civil service clerk. I've always thought him a weak dull mediocrity (although he was at my tutor's) and here is proof positive. He deserves to have these tedious pages read back to him at dictation speed by a Foreign Office Spokesman.

21 January 1960   *Grundisburgh*
This is really the dead vast and middle of the winter—when, according to M.D. Hill, all the great frosts of the past century have begun. The neighbourhood is stricken with fowl-pest and an obscure hepatic complaint is wiping out all the foxes. Not that I was ever a hunting-man. To sing 'John Peel' in my bath was as near as I ever got to being one. It was a kindly dispensation of Providence to see that I weighed thirteen stone when I was sixteen, so that my economical father would not run to what would practically have been a shire horse—certainly by the time I was eighteen and weighed fifteen stone I should have needed one whose neck was clothed with thunder, like the great Suffolk punch, Naunton Prince, over whose demise his late Majesty and I shed tears together.

I am *pro tem.* up-to-date with my R.H.-D. books, so got yesterday from the library Coleridge's Letters Vol IV, but they look a little daunting. You know of course Carlyle's perfect picture of C. in *John Sterling* 'Glorious islets too I have seen rise out of the haze (of C's talk)—islands of the blest and the intelligible'. Ten per cent genius and ninety per cent bore—an uncomfortable blend, but perhaps not a very uncommon one, e.g. daddy Wordsworth too—in his poetry as well as (I expect) his conversation.

I must go and hew wood.

Adam went back cheerfully on Wednesday with an enormous stack
of kit and rations. The night before, Ruth and I took him to dine in
Soho (whitebait, steak, Beaujolais, cream cake) and on to the old Vic,
where we all three thoroughly enjoyed *The Importance of Being
Earnest*. The production wasn't frightfully good and Fay Compton
couldn't get anywhere near Lady Bracknell, but the words and jokes
are good enough to survive almost any acting (have you read the play
lately?). Edith Evans was the Lady B of all time, and, as John Gielgud
once said to me, any perfect performance spoils a part for a generation. E. Evans has similarly spoiled Millamant[1], and the Nurse in
Romeo, but her Cleopatra was an agonising disaster.

I am going to include FitzGerald in my Reynard Library series.
Except for *Omar* and a few oddments, the volume will consist entirely
of letters—and jolly good ones too. There is no edition in Everyman
or World's Classics. You will have to do your best to promote the sale
in Suffolk. The editor is a nice woman called Joanna Richardson: I
hope she won't make a mess of it.

I read *The Importance* a few years ago, when with a spurt of imbecil-
ity, unusual even for them, the Oxford and Cambridge Board set it
in the Higher Cert. Of course Edith Evans made any other Lady B.
impossible. And I often read how the other parts are spoilt by the performers' obvious consciousness that they are being funny. But, as you
say, the language of the play is unspoilable. Don't our sillier young
critics object to any attempt to use words with grace and point, or is
that fatuous little fashion on the way out? I am dubious. The hosts of
Philistia, constantly changing their uniforms, seem to me to grow
pretty steadily. But then I am frequently charged with pessimism.
Well, I don't know. It depends on how far you look. I am not one, as
regards friends and family etc., but I suppose that fundamentally
anyone who has no belief whatever in a future life may or must be
called a pessimist. Do you know that magnificent paragraph of
Arthur Balfour's about the almost contemptible brevity of the human

---

[1] In *The Way of the World* by William Congreve. Maggie Smith was the next great
Millamant.

race's sojourn on the earth, which some day, 'tideless and inert, will no longer tolerate the race which has for a moment disturbed its solitude'?[1] Nowhere that I know is the stark factuality of science so majestically garbed in language.

What a mysterious job is yours. How *do* you spot a best—or even a good-seller? I will do all I can for your Reynard FitzGerald. Isn't it time his letters were properly edited, or am I out of date? I have only Aldis Wright's two vols, which aren't really edited at all. Nobody and nothing alluded to ever have an explanatory note. A.W. was an old humbug. I remember him at Trinity—one of those absurdly formidable-looking old dons, grim, rigid, incurably 1850. 'Sound your alarum, sir' was his angry injunction to an undergraduate on a bicycle who nearly ran him down.

Must I read Coleridge's letters? In the vol I opened recently I read 'So beautiful a countenance [Byron's] I scarcely ever saw, his teeth so many stationary smiles, his eyes the open portals of the sun.' Of course I read on, but soon lost my way in the purple fog of his English. But perhaps I should have persevered?

30 January 1960   *Bromsden Farm*
It's usually impossible to forecast what books are going to sell, unless the author already has a steady public. I always assume that anything I particularly like will not sell at all, but publish it nevertheless. If one abandons one's own opinion in an attempt to gauge the market, one is lost indeed. It's a mug's game.

The only way to tackle Coleridge's letters is one or two at a time, skipping: otherwise you'll assuredly get bogged down.

Estimates on Oscar show that it will make 850 *large* pages, and if I can't somehow manage to print more than 3000 copies the price will have to be *five guineas*. (The setting up of the type will cost £1500, and the more copies one can spread this over, the cheaper each copy will be.) My chief hope is that the American publishers will agree to my printing their edition at the same time as mine. If they do, and I can print a total of 10,000 copies, I can publish at *three* guineas, which is a little better. See with what mundane considerations the purity of scholarship is beset!

[1] From *The Foundations of Belief* (1895).

Adam reports that his English Extra Studies are divided equally
between Keats (please send me an edition, he adds) and some novel
published last month. No such nonsense would have been permitted
in G.W.L.'s day.

I am gradually collecting objects for the London Library sale.
Leonard Woolf has sent copies of the first six Hogarth Press books,
which he and Virginia set up and printed by hand: they should fetch
a lot. And the splendid old G.M. Trevelyan says that he can never
repay the London Library, without which his early books could not
have been written. He is giving us drawings by Domenichino,
Romney and Edward Lear, as well as the manuscript of his own auto-
biographical essay!! He apologised for not bringing them to London,
as he is too blind, so I am to collect them at Cambridge on Monday
afternoon.

This morning my eye fell on *The Egoist* [by George Meredith] (I
have a battered first edition—three vols—which belonged to
Augustine Birrell) and I took down the first vol, found the first
chapter enchanting, and quickly put the book back on the shelf in
case I should be so beguiled that my work would go by the board. If
I ever have a free day I'll go a bit further: when did you last try it?

The railwaymen are obviously insane. We *may* escape something very
like a general strike, but hadn't the boil better burst? How obvious it
is that we can't go on in this atmosphere of perpetual strikes threatened or actual. But how is it to be tackled? The trouble is that dem-
ocratic government demands (1) more brains (2) more unselfishness
(3) more patience, and (4) more imagination than there is the smallest reason to suppose human nature will be able to produce for several
hundred years. Aphorism by GWL.

Did you ever read the Tranby Croft baccarat case[1]—and if so tell
me *why* Sir William Gordon-Cumming cheated. His income was
about £7-8000 a year. But my uncle who was in his regiment said he
was suspected long before of cheating at cards by his brother-officers.

---

[1] For a full account of this famous case in 1891, involving the Prince of Wales, see
Cheating at Cards by John Welcome (1963).

The day after I saw you, old Jonathan Cape died suddenly, and his *Times* obituary, which I had promised to do eighteen months ago, had to be dashed off in a couple of hours. I am also supposed to be writing Diana Cooper's obituary for *The Times*, but I find the task unsympathetic to the point of impossibility when the subject is alive and flourishing.

I think Sir William cheated because he liked winning, so that his wealth had nothing to do with it.

Next Wednesday I have to take the chair at a Foyle's Literary Lunch (I've never been to one before) in honour of Priestley's massive new tome *Literature and Western Man*, of which I've read a good chunk: it's a remarkable achievement, though I can't quite understand why he took the trouble to write it, or who exactly is expected to read it.

The American publishers of Oscar's letters have proved most co-operative, and proofs should start coming in before the end of March. Then the fun begins!

E.M. Forster has offered to give the manuscript of *A Passage to India* for the London Library sale! He says it's messy and incomplete, but it should fetch a tidy sum. I fear I shan't get it without another journey to Cambridge, and I'm always so short of time. You've no idea how often I envy you your comparative leisure to do and read what you want.

The fly in the amber of leisure to read all one wants to is that it belongs to a period of life when one gradually becomes more conscious of 'Time's hurrying footsteps' and Winston's 'surly advance of decrepitude'. The grim Scottish aurist says a permanently flat drum in my left ear is not temporary but eternal, i.e. old age. But some kind of hearing-aid will probably materialise in a week or two. They tell me the defect of it is that what one hears most clearly is one's breathing and the beating of one's heart. We shall see.

Jonathan Cape's funeral on Monday was icy, and the clergyman so thin-voiced, old and doddery that I feared he might have to be shovelled into the same grave. The church at Petersham is a lovely old building with high pews, and a gallery round three sides of it. I travelled down by tube and taxi, but got a speedy lift back from a chartered accountant (Cape's and mine). He said that for years he had tried to persuade Jonathan to give some of his fortune to his five children, and so avoid at least part of the crippling death-duties, but the old boy always refused. Power to such as he is simply money, and if you part with any of your money you must lose some of your power. Jonathan was in fact, despite my obituary notice, one of the tightest fisted old bastards I've ever encountered, though his partner Wren Howard is even tighter. Still, one doesn't engrave a man's faults on his tombstone, does one?

The Foyle lunch was hard work. I took an old friend as my guest, a most amusing widow called Josephine Bott (see my *Hugh Walpole*, *passim*), and when we arrived Miss Foyle (dolled up to the tens and immensely refined) asked if I would receive the guests. I said I was her servant, so Jo and I stood solemnly inside the door and warmly shook hands with dozens of people as an enormous man in red called out their names with a roar. Tiny little old women with purple dresses and white fur hats and a surprising number of men. Jo almost got the giggles and tried to abandon me, but I made her stay, pointing out that we were in a strong position, since none of the guests had the faintest idea who *we* were, whereas we knew at least all their names. Several hundred people sat down to what proved a surprisingly palatable lunch (sole, chicken, ice-cream and peaches, white wine). I was between the two Priestleys, which was fun. After lunch I made a brief introductory speech, then Richard Church spoke well but dully about Priestley, and J.B.P. replied in his happiest and least combative vein. He said: 'When I arrived, the Chairman asked me why I always arrive at a function in my honour with a face of thunder (as I indeed had), and I'll tell you. Most of the time I'm glum because I'm not being praised, and on the rare occasions when I *am* praised I'm ashamed because I haven't done better.' Which I thought rather charming. The whole thing took more than two hours.

25 February 1960   *Grundisburgh*
My hearing-aid is not yet to hand, in fact I still await a summons to the clinic. It is a rather sinister fact that several people who have the thing quite rarely use it. Like another friend whose first action when

taking his seat at table, is to remove his dentures, which he says are just tolerable except when eating!

I notice in today's literary page in *The Times* that there is a sudden revival of interest in Southey, of all dreary dogs. Are you aware of this? It seems to be his political writings rather than his poetry.

I have been recently rereading all the *Martin Chuzzlewit* bits in which Mr Pecksniff and Mrs Gamp come (and *of course* the whole story of M.C. and Mark Tapley in America). Gosh! the man's mind was simply a *ceaseless* bubbling-up of fun and fantasy and the right words for embodying every notion, big and little. And how magnificently bad his character-drawing is! All his folk are black or white, e.g. Jonas Chuzzlewit and Tom Pinch—no iota of good in one or bad in other—and both therefore very tedious. And Macaulay called *Martin Chuzzlewit* frivolous and dull, and refused to review it because he had dined with Dickens—a lovely Victorian blend of stupidity and gentlemanliness!

27 February 1960   *Bromsden Farm*

I'm sorry to start this week by quoting your least favourite author, but Comfort has been reading *Pride and Prejudice*, and she says I am exactly like Mr Bennet: 'In his library he had been always sure of leisure and tranquillity; and though prepared, as he told Elizabeth, to meet with folly and conceit in every other room in the house, he was used to be free from them there.' I see what she means, and try hard to be charitable, but this room, which I made out of an old dairy so as to get away from the children, is now so much the warmest and cosiest room in the house that they tend to congregate here.

This morning I drove over to visit the Poet Laureate[1] at Burcote Brook, between Dorchester and Abingdon. One bumps up a dismal drive to a low-slung desolate-looking house standing in the midst of much unkempt grass, with the swollen Thames flowing sullenly past. He had ready for me three cartons, all packed and labelled by him, containing no fewer than *128* of his own books and pamphlets, in each of which he had written something—a quotation or other remark, sometimes about the London Library—and signed his name. It was all most touching.

---

[1] John Masefield (1878–1967).

Talking of millionaires, did I tell you that I have managed to extract £500 from Mr Roy Thomson, the owner of the *Sunday Times* and many other papers? We have now passed the £10,000 mark—half way there!

On Wednesday I travelled again to Cambridge and visited E.M. Forster at King's. I found the dear old man surrounded with sheets of the manuscript of *A Passage to India*, which he was vainly trying to put in order for me. I told him I'd do all that for him, swept it up and took it back to London. After two evenings of sorting (when I should have been doing a hundred other things) I've got it into pretty good order, despite his appalling handwriting, and it should fetch a pretty penny. After all this sweat and toil we've received only some fifty lots, and we need 120. Somehow I must try to assemble the other seventy by the end of March, so that the cataloguer can get to work. T.S.E. has been laboriously copying out *The Waste Land* in Morocco, and yesterday I got a postcard from him, beginning:

Oh Chairman, my Chairman,
The fearful task is done!

I long for further news of your hearing-aid. Perhaps you'll hear, not only your own heart beating and clothes rustling, but the bats squeaking in your belfry, the chip creaking on your shoulder, and the bees buzzing in your bonnet. Every man his own concert-party!

I can't help having a soft spot for old Southey, though I was quite unaware of any general feeling in that direction. Landor thought the world of him: a much greater poet than Wordsworth, said the old silly. But isn't the *Life of Nelson* rather good?

2 March 1960   *Grundisburgh*

Pride and Prejudice is the Jane Austen I like best. As to the others my resentment (as of course you know) is composed partly of annoyance at myself for not seeing what so many great and good men are apparently unanimous in praising, and partly impatience with the amount of *Schwärmerei* there is about her by Walkley and David Cecil and all those voluble women.

I was amused and pleased by the *Times* leader putting Harold Nicolson firmly and justly in his place about T.C.—one of what I

suppose to be the rare occasions on which H.N. spoke foolishly.[1]
Please read the very last paragraph in his *Reminiscences*, just after he
had finished with Wordsworth, and tell me how can one *not* love the
man who wrote that?[2]

Why does J.B. Priestley, in *Literature and Western Man*, give a
short parenthesis and no more to Milton; how can *he* be deaf to the
organ-voice? Another question. The excellent N. Bentley has a
lovely remark about M. Arnold's 'chilblained mittened musing',
which is shrewd and telling about a good many of his poems, but
what about Sohrab, Thyrsis, and Scholar Gypsy? Do tax him with
this little catechism.

5 March 1960   *Bromsden Farm*
I forgot to tell you that I asked J.B.P. about his unhappy trip to
Australia, where he clearly put the natives' backs up, as he inevitably
does wherever he goes. 'What did you say to upset them?' I asked.
'Nothing at all,' says he—and then, after a pause, 'I did say that their
big cities reminded me of Wolverhampton after a long dry spell—but
nothing else.'

On Thursday Christie's sent out a 'press release' about the London
Library sale, and I was rung up by every newspaper in London. After
lunch the B.B.C. telephoned to ask if I would be interviewed on television. I felt I must agree, but stipulated that I must be conveyed to
Alexandra Palace and back in a B.B.C. car. This they arranged. I was on
view for two minutes, twenty-one seconds, and the whole thing took
exactly *three hours!*

Next morning a widow sent the library a cheque for £2000, but no
amount of flattering unction can persuade me that this had any con-
nexion with my TV appearance. Also I have persuaded one of the
independent TV companies to subscribe £250 *a year*! I started my TV

---

[1] He had called Carlyle 'a horrid old thing'.

[2] 'In a few years, I forget in how many and when, these Wordsworth appearances
in London ceased; we heard, not of ill-health perhaps, but of increasing love of rest;
at length of the long sleep's coming; and never saw Wordsworth more. One felt his
death as the extinction of a public light, but not otherwise. The public itself found
not much to say of him, and staggered on to meaner but more pressing objects. Why
should I continue these melancholy jottings in which I have no interest; in which
the one figure that could interest me is almost wanting! I will cease.'

interview: 'The London Library was founded in 1841 by the *great writer* Thomas Carlyle ....' I knew you would approve.

12 March 1960   *Bromsden Farm*

Two little things I forgot to tell you last week: (1) when I looked out of my bedroom window here at 7.30 on Monday morning, just as it was getting light, I was enchanted to see five wild deer, grey and ghostly, in the field. By the time I had had my bath they had vanished into the wood, and now I only *just* believe in their existence. (2) Coming down exhausted in the train on Friday evening I was irritated from Paddington to Henley by two schoolgirls, who talked and giggled loudly without a break. I could have slapped them both with pleasure, and then one of them said, quite seriously, 'I've given up being beastly to Daddy for Lent,' and my wrath subsided.

What, if anything, makes you cry? I asked Harold Nicolson this question at the Lit. Soc. dinner, and he said: 'Three things only—patriotism, injustice righted, and misunderstanding explained. Tragedy never.' I agree whole-heartedly about patriotism: can't see the Queen on a newsreel without a lump in my throat; but am less sure about the other two.

17 March 1960   *Grundisburgh*

I told two noisy schoolgirls on the top of a bus recently that they shouldn't make so much din in a public place, and to my astonishment they never uttered another sound. I suppose they thought I really *was* the great Panjandrum with the little round button at top.[1]

I cry repeatedly (like Winston) certainly at some aspects of patriotism, some ridiculously obvious sob-stuff in e.g. a cinema, but mainly at *words*, used as they are in e.g. 2 *Samuel* ch. 18, *Matthew* 26, the end of *Earlham*, of 'Sohrab and Rustum', of *Lear* (which old Samuel couldn't bear to re-read, though he was editing it!) and of course the 'Thus with the year' at the beginning of *Paradise Lost*, Book Three.[2]

---

[1] From a rigmarole composed by Samuel Foote (1720–1777).

[2] The *Samuel* chapter describes the death of Absolom; the *Matthew* chapter, the woman coming to Christ with the box of precious ointment, the Last Supper, the Agony in the Garden, and Peter's denial; in the *Paradise Lost* passage, Milton laments his own blindness.

Oh yes, and I think I must tell *you*. My Aunt Lucy (Lady Frederick Cavendish)'s husband was murdered in Phoenix Park, Dublin, in 1881 and it broke her heart.[1] She was very religious and quite enchanting, so full of humour and understanding; we children all loved her. Well, the murderers were rounded up and several put to death. The ring-leader, Casey, nicknamed 'Skin-the-goat,' was to be hanged on a certain day, and the evening before Aunt Lucy sent his wife the little gold crucifix she always wore, as a sign of forgiveness—and other things. Of course *she* never told anyone, but Mrs. C. probably did. Anyway *old* George Trevelyan tells it in his Life of Macaulay, and says it is the most beautiful human action he ever heard of. That makes me cry whenever (very rarely) I have told it. It *could* be misunderstood, but Aunt L. was the most entirely genuine person that ever lived.

19 March 1960   *Bromsden Farm*

My friend Humphry House couldn't read aloud 'whose dwelling is the light of setting suns' and the lines around it, without tears.[2] On the other hand my Uncle Duff habitually cried when he was reading, and in the theatre, at almost any emotional passage, and in a way I rather envy that extra enjoyment of his.

Leonard Russell, the literary editor of the *Sunday Times*, asked me to lunch on Monday at a place called The Paint Box in a back-street near the B.B.C., which he had seen advertised. I arrived first and found it to be a pitch-dark basement with faint lights round the edges and a hidden gramophone playing incessantly. Two solitary men and a couple were sitting at widely spaced tables, groping for their food in the gloom. A strong smell of bad cooking pervaded everything. I sat down at a tiny bar to wait. Presently some curtains on one side were

[1] Lord Frederick Cavendish was Chief Secretary for Ireland when he was murdered by Fenians a few hours after arriving in Dublin.

[2] '. . . a sense sublime
Of something far more deeply interfused,
Whose dwelling is the light of setting suns,
And the round ocean and the living air,
And the blue sky, and in the mind of man:
A motion and a spirit, that impels
All thinking things, all objects of all thought.'
From 'Lines composed a few miles above Tintern Abbey', by Wordsworth.

pulled back to reveal a tiny stage, on which a stark-naked Eurasian girl was reclining on the floor, with her back against a chair. She had a fine figure, but was clearly not allowed to move an inch for fear of breaking the law. None of the half-dozen people in the room paid the faintest attention to her, but I thought it only civil to face in her direction until my host arrived. He was extremely embarrassed and kept his back firmly towards the girl, who must, I fear, have been frozen. We played for safety with cold ham and an omelette. After about half an hour the curtains were drawn again, and soon the girl appeared in the restaurant, rather scruffily dressed and far less prepossessing. Later she carried on a piercingly loud telephone conversation in what I took to be Malayan, a few yards from our table. Apparently London and our other cities are full of such places, where tired business men can eat nasty food with a frozen nude in front of them. Perhaps even in Ipswich...?

The best London Library news is that James Strachey (to whom I wrote soliciting) is going to give us the manuscript of Lytton's *Queen Victoria* for the sale! Willie Maugham is sending the manuscript of a long short-story, and Nancy Mitford a whole novel.

23 March 1960   *Grundisburgh*
                                                            (Summer-house)

Adam's scholastic career is most impressive.[1] I imagine you chatting with him on a summer evening about specific gravity. Who teaches him? In the Nineties all the science-beaks were absurd, though Porter had a touch of genius, and was a fine showman. He told K. Fisher who was brought in to re-organise Eton science (which P. thought was unnecessary) that all the science teaching at Eton except his own was mere wind, and got the Johnsonian retort: 'But even so, my dear Porter, is it not better that we should have organised wind instead of casual flatulence?' K. Fisher was a good man.

27 March 1960   *Bromsden Farm*

Yesterday I drove over and had tea with Lytton Strachey's brother James, a charming old boy with a white beard, blind in one eye, who lives with his psychoanalyst wife in a fine centrally heated, book-infested house in a wood above Marlow. He has now translated

[1] He had come second in the top Science division at Eton.

eighteen of Freud's twenty-three books into English and still seems quite cheerful. He gave me the complete manuscript of *Queen Victoria*, beautifully legible, together with corrected typescript, corrected page proofs, and a number of notebooks in which L.S. planned the book and took notes for it—what a haul! I found it difficult to thank him adequately.

30 March 1960   *Grundisburgh*

The line I have in mind for the Leys School in May is not anti-science (though I shall have a little swipe or two at Hogben and co) but rather to show how *clarity* of style is essential to both literature *and* science—and how they can and must almost entirely acquire that on their own, with very little help from the beak. Do you think that is at all a promising line? Of course I am not anti-science (it is important that Adam should not think that) but only arrogant ignorant scientists—e.g. Hogben.

There is a good deal of fun in the papers just now. Are you well up in Francis Bacon's painting? His 'Sleeping Figure' in to-day's *Daily Telegraph* has strong emetic value (hailed of course as of immense power and originality). And I like the brothers Cheeryble on p. 19 who are suing the Attorney-General and a brace of policemen for £10,000, for charging them (successfully) with swindling. America of course does well with a 'special tariff' for black men at an eating-house which charges them 17/9 for a cup of coffee and then summons them for making a disturbance.

2 April 1960   *Bromsden Farm*

The Oscar proofs have begun to pour in, and I am already overwhelmed with sheets and sheets of paper, all requiring checking and titivation. I shall not badger you at this tiresome stage, but perhaps when the proofs are paged and manageable (in some months' time) you might be amused to read them and look for howlers?

Francis Bacon's pictures are too revolting for words—stockbrokers with two heads and no trousers, elemental horrors crawling up walls.

My publishing activities, having lain dormant since January, will start up again on April 28: nothing very exciting, I fear, or very saleable—except for a frightful book about the Wolverhampton Wanderers football club. The ghost-author is always unobtainable and the book is almost a year late—luckily perhaps, since W.W. are now in the Cup Final, and may win the League as well. Our first edition of 5000 copies looks like being exhausted before publication, which is more than can be said of most of my precious literary books.

6 April 1960   *Grundisburgh*

Those who say that Carlyle's prophecies of disaster have been disproved, don't know or have forgotten that the *ultimate* crash that he foresaw might not happen for a century or two. *All* his lamentations a hundred years ago—love of money, lowering of standards, political humbug, impotence of religion etc—would surely be intensified today, if indeed the English language could carry any more than he put into it. If Gladstone on Ireland, and Dizzy on the Franchise, nearly killed him with exasperation, what would Barbara Castle have done?

At the moment my grandson Lawrence is on the way to Greece with a party. I hope he will see the Acropolis by moonlight, *and* with the southern sun on the rich marble of the Parthenon—quite unique and unforgettable. The light seems to be coming out of the marble. It is worth remembering (or is it?) that Bernard Shaw wrote to Ellen Terry that he was glad to get away from Athens 'with its stupid classic Acropolis and smashed pillars'. One of his pronouncements that make one's toes itch.

9 April 1960   *Bromsden Farm*

I have just finished the manuscript of Peter's book about the Younghusband expedition—at present called *Bayonets to Lhasa*. It's a fascinating story very well told, but I can't see it selling as well as *The Siege at Peking*: it lacks comedy, and the Dowager Empress, and a proper climax, but you'll like it, I'm sure.

Sunday morning

Last week I saw Diana Cooper, fresh from the De Gaulle banquet at Buckingham Palace. She reported Winston as totally *non compos*, and scarcely able to walk. I fear the old hero has lived too long.

I expect you saw that Peter Davies[1] threw himself under a train. The poor fellow had for years been dying of some incurable disease,

[1] Publisher.

243

but this does seem to me a particularly inconsiderate form of suicide: just think of the driver of the train, and the people who have to pick up the remains! Sleeping-pills are surely the most civilised means, and going to sleep is itself pleasurable, but I suppose they don't work instantaneously and might leave time for a change of heart. Hemlock itself wasn't all that quick, was it?

Last week I also got copies of the last nine Oscar letters which had hitherto evaded me, and now I know of none that I haven't got, though many more probably lurk here and there—especially in America. You must forgive my harping on Oscar: he is much on my mind just now.

13 April 1960   *Grundisburgh*

The *fundamental* difference between Carlyle and Macaulay is that C. never lost his sense of mystery, and M. never had one. I expect you may find C's lamentations for Jane a bit too much. In any recollections connected with her he writes as if she had died the moment before, and as if she simply was unique—body, soul, and mind. The old man had extraordinary tenderness, and yet you can see, from what she quotes in her letters of what he said, that this usually had a grumpy sound. I suppose the Scots are like that—his family especially. 'Pithy, bitter-speakin' bodies' some neighbour said about the whole clan.

I shall be greatly honoured by having the very smallest bit to do with the Oscar letters. Will the chorus of indolent reviewers see the immense trouble you have taken with it? Some will, no doubt, and the rest don't matter. You will have every right to be wholly indifferent to what they say—like T.C., content with the knowledge that you have done every blessed thing that you could.

Where did I read recently a complaint about T.S. Eliot's dullness in conversation? Not that he is alone among great men. Housman could be deadly—partly from disdain, partly because, just like Kipling, he didn't *want* to give his opinions about this and that, except on rare occasions in congenial company, and with just the right amount of the right food and drink inside him. Too often, as Max Beerbohm said, he should have had a poached egg in his room. But he was very greedy, so paid much attention to the fare and none to his fellow-guests.

I have had my aid fitted, but I doubt if I shall wear it much. There is too much fiddling with adjustment and parking of batteries etc.

They tell me I shall get used to hearing my own voice (my daughters rudely say that surely I must be *that* by now). I think I may find it useful when sitting on a committee, and so avoid announcing as the next item on the agenda the matter they had just finished discussing. On Tuesday I go to a Christie play just to test the thing. If I could resume playgoing that *would* be a great gain. *Nous verrons.*

Suicides are incalculable—wasn't it Brutus's wife who died by swallowing red-hot charcoal? 'Many the ways, the little home is one'.[1] I suppose a doctor can do it without pain or delay.

Easter Saturday, 16 April 1960   *Bromsden Farm*
I have just re-read *The Bridge of San Luis Rey* by Thornton Wilder, which I hadn't looked at since I bought and much enjoyed it when it first appeared—in 1927, when I was twenty. To my astonishment I now think it *first-rate*—a shaped and finished work of art—contrived, admittedly, but none the worse for that. Do read it again and see whether you agree. It seems to me to have improved and mellowed in thirty-three years, and I don't see why it shouldn't be read and enjoyed as long as books are read. I shall nervously await your reaction to this *ex cathedra* pronouncement.

You must give the deaf-aid a proper hearing, to coin a phrase, before you miss any of Cuthbert's witticisms.

The other day I was trying to find words to explain my dislike of Henry James's old-age revisions of his early work—and today I find that Max (I might have guessed) put it perfectly:

> One . . . wasn't glad that for the definitive edition of his works he did a lot of re-writing—a process akin to patching pale grey silk with snippets of very dark thick brown velvet. It was a strange sad aberration: and a wanton offence against the laws of art.

Sunday noon.
On the Resurrection morning I slept till 10.30, and over my breakfast (one slice of bread and marmalade, one mug of tea) I read the second volume of a book called *La Jeunesse d'André Gide*, from which I was happy to learn that the French translation of *Wuthering Heights* is called *Les Hauts de Hurlevent*.

[1] T.L. Beddoes, *Death's Jest Book*, act 1, scene 1.

Bridget has gone riding, Adam (after attending Holy Communion in the village church) is pursuing pigeons with his gun, Comfort is scrubbing the kitchen floor, Duff is with his sweetheart in Wales. There is much rough work to do in the garden—clipping and pathlaying and stone-carting: the sun is shining through the window, and I must away. I like to think of you sunning in your summer-house, perhaps thinking up a joke or a quotation for next week's letter. How many words, I wonder, have we now exchanged? A quarter of a million each? Sorry about this ink—fountain is the right name for my pen. A lovely nib but an incontinent belly.

20 April 1960   Grundisburgh

My hearing-aid. Well, yes I do hear better with it, but it is, somehow, not all that gain. One hears so much else, plus a sort of old gramophone background noise. But I missed very little at the theatre last night, where we all went to see *The Unexpected Guest* by Agatha Christie. Very good fun. She is really devilish clever in making one suspect *everyone* in the affair, except the right one in the last minute. I think I shall keep the aid for such occasions—and especially committee-meetings, where everyone mumbles, and one sits at a long table. I shall *not* bring it to the Lit. Soc. and Sir Cuthbert's acidities shall waste their sweetness on the desert air.

I am browsing in Johnson's Lives, *not* of the poets but of others, and constantly turning up nuggets, e.g. the reason for Blake (Admiral) not getting a fellowship at Merton, because of 'his want of stature, it being the custom of Sir Henry Savile, then warden of that college, to pay much regard to the outward appearance of those who solicited preferment in that society'. In fact Sir H.S. was a—? I will send you more as I find them. Meanwhile let me remind you that when Johnson and Boswell supped with a farmer at Armadale on Skye the fare put on the table was minced collops, fricassee of fowl, ham and tongue, haddocks, herrings, frothed milk, bread pudding, and syllabubs made with port wine. Those were the days.

23 April 1960   Bromsden Farm

Almost the only thing I have learned in thirty years literary life is that *all* authors, whatever they pretend, *love* getting appreciative letters from readers.[1] Authorship is a lonely business, and after the nine days' wonder of reviews etc, the ripples are apt to subside, and as far as the author knows no one is reading or enjoying his book. The most acceptable letters, therefore, are the ones that come after the initial splash has subsided. *Verb. sap.*

Dinner at All Souls was uphill work. Besides the Warden there were only three other Fellows there—a rather dried-up Professor of Comparative Religions, a young philosopher with long hair, and the black Fellow (from Ghana perhaps) who never spoke. When the daylight died and the only light came from the seven-branched candlesticks on the table, you couldn't see him at all against the dark panelling of the Common Room until he opened his mouth and his very white teeth flashed out. Sparrow told me afterwards that the servants had complained of this fact. I gathered that they all regret having elected the poor fellow—falling over backwards to avoid any hint of segregation—and I daresay he feels pretty miserable too.

On Tuesday I lunched with Sir Fordham Flower, brewer and chairman of the Stratford Theatre, and Alfred Francis, chairman of the Old Vic. As a result I think both these great concerns will contribute mildly to the Phoenix Trust. Flower was interesting about the results of advertising his beer on commercial TV, describing how the demand rose hugely *next morning*! whereas they reckon that ordinary advertising (press, posters and what they call 'point of sale') takes at least *three years* to produce any visible result. No wonder the TV companies are so rich.

On Wednesday at a meeting of the B.B.C. General Advisory Council, I spoke not a word. There was much discussion of B.B.C. interviews on sound and television, and it was generally agreed that, whereas private people being interviewed should be treated with care and consideration, public men were, as it were, fair game and could be more roughly handled.

This morning Comfort got a letter to say someone had left her £100 and I got a very grand one from Windsor Castle signed by Michael Adeane and saying that the Queen, God bless her, will present a book to the London Library sale. This was Harold Nicolson's doing, and the publicity value should be considerable.

---

[1] G.W.L. had doubted whether J.B. Priestley would appreciate a fan letter from him.

27 April 1960   *Grundisburgh*

You know practically all the modern remarks one comes across on
Carlyle are based, if not on sheer ignorance of him and his best work,
on a view of him which is limited to his *Latter-Day Pamphlets* pro-
Germanism, Might is Right, and the greatly overdrawn picture by
Froude of his inconsiderateness to Jane. It must not, too, be forgotten that the old man never meant his *Reminiscences* to be published
at all, with their morbid self-accusations, exaltation of Jane, and con-
sequent denigration of almost everybody else. There is a sort of conspiracy to ignore his rectitude, courage, independence, insight and
depth of feeling. Stimulated by your interest (which I find nowhere
else) I have just re-read his magnificent essays on Johnson and Burns
and am deep in 'The Diamond Necklace'.

30 April 1960   *Bromsden Farm*

I have spent most of this lovely sunny day kneeling in the garden,
picking stones out of the new November-sown lawn. Excellent
therapy, no doubt, but I am now suffering from some sort of double
housemaid's knee and move with groans. Whether or not Carlyle
intended his *Reminiscences* to be published, I am enjoying them almost
more than anything of his—certainly more as a whole, for in most of
his works one has to wade a good deal to get to the plums, if you will
forgive a peculiar metaphor. This book is *all* enjoyable, the writing
much more unbuttoned and less strained than elsewhere. I particularly
like the description of a Warwickshire serving woman: 'correct as an
eight-day clock, and making hardly as much noise', and when T.C.
rode over to Hagley and thereafter 'Lord Lyttelton's mansion I have
ever since in my eye as a noble-looking place', I raised a special cheer.

The Oscar proofs are now approaching the half-way mark, and the
galleys themselves are becoming a burden. The trouble with a book
of this length and complexity is that one needs an index at the typescript stage, and another for the galley-proofs, for unless one can
remember exactly where each letter and each note come (which one
can't) one wastes hours in searching. When we get to page-proofs
(which you shall see) I shall have to compile *the* index, which will take
many weeks.[1]

---

[1] It took six months.

On Thursday evening Ruth and I went with an American friend to *A Passage to India*, which we thoroughly enjoyed. The Indian lady dramatist has made an excellent job of it, and the leading part is brilliantly played by a Pakistani actor. Afterwards we had a first-class supper with John Gielgud at Prunier's (*oeufs en gelée*, steak, an excellent claret, and a melting-in-the-mouth piece of cake). John G. regaled us with a variety of good stage anecdotes, told with punch and finish. Vague and dreamy about most things, he is exact and always amusing about the theatre, having been, as he says, stagestruck all his life.

On Tuesday I dined with the James Lavers in the Boltons. Vyvyan Holland (Oscar's son) and his wife were there, and I was able to enlist Mrs V.H.'s support in my campaign to prevent V.H. from expurgating anything in the Letters. He owns the copyright and must be appeased.

7 May 1960   *Bromsden Farm*

Adam reports clean-bowling an opponent with his first ball of the season: perhaps the umpire hadn't called 'Play'. I have finished the first volume of T.C.'s *Reminiscences* and am keeping the second for Swaledale. (By the way, T.C. refers to the Yorkshire moors as 'those mute wildernesses and their rough habitudes and populations'.) I particularly enjoyed, and sympathised with, the plight of poor John Murray (Byron's one)—do you remember?

> Stupider man than the great Murray, in look, in speech, in conduct, in regard to this poor *Sartor* question, I imagined I had seldom or never seen! Afterwards it became apparent to me that partly he was sinking into the heaviness of old age, and partly, still more important, that in regard to this particular *Sartor* question his position was an impossible one; position of a poor old man endeavouring to answer yes *and* no!

My ageing publisher's heart goes out to the poor old fellow: I know that feeling so well.

After watching the royal wedding[1] yesterday (I hired a television set for the day, so that all the staff could see it—and we all loved it) I think £25,000 was a very modest outlay for such general enjoyment and beneficial outlet for emotions. Reflect also that a great deal of the

---

[1] Of Princess Margaret and Anthony Armstrong-Jones.

money goes in wages to the people who put up the decorations, and so benefits them. The royal yacht is permanently manned and maintained, so that fuel and food are the only extras for the honeymoon. As you see, I grow more militantly Royalist daily.

11 May 1960   *Grundisburgh*

You are now there [Swaledale]—browning, probably already, happy as a sandboy, whatever a sandboy may be, and Ruth somewhere in the immediate offing, looking quite lovely against the background of heather and hill—that endless sky which the children evacuated from London to the country in 1939 found so horrible and terrifying. Not that she depends on background. She would give grace to the goods-yard-wall[1] of St Pancras Station.

Poor old Murray. Publishing must be a very difficult vocation. For one thing the difference between silliness and genius must often be very hard to discriminate. One post brings Della Crusca[2] or Dada and the next *Tristram Shandy* or Ezra Pound (a good seller, I imagine, though to me unreadable). And would any sane man spot *Lucky Jim* as the book which everyone *must* read?

I had a heavy fall on the top of a bus yesterday and have cracked a back rib. The leech prescribes rest for at least a week and says at my age etc a cracked rib is not to be sneezed at. Not that I would dream of trying. Every movement is infernally painful. Dressing is purgatory; changing position in bed is hell; merely to clear the throat *very* gingerly would start Himmler or even Heydrich chuckling. And I always thought a cracked rib about equalled a mildly sprained ankle. The only *soulagement* to my feelings is that it was not my fault but that of the damned bus, which stopped with a hideous jerk as I was making my way to the steps, and hurled me to the ground.

The opera! It is an immensely ridiculous art-form surely; 'an exotic and irrational entertainment' the old man called it,[3] but it survives with apparent ease for all its absurdity. When King Mark found Tristan making love with Isolde, instead of laying T. out with one swashing blow, he merely lamented the situation for twenty-two

---

[1] The brickwork of which was particularly admired by John Betjeman.
[2] A group of sentimental versifiers in the eighteenth century.
[3] Dr Johnson, *Life of John Hughes*. R.H.-D. had been to *The Trojans*.

minutes in notes of indescribable fatness (he was a superb basso-pro-fondo). I have just read Roger's book.[1] The royal family circle must always have been fascinating—in one way. Not one single solitary remark ever made indicating the slightest understanding or appreci-ation of anything at all three inches below life's surface or two inches off the beaten track. What did George V and VI *read* in their spare time? Our little Queen I believe is fond of Jane Austen.

15 May 1960   *Kisdon Lodge, Keld*

The first night we slept exactly twelve hours (10.30 to 10.30), since when we have averaged ten hours a night. The first morning, when we were fetching water from the spring in the next field (six gallons, carried in two buckets and two plastic water-carriers given us by Elisabeth Beerbohm) in hot sunshine, Ruth spotted a ring-ousel's nest in the stone wall. The fields are thick with wildflowers, which Ruth arranges in the most enchanting way all over the cottage. Just now there are kingcups, primroses, cowslips, oxlips, forget-me-nots, anemones, heartsease and masses of deep purple orchids. We have been to one village sale, where in an afternoon of pure enjoyment we spent 21/6 on a looking-glass for the bedroom, two pillow-cases, three curtains and a quantity of plates and dishes. The weather has been Aprilish—hot sunshine between hailstorms—but we are just as happy inside as out. Oscar proofs arrive most days and we are busy checking the letters against photostats of the originals.

The grandfather clock is ticking placidly; the Aladdin lamp sheds its splendid light; the fire burns brightly, and another is already lit in the bedroom. There is no sound outside, save now and then the mournful cry of a curlew. If one stands outside the cottage door one can see four lights strung out along the bottom of the valley: three are in farmhouses and the fourth in the telephone-box in Keld. It is on all night, and doubtless we all pay for it. The lady who keeps the only shop in Keld is stone-deaf and has been courting for thirty-five years. This year we hear she has acquired a deaf-aid (*verb. sap.*) and has so far regained touch with life that she insists on shutting the shop at the regular hour of 6 p.m. (and then removes the deaf-aid to avoid hearing the knocks and shouts of the outraged villagers) instead of

[1] *Hanover to Windsor.*

obligingly staying open till all hours, as she has done for many years. The couple who run the Keld post-office are giving it up on July 31. They're sick of being tied all day and everyday for £4.10.0 a week, which is apparently all they get.

18 May 1960   *Grundisburgh*

The plot thickens. The doctor—like all of his trade a simple psychologist—told me I had a cracked rib, by which he really meant not cracked but broken, confident that the milder word would soothe me. But after two days it seemed to me that the pain was altogether on too majestic a scale for a mere crack, so I had it X-rayed, and that revealed *three* ribs temporarily but effectively bust. They are now sullenly mending. I can now clear my throat without feeling sick, and can walk much as usual, though, to adapt Flurry Knox on Miss Bobbie Bennett,[1] you would still look a long time at Deerfoot or Jesse Owens before you thought of me. But how bored you will be with all of this. Your letter breathes happiness, which is wonderfully refreshing in 1960.

I raced through the new life of Charles Kingsley. A tedious old hearty in many ways, but a goodish chap I expect. Not up to Newman's class with the foils, but wasn't he mainly right? And wasn't there something faintly repellent about Newman, described by Scott Holland as looking 'as delicate as an old lady washed in milk'. Remembering many boring pictures of saints in the galleries and churches of Rome I like K's calling them 'prayer-mongering eunuchs'. And after all he did write the finest English hexameter, *n'est ce pas?* 'As when an osprey aloft, dark-eyebrowed, royally crested.'[2] Do you know about N. saying of Manning: 'Ah yes, Cardinal Manning, ambition, ambition, ambition.' Some kind friend told M. who flushed and riposted; 'And shall I tell you what was wrong with Cardinal Newman? Temper, temper, temper.' Both bullseyes, no doubt.

My nephew was here recently. He says there is not much hope for Hagley. It is too near the Black Country and, there being only one park-keeper, toughs and teddies swarm at will in the park. When they want to come into it, they kick out three or four palings and come.

[1] In *Some Experiences of an Irish R. M.*
[2] From 'Andromeda.'

There is a good deal of fern and bracken in the park, and the sardonic keeper told Charles that much of the recent rise in Birmingham's population was the result of what happens in the Hagley bracken every summer evening. Old George finished building the house *exactly* two hundred years ago. *Tout passe, tout casse, tout lasse.*

22 May 1960   *Kisdon Lodge, Keld*
This week we had three sunless days of bitter east wind, which kept us at the fireside and greatly benefited the galley-proofs of O. Wilde. We have now checked 448 galleys against the photostats of the originals (finding just enough errors to make it worthwhile and amusing) and await more by tomorrow's post. The dear fellow has still two and a half years and a hundred or two letters to go. I should be doing lots of other work on the proofs, but our days seem all too short and full, and we still sleep our solid ten hours each night.

We have been for one long walk—a circumambulation of Kisdon. It took six hours, including two hours for picnic lunch and reading on the river-bank. It was hot and sunny, and we saw *no one* except a very distant farmer on a horse.

25 May 1960   *Grundisburgh*
There is a delightful holiday air about your last letter, slightly reminiscent of Tennyson's lotus-eaters reclining by their nectar, far away from everyday affairs. Just as it should be. And I fear you must find my half-baked observations on literary topics sounding very like the bloodless twittering of ghosts that Aeneas heard in Hades.

Hagley won't be got rid of till my nephew comes back from N.Z.— over two years, but I see no hope after that. The cussedness of things! My brother sold ten years ago a lot of land near Birmingham and got £110,000 for it. Very nice? Well, today it would easily fetch £1,000,000, and as my nephew says, you can do a lot with a million, and even get parlour-maids and gardeners.

30 May 1960   *Kisdon Lodge*
The final batch of Oscar galley-proofs (ending up with No 542) reached us on Saturday, and we spent most of yesterday (a still and warm but largely sunless day) checking them against the originals, finishing after tea. In the same bundle as the last Oscar proofs there

arrived *all* the galley-proofs of Diana Cooper's third volume. (What, you may ask, is holiday, and what work?) But there are only 160 of them, and I should be able to read and correct them all during to-day and tomorrow.

Last week we made two longish walking expeditions—one to Crackpot Hall, where we would like to live (jokes or no jokes), for its situation is superb, but the central part of the house collapsed some years ago—the result, they say, of centuries-old lead-workings under the hill. The other expedition was to various places, including Summer Lodge Tarn, a large and rather sinister mountain lake, miles from anywhere, in the midst of bog and heather, where thousands of black-headed gulls come every spring to nest—it must be a good sixty miles from the sea.

I have finished both large vols of Swinburne's letters. One can't *like* him much, and his shrill tirades against 'the Galilean'[1] and in favour of the Marquis de Sade are tedious and childish. But his devotion to poetry is fine, also his passionate championship of Shelley, Blake, Landor, Victor Hugo etc.

11 June 1960   *Bromsden Farm*

Last week in London, though a short one, was well-nigh intolerable. Apart from the noise, heat and stink, my office was seldom free of callers and the telephone rang incessantly. Everything had stood still during my absence, so all books are behindhand. Vyvyan Holland is trying to make me bowdlerise Oscar's letters. Of course I won't (still less will I falsify some of them, as V.H. suggests) but the copyright belongs to him and I see a deadlock looming. I can't tell you how fed up I am with it all—and how I long to retire to Kisdon's happy hill.

I met Leavis once and thought him quite revolting—dirty, messy, rude—but perhaps he grows on one. I shall certainly give him no opportunity of so doing.

16 June 1960   *Grundisburgh*

I asked him[2] a good deal about Waterloo, and you may (or may not) be surprised to hear that the [1st] Duke did not make all that many

---

[1] Jesus Christ.
[2] The 7th Duke of Wellington, at the Lit. Soc.

mistakes. But, as the D. himself said, there are so many different versions of what happened that he really became quite doubtful whether he had been there himself. Jonah and Ivor Brown and I sat for another hour afterwards. I like old Ivor very much, but doubt if he is a happy man. Yet as his old thrawn fellow-countryman said, nobody conscious of what is below the surface, i.e. the fundamental tragedy of man's life, can possibly be really happy—not even Leigh Hunt, 'idly melodious, as bird on bough'.

19 June 1960   *Bromsden Farm*

Even as Cuthbert at the dinner-table sheds around him a baleful aura of *ennui* and *malaise*, so do you, my dear George, surround yourself with an infectious gaiety and pleasure. Whenever my eye falls on you, your noble brow, towering above its brachycephalic neighbours, is always the centre of laughter and anecdote, wit and repartee. Truly your presence always raises the Lit. Soc. level to what it's supposed to be. You mustn't mind my slipping away after dinner: I have almost always had enough by then, and Ivor is delighted to have you to himself. No, I don't think he is a happy man—a disappointed one perhaps.

22 June 1960   *Grundisburgh*

What a very nice letter to get! I remember my old tutor (or 'tootor' as my aunts always pronounced it; and it was a dear old Victorian snob great-aunt who, when a relative married a Headmaster of great distinction, said gloomily, and frequently: 'No, I must say I do think it is rather—as in 'gather'—dowdy to marry a tootor') Arthur Benson saying (not that no one else ever said it) '*Everybody* likes praise, deserved or undeserved, though many will pretend they don't'. But if you *will* produce such easy and charming people to sit next to, how can I help bubbling away? I am not so sure about your reference to my noble (sic) brow '*towering*' above those of my neighbours. The Creator has a frequently malicious sense of humour. He sent me into the world with an outsize head, and fifty years later gave me Paget's Disease, of which one of the results is a slow but steady increase in the size of the head. I don't yet—like Jeeves—take no. 9 in hats, but am not so very far off. So I adopt the feeble but very human device of practically never wearing a hat. Don't sympathise about Paget: it honestly doesn't bother me at all; there are many varieties, some hideously crippling, some quite harmless, and it was worth the exorbitant (I thought) £5.5.0 that I paid to the great Rowley Bristowe twelve years ago to be told a) it would trouble me very little and b) don't waste any money going to Droitwich. I was glad especially to hear b), as, with the possible exception of Stourbridge and Dudley, Droitwich is the most unattractive of places. Wigan—like Hell—has something majestic about it. Not Droitwich. Hester Alington was nearly drowned there, as the water is so salt that if you go upside down in it you can't right yourself. Didn't that happen to Kinglake in the Dead Sea?[1]

26 June 1960   *The Swan Hotel*
                                              Newby Bridge, Lancs
                                  (My bedroom is called Coleridge)
The London Library sale exceeded all conceivable expectations—realising a grand total of £25,600!!!! Added to the £17,000 we have already collected in cash, this more than doubles the sum we originally appealed for, and should keep the Library solvent for some years. The high spot was the manuscript of Forster's *A Passage to India*, which, you remember, I travelled to Cambridge to fetch, and brought back higgledy-piggledy in my brief-case. Believe it or not, this fetched £6500—from America. Next highest was £3800 for two address-books belonging to T.E. Lawrence, and £2800 for the manuscript of *The Waste Land* which I persuaded T.S.E. to copy out last winter. The manuscript of Strachey's *Queen Victoria* fetched £1800, that of Maugham's *Up at the Villa* £1100, and so on. It was a very exciting, if hot, evening. Ruth and I dined first with the Eliots at their flat and went along with them. At dinner we spoke of Shaw, and T.S.E. said he thought S's best plays were *The Chocolate Soldier* and *My Fair Lady*—which I think better criticism than it sounds: there's nothing like a few good tunes for bolstering up a rather outmoded play.

There is mercifully no spare-room in Arthur Ransome's very uncomfortable cottage, so I am quartered in this excellent hotel. Ransome is pretty immobile—shuffling with a stick—so yesterday I drove him all day through the lakes—Esthwaite, Rydal, Grasmere,

---

[1] A.W. Kinglake (1809–1891) found it difficult to swim in the Dead Sea (*Eothen*, 1844, chapter xiii), but made no mention of capsizing.

Thirlmere, Ambleside, Derwentwater, Keswick (where I visited Hugh Walpole's grave), Bassenthwaite (we picnicked on the road above the lake) and on to Cockermouth (birthplace of Wordsworth), where we sat in the sun by the Derwent, from which Ransome has pulled innumerable sea-trout and salmon. He is much grieved by the (scarcely acceptable) realisation that he will never be able to fish again.

29 June 1960   *Grundisburgh*

To revert to O'N. and your grim dictum 'He couldn't forgive Agnes for behaving so well'.[1] Isn't that first cousin to D.H.L.'s insufferable trait of writing with the most venomous malice about those who had most helped him? Katherine Mansfield said there were three Lawrences—the black devil whom she hated, the prophet in whom she did not believe, and the man and artist whom she revered and loved. But I did not know him as a man, and am not clever enough to appreciate him as an artist, so all that is left is Nos 1 and 2, alas! But couldn't his executors have offered you something for the L.L. sale? Perhaps he thought it should be razed to the ground and the site sowed with salt, as that old ass G.B.S. suggested for Oxford.

Bad news in to-day's paper is that in a few years' time the larger apes will be no more throughout Africa. What will life be without gorillas? You mustn't anger them; if it comes to a showdown you won't win. An irate gorilla once gripped a gun-butt so tightly that his fingers sank into the wood, and in a tug-of-war he can pull over seventeen men with one hand. He has a very sensitive spirit and can suffer acutely from disappointment—like (also improbably but truly) the pike.

2 July 1960   *Bromsden Farm*

Your harping on an imaginary knighthood is a delightful fantasy. In the extremely unlikely event of one being offered, my instinct would be to accept.[2] I have no worldly ambition (only peace at Kisdon) but while one is engaged in the merry-go-round, it seems churlish to refuse any rewards from the sideshows. There is surely a great deal of snobbery—straight and inverted—in these matters.

[1] G.W.L. had been reading a biography of Eugene O'Neill, published by R.H.-D. Agnes was one of O'Neill's three wives.

[2] R.H.-D. did, in 1967.

July 5 or 6, anyway Wednesday   *Grundisburgh*

You are right about the snobbery of those who sneer at honours (or mere conceit, like Housman refusing the O.M. because Galsworthy had it). Surely old E. Garnett was quite wrong about the C.H. being given to dentists. Wasn't he mixing it up with the M.V.O., fifth class, which, the legend was, Edward VII gave to his bridge-partner who left the declaration to Tum, who had four aces.

You know, Rupert, the fundamental—and slightly depressing—difference between my letters and yours is that yours are full of interesting things you have done, and ditto people you have seen. I, having done neither, am reduced, largely, to not very inspiring chatter about what I have been reading—with an occasional diversion onto, say, gorillas or other large animals for which you do not share my taste. What can be done about it? Nothing that I myself can see. Shall I tell you what Miss Smith (nicknamed 'the Drip') said about teaching Eng. Lit. to girls who confuse Ben Jonson with Dr Johnson and are not in the least abashed by her horror? Shall I tell you how I scored off the Inspector of Taxes last week, or that the reason why George Dunnett the local carpenter won't now go up a ladder, is not because, at seventy-five, his balance (like mine) is untrustworthy, but because, his weight being eighteen stone, he is sure that sooner or later a rung will wilt beneath his foot and bring him 'with hideous ruin and combustion down'?[1] I can't (honestly) think why you like my letters, but I believe you do. One, I suppose, of the anfractuosities of the human mind. Well there it is.

Now a small problem. Henry James wrote to R.L.S. that *Tess* was '*vile. . .* pretence of sexuality. . . abomination of the language' etc. But in *The Legend of the Master* I read that in a later letter to R.L.S. he said that in spite of its faults it had 'a singular beauty and charm'. Well, where *is* that letter? He oughtn't to be left with that slightly obtuse judgment.[2] I am delighted to re-find that he regarded Carlyle as 'perhaps the very greatest of letter-writers'. But I suppose H.J. was not far wrong when he wrote 'your demolitions of the unspeakable

---

[1] Milton, *Paradise Lost*, book I.

[2] *The Legend* was a compilation, by Simon Nowell-Smith, of anecdotes about Henry James (1947). Henry James' complimentary remarks on *Tess of the D'Urbervilles* were in a letter to R.L. Stevenson on 19 March 1892, while the denigratory ones were in a letter to R.L.S. on 17 February 1893.

Froude don't persuade me that C. was amiable. . . perhaps the most disagreeable in character of men of genius of equal magnificence'.

Last week, for most of three days, Ruth and I escaped to the comparative peace of the Manuscript Room of the British Museum, where we checked the manuscript of Oscar's *De Profundis* (his longest, best and most important letter) against our proofs. The manuscript was given to the B.M. by Robbie Ross in 1909 (to ensure its not falling into the hands of Lord Alfred Douglas) with a fifty-year embargo on anyone's seeing it: R. and I are therefore almost certainly the first people who have scrutinised it properly, and to our surprise and great excitement we discovered that the so-called 'complete' version (first published in 1949) is a travesty of the original (it was printed from a wildly inaccurate typescript of Ross's). At least 1000 words were omitted, many hundreds misread, paragraphs transposed and goodness knows what.

You are quite right about Druon's *Alexander*.[1] It was intended as the first volume in a series of *biographies* of Famous Bastards: Druon is one, and is therefore interested in the subject: he prefaced the book with a long introduction proving that all the greatest men in history were illegitimate (this seems to me idiotic: who knows who's legitimate for certain?). Anyhow the series never materialised, and we were left with this isolated volume. I decided I couldn't possibly publish it as a biography in English, so I changed its title, removed the introduction, and put it out as a novel—to all which Druon most helpfully agreed. But it's nowhere near so good as his French history novels: I've just corrected the proofs of the new one, *The She-Wolf of France*, which will appear in the autumn. It includes an appallingly graphic description of the murder of Edward II in Berkeley Castle.

Here is a splendid piece of Oscar, rescued by us from the B.M. last week. It describes the recipient's [Lord Alfred Douglas] father, Lord Queensberry:

And I used to feel bitterly the irony and ignominy of my position when in the course of my three trials, beginning at the Police

---

[1] G.W.L. had been 'a little disappointed.'

Court, I used to see your father bustling in and out in the hopes of attracting public attention, as if anyone could fail to note or remember the stableman's gait and dress, the bowed legs, the twitching hands, the hanging lower lip, the bestial and half-witted grin. Even when he was not there, or was out of sight, I used to feel conscious of his presence, and the blank dreary walls of the great Court-room, the very air itself, seemed to me at times to be hung with multitudinous masks of that apelike face.

Good strong stuff, eh?, and you are almost its first reader. Mind you get the Peter Quennell book, *The Sign of the Fish*: it is reviewed in the current *Spectator* by Evelyn Waugh with a feline savagery which can only come from an old friend with a grudge.

19 July 1960   *Grundisburgh*
It is very wrong of you not to hand on anything nice that Ruth says. You don't perhaps realise that my generation of the family is profoundly diffident—quite the opposite of my uncles ('all cheek and charm' as Dean Inge said), who, as a result, all got jobs which they weren't quite up to—except my father who had no ambition at all. But you evidently think my head is easily turned, or perhaps, with the Doctor, that 'there are few things that we so unwillingly give up, even in advanced age, as the supposition that we still have the power of ingratiating ourselves with the fair sex'. Well, I don't care, and continue to send her my very best love, knowing full well though I do, what a peck of dry dust at seventy-seven she must think it (and quite rightly). What *would* life be without illusions?

24 July 1960   *Bromsden Farm*
I spent most of Friday and Saturday on a jaunt to Stratford. I was driven down by a charming widow whom I have known for thirty years. We stayed with my ex-wife, Dame Peggy Ashcroft, in a very comfortable cottage in the country nearby and in the evening saw P. act in *The Taming of the Shrew*—a negligible play which in this production they have made enchanting. I last saw it in 1927, when it was the first play in which I appeared (playing a non-speaking servant) as a student at the Old Vic. This fact, combined with Peggy's astonishing youthfulness and beauty in the part, took me back forcefully, and with

exquisite melancholy, to the time when we and the century were in our twenties. This in its turn made me long to write down some impression of those days.[1] My love for Peggy, which will be with me always, was (I now see) chiefly an intellectual and spiritual passion, tied up with poetry and music, drama, youth and spring. Basically it wasn't a physical passion at all—which is why the marriage foundered—but all the rest is still there, although we seldom meet, and a brief visit like this can be an inspiration. Forgive me for pouring it all out to you: it is still very much in my mind, and you are my conscience.

You're quite right about Cuthbert's frailty: when I helped him up from the sofa before dinner it was like lifting a parcel of bones wrapped up in tweed. As for Ezra Pound, he is (or rather was) one of those people whose *influence* is infinitely greater and more important than their writings. He undoubtedly had a great and beneficial influence on both Yeats and Eliot, and yet his own works seem to me largely wind and rubbish.

30 July 1960   *Bromsden Farm*

I dined with Veronica Wedgwood, where I met Sir Somebody Something, one of the joint heads of the Treasury, and so one of our chief rulers. He might have appeared, without make-up, as 'Self-Love' or 'Complacency' in a morality-play like *Everyman*, though his performance might have been thought a little exaggerated. As you will have gathered, I didn't take to him. When we left it was pouring with rain: he had a government car and chauffeur waiting but was too nervous to take us an inch out of his own way, so I and another chap were deposited in a streaming Oxford Street.

3 August 1960   *Grundisburgh*

I am delighted to hear of Duff's second in Greats. All the *best* men have got seconds from Newman downwards. Housman was ploughed, C.B. Fry got a fourth. People like Blue-tooth Baker[2] get firsts, do nothing very striking, and end up as Warden of Winchester. About the most brilliant scholar ever at Eton was Carr Bosanquet, of whom you have never heard—irretrievably lost as some kind of

---

[1] R.H.-D. did, in the second volume of his memoirs, *The Power of Chance*, 1991.
[2] Harold Trevor ('Bluey') Baker, Liberal politician (1877–1960).

permanent official.[1] But one thing he did which should not be allowed to die. He described *The Yellow Book* as a book 'which binders would buy to bind and bounders would be bound to buy'.

Did you see about Humphrey's loss of his trumpet and its return? It was actually in the 9 o'clock news, being apparently of equal importance with Lumumba and Castro and Cousins etc. No doubt some genial gossip-writer will hint that he had it stolen on purpose—like a filmstar's jewels.

Luncheon is imminent and I must stop. It will be a good noisy meal, though luckily not all at one table. The grandchildren are in the kitchen, the grown-ups in the staff-hall next door. Two of my grandsons are born teddy-boys, their motto being that anything like a book, hat, tool, or utensil of any kind is merely there to be destroyed, damaged or thrown away *quam celerrime*. One of the most boring traits in *all* the young is the irresistible urge to take away my stick.

I picked up the Shaw-Mrs Patrick Campbell correspondence after many years and found it *quite intolerable.* His voluble amorousness in letter after letter very quickly turned my stomach. What do *you* think?[2] Give my love to Ruth. The idea of her as a grandmother is wholly incongruous. But then Nature *is* incongruous. My aunt Georgina married Lord Leicester and found *two* stepdaughters several years older than herself.

P.S. I have just discovered that there was a saint Bugga (*D.N.B.*). It almost reconciles me to the approaching collapse of civilisation.

13 August 1960
Duff is expecting a call to begin his life's work as a journalist on the *Western Mail* at Cardiff, and meanwhile he is feverishly repainting the kitchen as a surprise birthday-present for Comfort. This evening he went to a cocktail-party nearby and on the way home shot three rabbits from the car with a .22 rifle. Nothing like being an all-rounder!

My trip to Edinburgh went according to plan. Very comfortable all-Pullman first-class carriage, in which, each way, I consumed a

[1] Robert Carr Bosanquet (1871–1935), archaeologist. Director of the British School of Archaeology in Athens 1900–1906.
[2] R.H.-D. reported Max Beerbohm as saying that he was so disgusted, he couldn't finish the book.

whacking tea and an immense dinner. The tea was especially good, and since it is a meal I usually miss, I particularly enjoyed it. I stayed comfortably with Hugh Walpole's brother, and woke on Wednesday morning to hot sunshine and a sky of unclouded blue. Edinburgh was looking its loveliest, and I rejoiced to see so many of its noble squares and crescents unharmed. The Estate Duty people proved very amenable, and the interview was over so quickly that I managed to fit in three-quarters of an hour in the best of secondhand bookshops. Altogether a most agreeable interlude. I have always liked Edinburgh, though I daresay one would tire of it eventually.

Last Thursday I went to Sotheby's to see about the approaching sale of Max's books etc from Rapallo. Across the room was the splendid library of C.H. Wilkinson of Worcester College, waiting to be catalogued. It isn't so much the worms who get everything in the end, as the auctioneers. Except for insurance, auctioneering is surely the safest racket imaginable—no risk, a sure percentage, and endless material (including often the same objects sold again and again). And they're all immensely pleased with themselves, as though they were creating the masterpieces they sell. But I suppose an annual turnover of £7,000,000 is enough to turn the solidest head.

18 August 1960   *Cambridge*

This will be rather a scrappy affair, I fear, as we are a good deal behindhand—owing to a posse of imbecile examiners who give three for a set of answers that deserve thirteen and vice versa, and then write reports which we spend half a day re-writing in English. Well you see what we are up against. We have been once or twice to the pictures— nothing much until last night when we saw Edith Evans in *The Importance of Being Earnest*. Excellent fun, though some of the wise-cracks date very emphatically. I was interested to see Dorothy Tutin, who is whole-heartedly adored, believe it or not, by Granny Gow. I don't blame him. Her Cicely was entirely charming. I haven't read the play for years, and please tell me if: Lady B. 'My nephew tell lies? Impossible! He was at Oxford' is a gag or not. I have a strong suspicion that it is—but it got the loudest laugh of the evening.[1] Margaret

---

[1] 'Untruthful! My nephew Algernon? Impossible! He is an Oxonian!' (*The Importance of Being Ernest*, act iii).

Rutherford was somehow wrongly cast for Miss Prism—too bulky and amiable, but the rest were all right. What a magnificent absurdity it is—and how O.W. must have enjoyed writing it. Leavis is only about 450 yards away from this hotel. I shall not call upon him.

20 August 1960   *Bromsden Farm*
The blessed day approaches. If you should suffer from insomnia on Tuesday night, think of us at 4 a.m. on Wednesday, when we shall set out from Soho Square in Ruth's tiny car, lights on, streets empty. Out through St Albans and Dunstable to Northampton. At 6 a.m. we stop by the roadside for coffee (from a thermos) and biscuits. Mounting excitement as the morning lightens. On through Market Harborough and Leicester to a road which bypasses everything till at 8 a.m. we reach Bawtry, just south of Doncaster and *inside Yorkshire.* There we breakfast at the Crown Hotel. Sundry shopping at Bedale, Leyburn and Hawes; a picnic luncheon high on the pass between Wensleydale and Swaledale—first taste of that incomparable air and silence—then drop down into Swaledale.

The question of my present from Max's sister-in-law is now happily resolved. She wanted to give me the plum of the whole collection (a biography of Bernard Shaw heavily annotated and extra-illustrated by Max), which Sotheby's have valued at £500+. I managed to persuade her to give me instead (1) a first edition of Oscar's *An Ideal Husband,* with a caricature of Oscar by Max on the flyleaf; (2) Max's copy of the first edition of *The Importance,* inscribed to him by Oscar, and with four most interesting notes by Max. These Sotheby's had valued at £150 and £200, I have done pretty well, and am quite delighted. Both books have suffered forty years of Rapallo sun, but inside they're fine.

I have been asked if I am willing to be called as a witness for the defence of *Lady Chatterley,* and shall reluctantly agree. I'm all against the prosecution, though in fact I think it a sentimental, contrived and occasionally ridiculous work. Anyhow they must surely have plenty of more important witnesses.

We usually have a coal fire in the bedroom at Kisdon, and dropping off to sleep there in the flickering light, in the certain knowledge that one won't wake for ten hours, is so unspeakably agreeable that I sometimes try to keep awake a little longer to prolong the enjoyment. Next week's letter will be pastoral-rhapsodical.

I get a vicarious glow from all you say about Kisdon—before, during, and after. My mind's eye reproduces it very convincingly as resembling that enchanting country along the Roman wall, or that surrounding the hamlet—it may be no more than a farm—which has the appealing name of Pity Me, which is somewhere up in the Walter Scott country, or at any rate Melrose. Please tell me exactly what you have for breakfast at Bawtry. It should surely be one of those great breakfasts of fifty years ago. The North used to be good at them. I still remember the one I had at Scotch Corner thirty years ago. Wensleydale and Swaledale!—you must by then be feeling as full of music as Milton was when he wrote of 'Horonaim, Seon's realm, beyond The flowry dale of Sibma, clad with vines'.[1]

Cambridge *wasn't* very gay—the whole day practically taken up with reading the work of the victims of very inept teaching. A name here and there pleased me. Among Browns and Joneses of some very English school there suddenly appeared *Parapolidikok* which I assure you is real, though it oughtn't to be. One good story I heard, which I hope you haven't. Old Maugham, talking to a girls' school about the art of writing short stories, told them that the essential ingredients were religion, sex, mystery, high rank, non-literary language and brevity. The schoolmistress next day told her young charges to try their hand at writing one according to this recipe. After a minute one said she had finished. The incredulous mistress told her to read it out, and she did: 'My God!', said the duchess, 'I'm pregnant. I wonder who done it.' That girl should surely go far.

Lady Chatterley. It is absolutely essential that you should not for a moment think that I am in *full* disagreement with you. I wholly agree that this police-court attempt at censorship is ridiculous. The fatuity of a lot of men in the jurybox, every one of them straight out of a drawing by the late George Morrow[2], listening to E.M. Forster testifying to the deathless beauty of *Lady C.* cannot be described in words. But what nauseates me is the flood of *cant* which so very many of those who support the publication pour out. I read that there are 250,000 copies ready, and what the defenders say (or imply) is that

[1] *Paradise Lost*, book I.
[2] *Punch* artist (1870–1955).

this mass of readers wants to read it because it is a (or *the*) masterpiece of the great genius D.H.L. And everybody knows that the great sale will be to all the adolescents in the country who, like George Forsyte, have a liking for the 'nubbly bits'. I have actually heard a man maintain that the book, expurgated, may be dreary, but the addition of D.H.L.'s fourth-form physiological crudities makes it a work of genius. If my view is Victorian, well I can't help it—but I would maintain that the inhibitions, the dislike of seeing all these crude words for the sexual functions flung onto the page, are every bit as 'natural' as the impulse to fling them. It was wrong to write the book, and it is wrong to print it.

29 August 1960   *Kisdon Lodge*
We did indeed have a fine breakfast at Bawtry—porridge and what they call 'a full house', i.e. egg, bacon, sausage and tomato, with masses of toast, butter, marmalade and tea. Since we got here we haven't left our hilltop except for a brief shopping expedition to Hawes on Saturday. Yesterday was my fifty-third birthday, and we celebrated it cosily in blissful isolation. Apart from its magical view, the first thing that strikes one with wonder here is the complete *silence*— a blessing almost unknown in most places today. At this moment for instance, with the door open, I can hear *nothing* except the tick of the grandfather clock and the faint bubbling of a milk pudding which R. is cooking on the range. We have never been to the Roman Wall, but I feel sure your comparison is pretty exact. We have often planned that and other such expeditions, but once we get here we never want to move, and our days seem so few and so fleeting. One day perhaps we shall have world enough and time. You ask about smells, and I don't quite know how to answer, for one's first impression is of the astonishing *absence* of smells, and of the purity and freshness of the moorland air. Just now, when the sun shines there is also the lovely smell of cut grass, for the wretched hill-farmers, who began their haymaking in June, are still not through with it. The field in front of us is cut but not gathered, and field behind not even cut. Three fine sunny days and we shall be helping with large wooden rakes, as we did last year.

How Green gets more and more reproachful on the shelf. Since we got here I have read a new Simenon, John Fothergill's *Innkeeper's Diary* (I find J.F. was a friend of Oscar's and so worth searching) and

266

part of the proofs of an immense (and immensely too long) biography of the Nineties poet Richard Le Gallienne (another friend of O's), kindly lent me by Martin Secker. I am also studying (with the aid of a tiny dictionary) the egregiously full notes to a German edition of *De Profundis*: '*Clapham Junction ist eine der belebtesten Londoner Vorortstationen*' and things like that.

30 and 31 August 1960   *Grundisburgh*
I am writing this at the club in Ipswich where I have finished the papers and am storm-bound by the punctual daily downpour. I do hope you are not getting all this monstrous hysterics of Nature, though it might be all to the benefit of Oscar. I still await some 300 papers from British Guiana, and have a faint hope that they may have been sunk on the journey. *Wednesday*. Still no letter.

I say, the *Times Lit. Sup*.!! The two main articles last week were on the Soviet Cinema and the poet John Oldham. Is this remotely sane? It looks as if Pryce-Jones's feelings as he contemplates his successor may be much the same as those of Sin when she first saw her offspring Death.

I was a good deal bored by Swinburne's letters. S's deep interest in flagellation is very odd to my Victorian mind, and his eulogies of Count de Sade, but I know little about such anfractuosities of the human mind. What I *should* like to know about is his friendship with Jowett, who cannot really have had much in common with de Sade. Where does the story come from of S., staying with J., sitting in a neighbouring room to one where J. was taking a tutorial, and from time to time a high triumphant screech from S. (who was reading some classical researches of J's) 'Another howler, Master, another howler!' and a demure 'Thank you, Algernon' from next door?[1]

Wednesday, second post.
All well; letter on hall-table. Thank you for breakfast menu at Bawtry. I was with you in spirit. Smells. Yes, cut grass is among the best. Almost my favourite is sacks in a coal-cart, especially after rain. Surely

---

[1] In *The Life of Algernon Charles Swinburne* by Edmund Gosse (1917), p. 213. Swinburne was actually reading the proofs of Jowett's translation of Plato's *Symposium*.

with the sheep in the offing you can't be smell-less? Hay-smell of course is superb. My old and very great friend C.D. Fisher (killed in the *Invincible* at Jutland. His brother the Admiral in the *St Vincent* swept into the battle past the wreck) maintained that his favourite smell was the top of a very small baby's head. And—*verb. sap.*—he wasn't far wrong. Gosh how you would have liked C.D.F.

I have given up all hope about *How Green*. Couldn't you get Ruth to read it while you are at some special proof-reading? Only a few pages are necessary; I would rely on her judgment with entire confidence—so would you. It really is a shame not to read it at Kisdon. It cries to Heaven, as the butler said about what was in Dr Jekyll's room. But I suppose, in fact I am sure, that being a publisher, you are very stubborn.

5 September 1960   *Kisdon Lodge*

I was both touched and conscience-stricken to read of your so eagerly awaiting my dull letter and being so often disappointed. I only hope that this week you will have learnt to expect nothing from Kisdon until (with luck) the second post on Wednesday. Your letter flew back and was in my hands by Thursday evening. Why have I not answered before? Because, as I've always found, the less one *has* to do, the less one *does* do, and how enjoyable that is! It has rained every single day since I last wrote, but so far not to-day, and this morning we helped the farmer, his son and daughter-in-law to turn their sodden hay in the field up here, which has lain cut and awash for sixteen days. Oscar is limping on: another three weeks up here and the job would be almost done: as it is, with the piles of proofs, manuscripts and letters which will certainly be waiting, I simply don't know how or when I shall be able to finish.

I once had Einstein's theory of Relativity explained to me so lucidly that for an hour or so I completely understood it: now nothing remains. In the same way have I several times been instructed in the meaning—and indeed the *working*—of *repêchage*, but alas! The French word must mean 'fishing up again', and I *think* here refers to some kind of proportional representation in timings—but who cares?[1]

---

[1] G.W.L. had asked its meaning after reading it in a report about the Olympic Games.

When Richard Le Gallienne, the long-haired poetaster of the Nineties, published a book called *If I were God by Richard Le Gallienne,* some wag commented: 'If I were Richard Le Gallienne by God I'd get my hair cut'.

What you say (rightly) about the note-excesses of Swinburne's American editor makes me ever so slightly shiver in my shoes, for it's much harder than perhaps you think to decide where to draw the line. Young people today seem to know almost nothing. When Oscar wrote to Reggie Turner in 1899 'I hear you joined the Fleet Street Kopje at the Cecil', I feel obliged to explain Kopje *and* Cecil, both of which would be obvious to you.

Ruth is revelling in *Middlemarch* and wants to know whether you have read it lately, so that she can talk to you about it in October.

7 September 1960   *Grundisburgh*
This is a notoriously dry corner of England, but we have had enough to hold up the harvest most days, and—as to-day—though dry, the sky is all over the colour of the belly of a dead fish. No doubt it is no more than we deserve, as an evangelical aunt of mine used to say— and how mealy-mouthed and soft was that generation which did *not* murder her. How right Thomas Hardy was in his remark 'It has been obvious for centuries that the Supreme Mover or Movers, the Prime Force or Forces, must be either limited in power, unknowing or cruel'. Can you see any way out of that?

But one thing makes me strike the stars with uplifted head, and that is that *Middlemarch* has always been my favourite novel. I read it first in 1904 and have read it at least three times since then. I am delighted to hear that Ruth likes it. It is simply crammed full of good stuff of all kinds. I often think of it when they babble (in speech or print) of the 'incomparable' Jane Austen, who just tinkles along in comparison. I could talk about it for hours, so dear Ruth had better look out. And if the British Guiana exam-papers still delay their coming, I may very well read it again. Didn't V. Woolf call it one of the very few really grown-up English novels? Even so one thing is missing, *viz* Dorothea's physical reactions towards her dreadful old husband. I wonder why G.E. called him Casaubon. Could one bring a great sailor into one's novel and call him Nelson? Because the real Casaubon was actually a great scholar.

Old Mortality, set for next year's G.C.E., is as you know full of full-blooded Scotticisms. Well, believe it or not, Everyman's edition has a glossary in which words like 'blithe', 'bracken', 'cannily', and 'feckless' are explained, but about 'grane', 'cess', 'tow', 'marts', and many others, no solitary word. I doubt if the Board, which chooses the books, are wise to choose Scott. He is so tremendously long-winded, and half the speeches of his ladies and gentlemen have the air of pieces set to be put into Ciceronian prose. And his young women!

Practically no undergraduates remember the declaration of war in 1939. An Oxford don told me recently that not one of the class to which he was lecturing had any idea what *Lebensraum* meant. A good many, of course, just don't read the papers. No one except me in the Ipswich Club ever reads the *Spectator* or *New Statesman*. I expect they regard them as just as devitalising as I find the *Express* and *Mail*.

10 September 1960   *Bromsden Farm*

I think it wonderful that, without having been there, you can so truly sympathise with, and enter into, our passionate love of Kisdon, our happiness there, and our ever-increasing sorrow at leaving. Everything you have ever written about it shows that you perfectly understand, whereas most people are perturbed by the thought of its primitiveness and isolation. On our last evening at dusk we watched *five* hawks hovering over the hilltop. Suddenly a huge owl got up, was attacked by the hawks, and gradually drove them away, one by one. We watched, spellbound, in the fading light. Stopping the grandfather clock wrings our heart—but I need say no more—you know it all.

The sort of thing that holds up Oscar interminably is this: a few months ago I managed to get from Paris photostats of two letters from Oscar to Mallarmé, the French poet. One is undated, the other clearly postmarked February 1891. I put them both together, only to be reminded by one of my invaluable helpers that in the Stetson Sale Catalogue (1920) there is a quotation from a Mallarmé letter to Oscar which is dated 10 Nov 91 and is clearly an answer to my undated letter. This entails moving my letter from February to November and shifting the main Mallarmé footnote to the other letter, which is now the first to him. Multiply this by several hundred and you will see the problem. Many things which I have laboriously read during the last five years (including this catalogue) couldn't then disgorge their full relevance, and there's a limit to what one can keep ready in one's head.

14 September 1960   *Grundisburgh*

I glanced yesterday at *Middlemarch*, and put it to you confidently that the very first three pages have more satisfying food for thought than fifty pages of—but I won't specify! I hope Ruth agrees in loving that charming prig Dorothea. In the story of Mr Casaubon's arid, indeed bloodless, courtship there is one quite delightful sentence: 'D. said to herself that Mr C. was the most interesting man she had ever seen, not excepting even M. Liret the Vaudois clergyman *who had given conferences on the history of the Waldenses*'. What a lot of the Victorian age, as well as of D., is in that sentence.

Do you know Leonard Woolf, whose reminiscences are interestingly reviewed? It isn't quite easy to take Bloomsbury very seriously in 1960. Did they, in spite of the good things they wrote, amount to much *collectively*? And isn't the last word on them in Max B's devastating 'From Bloomsbury to Bayswater'?[1] Is anything less attractive than faded arrogance—or more ridiculous? One gets the impression of rather pinchbeck Ozymandiases. I find that much the really best things in Lytton Strachey's writings are those in which he is *not* mocking, however subtly—though these can still amuse when, like e.g. Monsignor Talbot,[2] the victims really were absurd.

18 September 1960   *Bromsden Farm*

I fear you won't get this before Tuesday. My whole week-end was disjointed by yesterday, when we were obliged to drive over to the Victor Gollanczes' new cottage near Marlow and play bridge with them for *six hours*. I am very fond of them both, but as you know I seldom play bridge (or anything else) and have a great deal to do. However, I think Comfort enjoyed it, and we eventually staggered home the richer by 7/6.

Last week in London was most exhausting. No one could be a less

[1] Published in Max Beerbohm's *Mainly on the Air* (1946).
[2] George Talbot (1816–1886), fifth son of the third Lord Talbot de Malahide. Private Secretary to Pope Pius IX, who helped Manning to become Archbishop of Westminster. He ended in a lunatic asylum. See Strachey's *Eminent Victorians* (1918).

demanding guest than my dear friend Leon Edel, but Ruth and I have come to depend on the flat for moments of escape and peace—coffee and the crossword at 10.30, often lunch, a quiet whisky-and-soda after the office, and so on—and to find even the nicest of guests always there, having to talk when one longs for quiet, is persistently frustrating. However, the dear fellow flies home next Saturday.

My spies tell me (*this is frightfully private*) that the big City invest-ment firm which owns Heinemann (and me along with it) is nego-tiating to sell the whole caboodle to an American tycoon. Nobody can guess what this would mean, but I don't much like the sound of it. I'll let you know as soon as I know any more.

Peter is meditating a book on Siberia 1918-1919, Admiral Kolchak, and the Russian civil war—but this too is secret for the moment. His present (Younghusband) book we have postponed till January. Diana's third volume[1] begins in next week's *Sunday Times*, but please don't read it there: I'll soon send you a proper copy. I dined last week with her and her son, and although it was all very nice I didn't enjoy myself much. Maybe I have reached some kind of climacteric or change of life, but I certainly feel ever less social, gregarious and tolerant, and long to do what I want to do in a place of my own choosing. Perhaps one day it will work out that way, and meanwhile I must grit my teeth and carry on.

22 September 1960   *Grundisburgh*
I have at last finished my exam-papers—about three hundred of them from overseas. And am I sick of vague and vapid jaw about Brutus and Cassius, or am I? But they are well up-to-date in British Guiana. One candidate stated that Caesar was a homosexual, the proof being his saying 'Let me have men about me that are fat'—which recalls a scabrous limerick which I found in my psalter in Eton chapel in 1896—which I shall *not* tell you.

I go nearly as far as Southey in finding my cheeks 'often bedewed with tears of thoughtful gratitude', whenever I contemplate my revolving bookshelf, *entirely* filled with gifts from R.H.-D. And now the beloved Tim has sent me Alan Ross's cricket anthology,[2] which I

---

[1] *Trumpets from the Steep.*
[2] *The Cricketer's Companion* (1960).

was on the brink of buying last week at The Ancient House, and was stopped by a spasm of economy. There are splendid things in it, and a good deal I have *not* read, plus old favourites. I wish R. had found room for C.P. Foley's superb account of Alletson in 1911, when he ended his vast innings by getting 139 in half-an-hour, *89 of it in fifteen minutes*. He clearly went quite mad—and remained so, for he never made another run practically, nor even tried to hit, though A.O. Jones told him that if only he would hit he should play in every match, however few runs he made. But of course, half the fun of an anthology is picking holes.

Adam, I hope, had (till last week) his feet on the fender reading non-scientific literature.[1] Warn him that Darwin, when he ultimately found himself at leisure, realised that he had completely lost any taste for literature, especially fiction (not that that matters) and Shakespeare.

25 September 1960   *Bromsden Farm*

I brought Leon Edel down here on Friday night, and we set off for London Airport (25 miles) at 11 a.m. yesterday. L.E. is a nervous traveller with ever-mounting gangplank-fever. We got to the airport at 12 and I took him to the huge central section, where 10,000 cars were parked. With some difficulty I found room for ours, lugged his heavy suitcase a long way to the first floor, only to be told that we were in quite the wrong part of the airport. Lugged the suitcase back, de-parked the car, was roundly ticked off by motorised police for going the wrong way (it's very confusing) and drove off to the *right* place. Here we were told that the flight had been postponed from 1 p.m. to 5.30 p.m. It was by now 12.30, the sun was shining hot and strong, and I felt I simply *couldn't* leave the wretched fellow to hang about for five hours. So I put him firmly back into the car and drove off.

Meanwhile, as they say in clumsy old novels, Duff had come over from Cardiff to pick the apples, found there were *far* more than we could use or store, so rang up Julia Coleridge[2] and sold her 200 lbs at threepence a pound. *Meanwhile*, again, Adam had telephoned

---

[1] He had gained distinctions in Chemistry, Physics and Maths A Levels.
[2] Wife of Adam's Eton housemaster.

delightedly to announce his election to the Library[1] and to ask for his tape recorder, portable wireless, box of electrical equipment, two spare recording-tapes, some eggs and other food, and (once again) his braces.

So, laden with all this clobber, and the undeparted guest, I drove to Eton. As we reached Fred's Boys' Entrance a boy, twitching and groaning with pain, was carried out on a stretcher and driven off in an ambulance. We found Adam, and with some difficulty persuaded the dame to cough up £2.10.0. for the apples. We admired the Chess Cup in the dining-room; Adam said he was playing football at 2.15, so didn't want to come out to lunch. Leon acquiesced in all the hurly-burly—and then I drove him to Monkey Island, which was looking very beautiful, and had a good lunch. I could see that L.E.'s anxiety-neurosis was growing rapidly, but managed to divert his attention by asking him to tell me about the time when he was psycho-analysed. This kept him going happily through a protracted lunch, but at 3 p.m. he said he'd be happier if we rang up the airport for confirmation, so I sat in the sun by the river while he got the necessary pennies. Soon he came disconsolately back to say he'd pressed the wrong button and lost all his pennies, so I got some more, rang up the airport, and was told the flight had again been postponed—till 8.30 p.m.! I drove him to Windsor and we pottered in the bookshops, buying a few odd books. Then he said he must telephone again, so we sweated to the Post Office at the very top of Windsor Hill, and got some more pennies, and the flight was still 8.30.

L.E. was really very touching, saying he realised I was being very kind, and he knew he ought to be enjoying the sunshine and the adventure and the bookshops, but that he simply couldn't control his exasperation, so after giving him a cup of tea I drove him back to the airport and left him there at 5.30, with three hours still to go. I got back here at 6.30 utterly exhausted, having driven eighty miles and spent all the apple-money.

28 September 1960   *Grundisburgh*
Alan Ross's anthology has lots of good stuff in it, and—as one might expect—plenty that one could spare. In fact, to come out into the

---

[1] The boys' governing body of an Eton house.

open with trailing coat, I am not permanently a-giggle over Macdonell's famous match in *England, their England.*

I get some definite pleasure from the *T.L.S.* reviewer who begins a paragraph about Kingsley Amis's last novel: 'This is a very nasty book'. He is, as you know, one of my steadily lengthening list of *bêtes noires*. A sure sign of old age. I become steadily deafer, the arch of my right foot steadily descends, my shins steadily itch, one deltoid muscle creaks and stiffens. Otherwise, thank you, I am perfectly well, though, as Lord Clive who is no longer alive said, there is a great deal to be said for being dead.

1 October 1960   *Bromsden Farm*

I have just read three hundred pages of a draft of my old friend Wyndham Ketton-Cremer's history of Felbrigg, his house in Norfolk. It's not exactly sparkling, but I know the house well, and any competent and documented family history of three hundred years is interesting as a sort of microcosm of history. Before Monday I must also read *six hundred* pages (typescript) of the first volume of Guy Chapman's history of the French Third Republic (1871–1940). Also a French book on the Algerian war, which I fear would be out of date before it could be translated. Also I must cut, edit and partly re-write Jock Dent's sloppy introduction to the Agate anthology I am to bring out next year. And, in case I have time to spare, I have brought along a 300-page (typed) 'extravaganza' by Arnot Robertson.

T.S.E.'s birthday party was most touching and enjoyable. I doubt whether he is writing anything much now, though I fancy he's continually brooding over a new play—and I wish he wasn't, for his plays aren't getting any better, and he has probably written enough. Reminiscences—I fear not, though I will try and raise the subject one of these days.

The Society of Authors rout in the H. of C. turned out (as so often happens with something one has long been dreading) to be rather fun. Some two hundred authors were crammed together, each with his (or more often her) name pinned to the lapel. (Most of them seemed to be called Margaret Bulge or some such.) The main attraction was the Brains Trust, which lasted well over an hour, and seemed to give general satisfaction. A.P. Herbert was on the right wing, then Compton Mackenzie, then the chairman Denzil

Batchelor, then Rebecca West, then me. The drink I had had (two whiskies-and-sodas and one glass of claret) must have been just right, for I suddenly felt on top of the Brains Trust and more than able to cope. The questions were quite sensible, and enabled everyone to speak a little about themselves.

I am much too ignorant of Gilbert to advise you about your speech, but it seems clear that neither he nor Sullivan was any use without the other, whereas in partnership their complementary second-rateness became in its way first-class. And I *still* haven't seen a single G. and S. opera!

5 October 1960   Grundisburgh

'October *rediit, rediit pars tristior anni*'.[1] Do you remember your Clivus? O. is very often the best of months in Suffolk, but it has made —meteorologically—a poor start. But all horizons are lightened by a parcel with a lovely quintette of books from R.H.-D. And I have just finished Quennell's book, a great deal of it with great pleasure. I found the Prologue and Epilogue a bit dry and difficult, like—to me—all writing about the principles of art, but whenever he gets on to people he is fine.

By the way, Cyril Foley in his excellent account of Fowler's match makes a very grave error of fact in saying that T.O. Jameson was laid out for a bit through being hit 'on the head'. It was really a much more vulnerable place—and a commoner, especially *on a wet wicket with none but slow to medium bowlers*. I read that old Maugham contemplates death with perfect calm—what would appal him would be the prospect of eternal life, and how right he is, especially if, as Arthur Benson said, there are many people who appear to think that in the next world they will have a prescriptive right to one's company. The old S.M. is very corrugated now, but after all at eighty-six one has a right to be.

9 October 1960   Bromsden Farm

Is this the second Flood? Have you an arkwright handy? Goodness knows what our rainfall has been to-day alone. Jonah's short stories are in the printer's hands: the book is to be called *The Bishop's Aunt*,

---

[1] October has returned, a sadder part of the year.

after what I think the best story in it. Last Tuesday I dined alone with Jonah and Evy in their St John's Wood eyrie. They gave me a superb dinner (they have a daily Viennese cook) of smoked salmon, a huge melting *vol-au-vent*, a fine bottle of Mouton Rothschild, and a wonderful *soufflé surprise*, topped up with coffee, liqueur and an excellent Partagas cigar. Afterwards we sat and gossiped most agreeably. Jonah is definitely much better: his breathlessness greatly reduced and his colour better. Ruth and I will be waiting for you at six on Tuesday, expecting you to be deaf, breathless and drenched; we will stay you with flagons.

Barbon Manor
Kirkby Lonsdale

19 October 1960

I imagine this country is very like Kisdon—rolling moorland and vast horizons (usually obscured by cloud). When they come in I will look at a map and see how near we have ever been to Kisdon. The name has never passed my lips to anyone but Pamela.

You will, I hope, be pleased to hear that both Pamela and Roger greatly like Diana Cooper's book, and both were quite expecting *not* to. Roger has many of the latest books and I batten on them. Lloyd George by his son: my Victorian view is that it *may* be interesting, amusing, and important to reveal that a big man's chief relaxation was promiscuous fornication, but that the revelation ought not to be made by his son. R. is a bit cagey about it, but I rather gather that to his cynical, 1960, man-of-the-world eye the bulk of readers may well praise the father's contempt for old-fashioned conventions and the son's courageous frankness. If they do, my conviction of the Gadarene course of all standards will be still further strengthened.

L. Woolf's *Sowing* did not wholly please me, though full of interest. Doesn't he jeer too much at all other views and convictions than those held by the Stracheys and Stephens and Keyneses etc? Do you know all about G.E. Moore and his philosophy? He is, as always, extravagantly lauded in this book—though represented by two curiously dull letters. When I went up (October 1902) I was urged to read his *Principia Ethica*, but I made no more of it than Dr Johnson did of playing the flageolet. But he does appear to have impressed a great many very intelligent people, though for many years his name has very rarely been mentioned, so far as my observation goes.

I look forward to seeing you reported as an enthusiast for *Lady C's Lover*. Please tell me all about it. It is all a fine piece of fantasy—jurymen quite clearly mystified, almost certainly shocked, very probably flattered by being told they are men of the world into denying what they *really* think. I wonder who will be the judge. Will passages be read *aloud* in court? Will there be women on the jury? Gosh, how I feel like Housman's Terence: 'I, a stranger and afraid In a world I never made'.[1]

I asked about Swaledale and Sibell says we will go there to-morrow, as it is superb.Roger to-day is at some function at Giggleswick School of which he is a governor. Yesterday S. took me to Sedbergh where Brendan Bracken [Old Boy] fitted out for them the nicest library I have ever seen—quite perfect. We talked to a nice prefect. When I told him I was Humphrey's father his jaw fell.

23 October 1960   *Bromsden Farm*

On Friday about 6 p.m., when Comfort was driving to Henley to meet me at the station, an idiotic little man, coming the other way, suddenly swung across C's bows and she hit him at about 55 m.p.h. That the fault was entirely his is little consolation, and it's a miracle that Comfort wasn't killed or badly hurt. In fact she is only very bruised and shocked. By the time I had been to the hospital, seen the police and collected Bridget from the station it was almost 9 p.m. We put Comfort straight to bed, where she has been ever since. She has a fever each evening, aches all over, and her teeth chatter if she gets out of bed. The doctor says these are all normal shock-reactions, and he thinks she will be all right in a few days. I didn't like the idea of her being alone here at night during the week, so this afternoon I bundled her up and took her over to a friend's where she is now in bed. All yesterday she wanted me to sit by her (very unlike her usual isolation), so one way and another Oscar has once again suffered.

I couldn't help being a little cheered by this morning's *Sunday Times*, where Leonard Russell (the Literary Editor) writes: 'There are three men on my beat in London whom everyone loves—Sir Compton Mackenzie, Rupert Hart-Davis, and John Betjeman'.

Lady Chatterley has been adjourned till Thursday. I am apparently

[1] *Last Poems*, xii.

still on the short list of thirty defence witnesses (selected, I am told, from four hundred volunteers), but can hardly think I shall be called. I hope however to see a bit of the fun. The defence were very keen to get some women on the jury, believing them to be more tolerant: please tell Pamela this.

27 October 1960   *Grundisburgh*

There was quite a lot of rain at Barbon and unluckily the worst day was that on which we meant to go to Swaledale. At Hawes we found ourselves in the middle of a wet dark cloud and could only come home. I never felt more sure of anything than that *Lady C.* should *not* be published unexpurgated. I hope you won't be summoned as a witness, for, if you are, I can't imagine what answer you will give to the question which any decent counsel must ask, *viz* 'How do these dozen passages lift the book from what it has been for thirty years in its unexpurgated form (which many think dullish) into a work of genius which mankind simply cannot do without?'

The last book I read at Roger's was the life of Dr Arnold. I found myself hating him. That episode of his giving *eighteen* blows to a boy for lying merely shows him up as foully cruel and dreadfully stupid and impatient and self-assured; he made no attempt to find out if the boy might be telling the truth (which he was). And when the boy stayed out for two days the egregious old ass was convinced he was malingering. He should have been sacked after that caning—and nowadays, would be. It is clear Strachey didn't know about it. I wish he had. What portentous prigs Arnold's sixth-form boys were when they went to Oxford. The uncle in Clough's 'Dipsychus' described them very well.[1]

29 October 1960   *Bromsden Farm*

Your insistence on the suppression of *Lady Chatterley* is the only symptom of age that you have ever shown me, and I realise that the

[1] From the epilogue to 'Dipsychus': Consciences are often much too tender in your generation . . . It's all Arnold's doing; he spoilt the public schools . . . My own nephews seem to me a sort of hobbadi-hoy cherub, too big to be innocent, and too simple for anything else. They're full of the notion of the world being so wicked, and of their taking a higher line, as they call it . . . Arnold used to attack offences, not as offences – the right view – against discipline, but as sin, heinous guilt, I don't know what beside!

longer a tabu has been cherished, the harder it is to eradicate. Surely if you remove words from smoking-room stories and lavatory walls, and allow them to be printed in their proper context and meaning, they cease to be obscene and become ordinary—not in a moment, but in the course of time. As far as *Lady C.* is concerned, the expurgated passages seem to me the whole point of the book—but you will have read the evidence in *The Times*, and indeed I shall be thankful when the trial is over, for (being readily accessible by telephone) I have become a sort of Perpetual Twelfth Man for the defence witnesses. They never know whether any particular person is going to be five minutes in the box (E.M. Forster) or an hour and a half (Hough and Hoggart), so they keep having too few or too many witnesses waiting. At lunchtime on Thursday they thought they were going to run out, so sent out a three-line whip, as a result of which I sat from 2 till 4 gossiping with Tony Powell and Anne Scott-James. Asked to reappear at 10 a.m. on Friday, I found *fifteen* waiting. I sent in a message to the solicitor, saying that there were more than eleven waiting to bat, and if we had a batting-order, some of us could fall out. On this I escaped, but was urgently recalled for 2.30, when I probably *should* have been called if a legal argument had not occupied an hour and three-quarters. As it was, I talked to Dilys Powell, and for a short time watched Mr Justice Maude dealing with a teddy-boy knife-slasher in the next court.

I am travelling to Rapallo next Thursday to attend the unveiling of a plaque on Max Beerbohm's Villino. It will mean forty-eight hours' travelling and ten hours there, but it will be a good change, and I look forward to the meals on the trains.

There seems to be a chance of Andrew Young's *Collected Poems* getting the Duff Cooper Prize this year, but it's not certain, so mum's the word. I should be delighted if it happened, for A.Y. is seventy-five and pretty hard up. The prize is worth only £150, but that's tax-free, and the publicity is bound to sell some copies of the book.

The Gerald Durrell book (*Zoo in my Luggage*) has gone off with such a bang that the first edition of *25,000* copies is almost exhausted: another 10,000 will be ready on November 18. A few more winners like that, and publishing would be a lot easier. Oh, yes—yesterday I talked to Bernard Levin in the Old Bailey. He looks about *sixteen*, and at first I thought he was someone's little boy brought along to see the fun—

very Jewish, with wavy fairish hair, very intelligent and agreeable to talk to. I imagine he is 'covering' the trial for the *Spectator*. Look out for it.

2 November 1960   *Grundisburgh*
The rock I founder on is this. No doubt all those high-minded experts were quite sincere in their views about D.H.L.'s loftiness of aim, his support of marriage, and hatred of promiscuity, the book being an allegory etc etc, but how many of the 200,000 new readers will take it like that? Some day, you say, the essential beauty of all that frankness will be seen. A devilish long time, surely, before the giggle will be taken out of sex?

I think you will have to read Christopher Hollis's history of Eton, just out. As he says, much of it is based on Maxwell Lyte,[1] but M.L. had nothing about the last 96 years, and, even on ground common to both, H. is much the livelier. How Eton survived rapacious and hostile kings, the ineptitude and brutality of some of her headmasters, and her own fantastic and ridiculous ways down the centuries, is a mystery. The book is dedicated, if you please, to *me*.

Thursday
Well, so *Lady C.* won. The judge, surely, really summed up against it, but the jury, as I thought they would be, were either intimidated by that highbrow phalanx, or resolved to show that they were as jolly broad-minded as anyone. And I remain in (I suppose) a small minority —with however the brother and nephew of D.H.L. (his sister hails the verdict with rapture, but her face in the *Daily Telegraph* rouses a strong suspicion of insanity). I see that lofty moralist Sir Allen Lane[2] hopes to publish a further 300,000—making half-a-million. What an unsuspected love of culture the public are showing! It is all very odd. And now we shall see what we shall see. I shall be surprised if we like it much.

6 November 1960   *Bromsden Farm*
I was told on Monday morning that I wouldn't after all be called, so Ruth and I spent the morning in court as spectators and then went

---

[1] Sir Henry Churchill Maxwell Lyte (1848–1940), deputy keeper of the public records, published in 1875 *A History of Eton College 1440–1875*.
[2] Founder of Penguin Books.

back to work. Everyone seems agreed that Richard Hoggart was the star-witness. I honestly don't foresee any evil consequences to this trial: pornography can still be prosecuted, and if a wedge has been driven between it and literature, as I think, *tant mieux*.

On Monday night Ruth and I were taken to *The Playboy of the Western World*, which I last saw in Dublin thirty years ago. I enjoyed it all over again, but shan't mind if I don't see it again for some time. By the end of the evening that poetic idiom of speech begins to sound like a trick, which is only *just* strong enough to support the Irish-whimsy anecdote.

Now for my journey. Altogether I ate five huge meals (four on trains and one at Rapallo), each of five courses and a half-bottle of wine, and felt all the better for it. I got to Paris at 5 p.m. (6 p.m. by French time), transferred my bags to the Rome Express, and strolled round the Gare du Nord till 7. A superb dinner (soup, a trout cooked with almonds, chicken, cheese and ice-cream), an hour's work on Oscar and a pretty good night in my sleeper. Got out at Rapallo at 10 a.m. A grey day, no sun but warm and dry. The little town put on all it knew for my benefit: first a fine funeral with purple-robed priests and much ornament, then banners bridging every street in honour of forthcoming elections: VOTA COMMUNISTA, DEMOCRAZIA CRISTIANA and so on. I had scarcely had a bath and changed when, right outside my window on the sea (by which open horse-carriages ply for hire under the palm-trees) an Armistice Day procession (the Italian armistice with Austria was on 4 November 1918) marched up with wreaths, bands, veterans and much fancy dress. Half an hour later when I went out for a walk I saw them all returning in a huge motor-boat—where from? I had some delicious coffee in a café, made a few purchases, and then worked on Oscar in my very comfortable hotel-room until 1.30, when I descended for the luncheon-party, twenty-two strong, given for the Ambassador (Ashley Clarke) by the Consul General from Genoa. I was between the retired C.G. (a Scotswoman called Fowler) and a writer called Cecil Roberts, a tolerably agreeable old queer. The lunch was Italian—shellfish (assorted), ravioli, *fritto misto* of local fish (so good that I had a second helping), excellent cheese and a fine chestnut pudding. Local wines, white and red. At 3 p.m. we were conveyed in three cars to the Villino, where a small crowd was waiting. As the Ambassador's Rolls pulled up opposite the house, the police stopped the traffic both ways on the narrow steep crowded road. The local mayor read out a speech in Italian, which I naturally couldn't understand. Then H.E. spoke (also in Italian) about Max, and I could follow most of it. By the time he pulled the cord which released British and Italian flags from the plaque, the traffic jam stretched for several miles in both directions, with every horn hooting. Nevertheless there was just time for a last look at the terrace and garden, all very desolate and wintry, with house and study shuttered. Ichabod! As I was driven back to my hotel, infuriated motorists were still hooting, bumper to bumper, for miles.

I then had a nap and worked on Oscar till it was time to catch the Rome Express at 7 p.m. Another good dinner (Italian—the restaurant car changes over at the frontier), more Oscar and another goodish night. At 8.30 a.m. yesterday I had *brioche* and *café-au-lait* in the dining-car and then settled down to a couple of hours of Oscar while the train first waited in the Gare de Lyon and then trundled round the *ceinture* to the Gard du Nord. Altogether I corrected more than a hundred galley-pages of Oscar, the longest consecutive stretch I've managed since Kisdon. A last delicious lunch on the Calais train, a smooth crossing, tea in the London train, a blissful reunion with Ruth at Soho Square, and down here by the 9.30 p.m. train.

13 November 1960   *Bromsden Farm*
No letter this week, as arranged, but here, instead, is a one-question exam-paper. *Who* wrote this and *when*?

If I am right it will be a slow business for our people to reach rational views, assuming that we are allowed to work peacefully to that end. But as I grow older I grow calm. If I feel what are perhaps an old man's apprehensions, that competition from new races will cut deeper than working men's disputes and will test whether we can hang together and can fight; if I fear that we are running through the world's resources at a pace that we cannot keep; I do not lose my hopes. I do not pin my dreams for the future to my country or even to my race. I think it probable that civilization somehow will last as long as I care to look ahead—perhaps with smaller numbers, but perhaps also bred to greatness and splendour by science. I think it not improbable that man, like the grub that prepares a chamber for the winged thing it never has seen but is to be—that man may have cosmic destinies that he does not understand. And so beyond the vision of battling races and an impoverished earth I catch a dreaming glimpse of peace.

The other day my dream was pictured to my mind. I was walking homeward on Pennsylvania Avenue near the Treasury, and as I looked beyond Sherman's Statue to the west the sky was aflame with scarlet and crimson from the setting sun. But, like the note of downfall in Wagner's opera, below the skyline there came from little globes the pallid discord of the electric lights. And I thought to myself the *Götterdämmerung* will end, and from those globes clustered like evil eggs will come the new masters of the sky. It is like the time in which we live. But then I remembered the faith that I partly have expressed, faith in a universe not measured by our fears, a universe that has thought and more than thought inside of it, and as I gazed, after the sunset and above the electric lights, there shone the stars.

You shall have the answer next week.

16 November 1960   *Grundisburgh*
Thank you for that very fine passage. It might well have been written by Judge Holmes, a very great man. In his letters there is often that deep bourdon note—he often looks at things *sub specie aeternitatis*, but not, of course, usually for as long a spell as this. Tell me all about it next week. G.K.C. sometimes strikes this note, e.g. in the account of the Battle of the Marne.

How *devilish* difficult it is to be brief and not dull. I told every new division at Eton of Wellington's apology for the length of his despatches from Spain: 'I had not time to make them shorter', which I suspect may be as '*crambe repetita*'[1] to you as Habakkuk.[2] Levin, by the way, begged too many questions; it is a little schoolboyish to over-praise all who take one view and sneer at all who take the opposite one. How hard our journalists find it to make *balanced* comment.

I suppose you don't yet loathe the winter as much as I do—more

---

[1] 'Cabbage hashed and rehashed.' Juvenal *Satires*, vii, 154.
[2] 'Write the vision, and make it plain upon tables, that he may run that readeth it.' *Habakkuk*, ii, 2.

every year. It rains every night—not very much but enough to keep everything dank. Indoors is pleasant of course and would be even more so if coal cost the pound a ton that it used to. But let us count our blessings. Books are much easier to handle, print is better, and e.g. the Pastoral Symphony, now playing on a long record, is better than my aunt Sybil's piano-playing and Jack Talbot's throaty rendering of Maude Valerie White's 'Devout Lover'—'It is not mine to sing the stately grace, The great soul beaming in my lady's face' etc. The second line rather puts the lady with Mrs Wititterley who, you remember, suffered from being 'all soul'.[1]

Have you read Hollis's *Eton* yet? Eton in the first half of the nineteenth century was a ridiculously bad school. I can't think how it survived. I am glad too that Hollis—not *too* strongly—shows up the snobbish arrogance of Julian Grenfell and co at Oxford; they were as bad as the segregationists of Louisiana and Milton's 'sons of Belial flown with insolence and wine'. Eddie Marsh loved them, but also hints at this unlovable trait in his autobiography. Still there remains 'The naked earth . . .'[2] and their deaths. *Per contra* Sir Philip Sidney wrote 'With how sad steps, O moon, thou climb'st the skies' and 'Fool said my Muse; look in thy heart and write', and was loved by *everybody*. Would Julian Grenfell have given his water-bottle to a wounded Philip Sassoon?

19 November 1960   *Bromsden Farm*

Those words *were* by Judge Holmes, and the astonishing thing is that they were spoken at a Harvard Law School dinner in New York on 15 February *1913*. The Duke of Wellington's admirable remark about brevity in writing was quite new to me—so there! And I'm prepared to bet that I *do* hate the winter as much as you do. Hibernation or Jamaica seem the only tolerable cures.

Last Tuesday I attended the sixtieth birthday celebrations of my old friend Hamish Hamilton, the publisher, who first insinuated me into the lamentable trade. The proceedings began with a gala performance of *Romeo and Juliet* at the old Vic. Then at midnight we sat down eleven strong to a sumptuous dinner (bortsch, pheasant, and a

[1] In *Nicholas Nickleby*.
[2] In Julian Grenfell's poem 'Into Battle'.

superb Italian sweet—Mrs H. is Italian—good white and red wine, champagne and brandy). I was blissfully placed between Lady Drogheda (an angel and old friend) and no less a person than the Duchess of Kent, for whom I fell hook, line and sinker. Very attractive, intelligent, charming and cultivated. Her sister, Princess Paul of Yugoslavia, to whom I talked after dinner, is another charmer. She speaks countless languages, including Yugoslav and Swahili. I said 'I'm sure your sister can't speak them', and she said 'But, you see, she's much younger than me'.

I had sent my host, as a birthday present, a fountain pen, which I knew he wanted, and in an accompanying note I described him as 'just the man to put the sex into sexagenarian', which seemed to please him.

26 November 1960   *Bromsden Farm*
I paid a brief visit to my old father, and couldn't help being moved by the pathos and irony of two excellent women (nurse and physiotherapist) *forcing* the old boy to walk again, when he has nowhere to walk to, and no desire to move. I am once again deep in Oscar, pausing only to read through the *Satires* of Juvenal in search of a quotation or to seek for French Anarchists in the *Encyclopaedia Britannica*.

St Andrew's Day 1960   *Grundisburgh*
Thank God I am not playing at the Wall to-day. It is anyhow an immensely absurd game, but on the whole I am glad we *don't* live in a completely sane world—partly of course because that is what E. Summerskill[1] and others of her kidney would like (how nauseating to think of E.S.'s kidney!).

There would surely be literally nothing to be said against euthanasia if it wasn't for nears and dears. I like the story of the old Roman who lay in a hot bath with a vein open, chatting with his friends, and plugged the vein whenever the talk was interesting, and removed it when the interest faded.

3 December 1960   *Bromsden Farm*
I have just been listening to Mahler's Second Symphony on the radio—did you hear it? I enjoyed it enormously, and all the more in

---

[1] Labour politician.

contrast to Alban Berg's opera *Wozzeck*, which I heard last night at Covent Garden. It is based on a German Expressionist play (someone in the interval said it was like *Carmen* written by Freud) and is written in what I believe is called atonal music. To a non-musical novice this seems like a free-for-all in the orchestra-pit, with distressing results. Nevertheless I found it all interesting, and the Droghedas' box (which is really two boxes) is attached to a private dining-room in which an excellent dinner is served *seriatim* during the intervals. The French Ambassador was of the party but consumed only a glass of water.

7 December 1960   *Grundisburgh*
Drogheda's box sounds all right, but really the French Ambassador and his glass of water! Like Edward VIII when Prince of Wales being lunched by the Harlech golf-club, which scoured the principality for viands and vintages—and he asked for rice-pudding and lime-juice, neither of which they had. But that was either bad manners, or bad organisation by his major-domo. However we were still eating the lunch meant for him weeks afterwards, so good came out of evil.

I have just written short biographies of Spenser, Sidney and Marlowe. I wonder if I have sufficiently concealed my opinion that *The Faery Queene* is unreadable. Columbia University in their rather disgraceful plebiscite on 'the ten most boring classics' had it second to *Pilgrim's Progress*. *Paradise Lost* was third or fourth and later in the list came *Silas Marner, Ivanhoe*, and *Boswell's Life of Johnson*!! All of which makes me very dubious about alliance with America in spite of Abe Lincoln and Stonewall Jackson—oh yes and *certainly* Judge Holmes, as great as any. I must go and hew wood, but *not*, you will be surprised to hear, draw water. Really the rain!

10 December 1960   *Bromsden Farm*
On Monday we finally penetrated the fastnesses of the Home Office and were allowed to examine and check Oscar's prison-petitions and other documents—very interesting and touching.

We had a terrific German dinner with Elisabeth Beerbohm's sister and brother-in-law—a wonderful fish-dish of sole in a sort of bun, flooded with a delicious sauce of lobster and shrimps; very good pheasant with sour cream sauce, cherry jam, potatoes and sauerkraut; a superb almond cream sweet, and a heavenly Riesling (two bottles among four). We both felt stupefied afterwards but thoroughly enjoyed it all.

On Wednesday was the unveiling of the Duff Cooper plaque in the crypt of St Paul's—very well handled by the Dean and Harold Nicolson. On in a hired car to Hyde Park Gate, where Princess Alexandra very charmingly gave the Duff Cooper Prize to my poet Andrew Young.

Oh yes—in one of George Moore's books Max wrote:

ELEGY ON ANY LADY
by G.M.
That she adored me as the most
Adorable of males
I think I may securely boast . . .
Dead women tell no tales.

14 December 1960   *Grundisburgh*

It has rained all day. The glass is rather high, the forecast said there was an anti-cyclone over England. Such are the facts. I make no comment or complaint; only an occasional question like Sam Weller's crosses my mind, 'Ain't somebody going to be whipped for this 'ere?'

I expect you may have had news of Adam's venture[1] by now. I do hope it was successful. You are right about my knowledge of chemistry. One thing alone I retain from Tubby Porter, viz that 'a body immersed in liquid loses in weight the weight of the liquid displaced'. I have found it most useful in life. For the rest I am incurably nonscientific, and full of pro-humanity saws like Dr J's 'We are perpetually moralists, but we are geometricians only by chance'.[2]

[It had been established that both R.H.-D. and G.W.L. knew Joyce Grenfell.] Her father Paul Phipps was a delightful man. I remember a nice simple witticism of his. My sister on the way to church with large party said: 'I do hope the hymn books won't run out'. To which P.P. said 'If they do, I'll run after them'.

I have been reading *The Duke's Children*. I love Trollope—and am maddened by him. The snobbery thick—a slab of the times and circles he wrote about, and those infuriatingly virginal young women.

---

[1] To try for a scholarship at Oxford.
[2] *Life of Milton.*

They all need a soupçon of *Lady C*! Apropos of which I see Sir Allen Lane, contemplating the sales of one and a half million of 'em, expressed distress that many people had bought them from the wrong motives! I suppose that the tiniest whisper of 'humbug' would have made R. West, Joan Bennett, that bishop, K. Tynan, B. Levin (and R.H-D.?) red with indignation??

17 December 1960   *Bromsden Farm*

This has been an exciting week. On Tuesday night we heard (as you have probably since read) that Adam had been awarded an Open Scholarship (or, as they call it, Postmastership) at Merton, having apparently been placed top of all the scientific candidates! Much jubilation at Eton, as you can imagine.

Next day A. played (as substitute Goals) in the final of the House Cup, the only player on either side in a white shirt. It was *bitterly* cold, with ankle-deep mud. I went down by train to Slough, thence by taxi. It was an exciting fast game, but I walked round a good bit, trying to keep warm. Two-all at full time. Ten minutes extra each way. Still two-all. Darkness falling rapidly. After a lengthy consultation in midfield they agreed to play five more minutes each way. After some three minutes a boy called Perkins got the ball through Snow's goal, and Coleridge's had won for the first time, after four previous failures in the final (including Duff's year). Adam was given his House Colours on the field, and I almost wept with pride and joy. He hadn't had much to do (having Lumley, the Field Long, in front of him), but he did it adequately. I wonder if he'll ever have two such exciting days again?

Meanwhile Duff has finally clinched the job on the new *Sunday Telegraph* in London, and is to start work there on January 9 at £18.10. a week. This means he can get married, since his girl (Phyllida Barstow) already has a similar job in London. When they all arrived this morning (after a dance in London last night) we cracked a bottle of champagne in general congratulation. (Adam is in the final of the Chess Cup—to be played off next half.)

                                                              Holland House
Shortest Day 1960   *Eton College*

I did send you a card and the Postmaster a word of congratulation the moment I saw the great news, but I fear it didn't reach either before

Monday. It was a magnificent achievement, and already I gather the science staff here are walking about looking several inches taller, as Mr Shandy said all women look after producing a baby (and every right they have to do so). Duff's weekly wage sounds very handsome. In my day it would have been £4. Wage-earners of all kinds, grave and gay, are, roughly, the new well-to-do. The poor old *rentier*'s number is up, and there is nothing we can do about it.

Boxing Day 1960   *Bromsden Farm*

So far our Christmas has passed off peacefully. I have had a number of 'useful and acceptable' presents, including a superb case of Riesling from Max's sister-in-law, but the one which pleased me and Ruth most was two home-made cakes from our Kisdon farmer and his family. How I wish we were there now, with perhaps some of that snow on high ground of which the radio-announcer so fruitily speaks.

Last week, in the intervals of frantic, and largely abortive, last minute shopping, I lunched with Sir William Haley[1] at the Athenaeum (potted shrimps, liver and bacon, treacle tart—all of which would have been good if they hadn't been luke-warm). W.H. neither drinks nor smokes, but graciously joined me in a half-pint of rather good cider, which he apparently (and quite wrongly) considers non-alcoholic.

5 January 1961
University Arms Hotel
Cambridge

Now this really *is* a miserable affair—the cold fact being that we are kept pretty hard at work all day, and after dinner there has been a lot of 'Come and have a glass of port' which always dribbles on till near midnight. And one night my colleagues insisted on taking me to the pictures, if you please—a film called *The Man in the Moon* which they assured me was desperately funny, and indeed they laughed like prep-school boys at what seemed to me to be comicalities of marked insipidity. So what will you, as the French say?

Yesterday we were among bibliographers and such, who were talking of a publication of yours of immense size and complexity, full of anagrams and other word-puzzles which do sound very baffling. Someone put the point that there could be no money in such a

---

[1] Editor of *The Times*.

venture, to which another replied to the effect that R.H-D. didn't worry very much about that side of publishing.

I haven't sent you *Sir Richard Roos*[1] because in any ordinary sense it is unreadable. Don't tell your Cambridge friends, but it has been entirely paid for by its author, so its lack of sales leaves my withers comparatively unwrung. Today I have wasted much time observing the six long-tailed tits on the bird-table. None has ever come there before, but these six seem to have taken to it, and their combined weight deters even the bullying nuthatch.

I have finished Geoffrey Faber's *Oxford Apostles*, having enjoyed and admired it enormously. But how odious Newman was! A wonderful preacher and writer, no doubt, and of great personal charm—but chock-full of egotism, self importance, self-pity, self-concern, the most tedious aspects of femininity—a real stinker, I should say.

Somehow soon, dear George, I shall simply have to put a term to my Oscar researches and reach some sort of expedient compromise between perfectionism and practicality. Ruth says, truly, that at this rate I might go on for years (it's five and a half already) and many of the lacunae that worry me will never be noticed by anyone. I know that's right, but I hate letting anything go until it's as good as I can get it. And I so seldom get more than a consecutive hour or two. If this were an American venture (like the Boswell papers or Horace Walpole's letters) it would be limitlessly subsidised, with a team of fully-paid full-time research-assistants. English scholarship (I don't mean my nonsense) is badly handicapped, and the British Museum hasn't even got enough money to catalogue its manuscripts.

I got some good stuff out of Flash Harry about Sullivan for my Gilbert paper, and he told me a good, and unprinted, Gilbert repartee. They asked him how some play of his was doing and G.—a very conceited man—told them how good a play it was. A prim listener said 'But Mr Gilbert, you know self-praise is no recommendation'. To which Gilbert replied 'Perhaps self-abuse would be better, though

---

[1] By Ethel Seaton (1961). A study of a fifteenth-century poet.

it doesn't seem to have done *you* much good'. I fear that won't quite do for the G. and S. Society, even after *Lady Chatterley*. But it was a good retort in the Garrick Club in 1900.

After [the Lit. Soc.] dinner I did what I always (rather intrusively?) do, *viz* go and talk to the members I haven't met before (or is that perhaps being the perfect clubman?). Anyway I got some excellent chat with both Christopher Sykes and Laurence Irving.

On the way home to-day I expended a book-token on *The Intelligent Heart* by Moore. All about the man D.H. Lawrence. I saw it recently very well reviewed and so fell, probably to your derision. Diana[1] met the *Lady C.* prosecuting counsel recently and thought him about the dullest man she had ever met. *Lady C.* was not mentioned. I should have liked to ask him how he managed to make such a mess of it, or how he expected a British jury to decide against a side which produced thirty-five witnesses in favour of one which produced none. The man must be an ass.

Tell me exactly what you think of the new Betjeman poem.[2] The brief verdict at Cambridge was 'It stinks', which is surely a little exaggerated. Dick Routh *per contra* puts it at the very top of all the poems he had read, which again seems to lack balance. It appears to me to have every merit except the poetic. Amusing, vivid, moving, full of stuff, obviously the work of a delightful, wise and excellent man. And I suppose it *does* gain by being in blank verse rather than prose? If I say that it doesn't do to me what poetry does—or did—you will answer: 'You must remember you are old and grey and full of sleep'. Leavis has not yet pronounced; he probably thinks it beneath his notice. His disciples at Girton, it is said, send to Coventry any girl who likes it.

I hadn't a book at Diana's and re-read with great pleasure in Winston's history of the first war. With not a word of censure he shows that Joffre, Haig, Robertson and even Foch were dreadfully lacking in ideas, and that we were saved only and entirely by Falkenhayn and Ludendorff being equally lacking. The French and our losses were consistently higher than the German, whether in defence or attack. It is a grim story—but very good reading.

[1] George's daughter, Diana Hood.
[2] *Summoned by Bells* (1960).

Tommy rang up on Wednesday morning, to say what a good evening it had been, and added: 'Of course, George is a host in himself', to which I heartily agreed. So glad you had a crack with Laurence Irving, the most charming of men. He is a close friend of Field Marshal Alexander, whom he quoted at dinner as saying: 'The British are warriors, but not militarists', which I thought very shrewd.

As Betjeman is almost my exact contemporary, and I knew him (and most of his friends) at Oxford, I cannot pretend to be impartial. I read the poem with great interest, sympathy and pleasure, and towards the end I found I was reading it as prose. Clearly it's scarcely poetry, except occasionally and briefly. When John Wain said that B's huge sales were the measure of the English fear and dislike of true poetry, he spoke more than a little of the truth.

I was most interested in your remarks on Winston's first-war history. If you ever get through the long and full history of the Franco-Prussian War which I shall soon be sending you, you will see that there the ineptitude of both sides was equally appalling, and the Germans won simply because the *luck* was always on their side. When they marched the wrong way they accidentally split the French army, but when the French went wrong they marched into Switzerland and were interned. I wonder if things are any different today?

I have just read the new Graham Greene novel.[1] In technique and sheer skill there is no one to-day to touch him. The story is gripping despite the interminable arguments on God and love. I think you should read it. Now I shall relapse upon Carlyle and sleep.

How right you are about Newman. In the Holmes-Laski letters L. says 'I should have been slightly nauseated by N. had he not been too remote for anything but curiosity' and H. sums him up as 'a tender spirit, and born writer, arguing like a pettifogger'. I remember being rather repelled by him when I read that he had said his *one* thought was 'Shall I be safe if I die to-night?' It doesn't do to think too much about the next world. Old Holmes was always sound about that.

I have finished Moore on D.H.L. Very interesting, and I should

---

[1] *A Burnt-out Case.*

think well done, though he handles his (to me) uncivilised and sneery side too gently. L. seems to have hated every place he went to after a few weeks, and every friend after a few months. I find him tremendously rebarbative (if that is the right word). That letter of his to K. Mansfield, beginning 'I loathe you. You revolt me, stewing in your consumption' in 1920 surely touches a new low in sheer caddishness. Was he really sane at such times? And what of the man Leavis calling him 'the finest literary critic of our time'? Was that before or after D.H.L. had put Fenimore Cooper above Tolstoy, Tourgenieff, and Dostoevsky? The picture in the book of Frieda in the Fifties, with one eye apparently closed suggests that L. occasionally scored a bull's (or should I say a cow's) eye with his plate-throwing. Anyway Medusa would have thrown up the sponge if she had seen this photo.

I look forward enthusiastically to the Franco-Prussian War—one of those topics I can never read enough about. Bismarck fascinates me—a terrifying man. How nice to think that the one person *he* was afraid of was Queen Victoria. What you say of 'luck' in war reminds me that the French (Clemenceau?) sacked scores of generals merely on the grounds that 'they weren't lucky', and the people understanding this brings the corollary to Alexander on the English, e.g. that the French *are* militarists—or were. They certainly understood more about war in 1914 than the English.

Pamela has just finished Lady Lytton—much struck with the editor's cleverness in making so much of material that might often seem dull, and also disliking good Queen Victoria a little more than before.[1] Really to put Scott at the top of all poets, at the same time regretting his occasional *coarseness* (!!). Did she approve of the draping of pianoforte-legs? They really weren't sane in those days. When Gilbert put *Great Expectations* on the stage, the censor deleted 'a lord' in Magwitch's remark 'Here you are in chambers fit for a lord' and substituted 'Heaven'. And Lewis Carroll, whose amiable hobby it was to photograph little girls naked, protested against the female chorus in *Pinafore* singing 'Why damme, it's too bad'—'Those pure innocent-looking girls, those pure young lips sporting with the horrors of hell'. And I suppose you look on my disapproval of *Lady C.* as being as frumpish as the above.

[1] *Lady Lytton's Court Diary* 1895–1899, edited by Mary Lutyens, pub. R.H.-D.

I am just off to see my doctor. I expect he will give me six months —with luck. In which case I should be writing you some such letter as John Sterling wrote to Carlyle in similar circs. It isn't a very bad letter, 'written', as T.C. says, 'in starfire and immortal tears'. Do look it up.[2] Pamela sends her love. She almost girds at me for my luck in having a fairy godmother like you. She won't hear of your disclaimer of any special generosity. 'After all what other publisher acts like that?' she says with that thudding feminine commonsense. Ruth knows too, I bet. Please give her my love.

21 January 1961   *Bromsden Farm*

The advance sales of Peter's book[1] (which is out tomorrow) are more than double those of *The Siege at Peking*, which I take to be a good omen.

Nowadays most English publishers make an annual pilgrimage to New York to acquire American books—and most do well out of it. I went in 1950 and again in 1952, but have avoided the effort ever since. Now I feel I must go again, so have taken a deep breath and booked a passage on the *Queen Mary* on February 25. I shall be there for most of March, and get back in time for Duff's wedding, which is to be at Builth Wells on Easter Monday (April 3). The all-important thing about the trip is that Ruth is coming too. For propriety's sake we have to book separately (and so pay double), but we shall be together all the time and are hoping to stay with some very nice people called Gleaves, old friends of mine, whose daughter is married to Ruth's son. By saving all the ruinous hotel-expenses I hope to pay R.'s passage out of the

---

[2] *10 August 1844*   *Hillside, Ventnor*

My dear Carlyle, For the first time for many months it seems possible to send you a few words: merely, however, for Remembrance and Farewell. On higher matters there is nothing to say. I tread the common road into the great darkness, without any thought of fear, and with very much of hope. Certainty indeed I have none. With regard to You and Me I cannot begin to write; having nothing for it but to keep shut the lid of those secrets with all the iron weights that are in my power. Towards me it is still more true than towards England that no man has been and done like you. Heaven bless you! If I can lend a hand when *THERE*, that will not be wanting. It is all very strange, but not one hundredth part so sad as it seems to the standers-by.

Your wife knows my mind towards her, and will believe it without asseverations.

Yours to the last, JOHN STERLING

[1] *Bayonets to Lhasa* (1961).

firm's money. Having her there will make *all* the difference (and indeed our unwillingness to be separated for so long has played a big part in my nine years' insularity), since she will bear some of the brunt of the manuscripts and the overwhelming hospitality. I shall have to visit some six different people *every day* we're there—think of it! Except for a week-end in Boston and Harvard, I expect we shall stay in New York. Ruth has never before crossed the Atlantic and is wildly excited. It will be my fifth visit, so I shall be able to show her everything. If the sea is tolerable, the two crossings will be blessed interludes, without social obligations or interruptions. You will have to get some of those six-penny air-letter forms, and I will write by the same means. It sometimes takes as little as two days. I shall miss only the March Lit. Soc.

Meanwhile my sailing-date has also become the deadline by which the Oscar galley-proofs must return to the printer, and there is much to be done. When I finally parted with the proofs of *Hugh Walpole* I felt exactly, I'm sure, as a woman must feel after giving birth to twins— empty, proud and slightly bewildered—and now I can hardly imagine life without Oscar.

My clothes are all so old and shabby that I thought I simply *must* get a new suit for America, so Ruth and I went to Burton's in Regent Street, and found a Ready-to-Wear Sale going on. I bought two very nice suits for £8. 8. 0. and £11.11.0. and came away rejoicing.

I am reading a life of Oscar Browning (in search of material about *my* Oscar) and do not so far find O.B. very congenial. Did you know him?[1]

25 *January 1961*   *Grundisburgh*
I read my Gilbert paper two nights ago. The Society was a little sticky at first but all right in the end. I ended up my researches rather liking Gilbert, absurd though his touchiness was. He was not easy to score off. When a prima donna objected to being told exactly where to stand etc she flung out: 'Why should I? I'm not in the chorus.' All she got from G. was 'No, madam, your voice is not strong enough or you would be.'

Oscar Browning was repulsive and wholly absurd. The Eton affair

---

[1] Oscar Browning (1837–1923). Eton master 1860–1875, Cambridge don 1876–1909. Author of many books, mostly historical.

was badly managed by Hornby, but O.B. was really becoming rather a menace. He was openly idle about all routine work and frankly favoured all the nicest-looking boys. Arthur Benson once told me that O.B. was talking about Oscar Wilde, and said 'I knew a good deal about all that affair' and, added A.C.B.,'his face as he said that was the face of a satyr.' Of course both Hornby and Warre (like Elliott too)[1] were Victorianly suspicious of art and artists, and O.B. did do some good work encouraging such. Old Warre indeed was something of a Philistine, for all his knowledge of Homer.

1 February 1961   *Grundisburgh*

I refreshed myself with Max's *Around Theatres*. He reviewed two plays by Gilbert and put them neatly in their respective places, *viz* at the very opposite pole to *The Bab Ballads, qua* wit, neatness, light touch etc. Gilbert's prose really is! M.B. says it is as bad as Pinero's, implying that nothing can be worse than that. I suppose in Victorian times your sentences were expected to be dressed up.

Tell Peter how greatly I enjoyed his Younghusband book. What a mess the Government made of it. St John Brodrick[2] of course the chief villain. I met him once and thought him curiously stupid, though he shone in comparison with his brother Arthur, who talked one entire evening at Holkham without saying anything. And what about Kitchener of Khartoum? My uncle General Neville L. who served under him in South Africa always not only disliked him but thought nothing of his brains—in that agreeing with Lloyd George who summed him up as 'a good poster'. He certainly had a tremendous presence. I have now, with your books, got from the library Shirer's Nazi history—1200 large pages[3], and one has read all of it pretty well in Bullock.[4] But somehow one—or at least I—can't resist it. The horrid truth is that Adolf was a genius, and so, in that tiresome way such men have, inexhaustible.

Why do so many always think that a change of fashion must be an advance in wisdom? It is his realisation of this—*inter alia*—that

---

[1] Hornby, Warre and Elliott were all Head Masters of Eton.
[2] Secretary of State for India at the time of Younghusband's invasion of Tibet.
[3] *The Rise and Fall of the Third Reich* by William L. Shirer (1960).
[4] *Hitler—A Study in Tyranny* by Alan Bullock (1952).

makes old Judge Holmes's comments on men and books so good. His grasp of essentials was Johnsonian. Don't you like his remark to Lady Desborough that the Boer war 'would give England a chance to pay for some of its unearned exquisiteness.'

4 February 1961   *Bromsden Farm*

It is now 8 p.m., and I have been working on the Oscar galley proofs since 11 a.m., with briefest intervals for food. The sheer physical labour of transferring several thousand corrections accurately and legibly on to the printer's set of proofs, clipping on hundreds of new typed footnotes at the relevant places, and so on, is appalling, and I have grave doubts of my ability to complete the task before catching the *Queen Mary.*

David Cecil looked in on Thursday to gossip about Max: he hopes to finish his biography in a year, but as he hasn't yet begun the writing, I have my doubts. He says Leavis has *no* chance of being elected[1], though he may split and confuse the vote a little. Only M.A.'s have a vote, and in practice only those in Oxford exercise it.

Next week, Ruth and I are going to see Peggy Ashcroft in *The Duchess of Malfi*, which I've never seen before, I suspect it will make one realise all over again the excellence of Shakespeare.

Duff's paper, the *Sunday Telegraph*, makes its bow tomorrow after weeks of stress and anxiety. Last week they set up a complete 'dummy run' for practice, and were so nervous lest the Beaverbrook press might get a glimpse of it and mock, that every proof was carefully locked up in a safe each night. Now the worst will be known. Shall you ever see it? Not at home, I imagine.

9 February 1961   *Grundisburgh*
                                                 (summer-house)

Your Oscar labours make me feel like the Queen of Sheba—whom I do not otherwise resemble.[2] You are just like Boswell (not in all ways!) running, as he said, half across London to fix one date.[3]

---

[1] As Professor of Poetry at Oxford.

[2] 'And when the queen of Sheba had seen all Solomon's wisdom, and the house that he had built [etc, etc] there was no more spirit in her.'

                                             I Kings, x, 5.

[3] Advertisement to the first edition of the *Life of Johnson*.

I wonder what you will make of *The Duchess of Malfi*. One gets an impression of a fine grimness and resonance in the reading of it; I suspect it may be like so many Shakespeare plays, much better when acted. 'Butcherly rant' was all Shaw saw in Marlowe, but his feeling for poetry was far from strong—he really did think blank verse was easier to write than prose. And so of course Dickens found it. And certainly Mrs Siddons in speech: 'You've brought me water, boy; I asked for beer' is richer than many lines in Tennyson's *Idylls*. Also perhaps Anna Seward's 'My inmost soul abhors the bloody French.'

I have just finished Shirer's 1200 pages on the Third Reich. Quite absorbing. Do you realise on how many occasions Hitler had us *absolutely cold*, and, by (obviously) the grace of God, did exactly the wrong thing? It is almost terrifying to see every time how many and how narrow our squeaks were. And where else in human history do you find so tremendous a blend of genius and wickedness? As a human being he simply had not *one* good quality. I hope whenever you meet a German you will impress upon him that only the Germans regard 'brutal' as a eulogistic word, and that only the German language has to have a word meaning 'pleasure in others' misfortune' (*Schadenfreude*) because the trait is so common in the German nature. The library lets one have a book for a *fortnight*. I wonder who but G.W.L. in Suffolk will get through these 650,000 words in that time. (A neighbour's gardener read forty pages of *Lady C.* in a week and then left it as being 'not very interesting'.)

11 February 1961   *Bromsden Farm*

We didn't greatly care for *The Duchess of Malfi*: indeed we were thankful when the last two characters simultaneously stabbed each other and we could escape. Peggy Ashcroft was lovely, and the staging superb (some of the best I've ever seen), but the other performers were moderate, and the play! The idiocy of Shakespeare's plots is masked and redeemed by the poetry, but except for three or four lines, there is nothing here but rhetoric and wind. Bloodshed and horrors get steadily funnier and more absurd as they multiply. I'm quite glad to have seen it once, but please never again.

You have to be vaccinated before you can enter the Land of the Free, so today I drove down to Henley and was 'done' by our doctor.

I asked him for the necessary certificate, but he said I should have to get a special one from the Cunard Line, and after he has signed it I shall have to get the Town Clerk to vouch for his (the doctor's) signature. But who vouches for the Town Clerk's? How much red tape can people think up?

The first issue of the *Sunday Telegraph* sold out all its *one million* copies, but they can't tell how much of that is due to curiosity. Most of the other papers' remarks have been fairly acid, as one would expect.

Q. What are Chitterlings?

A. Lady Chatterley's children.

16 February 1961   *Grundisburgh*

How right you are about counsel's opinion.[1] I remember once, when a housemaster asked the Governing Body some question about responsibility in case of fire. They got counsel's opinion (price five guineas) and sent it to me. I rejoined that it was an exact parallel with the old problem and its answer about how to find the sex of a canary. 'Give the bird a lump of sugar; if it is a he, he will eat it, and if it is a she, she will.' This went to the Bursar who read it out to the G.B. and a loud cackle of laughter from Provost Quickswood prevented my being hauled over the coals for impudence.

I have just written to nephew Charles about a New Zealand village called 'Taumatawakatangihangakoanstameataturipunakapikimaung-ahoronukupohaiwhenuakitanatahn'. It means 'The brow of the hill where Tamatea, the man with the big knee who slid, climbed and swallowed mountains, the discoverer of land, played his flute to his loved one'.

18 February 1961   *Bromsden Farm*

As you can imagine, my chief concern, far more compelling than American dollars or visas or office affairs, is to get Oscar ready for the printer before we leave. It's touch and go, with many desperate decisions and wily plans for leaving, here and there, sufficient space for small insertions in the page-proofs. For instance, where I know that a three-line footnote is needed and can't be done in the time, I either write 'leave space for three-line footnote', or write three idiotic

[1] R.H.-D. had said it is 'almost always *wrong*'.

lines, for which the right ones can be exchanged later without too much worry and expense. Most of them will pass unnoticed anyhow.

From New York I have already received invitations to lunch, dinner, theatres, operas, Sundays in the country, and God knows what. Their deep feeling of inferiority leads to a crazy excess of hospitality, and if one persists in praising the country and all its ways they are momently reassured. But oh how exhausting it all is! Almost all the food has been refrigerated into tastelessness—only coffee, orange-juice, ice-cream and oysters are always good. And most of the flowing drink is straight whisky or gin with a lot of ice.

22 February 1961   *Grundisburgh*
I am of course in the summer-house (only just, if you see what I mean). Being swathed in a rug, I am unwilling to move. I am only pretending that it is warm enough. What is the point of thick white cloud on a perfectly dry day? I frequently find myself in agreement with Mrs Besant in her fierce days. Genius on your part to send her life.[1] I am greatly enjoying it. Clearly one of those tremendous, admirable, intolerable women like F. Nightingale and B. Webb. Wonderful character and courage and achievement and all that. But uncomfortable for us humdrum folk whom they clearly despise. But Annie B. must have been less one-track than F.N. and B.W., who saw *no* point in talking or thinking of anything but nursing and gas-and-water respectively. I suppose there must be some of this sort; otherwise Mrs Gamp and Mr Bumble would be still with us. At present I am at the Bradlaugh[2] period—I remember Mr Gladstone fulminating about him at the dinner-table. But I suppose if you are sure about the Trinity you are fierce about its enemies—or still more perhaps if you are not *quite* sure.

Tell me what you thought of Britten's *Midsummer Night's Dream* (and Shakespeare's too of course). What can B's music do for S's which is often incomparable there? Old Agate always maintained that first-class poetry and ditto music spoilt each other, and that the insipid libretti of the Wagner operas were all right. I must tell you, the man Leavis's article in the *Spectator* on *Lady C.* seemed to me

[1] *The First Five Lives of Annie Besant* by Arthur H. Nethercot (1961).
[2] Atheist and Radical M.P.

excellent—both very intelligent and quite intelligible. And he ties the English language up in fewer knots than usual.

25 February 1961   *R.M.S. Queen Mary*

This is just a brief interim report, which can be posted at Cherbourg. Despite persistent catarrh and a hacking cough, I managed to get Oscar back to the printer, and everything else more or less straightened out. We are now blissfully ensconced in two comfortable and almost adjacent cabins. Any amount of excellent food, no letters, telephones or papers, and a free cinema show every day. Apparently President Kennedy is a great one for the girls, and during the election his opponents said that if he got to the White House they only hoped he would do for fornication what Eisenhower did for golf.

1 March 1961   *R.M.S. Queen Mary*

Heavy seas, mountainous meals, a movie each afternoon, ten hours of sleep each night (including the one caused by putting back the clock), an ever-open bar—all these have proved very beneficial. We are both thoroughly relishing these unreal days of suspended animation. Little walks on the icy deck, bowls of broth at 11 a.m., tea and light music after the movie, visits to the library (where this is being written) punctuate the steady rhythm of creaking timbers, throbbing floors and rushing waters. Two days were rough: now all is calm and speedy.

The food is excellent, and one can order almost anything one fancies. I have kept a typical menu to send you. Last night, for instance, became a Gala Night, by the general issue of gaily coloured miniature hats, and we consumed oysters (melon for R), turtle soup, skipped the fish, excellent tender fillet steaks, and a deliciously light American pudding called Nesselrode Pie. For breakfast one can have bloaters or minced chicken or onion soup, but we generally stick to the excellent bacon-and-eggs. We have a little table to ourselves, where we are waited on by a charming man who escaped from the 'Free City' of Danzig in 1936 and fought with the Royal Engineers in Italy. Now he is married to a Scottish girl and lives at Eastbourne.

My first written word to you, dearest George, and very little space for any outpouring of soul. The best thing so far is that R. seems so definitely rested and better and has thrown away ideas of diet and eats and drinks like his old self. Very, very satisfactory. I shall try and send you a separate word in the next days or weeks. My love to you. Ruth.

2 March 1961   *Grundisburgh*
I am at the moment in London, for two meetings. On the G.B.A. Committee, we shall now be dragooned by Sir Griffith Williams, one of those men who looks far more important than anyone can possibly be—knighted for some incredibly dull services in secondary school education, which have for some reason convinced him that he need not cultivate the graces. He has no manners at all, which I find invariably displeasing.

I am reading in bed a life of William Cory, whom I don't much like.[1] Too much sentiment, and though very learned, almost always wrong in his judgments, e.g. that Tennyson was far greater than Milton. His leaving Eton and changing his name was very mysterious and no one has ever really spoken out about it—any more than they have about Oscar Browning.

7 March 1961   *Grundisburgh*
Nice letter redolent of ozone arrived this morning (with a builder's bill which I had expected to be about £75 and was £184. But I suppose that happens to everybody—though one item on it was more than surprising, *viz* 'holidays etc'). You sound in good case (as Swithin Forsyte used to say).

Please give my very best love to Ruth, with warm thanks for her little P.S. to yours. It is a pleasant thought—you and she happily enjoying sea and sun and wind, wearing gay hatlets, and tucking into Nesselrode Pie. P. and I supped yesterday on boiled eggs, which Percy Lubbock once called 'stuffy little things' but we both enjoy them.

19 March 1961   *220 E 61 Street*
                                                          New York City
Do not fancy, my dear George, that an intermission of writing is a decay of kindness. No man is always in a disposition to write, nor has

---

[1] Presumably *William Cory, a Biography* by Faith Compton Mackenzie (1950). See pp. 47 and 62.

any man at all times something to say. I send you this mangled quotation for the same reason that Alice Meynell on her deathbed murmured 'my bluest veins to kiss'[1]—to show that I am still sentient and at least a fragment of my usual self. This is the first letter I have sent you from America, and it may well be the last, such is the pace here, without cease. Mostly freezing days with clear blue sky and all these topless towers glittering in the brightest sunlight. Two appointments in the morning, an enormous lunch at someone's expense, with much liquor. Two or three more appointments, drinks somewhere before a dinner-party or theatre, or both. Home by 12 or 1 to deepest sleep, and then another similar day. We have been to three plays, two revues, one movie and one opera.

Baghdad on the Hudson was a pretty good name for this city of fantasy. My reason is saved by my beloved Ruth's presence, and she so enjoying it all in the savage way one must. We have between us read, perused or sampled several dozen manuscripts and sets of proofs—most of them quite unsuitable for English publication. Have picked up one or two little things, but so far nothing major or important. We learn that the proof-corrections in the Oscar galleys will cost £500!! The compulsive friendliness and hospitality of Americans is both pleasing and exhausting, and seeing so many people in quick succession makes for endless repetitions. Needless to say, all dieting has gone by the board, all my clothes are tight, and Ruth says it's a very good thing. All helpings of food are enough for three, and enough food must be thrown away in this city to feed half the Congo.

Darling Rupert is a total success (Americanism) and adored by all these open-armed people. Which is, after all, much like being at home. A great deal of it is rewarding and stimulating, but they have no cubby-holes in their nature where one can curl up and rest. It's all outward striving and constant movement, and my heart yearns for the curlews of Kisdon. Keep yourself warm for our return. Love Ruth.

22 March 1961   *Grundisburgh*
Last night dinner with Wells (C.M.) at the United University Club—his ninetieth birthday, and he was one of the least decayed men in the

---

[1] *Antony and Cleopatra*, act two, scene 5.

room. John Christie[1] has had jaundice and has gout. No excuse for the former as he drinks *cream* by the pint (literally). Old Gow is vanishing—really frighteningly thin. He told me he now weighed eight stone odd (At Eton he was *twelve*!). I urged him to eat more food and he said that is the trouble—he hates the stuff. Well they know all about that; it is 'anorexia' and unless cured it kills you, because you become vulnerable to any germ that is about. His state partly comes, as he admits, from having lost *all* interest in life. I had a good crack with G.O. Allen[2] who was at his best—and that is very nice. He knows *all* about modern cricket. He corroborated what nephew Charles told me, *viz* that since Hutton's command of 'no fraternisation' the MCC sides in Australia have been very unpopular —and no wonder. And do you know, and can you believe, that D. Sheppard forbade his Cambridge side to fraternise with Oxford in the match? Unbelievable but true—and quite insufferable, as G.O.A. firmly said.

I stayed with my brother-in-law Lord Leconfield yesterday. A niece of his came in, and we chatted away. Afterwards he told me that I had talked him down—was, to put it shortly, intolerable. He is 83½ and I think had a rush of blood to the head—or is what he said true?

27 March 1961   *220 E 61*
                                                                           N.Y.C.

I need not tell you that Ruth is a *succès fou* with the American gentlemen and finds this very stimulating. We are astonishingly well, considering the life we're leading. We sail after lunch tomorrow. We find we need more and more liquor—mostly Bourbon whisky, which we love—to keep us going. The best building since I was last here is the Seagram (whisky) building on Park Avenue. It is some sixty storeys high and made of *bronze*. Very beautiful in sunlight and even more so at night when one of its thousands of windows is permanently lit up. On the ground floor is the world's most *chi-chi* restaurant, called The Four Seasons. It has a Picasso mural forty foot square in the entrance hall, and a pool the size of a swimming bath in the middle of the restaurant, with four *trees* at its corners etc etc. Everything is wildly

---

[1] Eccentric millionaire (1882–1962). For some years an Eton master. Founded the Glyndebourne Music Festival on his own estate 1934.
[2] Cricketer, Captain of England, 1936–37, 1948; President of the MCC, 1963–64.

expensive, except cigarettes, but the firm is paying, so to hell with that. Last week we found two new Oscar letters, which a kindly bookseller allowed us to copy and airmail home for last-minute inclusion.

Everything is brash and loud and brutal, but at night very beautiful. Most of the people are very ugly, but friendly and longing for praise. The subway is indescribably awful. There is no climate in New York, but rather a succession of violent extremes. The city is a vast melting-pot of races and colours and creeds which presumably will one day solidify.

29 March 1961   *Grundisburgh*

I grow old—physically—rather rapidly. Young ladies offer me their seat in buses—not wholly from kindness, partly in self-defence, for they see how a lurch of the bus shoots me into the lap of some unoffending matron slow in escaping. I expect to find myself sued, like the Rev. Thomas, for embracing. His plea that arthritis and copulation in a taxi were an impossible combination was rejected by the Consistory Court. Have you been reading the case? I met the sublime and the ridiculous in juxtaposition last week—viz the whitest magnolia in Suffolk and under it a poster announcing 'Mrs Brandy in the Box'.[1]

The Ancient of Days, who has a fine sense of humour, as we know, must be indulging in Olympian chuckles over the circulation of the New English Bible running neck and neck with that of *Lady Chatterley*. Have you seen it? They seem to me to have altered some things quite needlessly, and surely to fiddle about with the Lord's Prayer is hardly forgivable. So many people do not appear to realise that language *just a bit* above people's heads is right. 'Truly and *indifferently*' true and *lively* word': would the change to 'impartially' and 'living' attract those who are now repelled? But I expect introducing lucidity into the crabbed exhortations of St Paul is a wholly good thing, and after all for centuries St Paul's Christianity has really held the field for discussion. Our rector will have none of the *N.E.B.* Indeed if it was still in print I think he would have Wycliffe's on the lectern.

[1] It was not in a taxi but in his own car, outside Wandsworth Common railway station, and in other places, that the Vicar of Balham was accused of persistent adultery with Mrs Brandy, a forty-year-old school-teacher. He was found guilty on 28 March 1961 and subseqently defrocked.

Good Friday, 31 March 1961   *R.M.S. Queen Elizabeth*

First class on this ship is indeed something, and I have decided that luxury is all right, provided you experience it only occasionally and for short periods: otherwise you simply begin to complain about the quality of the caviare.

We have two *huge* cabins with an open door between. When we embarked we found three enormous bouquets for Ruth, three bottles of champagne, a bottle of Bourbon whisky, a vast box of chocolates, sundry books and a cable or two. We managed to restrict the seeing off party to three faithfuls. So far the sea has been glassy, and all yesterday we sat out on the sun deck in comfortable chairs, swaddled in rugs, enjoying bright warm sunshine. We try to eat only a small luncheon, though one can have *anything* one wants, and work our way through afternoon tea, a rest with books, a bath and change, cocktails in the bar, and a superb dinner. Last night we had oysters (smoked salmon for Ruth), delicious poached turbot cooked with mussels and shrimps, the breasts of ducklings done with cherries, and a marrons-glacées ice, washed down by some excellent Montrachet. Each evening at 9.30 there is a free movie in the huge theatre. We saw five on the outward journey, and so far two on this—*Tunes of Glory* with Alec Guinness, and a goodish New York one called *The Rat-Race*. Then bed, and it's an hour later than you think.

Easter Monday. Cherbourg

We have bought a copy of *The Times* so that we can do our first crossword for five weeks. Perhaps we shan't be able to. And a rather tragic little concourse of elderly gentlemen are playing us to our tea with tunes from *The Merry Widow*—so we must go. My love. Ruth.

8 April 1961   *Bromsden Farm*

We landed at 7.15, a.m. on Tuesday in dark grey rain. A most officious Customs man disarranged all our luggage and made us pay £3. 12. 0 for sundry nonsenses. Finding an English translation of *Madame Bovary* in my bag, he made sure he was on the trail of dirty books, but a couple of pages of the learned translator's preface calmed his ardour. The office was piled high with this and that, and we longed for the peace of the *Queen Elizabeth*. Adam *lost* the Chess

Cup—I suspect through idleness and other distractions. I have put back seven and a half of the ten pounds I had previously lost, but am quickly dropping my American accent. One's first impression of England in the train from Southampton is of incredible *greenness*. All grass in New York, Boston and between is at this time of year a dark brownish-grey.

15 April 1961   *Grundisburgh*

How very nice it was to see you again. Two families have just left here and two more just come—the larger ones. But happily only two grandchildren are spoilt and therefore unpleasing and they have gone.

Two thousand more members for the MCC! And the only match I ever go up for is the Australian Test Match when the pavilion is cram-full one and a half hours before play begins—and I only got a seat in 1956 because a man (in the best seat of all) died ten minutes before I arrived, and in Housmanly fashion I took it.

Last week I lugged a waggon, full of timber, a good deal impeded by several grandchildren, though when Henry *(aetat* three) was asked by his mother where I was, his answer was 'He's just been helping me bring in the wood.'

16 April 1961   *Bromsden Farm*

I entirely agree with your remarks on the New English Bible. A few fragments of mystery are surely an *asset* to religion, and to slaughter one of the greatest glories of our language and literature to make a Sunday-school holiday is monstrous.

The Eichmann trial seems to me all wrong, because one simply can't help feeling a trace of sympathy for the victim in the glass cage, and clearly one *shouldn't*. I should be happier if they had shot him like a mad dog when they found him. But I suppose the Jews don't want the world to forget what they have been through.

Robert Birley[1] has sent me his Clark Lectures, which I shall certainly publish. They are called *Sunk Without Trace* and deal with six works of Eng. Lit. which were tremendously popular in their day and are now unread and almost forgotten. They are Warner's *Albion's England* (Elizabethan), Nathaniel Lee's *The Rival Queens*

---

[1] Head Master of Eton, 1949–63.

(Restoration), Young's *Night Thoughts*, Robertson's *History of the Reign of Charles V*, Moore's *Lalla Rookh*, and Bailey's *Festus*. The manuscript is in longhand: the writing is legible, but it takes much longer to read than a typescript.

Ruth has gone to Essex to spend the week-end with her son and grandson. The simple truth is that I miss her every moment she isn't there, and that after fifteen years! It must be the real thing—and how rarely is that found!

20 April 1961   *Grundisburgh*
Pro tem I am reading Daphne du Maurier on Branwell Brontë, whose appearance was seemingly like the mildest of spectacled curates. No wonder he could not stand up against his terrifying sisters, but I wonder who could have. Some blend of Heathcliff and Rochester, I suppose.

Do you get any kick out of the Budget? I hope the surtax cut benefits you. It doesn't me. I find it annoying that after saving what I could through a working life of thirty-seven years, and investing it in gilt-edged (which have steadily depreciated) and living in my old age modestly and mainly on my dividends, I am regarded (and called) a parasite by half the Socialists, my income is called 'unearned', and I continue to be taxed up to the hilt. And hundreds of thousands of retired professional men—doctors, dentists, lawyers, schoolmasters, dons, deans etc—are in the same boat.

All decks here are stripped for Oscar. I will go through anything you send with a small toothcomb (whatever a tooth-comb may be). But you remember what James Agate said about proofreading, viz that real efficiency is impossible. He advocated reading upside down, but even so found that as soon as you recognise a word by its first half you take the second half for granted. Anyway I will do the best I can.

23 April 1961   *Bromsden Farm*
Yesterday Duff's wedding entailed a marathon drive for us. We left here at 8.30 a.m. and got back soon after midnight, having covered 305 miles, mostly in heavy rain. Most of the lovely hills and valleys of the Wye were obscured by rainclouds, but all went off gaily and well. The tiny church of St Bridget at Llansantffraed-in-Elfael is as remote

as can be imagined, at the dead-end of a tiny valley, so that all the cars had to be left in wet grass four hundred yards away and the ladies' wedding hats and shoes were sorely tried by two muddy walks in steady rain. Every seat in the church was occupied, and we were so packed in the pews that we had to get up one at a time. The young couple looked exceedingly handsome, and it was all most touching and suitable. The registry was a leaking tent adjoining the east end of the church, but by then we were prepared for anything. Afterwards champagne flowed, with Adam as chief pourer, and we shook innumerable hands and complimented everyone.

The garden here is lush and green and badly needs mowing. Every drainpipe and gutter is blocked with birds' nests, and the lilac is in bloom. The wallflowers are wonderful, but it's always too wet even to look at them. This morning I burned dozens of old newspapers and clipped a few edges before I was driven in by bouncing hailstones. Oh to be in England . . . !

27 April 1961   *Grundisburgh*

Llansantffraed-in-Elfael. Perfectly superb, a poem in itself. I should like to hear you pronounce it. The champagne, poured by Adam, sounds all right, inferior and vulgar wine though it is, though its effects are good, convincing one without much difficulty that the world is in a better state than in fact it is.

Please tell me whether, in the effort to keep up to date, I ought to read the plays of Wesker and Miss Delaney. They cannot surely be as bad as *Lucky Jim* or *Look Back in Anger*.

The Australians, I shall be watching with Gerald Kelly on the middle gallery at Lord's, where seats are kept for us by a man who, I think, sleeps there all night. I wish my nephew was at Hagley. I saw the Australians at Worcester in 1948. Charles Fry[1] was there. Bradman of course got 200 and C.B.F. watched every ball through a pair of vast field-glasses. In the evening he said he had never expected to see another batsman who saw the ball as quick as Ranji,[2] but Bradman certainly did—and was R's superior in concentration, which C.B.F. said he had never seen remotely equalled. Interesting.

[1] Famous cricketer and all-round sportsman, once offered the throne of Albania.
[2] Prince Randjitsinhji, famous cricketer.

I don't really much *like* champagne either—Belloc once described it as 'wine, yellow and acid, with bubbles in it'—but it's a great morale-booster, don't you agree?

I certainly should *not* read the plays of Wesker and Miss Delaney. They may some of them be just tolerable in the theatre (*A Taste of Honey* was more than that), but to *read*—no, my dear George!

On Wednesday Marjorie Linklater (Eric's wife and a friend of more than thirty years) paid one of her rare visits to London, and I (in all good faith) took her to the longest and dullest film either of us had ever seen—the Italian *La Dolce Vita*.[1] It lasts for *three hours,* and there is no plot, only a sequence of incidents. The famous 'orgy scene' is pretty tame, and the whole thing seemed to me pretentious and wearisome.

I am reading a life of Maupassant by a charming American called Francis Steegmuller, whose future books I am going to publish. He writes with style and learning: it's an excellent book, which you would enjoy. My bedtime reading has for so many years been largely conditioned by Oscar and the search for quotations used by him, that I suddenly feel liberated, and able for a few minutes most days to follow my fancy in an agreeable way.

Assuming that you want them *quam celerrime* I send the mild little results of my tooth-comb now instead of waiting till my Thursday letter. I find no solecisms by R.H.-D. and let me say at once, surely no book since Birkbeck Hill's Boswell has been so comprehensively and beautifully annotated. You will laugh at my one suggestion for the alteration of your English. What the split infinitive is to some (on the whole silly) people the double pluperfect has always been to me.

Very many thanks for your note of April 29 and for your extremely valuable comments on the first thirty-two pages. They are just the sort of thing I was hoping for. Here is a note from the *Oxford*

---

[1] Directed by Frederico Fellini.

Companion to Music which will answer your query about the Skye Boat Song:

> One half of the tune is a sea-shanty heard in 1879 by Miss Annie MacLeod (later Lady Wilson[1]) when going by boat from Toran to Loch Coruisk; the other half is by Miss MacLeod herself. The words, by Sir Harold Boulton, Bart, (*Speed bonnie boat, like a bird on the wing*) date from 1884. Later some other words were written to the tune by Robert Louis Stevenson, who apparently believed the tune to be a pure folk-tune and in the public domain.

I sent you another thirty-two pages yesterday and more should follow tomorrow. Keep up the good work.

3/4 May 1961   *Grundisburgh*

Just before the first proofs arrived I was reduced (wrong word) to re-reading *Mansfield Park*. At first my anti-Austen feelings were re-inforced by the immensely insipid and trivial conversations in Chapters 6 and 9 (please have a glimpse and tell me if I am really as wrong as all that). But I frankly confess (who is humble and I am not humble?, as St Paul obscurely put it) I enjoyed it—so much so that I must shortly have another go at my *bête noire, Emma*. I fear I dislike *her* too much.

I am delighted to hear there is to be a sequel to *How Green*, though the fate of sequels is grim—apart from *Alice, The Jungle Book, The Prisoner of Zenda, The Newcomes* and no doubt several others which I have forgotten.

When I grouse about aches and pains to my doctor, he unsympa-thetically says that such are *en règle* at my age, and that he knows no man of seventy-eight fitter than I am. And my only way of scoring off him would be to die suddenly to-morrow, and then I should miss Oscar. So he has me, damn him, in a cleft stick. Do you remember in that admirable second act of *The Truth about Blayds*[2] the old man's answer to the family's wishes of 'many happy returns' on his ninetieth birthday 'Happy I hope; many, I neither expect nor want.' A good answer, and in fact he died that very night.

---

[1] Her enjoyable *Letters From India* were first published in 1911.
[2] By A.A. Milne (1921).

On almost every page one detects *weeks* of hard research, and I like to see you sometimes enjoying yourself. E.g. p. 125 the 'American lobbyist, financier, talker and gastronome' and just below after O.W's ecstatic praise of *A Daughter of the Nile*[1] produced on September 6, your laconic statement 'It was withdrawn on 23 Sept.' What an extraordinarily *nice* man O.W. was, so kind and courteous, till pricked. Did his extremely beautiful wife remain loyal to the end, or was her stuffy family too much for her? It was a dreadful business really and need never have come to a head at all. O.W. didn't corrupt anybody, and everyone now knows that the clause in Labby's[2] bill making private behaviour a public offence was passed at the end of the day when all MPs wanted their dinner, and weren't attending.

Why is T.S.E. not among the 'Companions of Literature,' the new order just started? He is a better man than either old Maugham or E.M. Forester (*sic* in *Daily Telegraph*).

I have also just got Cyril Connolly's *Enemies of Promise* which I remember finding interesting years ago. Do you know him? Shall I write and tell him that he is in error saying the book was banned at Eton? Eton is particularly good at *not* being thin-skinned about hostile opinions (partly, of course because she does, or did, not, like the Duke, care one twopenny damn what hostile critics think). I remember Tuppy Headlam being much pleased by C's eulogy of him as teacher and influence, but I fear it was much too favourable. T.H. never had 'much the best house at Eton', and if as C. says he 'hated idleness' he got over it: for in his last years he was conspicuously idle in school (golf at Swinley *every* Sunday!) partly because he had formed the opinion that history was not a good subject for teaching to the great majority of boys. And he may have been right.

Slightly comic Governors' meeting of Woodbridge School yesterday. Next year we are to have tercentenary celebrations. What big noise shall we try to get? The Duke of Edinburgh? Well who do we

[1] A play by Laura Don.
[2] Henry Du Pré Labouchère (1831–1912). Radical M.P. for Northampton 1880–1905. Founded *Truth* 1876.

approach to find if he could or would? The Lord Chamberlain. Who is he? Lord Nugent. Does anyone know him? G.W.L.: 'My first pupil'—but he isn't the Lord Chamberlain. Who is? Eric Penn. Does anyone know him? G.W.L: 'He was in my house', but he isn't the man. Some governor: 'No, the man to go for is Sir Edward Ford. Does anyone know him?' G.W.L: 'He is my cousin.' Another governor: 'I believe the right man is Sir Michael Adeane; does anyone know him?' G.W.L: 'He is my wife's cousin.' Another: 'Suppose we can't get him. What about the Queen-Mother? Does anyone know her?' G.W.L: 'She was a great friend, before marriage, of my wife's.'

So now I am in the eyes of my fellow-governors either *very* highly connected or the biggest snob in England. *Que voulez-vous?*

13 May 1961   *Bromsden Farm*
T.S.E. refused that ridiculous award, and I encouraged him to do so. The Royal Society of Literature—a miserable institution—is simply trying to bolster itself by crowning five octogenarians, who were too vain, gaga or polite to refuse. In any case, I told Tom, a stripling like him is far too young for such a questionable *galère*.

Yes, Constance Wilde behaved well all through, as you will see, though at the end she was quite out of her depth. Hold on—the best is yet to come.

I had a protracted and pathetic luncheon with my old father at White's on Wednesday. He has to totter with two sticks, seldom recognises anyone, and if he does can't remember their name. He reads all day and night, but enjoys very little, finding his adored Dickens now quite unreadable. Self-pity is surely the least attractive of all faults, and it prevents one's own pity from functioning. He never stops saying he has made a mess of everything and wishes he was dead. What can one answer? He refuses to have TV and seldom switches on the radio—what a life! He has day and night nurses permanently in attendance. Sorry to be so depressing. You could easily be my father—what a difference!

18 May 1961   *Grundisburgh*
Rather a moderate harvest this week, I fear. You and your minions are wonderfully accurate on the whole. I am greatly enjoying the job and childishly pleased when I discover an error. The letters are crammed

with interest. I have a *very strong* feeling that Carlyle said 'Gad' and not 'God'. I hope you will find it. I continue my search.

I much enjoy your dislike and contempt for literary societies and—to a great extent—men. Do you remember Henry James's reply to John Bailey when asked to be chairman of the English Association?[1] Edel missed it in his volume of selected letters (published by you) just as he missed another immortal one to Walter Berry who had presented him with a dressing-case.[2]

I am sorry about your father—knowing enough of the stresses of senescence to sympathise with him—knowing too how many people wish they were dead but manage to refrain from saying so.

20 May 1961   *Bromsden Farm*

Sure enough you're right: the phrase is given as part of a conversation between T.C. and Margaret Fuller: 'I accept the Universe'. 'Gad, you'd better!' I am most grateful. What should I do without you?

I do indeed know the James letter to Walter Berry, and in March when I was staying in the James home in Cambridge, Mass, I made

---

[1] '. . . Let me, for some poor comfort's sake, make the immediate rude jump to the one possible truth of my case: it is out of my power to meet your invitation with the least decency of grace. When one declines a beautiful honour, when one simply sits impenetrable to a generous and eloquent appeal, one had best have the horrid act over as soon as possible and not appear to beat about the bush and keep up the fond suspense . . .'
After which he delightfully beats about the bush for several pages. See also p. 105.

[2] '. . . You had done it with your own mailed fist—mailed in glittering gold, speciously glazed in polished, inconceivably and indescribably sublimated, leather, and I had rallied but too superficially from the stroke. It claimed its victim afresh, and I have lain the better part of a week just languidly heaving and groaning as a result *de vos oeuvres*—and forced thereby quite to neglect and ignore all letters. I am a little more on my feet again, and if this continues shall presently be able to return to town (Saturday or Monday;) where, however, the monstrous object will again confront me. That is the grand fact of the situation—that is the tawny lion, portentous creature, in my path. I can't get past him, I can't get round him, and on the other hand he stands glaring at me, refusing to give way and practically blocking all my future. I can't live with him, you see; because I can't live *up* to him. His claims, his pretensions, his dimensions, his assumptions and consumptions, above all the manner in which he causes every surrounding object (on my poor premises or within my poor range) to tell a dingy or deplorable tale—all this makes him the very scourge of my life, the very blot on my scutcheon . . .'

315

Billy James (H.J.'s nephew) read it aloud. He has a barely percepti-
ble and rather attractive hesitation in his speech; and it might have
been the Old Master himself—a delicious experience. In justice to
Leon Edel, it's fair to remind you that in his introduction to the
Selected Letters he explains that he has deliberately omitted famous
letters already known or printed, in favour of others hitherto
unknown.

24 May 1961   *Grundisburgh*
I have just read a book (*Mirror for Anglo-Saxons*[1]) in which the author
condemns the English wholesale for being 'gentlemanly'. U.S.A.
writers are praised heartily for their 'brashness'. Have you seen the
book? It says some sensible things but very many silly ones. How tiresome these young men are who complain of having been 'ruined' by
being sent to Oxford or Cambridge.

Are you hot under the collar about the latest plan for the Oxford
road? A.W. Whitworth[2]—*not* a Christ Church man—says a lot of rot
is talked about the incomparable beauty of Ch. Ch. Meadow. I don't
know it. What would be a real crime would be to spoil the Parks. But
I suppose you all realise that you have literally the loveliest cricket
ground in the world. It would *not* be improved by a motor-road
across the pitch. Fenner's [at Cambridge] on the other hand would.
It might also improve their cricket. Annoying your missing the Lord's
Test. We could have split a ham sandwich.

I am just off to judge a reading competition at Ipswich—the first
at which I shall be using my hearing-aid. Old Rendall[3] went on
judging when he could hear only treble voices, so all the prizes went
to the small boys—which gave rise to the murkiest and most un-
reasonable theories.

28 May 1961   *Bromsden Farm*
Your question about the change in Oscar's attitude to Bosie between
May 1895, and May 1896 has probably now been answered by your
reading the *De Profundis* letter. He had had a whole year to think

---

[1] By Martin Green (1961).
[2] Former Eton master.
[3] Montague John Rendall, 1862–1950. Headmaster of Winchester 1911–1926.

about it all: Bosie had never once even written to him: the attempted publication by B. of O's letters and the suggested dedication of B's poems—all combined to this end.

Yesterday was joyful. Lord's only half-full, and a bitter north-eastern blowing. I had failed to get a Rover for Ruth, so we paid six shillings each and sat in the front row, ground floor, in the middle of the Grand Stand, whence we had a splendid view. The sun shone on us all the morning, but in the afternoon we got colder and colder, and at the Tea Interval went back to Soho Square for a hot bath to stave off *rigor*.

After our bath we went to a revue called *Beyond the Fringe*, which is the talk of the town. I expect you have read of it—just four young men, who wrote it all—and I must say it was vastly amusing. The best things were a skit on Macmillan speaking on TV, and a mock-sermon. I hold no brief for Christ Church Meadow—a dreary flat expanse.

7 June 1961   *North Foreland Lodge*

I am in the headmistress's study at North Foreland Lodge. We (a small sub-committee) met yesterday to tell the staff they were, in one or two respects, inefficient, and to do so without hurting their feelings — and staff's feelings are very near the surface. Well I, as chairman, poured melted butter over them and all was well—except that I think they dispersed, unanimously convinced that we had come down solely to congratulate them. I used the old trick of describing one or more of their bad practices as what other schools I knew absurdly and lamentably did. I think I deceived all except the cynical old man who teaches art and fencing who was clearly enjoying hearing his colleagues hinted at and not himself.

Do you know about girls' schools? Virginal starry-eyed, angelic, do you think? Well the headmistress showed me a letter from another school to the girls here, challenging them to a novel contest—how many girls they could get into a bath all at once. The challengers' record was nineteen. And would they kindly send a photograph of the proceedings before, during, and after. The headmistress asked me (non-committally) what I thought, and was delighted when I said what she thought, *viz* that it stank.

There is literally nothing that I can find in this O.W. instalment, though I am a little distrustful, as I read it against a prattle of child-ish voices and a backfisch playing the Moonlight Sonata with the forthright vigour that one expects in 'Rule Britannia'.

11 June 1961   *Kisdon Lodge, Keld*
Our farmer's son has gone away to work in Kirkby Stephen, and now there is no milking on Kisdon, so we get our post only when we walk down the hill (which isn't every day) or when the farmer comes up on his motor-bike, ostensibly to look at the non-milking cows ('drybags,' he calls them) but in fact to bring us milk from below. The hired car—a Ford Anglia—went like the wind, and by making use (for the first time) of the M.1. from its beginning to the Northampton turn we cut *forty minutes* off our total time, without covering any fewer miles!

I have been reading for the first time John Buchan's last (or perhaps penultimate) novel *Sick Heart River*, which I much enjoyed: he is surely under-rated as a story-teller. Now I am ready for Priestley's new novel, and the life of Wilfrid Blunt by his grandson. But in daytime I am mostly occupied with the Oscar proofs. Just finding and filling in those cross-reference page-numbers in the footnotes takes longer than you would think. So far you have said nothing of your opinion of Oscar as letter writer.

To you I can confess that I carry a heavy burden locked in my heart for, quite inadvertently, when buying stamps in the post office at Hawes yesterday, I overheard the latest Test Score and may not tell it for fear of spoiling the papers for days ahead (we are always two days behind). I feel dreadfully guilty and may even give it away in my sleep. You would have laughed to see R. wrapped up to his ears in a rug and crouched over the fire and his O.W. proofs; a tempest without and our last drop of paraffin gone. Dear George, forgive these crooked words but I write on my knee which is nearer the fire. And they bring you my love and the nice thought that I shall one day soon again hear the tap tap of your stick on that interminable flight of stairs. My love. Ruth.

14 June 1961   *Grundisburgh*
How lumpish of me not to have said what I have all the time felt, *viz* that O.W's letters are *fascinating*. But I was, before your letter arrived,

intending to tell you how steadily one's liking for him grows. His bed may have been as full of boys as that bath I told you of was of girls, but what is that to me? It didn't prevent him from being far kinder and nicer and wiser and wittier than most of his precious friends. The Victorians really could be unbelievably stupid and grossly unchristian, whatever their lofty professions. His unending poverty in '97 and '98 is a heartrending tale. Why did no man with money and imagination send him £1000? But perhaps the two things never run in harness.

You praised Constance in one letter, but wasn't she pretty harsh and unforgiving at the end? Of course she loathed Bosie—and who shall blame her? Except of course D.H. Lawrence, it is hard to think of anyone who could behave more caddishly. And one finds it hard to forgive coarse second-raters like Henley running down the incomparable *Ballad*.

I agree about John Buchan—a first-rate story-teller—and who is there except V. Woolf and others who profess not to like a story? Did you know him? A very friendly fellow, excellent company. A pretty stout chap too; he paid practically all his Oxford fees by literary work. He died too young. I must get *Sick Heart River*.

I have lately been re-reading about two great heroes of my youth (and old age) Wellington and Lincoln. Do you realise what a vast volume of opposition, dislike and contempt both were consistently treated with *by their own side*? And neither turned a hair. That picture of Abe—a broken-hearted man—in the last year of his life is one of the most moving things I know. Also the wonderful beauty of the Duke as drawn by d'Orsay. You know it of course. And please look up Carlyle's pen-portrait of him in his journal 25 June 1850.[1]

---

[1] 'By far the most interesting figure present was the old Duke of Wellington, who appeared between twelve and one, and slowly glided through the rooms—truly a beautiful old man; I had never seen till now how beautiful, and what an expression of graceful simplicity, veracity, and nobleness there is about the old hero when you see him close at hand. His very size had hitherto deceived me. He is a shortish slight-ish figure, about five feet eight, of good breadth however, and all muscle or bone. His legs, I think, must be the short part of him, for certainly on horseback I have always taken him to be tall. Eyes beautiful light blue, full of mild valour, with infinitely more faculty and geniality than I had fancied before; the face wholly gentle, wise, valiant, and venerable. The voice too, as I again heard, is "aquiline" clear, perfectly equable—

Wilfrid Blunt I always suspect had a good deal of the four letter man about him—but he was a good friend to some. Why not—after your gargantuan labours on O.W.—produce a biographical sketch of *Skittles*[1] and her sleeping-partners, among whom, did you know it? was the old Duke of Devonshire. I suspect she was pretty good fun.

18 June 1961   *Kisdon Lodge*
The weather is turning this holiday into an endurance test, and though we are winning, we do long for a few days of hot sun. So far in twelve days we have sat out for only two hours. Here we do the index together, Ruth controlling the hundreds of cards and fishing them out as I need them. This demands table-space, concentration and no intruders. The final proofs will have reached you by now, and your labours will be done. If mine are ever concluded I shall have to turn to

SKITTLES
The Story of a *Poule de Luxe*
by R.H-D.
with an introduction on Victorian Prudery,
and special reference to the bathing
accommodation at girls' schools,
by G.W.L.

Am I right in thinking that there is no really adequate biography of the Duke of Wellington? Guedalla is too slick and sly and second-rate. Shouldn't I commission the right chap to do one? Who is he? Gerry Wellington is very choosy about showing people the documents, having been much harassed by journalists and Yanks, so his approval is essential.

I'm sure I've told you before of the tiny shop in Hawes where the eccentric owner of the Wensleydale cheese-factory deposits all the books he doesn't want, on sale for sixpence or a shilling each. In the past the shop has always been shut, and we got the key from the

uncracked, that is—and perhaps almost musical, but essentially tenor or almost treble voice—eighty-two, I understand. He glided slowly along, slightly saluting this and that other, clear, clean, fresh as this June evening itself, till the silver buckle of his stock vanished into the door of the next room, and I saw him no more.'

[1] Nickname of Catherine Walters, a famous courtesan, to whom Wilfrid Scawen Blunt wrote many of his love-poems.

grocer next door, to whom we returned it with our shillings and six-pences. Now the shop is intermittently cared for by an octogenarian retired railway-signalman, who delivers the morning papers in Hawes and then potters about the shop. He knows the Bible by heart, a great deal of Shakespeare, and has a good library at home, he says, includ-ing a complete set of the English Men of Letters series. He was much delighted with a life of Beethoven which he recently bought in Kendal. He used to make a day-trip to York, so as to browse through all the secondhand bookshops. There were no books in his home when he was a boy, and none of his family or fellow-railwaymen shared his interest. Isn't it extraordinary? He is a charming old chap.

E. Blunden has arrived at Soho Square, and is to be there, on and off, till August 20, when an old lady from America moves in. What hope for the index? Now comes Ruth.

I *did* love having a letter from you all to myself and wish I had some fascinating story to fill in my tiny quota of space. One thing I can say. *How G. was my V.* has been taken from its shelf and laid on the win-dow seat. What this portends I cannot guess, but I will let you know any developments there may be. I read it years ago with enjoyment but shall not press it upon R., as that would be fatal at this stage. My love. Ruth.

23 June 1961   *Lord's Cricket Ground*
                                                            London NW8

From the holy of holies—but all the writing-seats are full and this is practically on my knee. And it will only be a wretched scrap. I leave Highgate Village too early for any letter-writing; I wait a long time for a 210 bus to Golder's Green, of all dim spots, then catch No. 13 for Lord's, and the walk from the stop to the nearest entry is curiously long. Then in the evening I wait aeons for a bus home and am expected to talk all the evening between yawns and so to bed, so what would you? Pamela optimistically opened our garden last Sunday, in spite of my prophecies of rain and murmurs that no one would pay a shilling, even on behalf of our fourteenth-century wall-paintings, to come and sit and listen to a loud gramophone playing the Water Music, etc. And of course I was quite wrong. Ancient village crones sat about like great loaves of bread (old fashioned shape), and all said how happy they were—*especially*, and surprisingly, *because* there were no lucky dips and guessing-games etc which most people think are what get the crowd to such things.

Last night I dined with some nice Old Boys at an absurd restaurant in Beauchamp Place in Knightsbridge lit—a big word—by glittering candles and cramped, but good food. I drank too many different liquors and slept uneasily. One of the Old Boys' wives whom I had never seen before insisted on kissing me goodnight. A very sinister sign surely, indicating that I am far too old for a kiss to have the smallest meaning. Never mind.

25 June 1961   *Kisdon Lodge*
If the publication of Oscar is unduly delayed, as seems likely, owing to the editor's failure to compile the index, the blame can be laid fairly and squarely on the shoulders of G. Lyttelton and R. Llewellyn. Almost since I last wrote I have been immersed in that infernal work,[1] enjoying it enormously, and quickly getting used to that lush-Biblical-Welsh idiom. I quite see what you mean about Bronwen.

29 June 1961   *The Painted Room, Oxford*[2]
How delightful that at last you have tackled *How Green*. Did the gentle but irresistible hand of Ruth play any part? I make private bets to myself—and always win them.

I had a very good evening with Tim. He tells me old Cuthbert is in a sad way—not *qua* health but finance. Has he been living on capital or what? I remember an old boy in Worcestershire who decided that he could not live past ninety and lived on capital which would last till then. When he passed ninety he quietly shot himself. They brought in the silly verdict that he was insane.

1 July 1961   *Bromsden Farm*
If I tried to describe our sadness at leaving Kisdon and returning to London, it would sound childish and unbecoming in a middle-aged man, but I think you realise a lot of it, and we try to cheer each other by reflecting that most people don't get even our glimpses of paradise. Yesterday, with the temperature at 85, we had our half-

---

[1] *How Green was my Valley.*
[2] In the Golden Cross Hotel in the Cornmarket.

yearly sales conference: thirteen people present for two and a half hours, and I talked almost the whole time—I hope with more conviction than I felt. Afterwards, exhausted, I fell asleep in my chair in the flat.

You are right about me and Keld. I *hate* your not having perfect weather as if it was my own holiday. Even so I don't see you spending your next summer holiday at Saxmundham, where incidentally lives the dullest man in Europe, whose sole interest is the Jewish plot against the world, which, with heraldry, is surely the hallmark of the bore.

I look forward to the batch of books from you, and hope confidently that they will lift the depression into which the perusal merely of the reviews of Iris Murdoch's new novel has plunged me.[1] I begin to agree with an old friend who maintains that incest and homosexuality are among the most boring of subjects. You will laugh when I tell you that I have been reading of an evening *The Idylls of the King*. The English is largely Wardour Street (a horse is rarely a horse; it is a steed or a charger, or, if a lady's, a palfrey) and the *dramatis personae* are china dolls. But now and then he brings off a charming little picture or a delicious chime of bells.

With briefest intervals for meals I put in *twelve hours* at my index today—10 a.m. to 10 p.m.—and covered *forty* pages. It's much the most I've ever done in a day, but I've still only got to p. 340, and the end is not yet.

Ruth—well it would be straining the truth to say that I was aware of her new dress, but it would *not* be to say that she was more attractive than ever to eye and ear. There again I suspect she was every bit as much so in April, but time scatters its poppy, and great charm always contains some surprise. I expect you are conscious of that every time you see her.

I am re-reading *A Passage to India* for exam-purposes. Is it as

---

[1] *A Severed Head* (1961).

good as some say it is, or is it a bit over-rated? The unpleasantness of Anglo-Indians seems to me rather over-stressed, just as does Jane Austen's irony, but as you can easily see, I am no judge. I was interested to be told by Anthony Powell that he cannot judge any novel, even his own. He has found Iris Murdoch's latest novel more readable than any of the others.

20 *July 1961*   *Grundisburgh*

Byron is as inexhaustible as Wilde, both of them mostly second-rate as writers, but not as men. I must have told you that Housman put B. top of all for an evening's company—perhaps because both were what Swinburne in his letters calls Bulgarians.

I have had another bout at my papers, and am ready to tell you that my interest in the character of Aumerle (*Richard II*) is every bit as small as Shakespeare's obviously was, and that I am tired of reading for the nth time half-baked dissertations on whether Malvolio, (*Twelfth Night*) was or was not 'notoriously abused'. All the beaks in England dictated what was to be said about Feste, except at Eton, where one candidate had the sense to say that the play could get along very well without him—whereas most of the rest invariably say that without Feste the play would be 'dreadfully boring'.

22 *July 1961*   *Bromsden Farm*

My life just now is overshadowed by my health—the gall-bladder, and this mysterious nuisance is to be x-rayed at the Middlesex Hospital.

I haven't yet tackled the Byron volume—it is huge and very heavy[1]—and instead am enjoying a gossipy book called *The Pilgrim Daughters* by Hesketh Pearson, all about the American heiresses who married English peers: very amusing. The first two volumes of the Swinburne letters are the best so far: the third and fourth seemed to me much duller. Watts Dunton[2] may have had a calming effect on the poet: he certainly damped down his natural propensities and flattened his style.

---

[1] *The Late Lord Byron* by Doris Langley Moore (1961).
[2] An indifferent novelist who took Swinburne under his wing and away from the bottle.

The gall-bladder is one of those residual organs which we can per-fectly well do without. Tell me all about it: all Lytteltons (male) have what others call a morbid interest in medical and surgical details. I used to enjoy a lot of shop with my London surgeon—the great Sir Holburt Waring. When he cut me he was plain Mr and I mischie-vously told him the provincial (Windsor) surgeon was a knight. When he heard the name Windsor he said coarsely 'Oh yes, those Windsor surgeons; he was probably knighted for cutting King Edward's corns', which, in fact, was not so very far from the truth; he had taken an appendix out of some royal child.

I have got the Swinburne Letters vols I and II. I quite enjoyed the 1880 or thereabouts volume, though it has its dull tracts. It is inter-esting to see that Watts-Dunton really did prolong S's life by about a quarter of a century. Was it you who told me some quite appalling things about W-D.'s sexual habits? Anyway no doubt you know them.

Pamela has just returned from a family gathering to the memory of her great-aunts, the one who died youngest being ninety-seven and the largest under five feet. She might say that was exaggerated, but it doesn't exaggerate my impression of them. Aunt Emily's mouth at tea was well below the level of the table, food found its way to it entirely by gravity. But she was a delicious old lady—full of fun.

The X-rays of Monday and Tuesday (when I reported as an out-patient) showed the gall-bladder blameless, so my doctor suggested further tests in here. On Friday morning I was subjected to tests so exhaustive, humiliating and exhausting that I have only just recov-ered. The worst of them—a barium enema—consists of their pouring a bucket of whitewash into one while the process is filmed and photo-graphed. The nurses, who are all gay and pretty and twenty or twenty-one, tell me that this is far the worst, so I await tomorrow's tests with comparative equanimity.

I have a little room to myself, quite comfortable but hellish noisy. Yesterday an electric drill outside operated for some six hours. I had the radio switched to the Test Match, but often drowsed off between the two noises. Today being a *non dies* and sunny, they told me I could dress and sit in an enclosed garden in the centre of the hospital block. I read the papers there, and have just come back to my room for roast chicken and a sweet made of bananas. Soho Square is only five minutes' walk, and the Matron (terrifying in dark green) has agreed to my walking gently there and back this afternoon, to change into some old clothes and fetch a few books.

I am toying with that new book on Byron, but find it hard to concentrate. Once one becomes a patient one loses all initiative and feels as helpless as a parcel, which may well be sent to the wrong place.

5 August 1961   *Bromsden Farm*

They have diagnosed my trouble as a diverticulum in the duodenum! Apparently it's not an ulcer but a little sac that fills up with 'roughage', and they believe that medicine and a strict diet will put it right. No raw fruit or salad, bread, pastry etc, nothing fried. I started it only yesterday (the whole week having been devoted to diagnosis), so feel little benefit yet—am, in fact, just as I was a fortnight ago, with a pain in the region of the gall-bladder, and *no* energy at all. Nevertheless I have resumed my labours on the index in a gentle way. Will this infernal task ever be accomplished? My love-hate for it is overpowering.

9 August 1961   *Grundisburgh*

I wonder why the 'roughage' should have behaved like that. 'Sir, you may wonder.' Your groans over O.W. are similar to Carlyle's over Frederick, but you have about another six or seven years to go. I can't think how it didn't kill him (and hasn't yet you!).

I expect the hospital rest did you good, but aren't the days long—partly because of their insanely early start to each one. One thinks it is nearly lunch-time and it is 10.45. How doctors do hate anything *fried*!

12 August 1961   *Bromsden Farm*

I'm glad to be able to report that I feel very much better than I did a week ago. For the first time in *many* weeks I begin to feel once again faintly on top of at least a few things, instead of that crushed and hopeless inertia which had for so long oppressed me, and which I now learn is a leading symptom of diverticulitis. You should by now have received Peter Fleming[1], *The Franco-Prussian War*[2], the Whiston book[3] and *Poor Kit Smart.*[4]

Sunday morning, 13 August.
A long but disturbed night, with bad dreams and some pain. My breakfast now is not your manly oatmeal porridge, but a sieved pap of groats designed for babies. As I mumbled this down I re-read Pater's *Renaissance.* Oscar says it influenced his whole life, so I thought I had better have another look at it, in case I had missed some references. So far this is not so, but the gentle tones and modulations of the old aesthete fit well into my frail mood of convalescence.

20 August 1961   *Bromsden Farm*
I am now poised for Italian sun. I am taking *no* Oscar or other work (I can't remember when this last happened), but simply a few paper-back detective stories and the World's Classics edition of *Middlemarch.* Ruth is as excited as a schoolgirl, and as she is paying for *everything*, I tell her that at last I shall experience the full pleasures of being a 'kept man', which has always seemed to me a consummation devoutly to be wished.[5]

Meanwhile the index, which is spread around me as I write, has reached p. 563, with another 300 to go. Darling old Katie Lewis (daughter of the first Sir George[6]) died last week, aged eighty-three, and left me, bless her, an exquisite drawing of Mrs William Morris by Rossetti—the gem of all her houseful of treasures.

As a bed-book I have been reading Pater's *Imaginary Portraits*, and find them just the thing—exquisitely written sketches of nothing much—four beautiful walls of tapestry with nothing in the middle.

---

[1] *Goodbye to the Bombay Bowler* (1961).
[2] By Michael Howard (1961).
[3] *The Whiston Matter* by Ralph Arnold (1961). An account of the running battle between the Rev. Robert Whiston, Headmaster of the Rochester Cathedral Grammar School and the Dean and Chapter of the Cathedral (1848–1852), which gave Trollope ideas for *The Warden* (1855).
[4] By Christopher Devlin (1961).
[5] They were going to stay with Ruth's daughter.
[6] See p. 214.

27 August 1961   *Via Agnelli 16*
                                                  Forte dei Marmi

So far the weather has been superb—a succession of cloudless blazing
days in the eighties, with three or four bathes a day, and the rest of
the time spent sunning, sleeping (including after-lunch siesta), eating
and reading—all done very slowly and with great enjoyment. This is
a nice little bungalow with modern plumbing, and I am writing in a
garden behind, which is entirely covered by vines and bunches of
grapes, rather like Max's 'vining-room' at Rapallo. The sea is an easy
ten minutes' walk. There are wide sands, all very clean and well organised. Under pretence of offending the Catholic Church, no one is
allowed to undress in public, and this enables countless little bathing-
huts to be let for the season, together with deck-chairs and large gay
beach-umbrellas. No English, thank God, and the chatter of the
numerous Italians is as unintelligible and harmless as birdsong or an
opera libretto—'*Ce qui est trop bête pour être joué, on le chante.*'

Close behind the little town, or so it looks when one is swimming,
tower the wonderfully dramatic peaks of the Carrara mountains:
black and pure white, and the lower slopes pine-tree-green with tiny
white villages dotted about. Florence is only an hour away, but I fear
we shall stick to the sea. We are both brown and well and, as I say,
relaxed to the point of inertia.

31 August 1961   *Grundisburgh*

I have just finished your massive book on the Franco-Prussian war.
Very interesting. I admit I skipped airily through some of the battles;
of which I can never follow the accounts. I have to write a tabloid
biography of Ben Jonson for Dick Routh. The awful truth is that I
have *never* been able to bear B.J., agreeing with Tennyson that
reading him is like wading through glue. No doubt I shall find that
Volpone is your favourite play, as it was A.W. Ward's and Saintsbury's.
Bernard Fergusson gets a good press for his sketch of Wavell. Old
Winston makes a slightly vindictive appearance. And he *ought* to have
attended Wavell's funeral—the only general who gave us a sniff of
success for two years. There has been some sad stuff in the recent cri-
tiques of war-books. What a pity Paul Johnson, Crossman, Alan
Brien, etc were not in command. They clearly know exactly what
should have been done.

This morning I had three long swims of perhaps half an hour each—
and except for the area of our bathing-kit we are a most satisfactory
brown all over.

I imagine that fifty years ago this was a strip of pine-trees and
sand, between the mountains and the sea, with perhaps a little village
in it. Now it has been 'developed' as a summer resort, but most
attractively—not at all like Peacehaven or Lytham St Anne's. In the
centre of the little town—a road's width from the beach—is a large
circle of shady pines, under which are a children's railway and
numerous carts drawn by donkeys and small ponies. All round the
wood there is held every Wednesday a most attractive market, where
we have bought this and that. My birthday turns out to be the day
of the local saint (St Ermete), in whose honour an extra day-long
market was held, followed after dark by superb fireworks on the
beach. I am just over half way through the magnificent *Middlemarch*
which I am enjoying inordinately. More of this next week, when I
shall have finished. Mr Casaubon is certainly a warning ('Oh, he
dreams footnotes, and they run away with all his brains'), but a fortnight here has so recharged my batteries that I positively look
forward to polishing off Oscar. The book is much *wittier* than I had
expected, and within its limits it is masterly—no fumbling or uncer-
tainty in the treatment.

I was sure you would enjoy *Middlemarch*—to my mind her best,
though what that old ass Ruskin called the 'disgusting' *Mill on the
Floss* is not far behind. The Rector of Hagley (a particularly good man
who hunted twice or thrice a week) wouldn't allow *Adam Bede* in his
house. *Tempora mutantur.*

I am setting G.C.E. papers for next year—a curiously sweaty job.
If you have in your mind a good question about Conrad's *Nigger* and
three other tales, please let me have it. A large general question about
the man Josef Korzeniowski.[1] They tell me he is out of fashion now;
he would be. But I like the story of a visitor to C. being kept for a bit

---

[1] Conrad's real name.

in the garden, C. still being in the throes; suddenly a window was flung open and a pale, sweating, haggard face looked out and gasped 'I've killed her.' He had just described the death—tremendously moving—of the young woman in *Victory*.

I must go in to tea. The garden reverberates with child-song.

I enclose half-a-sheet for Ruth—very poor measure I know. I am like the saint who had endless things to say to and about the Almighty, but eventually said only 'Lord, Lord!'

10 September 1961   *Bromsden Farm*

The weather held up wonderfully until the very morning of our departure, when, as though in anger at our going, thunder crashed out over the mountains, and rain fell in torrents. First we took a local train to Pisa, where we spent three hours admiring the Leaning Tower and other antiquities. The Campo Santo was badly bombed, but has been excellently restored. The rain had stopped by this time, but the air was hot and clammy. As we entered the very stuffy Baptistery, Ruth said 'I shall get a migraine if we stay here long,' so we withdrew immediately. We reached Florence in darkness, so saw nothing but the huge, clean, modern station, where we transhipped to our sleepers in the express.

Middlemarch was exactly right for that sun-drenched peaceful holiday, with only Italian voices in the offing. I finished it in the train to Florence, quite sorry to part from some of the characters. For the rest of the return journey I read *Weir of Hermiston* with sad pleasure: I think it might well have been R.L.S.'s masterpiece. This passage from it might be about Kisdon:

> All beyond and about is the great field of the hills; the plover, the curlew, and the lark cry there; the wind blows as it blows in a ship's rigging, hard and cold and pure; and the hill-tops huddle one behind another like a herd of cattle into the sunset.

Duff has brilliantly contrived to make the *Sunday Telegraph* pay £1500 for the serial rights (one article) of the Oscar letters. Of this £675 will come to me, and not a moment too soon, for I haven't a penny anywhere. Adam's year in India gives me a breathing-space to collect enough for his three years at Oxford.

14 September 1961   *Grundisburgh*

I fear you may not have been long enough in the Pisa Baptistery to hear its really gorgeous echo. The curator sings four or six notes and a celestial chord wanders to and fro about the roof for at least half a minute.

I am delighted that *Middlemarch* came up to expectation and hope. There are moments—I say this with bated breath—when *to me* she makes Miss Austen a little thin. I horrified a young woman who was here last week by saying that I thought *Mansfield Park* much better than *Emma*. And I am *quite sure* that *Northanger Abbey* is on the whole bad. *Nothing* can surely be said for General Tilney's behaviour—true neither to nature nor art. *Weir of Hermiston* I remember thinking a magnificent start. What an outstanding horror Weir's original, Lord Braxfield, must have been—like a formidable blacksmith in appearance, as Cockburn says. Illiterate, contemptuous, coarse, and often condemning a man to death with a savage joke. But Scotch judges have always been *sui generis*.

Do you admire that tiresome old ass Bertrand Russell going cheerfully to jail for his principles at eighty-nine? Because I do! And how can anyone be happy about our present bomb-policy?

16 September 1961   *Bromsden Farm*

Adam writes happily from India, where he apparently lives on curry and spends every evening playing bridge in Hindi with the beaks. His train-journey from Delhi took three and a half days owing to a landslide, but he failed to describe it in detail, so my letter to him this week is largely composed of searching questions.

I don't spend much time worrying about the Bomb, having plenty of other things to occupy me. As you will long ago have recognised, I have gone stale on the Oscar job, and must somehow regain enough initiative to polish it off. At the same time I feel compelled to strive for perfection.

The papers announce parking-meters in Soho by November, and they should greatly lessen the noise and nuisance which now make the whole place hideous.

21 September 1961   *Grundisburgh*

My youngest daughter with family is just off to Kenya—perhaps for three years, maybe for one, or, if Kenyatta has his way, less than that.

I of course am obsessed with the morbid notion that I may have passed on before I see her again. I always hate the holidays here coming to an end; I like seeing the place swarming with children. The £50 or £60 extra catering etc is merely equivalent to the trip abroad which e.g. Roger and Sibell take every year.

Old Bertrand Russell suffers from that last indignity of the old; worse than bladder, heart, knees, ears, i.e. his judgment is gone. Fancy not seeing that these sit-downs and marches merely encourage the Russians. But really our governors! The captain of a boys' house in a weak year would have spotted that the way to treat a crowd in Parliament or Trafalgar Square was to do *nothing*. Let 'em sit. If they get in the way of traffic, give abundant warning and then clear a way with a hosepipe. How long would a crowd's spirit last such treatment?

27 September 1961   *Grundisburgh*

That disc I hope by now has yielded to treatment. We bid you to hope, as Carlyle was always quoting from Goethe, though none the less remaining plunged in melancholy all his life.

Did you hear Flash Harry on the Proms last evening? I wonder how cynical he—and the audience—feels when they all bellow 'wider still and wider, shall thy bounds be set' etc. Not a convincing picture of the British Empire, or Commonwealth, in 1961 surely. Did you hear or read of the young lady who greeted Flash's quotation from Bach that music should bring honour to man and glorify God, with a shrill cry of 'Alleluia'—which reminds me to tell you Housman's exquisite poem:

> 'Hallelujah!' was the only observation
> That escaped Lieutenant-Colonel Mary Jane,
> When she tumbled off the platform in the station,
> And was cut in little pieces by the train.
> Mary Jane, the train is through yer:
> Hallelujah, Hallelujah!
> We will gather up the fragments that remain.

At the moment I am re-reading some Gibbon. But I am encouraged to find that Gow found exactly what I do, *viz* that one floats dreamily down the stream of that wonderful style, but remembers very few of the facts recorded. I am just approaching the chapter in which he busies himself in 'sapping a solemn creed with solemn sneer,'[1] but expect to be less shocked than e.g. Boswell was. What a good man Diocletian was! He has never been more than a name to me and I was quite prepared to find his record studded with startling notes 'in the decent obscurity of a learned language.'[2] But not one.

30 September 1961   *Bromsden Farm*

Too many of the wrong people are dying. Today I drove over to the Devlins', near Marlborough, where Christopher D., who wrote the book on Smart, is fading rapidly from cancer. He looked like a ghost of himself, and one can't wish him any long continuance of this agony of pain and drugs.

Adam writes cheerfully and at length from India. There seem to be a lot of holidays of various sorts, and next week a beak called Mr Purohit is apparently going to take him tiger-shooting! He says the boys love learning English poems by heart and reciting them in class. Also they often ask for more homework!

Did you see that Victor Gollancz broke his thigh watching the nonsense in Trafalgar Square? I went to see him in hospital on Monday and found him in roaring form. Canon Collins was there— a much nicer man than from his antics one might imagine.[3] Tomorrow I have promised to go back and play bridge round the bed for two hours (6-8) with V.G., his wife and some other lady.

Siegfried is coming to the Lit. Soc., but Ivor can't come because he is proposing the toast of Literature at the Guildhall, poor fellow. His word-book, so judiciously dedicated, won't be out till November.[4]

---

[1] Byron, *Childe Harold*, canto 3, cvii.
[2] Gibbon, *Autobiography*.
[3] He was a leading figure in the Campaign for Nuclear Disarmament.
[4] *Words in Season* (1961). Its dedication runs:

TO
GEORGE LYTTELTON
whose teaching of English
has done so much for
others in youth and
for me in age

5 October 1961   *Grundisburgh*

Yes, I do wish people wouldn't die the way they do. One feels a sort
of indignation like James Forsyte: 'What did *he* want to die for? He
was no age.' You probably never saw Reggie Spooner[1] bat. You would
not have forgotten it—the purest champagne. Even bowlers enjoyed
his punishment of them—the lovely grace of the stroke itself and the
courtesy, so kindly without anything remotely condescending. It was
Colin Blythe who after being despatched through the covers said to
him 'Mr Spooner I would give all my bowling to make a shot like
that.' Trueman would not have said that. He was one of Cardus's great
heroes, and got compared with every kind of operatic and musical
figure down the years—none of whom dear R.H.S. had ever heard of.

7 October 1961   *Bromsden Farm*

My dear friend Christopher Devlin died peacefully on Thursday night.
He was saying Mass daily up to the last, and in that sense certainly died
happy. How difficult it is to imagine oneself similarly comforted!

Victor Gollancz was in great form on Monday, smoking a large
Henry Clay (he gave me one) and using a pâté-de-foie-gras pot as an
ashtray. After three hours of bridge on his bed I was the richer by 6/6.

12 October 1961   *Grundisburgh*

Yesterday when I lunched at White's with my beloved Tim we met
Bob Boothby who said that Winston is hardly compos and fills much
of the brief periods when he is with angry lamentations at still being
alive. When F.E. Smith died who, according to B.B., was W's only
great friend, W. said 'Well at least he went out with a bang—one
thing I pray against is a protracted old age.' and not long ago he was
in a little company which was talking of the Jutland battle and W
sadly said 'Once you know I knew everything about it, but now it is
as remote and vague as the Battle of Salamis.'

14 October 1961   *Bromsden Farm*

We thought you were in excellent form on Tuesday, and at dinner I
could see that Flash Harry was eating out of your hand. When you
see Willie Maugham ('that old iguana', as Harold Nicolson calls him),

---

[1] Lancashire and England cricketer (1880–1961), recently dead.

334

it's possible, nay likely, that the subject of his leaving his fortune to the Society of Authors may crop up. If it does, see whether, with the utmost tact, you can suggest that one certain way of helping young authors (his avowed intent) would be to leave some money to the London Library. W.S.M. did give us £1000 at the time of our appeal, but that is chicken-feed to him.

Jonah is not yet strong enough for visitors, but soon I shall have to fight my way to St John's Wood—'the shady groves of the Evangelist', as a fanciful old baronet of my early acquaintance used to call it.

My index has reached p. 790, and as I sniff the smell of the stable-door (p. 868), I begin to get the bit between my teeth and bolt for home. When I finish there will be a lot of re-writing, arranging and tidying-up to do, but those are trifles compared to this slogging compilation.

18 October 1961   *Grundisburgh*
Thursday. Well there is nothing much to report. Old Maugham was friendly, intelligent, forthcoming, unaffected. He might have been a member of the Lit. Soc.! The London Library was mentioned, but he didn't rise much. He knew of your fine work, but censured the 'intelligentsia', whosoever he meant, for the meanness of their contributions. So I fear he may be thinking he has done enough. He looks younger than his years and less corrugated.

21 October 1961   *Bromsden Farm*
My best news is that the index is finished—or rather, the first draft of it, for I now have to read it through and rewrite some of the messier cards.

Siegfried has been asked to unveil the tablet to Walter de la Mare in the crypt of St Paul's at the end of November. Tommy has promised to chaperone him, but already S.S. is saying he is sure to be having bronchitis just then.

T.S.E. is much delighted with the French translation of *The Owl and the Pussycat*.[1] Have you looked at it, or hasn't it reached you? I think we ought to sell quite a lot of it. But everything depends on the

---

[1] *Le Hibou et la Poussiquette*, freely translated into French from the English of Edward Lear by Francis Steegmuller (London, 1961).

Durrell book, which appears on Monday week.[1] I have printed 50,000 copies, and have already orders for more than 23,000. If only I had a few more authors of that selling-capacity!

Heinemann, and their big-business owners, are getting increasingly restive at the unprofitability of my business, and I foresee a fairly early crisis. If they would let me go I think I could find someone else to buy the business and leave me to run it, but Heinemann seem to think my leaving would in some way damage their prestige. Nonsense, I say, but if you really think that, you must be prepared to pay for the privilege of keeping me. What I can't tell any of them is that in general I've had quite enough of publishing and would welcome retirement—but what should I use for money? It simply isn't on.

There I went to bed, and it is now a weeping Sunday morning. Comfort is making Christmas puddings, with Bridget's assistance. (Now comes a crisis. They have peeled almonds and made bread-crumbs and mixed a great bowl of flour—and there is no candied peel! Comfort has driven to Henley to try and knock up a friendly grocer.) When I was in New York in March I paid £50 for an option to have first look at a full-length biography of Sherlock Holmes, which one of those crazy enthusiasts has compiled from the stories, and now the typescript has arrived—more than 400 pages of it, and my spirit quails a little at the prospect.[2]

Comfort has returned in triumph with peel and the Sunday papers.

25 October 1961   *Grundisburgh*

P.G. Wodehouse: I like to think I am in the company of Asquith, Balfour, M.R. James, Ronnie Knox etc, who at least were not trivial and foolish people. The simple truth is that we share an intense delight in seeing language *perfectly* handled, no matter what the subject. But I was amused by a recent review of him in which there was a complaint that his young men and women who fall in love are altogether too virginal—that the only idea the sight of a double bed puts into their minds is 'What a grand apple-pie could be made of it!'

---

[1] *The Drunken Forest* by Gerald Durrell (1961).

[2] *Sherlock Holmes, a Biography of the World's first Consulting Detective* by William S. Baring-Gould (1962).

And that is true. Did any popular author ever remain more constantly at his best?

I am no judge, but my impression is that all that clever Holmes investigation—which as you say, was rather overdone—has had its day. I too am a fan of the stories (especially *Adventures* and *Memoirs*, in which I once could have passed any exam) and S.H. still cuts a brave figure.

28 October 1961   *Bromsden Farm*

Last week was much occupied with publishing discussions. Just when my relations with Heinemann had reached breaking-point and there seemed to be no possible satisfactory solution except the closing down of my business, or my resigning and starving, a splendid *Deus* stepped *ex machina*, or rather out of a jet air-liner, and all may now be well. My saviour is a chap called Bill Jovanovich. His father was a peasant in Montenegro (as you may know, the Montenegrins are proud mountainy men who rightly consider themselves superior to all the other Jugoslavs), who managed somehow to emigrate to the U.S.A. and worked in the Pittsburgh steelworks. He married a Polish girl and produced Bill, who won every conceivable scholarship, ending with a Ph.D. in Eng. Lit. To cut a long story short, by the time he was thirty-four he was President of Harcourt Brace, one of the leading U.S. publishers for quality, though not then for size. He had worked his way up through the textbook department, and in the last six years he has turned H.B. into the second or third biggest publishing house in the world, with an annual turnover of $33,000,000.

Bill would leave me to run my business, as now, helped by books from his list, and would bolster it with a textbook business, which today is the only hope of survival. It's all too good to be true, and the chief hurdle is to get Tilling's (who own Heinemann) to agree.

I have said I will publish the Sherlock Holmes book, if all questions of copyright can be cleared up, and in due course you may be called on to read its proofs as an expert.

4 November 1961   *Bromsden Farm*

I gather that Conan Doyle's son Adrian is both dotty and litigious. He recently tried to sue someone for saying that *Holmes* was Semitic! Also he lives in Geneva, which doesn't quicken things up.

Here is the joke I promised you. A couple, twenty years married had a fearful row. The wife told the husband exactly what she thought of him, ending: 'And on top of all that, we've had your mother living with us for ten years.'

HUSBAND '*My* mother? I always thought she was *your* mother!' End of story.

Can you get old novels (1946 or so) from your library? If so, and you haven't read it, ask immediately for *States of Grace* by Francis Steegmuller. He gave me a copy, which I have just finished with chuckling delight. It's light and witty and altogether a joy. Now I am reading Evelyn Waugh's latest[1], which as usual is compulsively readable, I find.

9 November 1961   *Grundisburgh*
I have just got from the library Mrs Langley Moore's immense book on Byron. It looks good browsing, but how can one remember all the ramifications? Luckily she tells us many things more than once. I suppose B. shares with O.W. that extraordinary posthumous vitality. We simply cannot let them rest in peace.

I look forward to further information about Holmes—and the imbecile Conan Doyle. But I agree with him in rejecting the theory that Sherlock was a Jew. I cannot think what evidence supports it. He was a misogynist—except for Irene Adler—and I am surprised no one has yet suggested that he was a homo. What about that gang of Baker Street Irregulars? Highly suggestive surely to anyone but Watson ('You see it, Watson, you see it?' 'But I saw nothing.' Might be the motto of the whole chronicle).[2]

11 November 1961   *Bromsden Farm*
Doris Langley Moore's book on Byron is on the short list for this year's Duff Cooper Prize. I think Duff would have found it fascinating. And surely the last thing either Byron or Oscar would have asked was to be allowed to rest in peace. By the way, the German and the

---

[1] *Unconditional Surrender* (1961).

[2] In Billy Wilder's witty film, *The Private Life of Sherlock Holmes* (1970), starring Robert Stephens, just this imputation is made.

French translation rights of Oscar have been sold—each for £400 advance, of which I get half. I am now sure that this book will pay for the whole of Adam's Oxford career. Perhaps one day I'll produce a book whose royalties I can spend on myself?

Last week I dined out twice, and on the second occasion at the Droghedas' in Lord North Street, I met Hugh Gaitskell for the first time, and to my surprise found him most charming, intelligent, amusing, and easy to get on with. An admirable Lit. Soc. member, I should say. I wonder if you know him. My chief impression was astonishment that anyone so seemingly sensible should want to spend his life in the filthy power-grabbing welter of politics. If I ever see him again I must ask him why.

Diana Cooper, who was also of the party, lent me her Mini (Morris) for the evening. 'It's like driving a swallow,' she said, and indeed it was: an ideal car for traffic. When I fetched the car I found stuck under the windscreen-wiper a piece of paper on which Diana had written 'HAVE MERCY. AM TAKING SAD CHILD TO CINEMA.' Apparently it had effectively prevented her being charged for parking in the wrong place.

18 November 1961   *Bromsden Farm*

You will be pleased to hear that the great deal is safely through. There was a nasty period—about three quarters of an hour—on Thursday morning, when the negotiations broke down altogether, and I had lost the business and everything. I think that perhaps the opposition had a faint hope that I might cave in, but luckily I didn't, so they capitulated instead. I can't tell you what a relief it is to have escaped from the Heinemann Group, which I'm sure was the cause of all my recent illnesses. Incidentally I shall also be earning a bigger salary, which will be a great help. I feel a great resurgence of hope.

Only twelve more days of Oscar, and much still to be done, though the index, thank God, is checked and ready. I'm delighted to say *Le Hibou et la Poussiquette* is selling like hot cakes: the 10,000 copies I printed won't last till Christmas, and I'm desperately trying to get some more printed in time. That's the worst of publishing—either one has far too many copies, or far too few, usually the former. Durrell too is going splendidly.

I really am delighted about the great deal which you must have trans-acted in the most masterly fashion.

I am going to tell the girls of North Foreland Lodge on Monday what a lot they can do to educate themselves by merely reading what they like—*and ruminating* about it. The English mistress will not like it when I tell them that at their age it is quite right that they should enjoy flamboyant verbiage and urge them to indulge in it sometimes in an essay. 'Probably your teacher will be sick, but that is one of the things she is there for.'

Did I tell you I had been reading about the intolerable *Prof*?[1] I cannot remember so strongly disliking anyone whom I had met only in a book. He seems to have had all the faults commonly charged against scientists, *viz* arrogance and narrowness and Philistinism. He had some very odd habits, e.g. his refusal ever to wipe his brow in public, however hot the day: and his diet seems to have been largely confined to olive oil and the white of egg. He would have been no good at a Lit. Soc. dinner.

Also Hankey's vast book all about the running of the 1914-18 war—one of the very few men who was really indispensable.[2] And how on earth we survived the incessant disasters of three and a half years is ungraspable. I suppose the solution is that, though we did not realise it, the Germans were really more incompetent than we were—and their top men more quarrelsome among themselves even than ours with the French—a very huffy and pigheaded lot these, conspicuously and persistently devoid of anything remotely resem-bling gratitude to any of their allies—and in fact I read not long ago that gratitude has never been one of the French virtues—coupled closely with conceit, for what else are you to call the settled convic-tion that only the French are and always have been truly civilised?

[1] Frederick Alexander Lindemann (1886–1957). Professor of Experimental Philosophy at Oxford. Personal assistant to Winston Churchill from 1940. Created Viscount Cherwell 1956. Known as The Prof. His biography, *The Prof in Two Worlds* by the second Earl of Birkenhead was published in 1961.

[2] Maurice Pascal Alers Hankey (1877–1963). Secretary to the Cabinet and the Committee of Imperial Defence 1916–1938. Knighted 1916. Created Baron 1939. His book *The Supreme Command 1914–1918*, after being banned by three successive Prime Ministers, was published in two volumes in 1961.

25 November 1961   *Bromsden Farm*

The news about my publishing plans broke in Tuesday's *Evening Standard*, with a piece on the front page headed by a blown-up reproduction of my fox.[1] Thereafter I had long telephone conversations with chaps from *seven* daily papers, all of which printed the news, more or less accurately, next morning. I was particularly anxious not to cast any aspersions on the efficiency of Heinemann, and mercifully all was well: no feelings hurt or umbrage taken.

Did you see the leader about Henry James in this morning's *Times*? It was written by the Editor[2], as a result of my lunching with him at the Athenaeum on Monday, and is a splendid Puff Preliminary.[3]

On Wednesday I took most of the day off and travelled to New College, Oxford for the choosing of this year's Duff Cooper Prize. After some discussion the Prize was awarded to Jocelyn Baines's Life of Conrad and then we were shown some of the College treasures, including the superb El Greco which Major Alnatt presented to the Chapel. He suddenly wrote out of the blue to say that he had been looking round the Colleges and thought the El Greco would look best there! I imagine he did just the same with the Rubens and King's, Cambridge.

30 November 1961   *Grundisburgh*

Did you read Connolly on *A Christmas Garland*[4] in the *Sunday Times*, in which he said that of the authors parodied only five were really familiar to-day (Conrad, Hardy, Kipling, James, Shaw) 'not because the parodies killed Baring, Benson and Co but . . . because their eclipse forms part of the *general subsidence into oblivion of the whole of English Literature.*' Is this really the truth—outside the schools who are still set books by Galsworthy and Wells and Bennett (who C says are 'under eclipse')? And if so, cannot one say that it always was true? C. implies that 'the leisured reader' is vanishing.

I read the girls of North Foreland Lodge last Monday Conrad's account of the return of the *Narcissus* 'Under white wings she

[1] The emblem of my publishing firm, engraved by Reynolds Stone.
[2] Sir William Haley.
[3] For the first two (1961) of the twelve volumes of *The Complete Tales of Henry James.*
[4] By Max Beerbohm (1912).

skimmed low over the blue sea like a great tired bird speeding to its nest', and they were wonderful listeners. Do you think I was fantastic to tell them that that sentence alone contained the ideas of speed, sunshine, loneliness, spaciousness, welcome, happiness, earth's solidity v. sea and sky's opposite, and to sum up drew a lovely picture? Well anyway I did and they seemed to swallow it. With equal avidity they delighted in Ivor Brown's officialese reproduction of the Lord's Prayer, though I didn't dare to quote more than 'We should be obliged for your attention in providing for our own nutritional needs, and for so organising distribution that our daily intake of cereal filler be not in short supply.'

Another book I have just read—with increasing dismay—is the Pelican *Modern Age* in their Guides to Eng. Lit. The language of modern criticism is to me so fearfully pretentious that again and again I cannot grasp the meaning, and am constantly merely guessing at it. Such a sentence as 'The final death of Gerald in the snow is only the symbolic expression of the inexorable consequence of his life-defeating idealism' means so little to me that I have decided to avoid modern criticism in future.

3 December 1961   *Bromsden Farm*

Oscar is done! The proofs go back to the printer tomorrow, and thereafter only proofs of the index will remain to be done.

That's a magnificent sentence about the *Narcissus*: no wonder the girls were good listeners. You simply *must* stop worrying yourself by reading rubbish like that Pelican book about modern literature.

Meanwhile the advent of parking-meters in the Square has proved an immense blessing. One can now drive right up to the door of the house, and the vans can load and unload in peace. No one is allowed to park for more than two hours, and that only in fixed areas on payment. This knocks out all the monsters who used to leave cars there every day for eight hours. The meters stop working at 6.30 p.m., so it fills up again for the evening as of old, but no cars are left there all night, and the tireless Jamaicans have a chance of sweeping the roadway before the office-workers start to arrive.

Last Wednesday Ruth and I took her guests to the dramatisation of C.P. Snow's novel *The Affair*, which proved an excellent evening's entertainment, somewhat in the Galsworthy manner. If all Snow's works could be served up in this painless way I might find them less rebarbative.

6 December 1961   *Over New Brunswick*

I daresay, with perhaps pardonable pride, that this is the first letter you have ever received which was written at 35,000 feet above the earth. So far on this trip I have found the preliminary dread greater than the fear in the air, though that is ever with me. This plane (a Boeing 707) is so much bigger than any I have ever been in before that it's more like a train, and therefore a little reassuring. I am sitting next to the President of the Shell Oil Company of America, who might well be most useful to Adam after he gets his degree—a most charming and civilised man. For lunch I consumed two large Bourbon whiskies as an aperitif, then caviare, lamb chops and beans, fruit tart, Stilton, *three* glasses of claret, coffee and brandy—all very good and boosting to the morale. I have also been able to smoke my pipe with impunity. We are due to arrive in another hour, and the terrors of landing still lie ahead.

8 December 1961   *Grundisburgh*

I must tell you that, having so repeatedly read that *Women in Love* is one of the greatest of novels, I have again started re-reading it, after about twenty years, and am about halfway through. There are fine things in it, but I remain convinced that when the D.H.L. *Schwärmerei* has died down the general opinion will be a lot of it is pretentious and unconvincing. So many of his subtle probings into man-woman relations are far outside any of *my* experience or the furthest range of my imagination that they strike literally no chord in my mind. If your answer is that this merely shows I am too stupid or at least too old-fashioned, I shall be quite ready to agree. But do have a look at the chapter headed 'Rabbit' and tell me how and why it isn't pointless, not to say silly.

10 December   *Bromsden Farm*

The return trip was less attractive than the outward one. We reached London three quarters of an hour late. When the sickening, deaf-making descent was almost completed (down to a few hundred feet), the pilot decided there was too much fog, went into a steep climb, and announced our departure for *Ireland*! An hour later we landed in *pouring* rain at Shannon Airport. When I was last there (also unwillingly—I wonder if anyone ever goes there on purpose?) the building was a sort of converted shack. Now it is a huge emporium like the ground floor of Selfridge's, with dozens of counters at which one can buy *anything*, an efficient telephone service and a twenty-four-hour bar, at which all drinks were free (i.e. paid for by Pan-American Airways). I rang up Ruth in London, and Duff here, to find that Comfort was waiting with the car at London Airport.

Then followed an exceedingly tedious wait of two and a half hours. When I could take no more whisky I turned to coffee and ham sandwiches. Eventually we took off again in the still heavy rain, and after another hour's flight came down safely at London A. It was then almost 3 a.m. and poor Comfort had been there for five hours.

14 December 1961   *Grundisburgh*
Humphrey was once ordered—with the other passengers—to throw all his luggage out, and the plane, after avoiding one foggy place after another, eventually landed with fifteen minutes' worth of petrol left.

I am nearing the end of *Russia and the West* by George Kennan; it seems to me wonderfully good, though not making one exactly cheerful—except in comparison with Bertrand Russell's last book of essays, which literally hold out no hope.[1]

What a grand writer for the young Macaulay is—so lucid and emphatic. They have been tackling his great Chapter III and I am stifled with exhaustive information about the Navy in Stuart times, the country gentleman, the new advances in science etc etc. They love such climaxes as 'In Charles II's navy there were both sailors and gentlemen, but the sailors were not gentlemen, nor the gentlemen sailors.' Simple and obvious no doubt, but a good true point.

6 January 1962   *Bromsden Farm*
The snow was so deep here last Sunday morning and the roads so tricky that I went back to London that afternoon. Duff managed to

---

[1] *Has Man a Future?* (1961).

get me to Henley station in his little car, but we couldn't even reach the main road until we had persuaded one of the farm-workers to go before in a tractor to flatten out a track for us. Altogether it took me *four hours* to reach the flat from here, but I was warm all the time, and able to read. Next morning, I learned later, the roads were worse still, and to cap it all my usual Monday morning train crashed into the buffers at Paddington and twenty people were taken to hospital.

I finished the Kitchener book simply *loathing* K, and almost pleased at his hopeless bungling of the War Office and the War. The knowledge that a massive attack at Gallipoli when it was first mooted would probably have taken Constantinople and perhaps ended the war is almost unbearable. Winston was right all along in that matter.

Bridget and Duff are making plans for a fortnight's winter sports in the Italian Alps at the beginning of February. Twelve of them are planning to take a chalet. I can't think of anything I should hate more—nonsense, I can think of plenty—but all the same—

13 January 1962   *Bromsden Farm*
Despite your prohibition, I think you must have at least a half length letter to cheer you in your giddiness. You looked exceptionally well on Thursday, though I'm sure it only irritates you to be told so.

Yesterday morning I took my sister to the Augustus John memorial service at St Martin in the Fields. Apart from an abnormally high ratio of beards to pews, it was all immensely decorous and tasteful, and might have been in honour of any ambassador or social dignitary. A crowd of gypsies on a mountain-top, with plenty of wine and girls, would have been nearer the mark. I'm sure A.J. never set foot in a church after his childhood. David Cecil gave a well-written address, but his super-U accent, his tail-coat, and his position in the pulpit, made it all grotesquely unsuitable. Many of A.J.'s children and grandchildren were there, and I wondered how many illegitimate ones. He knew he was a genius and came to think it his duty to people the world with others. Did you know that Peter F's mother had a child of his? A pretty girl called Amaryllis, with his red hair and Mrs F's features. I remember the appearance of this baby when P. and I were at Eton, and even then in my innocence I thought Mrs F's account of how she had adopted this child, through Lord Dawson of Penn etc., rather unnecessarily protracted. Now she is a cellist of, I suppose thirty-seven, very good-looking and withdrawn. The most moving—the *only* moving—part of yesterday's service was when she suddenly appeared in the choir, looking very young and slim in black, with flaming red hair, carrying her cello, on which she played some unaccompanied Bach—rather too much I thought.

18 January 1962   *Grundisburgh*
My vertigo (I am pleased to find, in the teeth of all my Cambridge colleagues, that the i is long and not short as they said) is being held at bay *pro tem*, though I don't feel it to be very far away.

I have read *The Fleet that Jack Built* with great pleasure. What fine chaps good sailors always are. I particularly liked Tyrwhitt, who got into the navy at his third attempt; thirtieth out of thirty-one! He has a splendid face—in fact they all have. Odd that old Fisher should have ignored the defensive equipment of the big ships. Anyone who knew the Germans must have known they would hit hard and accurately. The fact must be faced that Jutland really was a defeat. That the Germans never came out again merely shows that they never really acquired the naval spirit. (Hitler didn't either.) But we had a lot of bad luck over those raids, when fog kept on saving them.

21 January 1962   *Bromsden Farm*
I travelled to Edinburgh on the Thursday morning train. After Darlington I had the carriage to myself, so could try out a few sallies *à vive voix*. Robin Walpole (Hugh's brother) met me at 3 p.m., and we just had time for a cosy tea of scones etc at his house before catching the train for Glasgow. There was a good deal of preliminary talk and drink in a stifling bar, and then the annual dinner of the Scottish Bookmen. My speech went down tolerably well, and we just caught the last train back to Edinburgh. Robin Walpole lives in great comfort with *two* maids! and it was rather fun to find one's pyjamas cherishingly wrapped round a hot-water-bottle, etc.

In his new book of memoirs, the actor Cedric Hardwicke is asked by an interviewer whether today he would recommend a young man to go on the stage, and answers: 'Certainly not: there's far too much competition. He'd do better to go into Parliament, where there's none.'

If you look at the current (February) number of a paper called

Encounter you will find an article by Sparrow which seeks to prove that *Lady Chatterley's Lover* is in fact a handbook to buggery. What next? Some old Wardens of All Souls must be rotating in their coffins. I much prefer *The Diary of a Nobody*,[1] which I am enjoying more than ever. When did you last read it? Have you got a copy?

24 January 1962   *Grundisburgh*
Is Hardwicke's book good? I always liked his acting. Yes, it must be a dreadful, fluky, up-and-down life. 'Overpaid casual labour' was what Gerald du Maurier called it, and he was a star—and apparently always plunged in depression. Old Arthur Benson once told me the most dreadful thing about melancholia was, as Shakespeare put it in one line 'With what I most enjoy contented least', for of course some quack told him to carry on with all his favourite ploys—and they all turned to dust in his mouth. Is it not odd that if A.C.B. came into the room, I should respectfully get up and generally kowtow—and he died when fifteen years younger than I am now? Once your tutor always your tutor is no doubt true.

I am re-reading *Pickwick*. Do you realise what an old tippler Mr P. was? I suppose they all were in the 1830's—just as a reader in 2050 will see our age as one of fornication, not of drink. I am also reading (don't laugh) Leavis's *D.H. Lawrence, Novelist.* I must try and find out what the man's greatness is supposed to be—particularly in that sticky *Rainbow* and *Women in Love*. So far F.R.L. is disappointingly peevish and sneery with those who don't agree with him, and anyway I know *that* is wrong. You seem to be wavering in your support of *Lady Chatterley*. I shall certainly get the February *Encounter*.

I haven't read *The Diary of a Nobody* for a long time, but I remember enjoying it, though my favourite in that genre was always Burnand's *Happy Thoughts*.

27 January 1962   *Bromsden Farm*
Thank goodness you're reading *Pickwick* to counteract that frightful Leavis. One day you must just forget all about D.H.L. Life without him is fine, I promise you.

Last Monday I travelled down to Somerset and spent a delightful

---

[1] By George and Weedon Grossmith.

evening and extremely comfortable night with the [Anthony] Powells in their charming house near Frome. Next morning I drove over to the printer's to see the ritual printing of the first sixty-four pages of Oscar. Needless to say, after a few minutes the machine broke down, and to allay my disappointment they took me on a ruthlessly conducted tour of the works. Seeing round any factory soon produces a state of acquiescent coma, as the exact performance of each monstrous engine is bellowed out at one above the din. On Thursday we dined with the Reichmanns (Mrs R. is Elisabeth Beerbohm's sister) and were given a dinner so deliciously rich and enormous that we felt peculiar for the next twenty-four hours. First a soufflé filled with salmon and asparagus, then a haunch of miraculously tender venison, with cranberry sauce and sauerkraut; then a pudding of the shape and consistency of a cake, which was in fact a rum-laced trifle, then some cheese. All washed down by quantities of Rhine wine that tasted of grapes.

Sunday morning, 28 January

I am reading, with great enjoyment, that first volume of the life of J.A. Froude that appeared some months ago. I ordered it immediately, but the O.U.P. has only just vouchsafed a copy. The great merit of the book is that most of it is in Froude's own words (hitherto unpublished) and he wrote beautifully. His prose is a joy to read. Do get the book from the library. The author's name is Waldo Hilary Dunn, and he hails, believe it or not, from Wooster, Ohio. Here is Froude on his first school:

> The master, Mr Lowndes, was rector and patron of the living. He was assisted in the teaching department by his brother and by three ushers, as they were then universally called, though converted now into masters by the ambitious vulgarity of the age.

1 February 1962   *Grundisburgh*

Pickwick of course was very refreshing. I skip a good deal—all about the boring fat boy, Mr Winkle, Mr Snodgrass, Solomon Pell, but there is plenty of compensating richness. I am now re-reading all the U.S.A. part of *Martin Chuzzlewit*. The Yanks' chief claim to greatness is that they forgave Dickens his really blistering picture of them. Jefferson Brick, Hannibal Chollop, Mrs Hominy, Elijah Pogram—

they all scintillate with gems of absurd speech whose appeal never dims. But what an ass Dickens could be. Pecksniff should have been left a figure of fun, not become a plotter and a villain. Similarly Squeers in *Nicholas Nickleby* should have been left a grisly comic instead of developing into a serious swindler. And all the Gride etc part of *N.N.* I find unreadable, in fact I finish more or less when N. has met the Cheerybles. Sir Mulberry Hawk won't really do. (By the way, have you ever heard any explanation of the *twenty-five*-mile walk which Dickens sent old Wardle, Pickwick etc on on December 24? They would hardly have got home before breakfast on December 25. I believe Bernard Darwin maintained that D. meant it as a joke— surely a very inferior one?)

4 February 1962   *36 Soho Square*

Yesterday Ruth and I went down to Brighton. It was a soft grey misty day, the sea calm and benign, as we walked the length of the front, breathing in the lovely seaweedy air. I was distressed to find that the secondhand bookshop in Hove that I had patronised since my earliest bookbuying boyhood had gone out of business. I can remember my mother urging me along the promenade with promises of this shop at the end of the walk, and I grieved at this snapping of another link with what Henry James called 'the visitable past'. However, we picked up a few trifles at other Brighton bookshops, ate an excellent lunch of fish-and-chips followed by treacle roll, breathed in a little more ozone and came peacefully back to Soho Square.

I must soon read *Martin Chuzzlewit* again: it used to be one of my favourites. I'm sure that the changes in so many of Dickens's characters (Pecksniff, Squeers etc) were due to the difficult and unnatural way he had to write his novels, for the monthly part-issues. He was seldom an issue ahead, and I imagine had only a rough plan of what was to happen, and how the characters were to develop. Also, he several times wrote two novels at once. In fact it's a wonder the plots hold together as well as they do.

8 February 1962   *Grundisburgh*
                                              (Summer-house)

I was pleased to read a strong complaint by Connolly in the *Sunday Times* about modern criticism, which never says that a book is good reading, but talks aridly about technique. Apropos of Leavis's remark recently about Max Beerbohm in the *Spectator*, I nearly wrote quoting Lamb's very sharp-pointed question to Coleridge, 'whether the higher order of Seraphim *illuminati* ever sneer'.

10 February 1962   *Bromsden Farm*

In the middle of my last bout of correcting this afternoon, I took half an hour off, to clear my head, and read the opening chapters, one after the other, of *Oliver Twist, Nicholas Nickleby* and *Great Expectations*. All are good and made me want to re-read all three books immediately, but *G.E.* is infinitely the best—much the most sharp and assured. I wish I had time to read *all* Dickens in the right order, so as to observe his growing mastery of technique (the overflowing genius of creation was always there).

Sunday morning, February 11

The sun is shining, and Comfort is putting me to shame by digging outside the window. If I had one of those jobs that finish when one leaves the office I should probably be a busy (if fine-weather) gardener. As it is, each week-end I hopefully bring home more work than I can possibly do, and the garden suffers. Don't misunderstand me: all I do anyhow is the rough work—weeding and repairing the brick paths, tidying, clipping and so on. All the real gardening is done by Comfort, and she is very good at it.

15 February 1962   *Grundisburgh*

I still remain the leech's headache. A liver-complaint hitherto confined to the entourage of the Akond of Swat is *my* diagnosis. The faculty's only suggestion is that in about a week, if no better, I should go and be investigated and x-rayed etc at the Ipswich hospital, so no doubt some day all will be as serene as it ever can be at seventy-nine.

I like the idea of your taking a spell of *Dickens* to *clear* your head; but I suppose he is rather like a plunge into the sea. I have left off *Dombey*—found I must have read it too recently and remembered it too well. Also I found Miss Tox and Captain Cuttle a bit wearisome—as also is the incredible Dombey himself. Carker's teeth are mentioned every time he appears; so are Captain Cuttle's signature remarks. But I am embarking on *The Moonstone*, which I last read when a boy at Eton and have forgotten every word of. Tell me what you think of it—it may I suppose be called the first detective story. Shall I be disappointed? The Clough book is on my list.[1] The young reviewers have been, *me judice*, all wrong about him. He was much better than they say. Of course there is something faintly absurd about a man who loses his faith and then bemoans the fact, but I am blowed if there isn't a lot of good stuff in 'Dipsychus'. Easy enough of course to be superior and sniffy about hexameters and varsity reading-parties of a hundred years ago, but I enjoyed 'The Bothie' at Cambridge.

P.S. Clough. I should of course have mentioned 'Amours de Voyage'.

17 February 1962   *Bromsden Farm*
It was a week of ceaseless activity. On Monday Ruth and I attended a cocktail (or rather, thank heaven, a champagne) party on Campden Hill in pouring rain, then went on to dine at the Café Royal with Allen Lane, the originator and head of Penguin Books. It was the night of the National Sporting Club's annual do, and the whole place was swarming with outsize bruisers in dinner-jackets. Tuesday was the Lit. Soc. On Wednesday I went to the theatre with Flash Harry, Princess Marina and her sister Princess Olga. The play was *Becket*,[2] which I saw in New York last year but enjoyed again. After it we were conveyed in a huge Rolls to the Savoy Grill, where we had an excellent dinner. Flash H. told a number of near-dirty stories, which the royal ladies clearly knew they couldn't avoid, and then Princess Olga told a charming one: 'Once upon a time there was a king who had two daughters, one blonde and beautiful, the other dark and exceedingly plain. The son of a neighbouring monarch came in search of a wife, and the two girls were paraded for him, the dark one in superb clothes and the blonde one clad only in her flowing hair. Which one do you think he chose? The answer is that he chose their father, for this is a fairy story.'

[1] *Arthur Hugh Clough: the Uncommitted Mind* by Katherine Chorley (1962).
[2] By Jean Anouilh.

On Thursday Ruth and I went to *Don Giovanni* at Covent Garden: a superb production of a superb opera, but it went on for three and a half hours with only one interval, and the seats weren't made for anyone my size.

21 February 1962   *Grundisburgh*

Roger told me that Bruce Lockhart's mind seemed to be giving way—like my old uncle, who was however eighty-six; he used to be reminded, when he got to the end of a story, of the beginning, so it went like chain-smoking—very hard for the audience to keep its face. *The Moonstone* is fine—no sign of it coming to an end for several more days. I feel there may be some tragedy to come, either via the Indians or the Quicksand which has already had one victim.

I have paid another visit to the leech and am now to go and be examined by the hospital consultant. There is something vaguely wrong round about the liver. You can't surely have gall-bladder adhesions thirty-seven years after the operation. Nature is a good deal of an ass but surely not such an ass as that.

Sorry about your constricted seat at the most delicious of all operas. It always takes the edge off one's enjoyment. As Winston once said of oratory 'The head cannot take in more than the seat can endure.'

24 February 1962   *Bromsden Farm*

I have begun, in a desultory, shuffling sort of way, to assemble the materials for two minor projects which have been held off for ages by Oscar's continuance. They are (1) the editing of Max's letters to Reggie Turner[1] and (2) the compiling of the definitive bibliography of the works of E. Blunden. This last is a labour of love and requires only time and a clear head, for in my office I have the most complete collection of his writings that exists. I am so accustomed to having some editing or kindred work on hand that I feel rather empty without any, and neither of these jobs will tax me unduly.[2]

---

[1] Published in 1964.
[2] The Blunden bibliography eventually passed from my nerveless grasp into the capable hands of Miss Brownlee Kirkpatrick, who published it triumphantly in 1979.

28 February 1962   *Grundisburgh*

I note your recommendation of *The Woman in White*.[1] Is it still in print I wonder? How refreshing it is to make one's way through a long story full of human beings who behave as such, and when one really wants to know what is going to happen.

I have now read *A Question of Upbringing*[2] and much enjoyed it though I am mystified about its exact significance. I like his neat and pertinent English. Le Bas has a good deal of Goodhart, not much of McNeile I think, who was a frightful ass. He succeeded to my beloved Arthur Benson and had every boy agin him in three weeks with his persistent fussiness and suspicion, and all the staff too. How good Tony P's picture of that French *pension* is and its inmates, and I feel I know Widmerpool nauseatingly well. What is Tony P's next one?

(Later) I have just had an immense interview with the leading Ipswich doctor and am in for a spell of x-rays and blood-tests etc with God knows what results. I shall report to you what they say—obstinately ignoring the truth that you do not in the least want to hear it. But even Dr Johnson did sometimes report, e.g. 'Dropsy threatened, but seasonable physic averted the inundation.' I hope to feel less of a worm in a week or two. I couldn't feel more.

10 March 1962   *Bromsden Farm*

I am outraged at the way these doctors keep you waiting for their idiotic opinions. No wonder you're depressed, but you must try not to be. The spring is coming, and you will soon be holding the Lit. Soc. table in thrall once again.

I think you will enjoy the book on the Marconi Scandal.[3] The author started out without any *parti-pris*, and wrote the book for the best possible reason—that she wanted to read a book on the subject, and there wasn't one. Gradually she came to realise, as any unprejudiced reader must, that Rufus Isaacs and Lloyd George were saved by Asquith and the Liberals, who covered them up with whitewash. It's a disgraceful story, and I think Isaacs was one of the nastiest bits of

[1] By Wilkie Collins, like *The Moonstone*.
[2] The first volume (1951) of Anthony Powell's *A Dance to the Music of Time*. The character Le Bas is an Eton housemaster.
[3] *The Marconi Case* by Frances Donaldson (1962). It was a matter of insider dealing in Marconi shares.

353

work that ever schemed his way to the top in everything. Kipling's daughter, who is a friend of Reading's widow, has refused permission for the reprinting of 'Gehazi', though it has already been printed in countless other books.[1] G.K. Chesterton's executor was similarly churlish about a relevant and amusing poem of his.

Have you read your friend Leavis's swingeing attack on C.P. Snow in the current *Spectator*? It's high time someone took this line, and I only wish it had been a less woolly and repetitive writer than Leavis.[2]

17 March 1962   *Bromsden Farm*
(St Patrick's Day)
I told Tony Powell you had enjoyed his book, and he was much pleased. He said the only characteristic of Goodhart's that he had deliberately given to his housemaster was G's habit of standing with both his feet pointing sideways in the same direction.

Osbert Sitwell's *Tales My Father Taught Me* are most entertaining, and short enough to prevent O's getting involved in those endless sentences that made some of his autobiography such heavy going. Sir George Sitwell is a superb character—and this whole book is about him.

22 March 1962   *Grundisburgh*
Grand man you are! I have sent you practically nothing for a fortnight and here you are with four excellent sides. What can I do in reply? I tell the doctors I am very ill and they deny it, pointing to thoroughly well-behaved heart, lungs, and kidneys etc. I say 'What do they matter in view of the fact that I am tired all the time, sunk in apathy and lassitude, and faintly sick-feeling much of the time?'

I have been too tired to read much lately. I tried Crabbe whom I hadn't read for fifty years, but it didn't do. That thudding relentlessness got me down with which he grimly shows up every friendship and love-affair ending in disaster. His pictures of Suffolk do nothing to enamour one of the county.

I didn't know that habit of Goodhart's, but please ask T.P. if he knew

[1] Kipling wrote the poem later, when Rufus Isaacs had become Lord Chief Justice, and Lord Reading. It described the denial of wrongdoing to Parliament as 'the truthful, well-weighted answer that tells the blacker lie'.
[2] This was the 'Two Cultures' controversy.

354

that G. had in a drawer numberless advertisements of women's shoes. Mat Hill of course recognised at once one of the commonest signs of suppressed or sublimated sex. Human beings get odder and odder. Do you ever dream about snakes or keys? Because if so you must look out.

Leavis does reduce poor old Snow to monkey-dust, but one doesn't like or admire L. any the more. He writes as if his opinion was clearly the truth, and anyone who disagreed with it must be fool or knave. Surely Snow *must* reply: in old days he would have with sword or pistol. But I doubt if he carries the guns.

This letter is a striking example of the victory of mind over matter. I got up feeling like death and very nearly fell asleep in the bath. But I formed *one* resolve—to ignore all else but to write four sides to you, and though I must now go and lie down for a bit, I feel all the better for having done so.

Bless you Rupert and give my best love to Ruth. Pamela is a wonderful nurse—and wife generally, but I have plenty left over for R.

24 March 1962   *Bromsden Farm*

I'm glad to say I never, to my knowledge, dream of snakes or keys, but I'm sure Rayner-Wood dreamt of little else. You were clearly right to resign from North Foreland Lodge, and I think you ought also to give up all that correcting: you have done more than your whack, and earned a rest, surely. I can hear you answering: 'How the world is managed, and why it was created, I cannot tell; but it is no feather-bed for the repose of sluggards,' and I can only say that I often wish it was. From that quotation you will know what I have been reading, and here's some more of it, just for the fun of copying it out, and despite my fear that you may earlier have copied it out for me:

If a man will comprehend the richness and variety of the universe, and inspire his mind with a due measure of wonder and of awe, he must contemplate the human intellect not only on its heights of genius but in its abysses of ineptitude; and it might be fruitlessly debated to the end of time whether Richard Bentley or Elias Stoeber was the more marvellous work of the Creator: Elias Stoeber, whose reprint of Bentley's text, with a commentary intended to confute it, saw the light in 1767 at Strasburg, a city still famous for its geese. . . . Stoeber's mind, though that is no name to call it by, was one which turned as unswervingly to the false, the meaningless, the unmetrical, and the ungrammatical, as the needle to the pole.[1]

Sunday morning, March 25
Bill Jovanovich's week in London consisted largely of conferences lasting several hours each—stimulating but at the same time exhausting. He stayed at Claridge's, where I ate several meals with him. In my youth it was a resort of riches and distinction: now most of the *clientèle* look as though they had been swept up in a third-class international air terminal. Ichabod! The gradual but complete social revolution which we have lived through has undoubtedly improved the lot of millions, but it has largely destroyed elegance and *la douceur de vivre*. What would Old Jolyon Forsyte say to the bearded youths in jeans and open-necked shirts that one sees in stalls at the theatre and Covent Garden?

Tomorrow I am promised the final pages of Oscar for approval—the index and the first thirty-two pages of the book (which they always print last). I shall return them to the printer on Tuesday, and all will be over—very nearly seven years since I took over the job in July 1955. I hope to have complete copies by Easter. So far we have orders for just over 1000 copies, but that is without the London shops, which should take as many again. They won't order at all until they see the complete article, whereas the wretched booksellers in the provinces and abroad see only a 'blurb' and sometimes a dust-jacket.

Months ago *The Times* sent me Edmund Blunden's obituary to revise and tidy up, but I find it almost impossible to do. If, which Heaven forbid, the dear fellow died tomorrow, I could do all that is needed in an hour or two, under pressure of emotion, but in cold blood it's another matter.

28 March 1962   *19 Burton Ward*
[Dictated to Pamela]   *East Suffolk & Ipswich Hospital*
                                                                     Ipswich
My life is one of crushing boredom, often variegated by discomfort and sometimes by pain. What more need of words? There shall be none.

---

[1] A.E. Housman, preface to his edition of Manilius, Book I (1903), re-printed in *A.E. Housman, Selected Prose*, edited by John Carter (1961).

I say, Leavis! Have you ever known opinion so unanimous about a man's spite, bad manners, injustice, bad English and conceit? It will surely do him a great deal of harm. I don't know why you have your knife into old Snow, though I admit I don't know much about him. He is perhaps a bit too omniscient.

Obituaries. I was for some time in charge of them for Eton Masters, and did several. I had a certain amount of grisly fun, e.g. in getting Eggar to do Mat Hill's, and Mat Hill to do Eggar's.

Well I mustn't fag poor Pamela any longer. I had an enchanting letter from Ruth which I will answer with my own hand as soon as I can. Give her my love.

31 March 1962   *Bromsden Farm*

I am delighted to learn from Pamela that you're probably going home tomorrow. I haven't in fact got my knife into Snow, but I do dislike his literary scheming, superiority and self-election as pundit. I find his novels third-rate, dull and humourless, and the sight of his fat face reproduced life-size in newspaper advertisements for the *Daily Herald* is enough to put anyone off their breakfast.

On Thursday I lunched with Tommy Lascelles and Joan in their royal stables. Clemmie Churchill, Veronica Wedgwood and Peter Lubbock were the other guests, and we ate a delicious steak-and-kidney pudding. One simply can't believe that C.C. is seventy-seven, so young and alert and active and pretty is she, and so charming. Tommy was at his gayest and most mellow. He said that the only stinker of a letter he ever knew George VI to write was to Ambassador Kennedy, about his defeatist pronouncements. Winston and others persuaded him to water it down to the version that is printed in Jack Wheeler-Bennett's biography.[1] Later Tommy referred to Jack's Appendix B as the best, indeed the only accurate, account of the duties and difficulties of the sovereign's Private Secretary. Last night I read it with interest and pleasure, suspecting that Tommy inspired all of it that he didn't actually write. Then I realised that I hadn't time to read the book properly when it appeared, so I am at it now. It's pretty good,

---

[1] *King George VI: His Life and Reign* by John W. Wheeler-Bennett (1958). Joseph Kennedy, the father of President John F. Kennedy, was US Ambassador in London in 1940.

I should say, but Jack hasn't got Harold Nicolson's magisterial sureness of touch in English prose,[1] and occasionally slips into careless cliché.

Ruth is very pleased because last week she sold at Sotheby's a dreary Henry Moore drawing which she had had for years and didn't care for. They told her it might fetch £300. She went to the sale, and it was knocked down for £550!

5 April 1962   *Grundisburgh*

George has asked me to write and say that he feels too ill to write any letters, but is most grateful to you for yours. At the moment he says he feels he can't cope with either receiving them or writing them. I am afraid he does feel horribly ill and I have an awful feeling that there is nothing they can do. We have not yet had the hospital report. Your friendship and letters have meant so much to George, I really can't tell you *how* much, and by the same token I do thank you so much for your sympathy and understanding. Love from Pamela.

6 April 1962   *Grundisburgh*
[Dictated to Pamela]

I send a postscript to Pamela's of yesterday to tell you that they have at last found a name for the damned thing. It is Hepatitis. It is rarer but apparently much the same in foulness and duration of time as Jaundice, and you know all about that. So evidently I am out of circulation for some time. The odd thing is that when I had jaundice ten or twelve years ago, though it was unpleasant, I was nothing like so miserably depressed as I am now. But in some queer way it is a relief to know that the beastly thing has a name.

P.S. The doctor told me that the tests were inconclusive. A clear negative would have been better. The above, i.e. Hepatitis, *is* true and a good answer to kind enquirers, and one which I am adopting. He is a bit happier having a name and some treatment.[2] Love Pamela.

7 April 1962   *Bromsden Farm*

Hepatitis, rather than jaundice, is what I had in 1959, and I remember your once or twice commenting on the depth and extent of my

[1] In his biography of King George V.
[2] He was in fact suffering from cancer of the liver, but he wasn't told so and apparently never suspected it.

inertia and depression, so I can utterly sympathise with all you are going through, and to cheer you can only say that though I was heavily under the weather for several months, I thereafter got quite all right, as you assuredly will.

I am reading a forthcoming book called *Great Cricket Matches*,[1] which I am enjoying. I have ordered a copy to be sent to you, ready for you to read lazily in your summer-house a little later on.

I can't tell you how *delighted* Ruth was with your letter. It was angelic of you to write it when you were feeling so low.

17 April 1962   *Grundisburgh*
[Dictated to Pamela]
We both love your notes and enquiries. That cricket book is full of interest and also strange omissions. Fancy leaving out Jessop's great match at the Oval in 1902, and the famous, though possibly apocryphal, 'Come on Wilfred, we'll get 'em in singles.' Uncle Edward on Fowler's Match I find a little prolix in places and I think there are better accounts, but it is all right. It calls up numberless memories, and as you may imagine I live during the day largely on reminiscence. One of the most persistent is those hours before the Lit. Soc. Bless you. I do wish I didn't feel so awfully ill, but *tout passe* no doubt.

P.S. The poor darling is very low today and I'm afraid feels very ill, but no pain and no nausea which is something to be thankful for. He doesn't feel able to do anything but he has enjoyed the cricket book.
    Much love Pamela.

25 April 1962   *Grundisburgh*
[Dictated to Pamela]
There is nothing in anything except my gratitude and the wonderfulness of Pamela (she mustn't cross that out). So what then? I am not even a chaos—I am a vast infinity. She will write you any more, if there is anything. Love to Ruth and bless you both. Oh the boredom!

---

[1] Edited by Handasyde Buchanan (1962).

INDEX

Conybeare, A.E. 21
Cooke, Alistair 137
Cooper, Artemis 45
Cooper, Diana 32, 45, 61, 94, 102, 116, 119, 121, 124–5, 168–9, 171, 188–9, 192, 224–5, 228, 234, 243, 254, 272, 339
Cooper, Duff 10, 32, 45–6, 61, 69, 74–5, 94, 109, 116, 121, 188, 193–4, 228, 240, 288, 338
Cooper, Lettice 128, 163
Cora, Lady Strafford 51
Corbett, Jim 68
Corday, Charlotte 198n, 203
Cory, William (*previously* Johnson) 47, 62, 303
Cowles, Virginia 51
Cowley, Abraham 140
Cowper, William 136n
Cozzens, J.G. 169–70
Crabbe, George 186, 354
Craig, Gordon 78
Cranmer, Thomas 23
Creighton, Bishop 35
Crippen, H.H. 200
Crossman, R.H.S. 194, 328
Crutchley, Brooke 114
Cubbitt, Sonia (*née* Keppel) 154
Cunard, Lady Nancy 28n 36, 57, 59, 114
Curzon, George Nathaniel, Lord 120

Daman, Hoppy 79
Damien, Father Joseph 178
D'Annunzio, Gabriele 47
Darwin, Bernard 183
Darwin, Charles 183, 273
Davies, Peter 38, 243–4
Day Lewis, Cecil 8
De Gaulle, Charles 243
de la Mare, Walter 229, 335
del Sarto, Andrea 3
Delaney, Shelagh 310–11
Denham, Sir John 17
Dent, Alan (Jock) 275
Desborough, Lady 298
Devlin Christopher 228–9, 327n, 333–4
Devlin, Patrick 228
Devlin, William 228
Devonshire, Duke of 56
Devonshire, Duchess of 165–6
Dickens, Charles 60, 67, 112–14, 136, 174–5, 200, 236, 294, 299, 347, 348–50
Dilke, Charles 167, 223–4
Dinesen, Isak *see* Blixen, Karen
Disraeli, Benjamin 243
Don, Laura 313
Donaldson, Frances 353
Donne, John 89, 95, 140

Donnelly, Desmond 14
Douglas, Lord Alfred 59–60, 142–3, 259, 316–17, 319
Dreiser, Theodore 170, 205
Drogheda, Lady 286–7, 339
Drogheda, Lord 287, 339
Druon, Maurice 259
du Maurier, Daphne 309
du Maurier, Gerald 347
Dulles, John Foster 18, 76, 100
Dunn, Waldo Hilary 348
Dunnett, George 258
Dunsany, Edward, 18th Baron 209
Durrell, Gerald 280, 336, 339
Durrell, Lawrence 82, 116
Duveen, Joseph 36

Edel, Leon 19n 46, 107, 129, 134, 272–4, 315–16
Eden, Anthony 18, 32, 123
Edward VII, King 51, 154, 258, 287
Eichmann, Karl Adolf 308
Einstein, Albert 268
Eisenhower, Dwight 302
Eliot, George 127, 129–30, 187, 216, 269, 271, 327, 329–31
Eliot, T.S. 58, 88, 119, 143–4, 147, 157–9, 164, 200, 213, 237, 244, 256, 261, 275, 313–14, 335
Eliot, Valerie 88
Elizabeth, Queen, the Queen Mother 116
Elizabeth I, Queen 5
Elizabeth II, Queen 74n, 247, 251
Elliott, Claude 24
Ellis, Havelock 173
Elton, Lord 130
Emerson, Ralph Waldo 117
Epstein, Sir Jacob 157–8, 169
Eugènie, Empress 51, 186
Evans, Edith 10–11, 231, 263

Faber, Geoffrey 21, 123, 291
Fahie, Norah 45
Falkner, John Meade 39
Fellini, Federico 311
Fergusson, Bernard 104, 328
Fisher, Charles 146–7, 268
Fisher, Geoffrey, Archbishop of Canterbury 212
Fisher, James 138
Fisher, K. 241
Fisher, Admiral 268
Fison, Sir C. 107
FitzGerald, Edward 93, 111, 168, 180, 186, 196, 216, 231–2
Flanders, Michael 118
Flash Harry *see* Sargent, Sir Malcolm

Morley, Edith J. 83
Morley, John 28
Morris, John 214–15
Morrow, George 265
Mortimer, Raymond 226–7
Morton, J.B. 20
Muggeridge, Malcolm 77
Munnings, Sir Alfred 35, 102
Murdoch, Iris (Iris Bayley) 89, 193, 323–4
Murray, John 249–50

Nabokov, Vladimir 171–2, 218–20
Napoleon I, Emperor of France 4–5, 13, 193
Nashe, Thomas 203n
Neguib, General Mohammed 18
Newman, Henry 21, 70, 222, 252, 261, 291, 293
Newsome, David 190n
Nicholson, Edie 158
Nicholson, William 30, 132, 158
Nicolson, Harold 61, 63–4, 67, 79, 100, 156, 211, 237, 239, 247, 288, 334, 358
Nightingale, Florence 146, 301
Nijinsky, Vaslav 78
Nuffield, William Richard Morris, first Viscount 37

O'Casey, Sean 206
Oldham, John 267
Olga, Princess 351
Olivier, Laurence 109
O'Neill, Eugene 257
Oppenheim, Phillips 62–3
Oppenheimer, Sir Ernest 91
Orwell, George 3, 62–3
Osborne, John 99, 108–9
O'Shaughnessy, Arthur 26n

Palmerston, Lord 5
Pardon, Stanley 174
Parry, Hubert 3
Pasternak, Boris 212–13, 219
Pater, Walter 327
Pattison, Mark 28, 140
Paul of Yugoslavia, Princess 286
Pavlova, Anna 78
Pearson, Hesketh 121, 324
Pepys, Samuel 191
Phillimore, Lord 165
Phillips, Sir Lionel 103
Pinero, Arthur 297
Piper, John 73
Pius IX, Pope 271n
Plinlimmon, David 201
Plomer, William 10, 128, 136, 155, 167
Pollock, Sir Frederick 27n, 76
Pooley, Ernest H. 210

Pooley, Lady 210–11
Porson, Richard 119
Potter, Stephen 130, 132, 187
Pound, Ezra 8, 16, 261
Powell, Anthony 127–8, 280, 324, 348, 353, 354
Powell, Dilys 280
Power, Manley 87
Priestley, J.B. 10–11, 46, 63, 79–80, 226–7, 234, 238, 247n, 318
Prodger, Dr 200–2
Pryce-Jones, Alan 3, 119, 267
Pusey, Edward Bouverie 21–2
Pye, Henry James 74

Quennell, Peter 25, 260, 276
Quiller Couch, Sir Arthur 83, 111, 197
Queensberry, Lord 259–60

Racine, Jean 77
Raleigh, Walter 50, 98
Ramsay, A.B. 50, 124
Randjitsinhji, Prince 310
Ransome, Arthur 9–10, 256–7
Raverat, Gwen 183
Ray, Gordon 134
Raymond, John 97
Reade, Charles 2
Reeves, Miss 164
Regler, Gustav 181n
Reichmann, Mr and Mrs 348
Renan, Ernest 128
Rendall, Montague John 316
Richardson, Joanna 231
Richardson, Tom 110, 148, 213
Ridley, Ursula 122
Ritchie, Lady 90
Roberts, Cecil 282
Robertson, Arnot 275
Robertson, Sir William 177
Robespierre, Maximilien Marie Isidore de 40, 127, 199
Robins, Elizabeth 90
Rockefeller, John Davison 37
Ross, Alan 272–5
Ross, Robbie 104, 259
Rossetti, Dante Gabriel 214
Rothenstein, Will 150
Rouse, Pecker 79
Routh, C.R.N. (Dick) 157, 179, 199, 292, 328
Rowse, A.L. 19, 118
Runyon, Damon 197
Ruskin, John 93, 130, 220, 329
Russell, Bertrand 331–2, 344
Russell, Conrad 189
Russell, Leonard 240, 278
Rutherford, Margaret 263–4

Tillotson, Kathleen 67
Trevelyan, G.M. 28, 233, 240
Trevor-Roper, Hugh 19, 118
Trollope, Anthony 101, 103, 140, 174, 190–1, 202–4, 227–8, 288–9
Trueman, Fred 91–2
Truman, Harry S. 134–5
Turner, Reggie 41–2, 269, 352
Tutin, Dorothy 263
Tynan, Kenneth 289

Udall, Nicholas 32

Vaughan, Toddy 69, 79
Verlaine, Paul 103
Victoria, Queen 51, 211, 294

Wagner, Richard 14
Wain, John 10, 14, 98, 227, 293
Walkley, A.B. 237
Walpole, Dorothy 220
Walpole, Horace 1, 86, 126, 291
Walpole, Hugh 10, 18, 88–9, 107, 217, 220, 235, 263
Walpole, Robin 220, 263, 346
Walters, Catherine (Skittles) 320
Ward, A.W. 328
Ward, Mrs Humphrey 48, 107, 225
Waring, Sir Holburt 325
Warner, Sir Pelham 84
Warre, Edmond 297
Warre, Mrs 12
Watts-Dunton, T. 325
Waugh, Evelyn 45, 192, 222, 226, 260, 338
Wavell, Archibald Percival, Field Marshal 328
Webb, Beatrice 107, 301
Webster, John 202, 298–9
Wedgwood, Veronica 261, 357
Welcome, John 233n
Welldon, Dean 35, 115
Wellington, Arthur Wellesley, Duke of 284–5, 319
Wellington, 7th Duke of 254–5
Wells, C.M. 124, 131, 148, 185–6, 304
Wells, H.G. 127–8, 130, 168, 177, 200
Wells, Mrs H.G. 68
Wesker, Arnold 310–11
Wesley, John 14
West, Anthony 130

West, Rebecca 130n, 139, 159, 276, 289
Westminster, Loelia, Duchess of (née Ponsonby) 124
Wheeler-Bennett, J.W. 357–8
Whiston, Robert 327
Whitman, Walt 86
Whitworth, A.W. 316
Wigg, Colonel 31
Wilde, Constance 314, 319
Wilde, Oscar 42, 46–7, 52, 59–61, 65–7, 83, 89–90, 104, 118–19, 132, 142–3, 145, 148, 154, 158, 164, 176, 179, 197–8, 204–5, 208, 210–11, 214–17, 231–2, 234, 242, 244, 248–9, 253, 259–60, 263–4, 266–7, 269–70, 278, 283, 286–7, 291, 296, 298, 300, 304, 306, 309, 311–13, 316–20, 322, 324, 326–7, 330, 338–9, 342, 348, 352, 356
Wilder, Billy 338n
Wilder, Thornton 245
Wilkes, John 168
Wilkinson, C.H. 263
Wilkinson, Ellen 194
Williams, Sir Griffith 212, 303
Wilson, Angus 26–7
Wilson, Sir Arnold 38
Wilson, Colin 101–2, 169
Wilson, E.R. 84
Wilson, J. Dover 159
Wilson, Mona 38–9
Wilson Knight, G. 75
Wodehouse, P.G. 22, 135
Wolsey, Thomas 32
Wood, Henry 119
Woodruff, Douglas 125
Woolf Leonard 233, 271, 277
Woolf, Virginia 3, 44, 64, 127, 182, 184n 233, 269
Wordsworth, Dorothy 35
Wordsworth, William 35–7, 71, 110, 215, 230, 237–8, 257
Worsley, T.C. 108
Wright, Aldis 180, 232
Wright, Almroth 101
Wright, Hagberg 101
Wyndham, George 186

Yeats, W.B. 9, 111–12, 261
Young. Andrew 280, 288
Young, G.M. 159, 187, 221
Young, R.A. 189